Remembering Keith Again
For Deb

All rights reserved. No part of this publication may be reproduced, distributed, or transmitted in any form or by any means, including photocopying, recording, or other electronic or mechanical methods without prior written permission of the publisher except in the case of brief quotations embodied in the book reviews and certain other non-commercial uses permitted by copyright law.

Copyright 2023

First Edition

Although inspired by actual events and people, this story is entirely fictitious and is a product of the author's imagination. Any resemblance to actual events or persons, living or dead, is entirely coincidental.

1

Jack made most of his living by performing in supporting roles for television but he still loved the stage. Acting had always been his way of life and his fondest memories were those when he had traveled with his father to watch him perform on Broadway. At thirtythree, Jack had hoped to be more successful than he was. He had learned a great deal from his father and graduated from San Francisco State with a degree in drama and music. He had learned over the years that acting was more than skill and depended a great deal on luck, being in the right place at the right time and knowing the right people.

His family life while growing up had been rocky, his parents fought constantly often leaving Jack feeling responsible. At the age of nine, Jack had tried to hang himself but his father had discovered him and saved his life. Unfortunately, the unhappy childhood continued and as Jack grew older he often acted out. His parents eventually divorced but that didn't save Jack from being placed in boarding schools during his prepubescent years. As a teenager he had experimented with drugs and the fondness he developed for the numbing effect he got from them, continued as he aged.

Over the years, he had become defiant. Jack was often angry with the way the world worked, especially hollywood. He made a decent living with his craft, but he thought that he was better than the roles he was being offered and he wanted more. He argued with his agent about everything and had a disagreeable reputation that was slowly growing with each passing year. When his agent called and commanded that he come pick up a letter, Jack was curious yet angry. He didn't like being ordered to do anything, yet his agent had made it clear to Jack that he must come pick it up.

Most correspondence came by way of his agent but he could pick those letters up at his leisure. The letters were usually nonsense, ideas for scripts, fan mail, requests for autographs or just bizarre letters. Admittedly, most of these remained unanswered and were filed in his trash can. Jack really had little interest in pleasing anyone other than himself but something about this letter was different. After arriving at his agent's office he had been handed a manilla envelope and was told there was a letter inside of it. His agent had explained to him that the letter wasn't to Jack, but rather to his unknown younger half brother, Keith.

Keith was 19 years old and a little lost in the world. Jack had invited him to stay with him at his small bungalow, knowing what living with their mutual father was like, he had taken pity on the boy and offered him refuge. Keith had gratefully accepted the offer while he assessed his life and decided on some needed life changes.

The letter Jack had been commanded to pick up, had started out in the hands of Dorothy White. She was a film editor and had a decent reputation. She had received the letter from her former sister in law Ruth Meeks. Dorothy's brother Jim, had been married to Ruth and was a decorated national hero; he had been a pilot for the United States Air Force. He was a very colorful man, ranking Major and an instructor pilot for B-47's and had been stationed at the air base in Lincoln Nebraska. On a routine training flight, his engines had caught fire on take-off, Jim had stayed with the plane and gained enough altitude so his crew could safely bail out, then he steered the plane away from a school and a farmhouse below before bailing out himself. His parachute never opened and they found him still strapped to the ejection seat. He had left behind his wife Ruth and his daughters Terry and Elizabeth.

Elizabeth, who had been nicknamed Izzy, was an unusual child. Her mother said she was psychic, but that really wasn't the case. Izzy couldn't predict the future, she remembered it, so as a young child who couldn't explain her memories, it seemed as though she just knew things, things that she wasn't capable of explaining. She was also in tune with the world that surrounded her. Her feelings extended beyond the room she was in, beyond her immediate family, it was as if she was a small part of a living, breathing world and understood when another part was in trouble. The world was simply an extension of herself. At times, she would be so insistent about something that seemed arbitrary to anyone else, but incredibly urgent to Izzy. Ruth would be at a loss how to cope with it. The latest of these incidents was about a letter she had written to Jack's brother Keith. Ruth had no idea what was in the letter, but Izzy wouldn't let it go. Izzy had insisted that she had to get the letter to Keith and it had to be done quickly. In desperation, Ruth had reached out to Dorothy, Jim's sister. Dorothy had spent an hour on the phone with Ruth, wanting to cry over Jim and drinking heavily while she did so. She assured Ruth that she could get the letter to Jack who was Keith's older half brother. Being in the business, she had lots of connections and she was quite good friends with Jack's agent. All Ruth needed was to mail Izzy's letter to her and she would take care of everything. Ruth agreed to do so, assuming that would be the last of it. She wasn't even sure if Dorothy would get it to Jack, but at least she could tell Izzy it had been sent and the little girl would settle down.

Ruth had wondered why an eight year old girl would so desperately want to get a letter to the brother of a small-time Hollywood actor. She wondered how Izzy had even heard about him. Izzy had been adamant about it, saying she had promised. Ruth was curious about to whom Izzy had promised this letter and what it was about, but Ruth respected her girl's privacy. She had never read their diaries or Izzy's journals, she never snooped in their rooms, she wanted the girls to know that they both could trust her and so when Izzy didn't offer Ruth more of an explanation, Ruth didn't pry.

Ruth had mailed Izzy's letter to Dorothy the next day as promised. The letter was put in a manilla envelope and sent to Dorothy's home address. Ruth had loaded the girls into her blue chevy impala and had taken both girls to the post office with her. Dorothy hand delivered the letter to Jack's agent who she knew quite well. His agent then personally handed it to Jack.

Jack took the letter home with him, he set it on the coffee table and then went to the kitchen and made a sandwich. It was turkey, tomato, cheese and a pickle. He ate the sandwich then licked his fingers, there was no mayonnaise on the bread, but the tomato had dripped a bit. He hadn't used a plate so he took a well used yellow sponge from the sink and wiped the crumbs from the table into his hand then shook his hand above the stainless steel kitchen sink. He turned on the faucet and washed the crumbs down the drain. He thought about drinking some lemonade but felt himself being pulled back to the letter. He returned to the living room and sat on the sofa in front of the coffee table.

Picking the letter up, Jack opened the envelope and discovered a sealed letter addressed to Keith inside of it which he also opened. He had intended to let this letter join the others in the trash can, despite the stern warning from his agent that he or Keith needed to answer this one, but for some reason, this letter intrigued him. It was clearly written by a child, it was just a few short sentences and was accompanied with another folded sheet of paper with song lyrics that the child had obviously not written. The letter said, " Here are the song words you wanted me to send to you, the ones that last time you didn't like. I kept my promise and reminded you." The lyrics on the second sheet of paper said "when it's a love you won't be needing you're not free" and were crossed out, then new lyrics were written beside them that said, "because my love feels so forbidden you're not free"

Jack had instantly recognized the lyrics, his brother had written the song not too long ago. Keith was very talented, he was excellent with written words and was also becoming quite adept at writing music. He had foolishly become involved with an older woman who was married. The two of them had met while performing on Broadway, Keith had fallen head over heels with the woman. They had a brief affair but despite her claims of freedom, Keith had issues with the fact that she was still married. Jack's brother was an interesting combination being both a hippy following in his brother's footsteps and also a cautious predictable man. He was far more traditional than he cared to let on and had learned a great deal from watching his older brother Jack's mistakes. How this little girl knew anything about Keith, much less the lyrics to his unpublished song was beyond Jack, Keith hadn't shared the song with anyone nor had he performed it anywhere. Jack read the letter and the lyrics over and over, at one point he even balled them up preparing to throw them away, but something made him stop and he gently re-opened the two pages and attempted to stretch out the creases he had caused. Jack laid them down on the coffee table in front of him. He continued to try to rub out the creases, then crossed his legs and stretched back on the brown leather sofa. "What to do..." He mused out loud.

A big gray tabby cat jumped on the coffee table and sniffed the letter. "You sense it too don't you buddy?" He asked. The cat cocked his head sideways and stared at Jack, then jumped from the table to the sofa beside him. He put his front paws on Jack's leg and made a chirping sound at his master. Jack stroked the cat's back in long smooth strokes starting at the ears and going all the way to the base of the tail. The cat seemed pleased and stepped off Jack's leg and laid beside him and slowly purred.

"What would you do boy?" Jack asked the cat. The cat closed its eyes and made bread on the sofa, Jack let him. So far the cat hadn't damaged the sofa, but Jack often had animals and was well aware of the fact that sometimes nice things and animals just didn't mix. He stroked the cat once more, this time he even gently tugged at the cat's tail, the cat stretched out onto his side, his legs sticking out away from Jack. Jack rubbed the cat's belly and scratched under the it's armpits. The cat closed his eyes and purred a little louder. "What to do." Jack said aloud again, still stroking the cat.

Jack was recently divorced and although he was fiercely independent, he liked having Keith stay with him. Keith idolized his big brother and Jack rather enjoyed it. He offered the boy real help, encouraged him and advised him, it made him feel needed. Jack had a dark side, a side that he hid from most. He displayed confidence outwardly, but secretly he was something else. Jack sought approval, he wanted admiration, he desired obedience and craved love. Having a doting little brother who worshiped the ground he walked on in his home, helped stave some of his needs. Keith had a lot of promise as an actor or a singer, whatever path the boy chose. Jack believed he would be successful at whatever he decided on doing. He liked taking on the role of being Keith's advisor, it made him feel connected in a human way that he desperately sought. Jack read the revised wording to the lyrics one more time and nodded," It is better." he said out loud. He stood up and walked to the phone that was on the wall by the kitchen. He lifted the phone off the cradle and called his agent.

"Hey, it's Jack." He said. "I want the phone number for that film editor friend of yours" He paused. "Yes, I will be nice." He said, rolling his eyes. He took a pencil from the top of the phone where he had kept it but the note pad was missing. He glanced over his shoulder and spotted it on the kitchen counter, he tried to reach it but the phone cord wasn't long enough. He rolled his eyes again.

"Say it one more time, I didn't have any paper." He commanded and using the pencil he wrote the number on the wall above the phone, then using the pencil's eraser end, he pushed down on the lever disconnecting the call without saying goodbye or thank-you. He paused for a moment, still pushing the lever down and holding the phone to his shoulder with his chin all while he thought through what he was going to say in his head. He released the lever and heard the dial tone and tapped the top of the phone nervously with the pencil in his right hand before dialing. After a moment he dialed the number using the eraser end of the pencil instead of his finger. The phone rang twice, then a woman with a business sounding voice answered.

"Dorothy White please." Jack said. It wasn't a request, it was a firm demand.

"This is Dorothy." The woman answered.

"Dorothy, this is Jack Enidarrac, I'm calling about the envelope you left with my agent this morning." Jack said matter of factly. "I need the name, address and phone number of the sender please."

The woman's voice changed and suddenly gushed sweetness. "I'm glad to know you received the envelope." Dorothy said. "The letter is from my little niece in Nebraska."

Jack paused. He wasn't sure why, but something about it sounded familiar. "Nebraska?" He asked. "I don't recall ever being in Nebraska and I'm sure that Keith has never been there." It was a statement, but it felt like a question.

"Oh Mr. Enidarrac, I'm sure you have never met any of my relatives who live there. My sister in law Ruth, well she called me because she knew I might know how to get the letter to your brother. I did try to locate his agent myself but I couldn't find that he had one. I wasn't even sure if he was in the business. I hope you don't mind that I dropped it off for you instead." She answered.

"No, I don't mind." He said, and he meant it. "We just need contact information so Keith can reply."

"Let me get it for you. I'm surprised it wasn't included in the letter, but Ruth probably didn't read it. She lets those girls have their privacy. I'm not sure if I agree with her parenting, but that's neither here nor there. Here it is, I have her phone number, it's 402-489-4165." Jack wrote that number on the wall beneath Dorothy's. He started to hang up, then caught himself. "Thank you Ms. White." He said, then hung up the receiver using his right forefinger this time before she could say anything else.

At this moment Keith walked in the front door. He had a sack of groceries in one arm. He nodded to his brother as he walked past him into the kitchen and set the bag on the counter just as Jack began to dial the phone. "Yes, is this Ruth?" Jack asked in a voice so kind that Keith stopped what he was doing and listened. "Ruth, this is Jack Enidarrac, Keith's older brother. I'm calling about the letter your sister in law left for him."

Keith didn't know what Jack was talking about, he knew better than to interrupt his brother but that didn't mean that he couldn't listen, he had never received a letter. He left the groceries in the brown paper sack on the counter and pulled out a kitchen chair and sat down on it. He was watching his brother who was not acting at all like himself, he wouldn't look Keith in the eyes and was pouring on charm while he spoke on the phone.

"We would love an opportunity to meet her. Are you ever in California or even New York, we could arrange a meeting." Keith's mouth dropped open a bit, Jack smiled mischievously and turned his back to his brother. "Keith really wants to meet her," He continued, pouring on charm. Keith stood up and walked around Jack and leaned on the wall next to him. He folded his arms across his chest and made Jack look at him. Jack just smirked and continued. "We typically don't travel in the middle," he laughed. "Nebraska is in the middle isn't it?" Keith furrowed his brows in confusion. "Ah, yes, horses. Do you know when?"

Keith could hear talking on the other end of the phone but couldn't make out what was being said. "That would be fine, we could meet for lunch, maybe Dorothy would like to join us too? I've never met her in person but she sounds delightful over the phone. Yes, Once you get the date decided on, let us know and we can plan a meeting. It was very nice speaking with you Ruth, and please let Izzy know how much we appreciated her letter." Jack hung the phone up this time placing the phone back in the cradle.

"Do I even want to know what that was about?" Keith asked. He was smiling but he kept a stern look on face at the same time.

"I think that you probably do." Jack laughed. Jack had a soft voice, almost a mumble. Sometimes when trying to be funny, people missed it because he delivered the line so matter of factly and in such a soft tone. Keith knew Jack was amused and wondered what it was about. Jack then motioned to the sack of groceries on the counter with a tilt of his head. Keith nodded and began unloading the sack. There was eggs, bread, cheese, milk and wheaties. "Did you get mayo?" Jack asked.

"I didn't know we were out." Keith said. "I'm not a mind reader. It wasn't on the list."

Jack laughed and mumbled "Mind reader" to himself then laughed again. Jack headed towards the sofa, that cat leapt from the sofa to the chair next to it while Keith put away the food. "I forgot paper plates." Keith continued. " We never put them on the list." He stepped out of the kitchen and sat on a green upholstered chair next to the sofa, he had to scoot the cat off of it before he sat down. The cat hissed at him when he did it.

"So?" He asked. "What was that about?" Jack handed Keith the letters from off the coffee table.

"Read." Jack commanded.

"This is to me." Keith said, slightly smiling at his older brother. Jack nodded. "Why is it opened.?" Keith asked, the smile he had earlier was returning to his face. Jack grinned in response,

"It was delivered to me through my agent." Jack answered. "Just read it."

"It's wrinkled." Keith said, now fully grinning at his brother. Jack just nodded and motioned for his brother to read it. Keith snorted and opened the letter. "From a kid?" He asked.

"Shut up and read it." Jack commanded his brother.

"Just my luck, I was hoping it was from a beautiful woman and included a picture." Keith said to Jack, still not reading the letter.

Jack picked up a toss pillow from the sofa and threatened to throw it at him, Keith laughed and opened the letter. A moment later Keith was staring at his brother. The smile was now gone and his brow was wrinkled. "What the hell?" He said. "Seriously what the hell?" He said again. "How?"

"It is yours right?" Jack asked. Keith stared at the lyrics that were hand written on the paper that he held in front of him.

"Yeah, it's mine." Keith confirmed. His hand trembled a bit. "You're telling me that a kid from Nebraska had my lyrics and improved them?" Keith asked.

Jack smirked at his brother. "At least you're able to see it is an improvement."

"Very nice Jack." Keith retorted.

"Do you have any idea how they were leaked?" Jack asked him. Keith shook his head. "Then we need to find out, there is just something weird about the whole thing. It feels strange to me."

"Weird? Yeah there is something weird about it. I'm pissed off, who is this person and who is Ruth and what does this mean that I asked her to send them to me?" He asked, shaking the letter in front of his brother as he spoke.

"Izzy is an eight year old. Ruth is the girl's mother. The mother doesn't know what was in the letter and she simply mailed it for the kid." Jack answered.

"A eight year old? Did I hear you right? An eight year old in Nebraska? What the hell Jack?" Keith tossed the letter on the coffee table, he searched his brother's face for answers.

Jack stretched back into the sofa again and the cat jumped from the floor onto his lap. He smiled at the cat, stroking its forehead with his thumb. "Hopefully we will find the answers soon little brother." He said. "Seems they are going to come out here and buy a horse."

2

It had been several months, Ruth had been in contact with Jack off and on. He was such a polite boy, he always asked how each of the girls were doing and made sure to personalize each conversation while he entertained Ruth with stories of his famous father. Ruth had grown up admiring Jack's father John; she hadn't been aware that the Enidarracs were his sons. The two boys had changed their last name once they had decided on a career in show business, not wanting to bank on their famous father's last name. Ruth admired their independence and determination to make their careers on their own and she truly loved hearing stories about the family's escapades. Dorothy had warned Ruth that Jack could be abrupt and cold, but Ruth found him charming. They had long telephone conversations and he was never anything except respectful to her.

When Jack had first started calling Ruth, she had hoped that he would reveal to her what Izzy had written to his brother. She was curious about what could have intrigued them enough to want to meet her little girl. It didn't take long before she realized that the boy would remain closed-lipped, honoring her youngest child's privacy. Ruth didn't pry, it was obviously important enough to the man that he wanted to know more about her child and Ruth admired his integrity, not many people would believe it worthwhile to keep the secrets of an eight year old girl.

Even though Jack wasn't much of a celebrity and his brother was mostly unknown, she knew that both men must be very busy.

Dorothy had told Ruth many times that actors were always hungry. Even the most popular of movie stars never knew for sure when or if another role would follow the last one. It was a stressful business, leaving many desperate for any audition. They were like hungry dogs waiting for someone to throw them a scrap of food.

Dorothy didn't like most actors. She believed them to be superficial narcissists and she had told Ruth that most Hollywood actors were stupid. They were uneducated and that the studio's preferred them that way. A less intelligent actor was easier for agents and studios to manage. Those who weren't stupid were ruthless. They would sell their soul for a great part and they always demanded more say in their contracts, roles, character behaviors and even how the shows were produced and directed. Dorothy told Ruth that Jack Enidarrac was the second type.

Ruth had been pleased to find that Jack Enidarrac was a well spoken young man with an excellent vocabulary. He didn't come across as ruthless at all to her, in fact he seemed very kind. It was apparent to Ruth that Jack loved his little brother deeply, she got the sense that whatever Izzy had written, had moved Jack. He wasn't simply being polite, this was more than fan mail but he never spoke to her of what was in the letter or what had inspired his need to meet the girl or even keep in contact with her family.

Ruth thought that Jack seemed a little shy at first which she had found endearing. As they grew to know one another better during their phone visits, she was impressed with his intellect. As a teacher, she appreciated those who wished to learn, she found Jack to be curious about religion and culture. She found that he was well read on both current subjects and classic literature. He had strong opinions on politics, both governmental and cultural but he didn't volunteer his opinions. He enjoyed explaining acting techniques to her and also knew a lot about music. He didn't seem to enjoy talking about himself, but was never at a loss of words on any other subject that he enjoyed. He reminded Ruth very much of her youngest child.

Izzy was also intelligent with a huge vocabulary, but like Jack, she was soft spoken and an introvert. It took effort to engage Izzy in conversation, she heard everything, never missing even the slightest inference, but she never willingly joined in the conversation. To most people, Izzy came across as extremely shy, if she were older Ruth imagined that the same behavior might be interpreted as arrogance. Izzy didn't waste time, she was direct, to the point and if someone wasn't open to her thoughts, she didn't bother talking to them. It was odd behavior for an eight year old, but her little girl seemed focused. She knew what she wanted in life, she just seldom shared her vision with Ruth.

The conversations that Ruth shared with Jack, left her feeling almost motherly towards him, he was a boy that silently asked for approval as did her little girl. The more they spoke, the closer Ruth became to him. She had grown to care about him much like she did her own children and the neighborhood boys who often came to the house to play with her girls. Ruth understood children, even grown children. All children crave approval and love, Ruth gladly provided it.

The summer had flown by quickly, it was mid August and the horse was finally ready to transport. The family had purchased a few horses across state lines in the past, but it had seemed there were far more hoops to jump through when the state involved was California. Terry was so excited that she scarcely spoke of anything else. She had settled on a mare, it was a beautiful quarter horse. Her interest in horses had begun with Arabians. Izzy didn't particularly like horses but she did think that Arabians were beautiful.

The girl's father came from a family that had bred thoroughbreds and quarter horses, supplying race horses in the western half of the country. During the depression his family had been forced to sell off their stock just to survive but Jim had never lost his love of race horses. They were beautiful, powerful horses and Ruth and Jim would frequent the race tracks. After Jim was killed, Ruth encouraged the girls to appreciate horses but only Terry really seemed to be interested. As Terry matured she became an accomplished young rider and started showing horses at shows for small prizes. She trained her horses herself. Her well mannered horses combined with her own brilliant personality made her a crowd favorite, so when she showed her horses, she usually won.

Terry competed at horse shows across the country and of course at the Nebraska state fair. Most shows rewarded winners with ribbons and trophies but monetary rewards were possible at larger shows. A winning horse that she could breed would provide income from the foals. Terry had initially started in beginning classes such as English and Western pleasure but as she grew, eventually so did her interests. She had grown tired of the limitations of Arabians and had begun showing in reining. Arabians weren't the right horse for that type of show, she needed a good quarter horse for that.

Terry had wanted to train her Arabians, they were smart beautiful animals and were certainly able to perform, but they weren't as physically strong as a quarter horse and were more fine boned. Terry felt that the compact body of the American Quarter Horse would be better suited for the intricate and quick movements required for reining. They would be better at cutting, barrel racing, roping and all other western events. She wanted a horse that was built to hold its head low, keeping it balanced. Izzy didn't really like the look of Quarter horses, she preferred the Ariabians. She loved the dished faces and the straight backs, she loved the height of the animals. Terry liked them too so she kept her favorite mare, thinking she might eventually breed her to a quarter horse but she sold off her geldings and replaced them with geldings of the other breed. A few of Terry's quarter horse geldings were doing well, but she wanted a quarter horse mare so she could produce foals. They had settled on a lovely gray, Ruth liked it because Jim had always bet on the gray at the racetracks. He had a weakness for any gray horse and Ruth smiled lovingly at her daughter knowing that Jim would have bought the gray for her in a heartbeat.

After arriving in Los Angeles at the airport they rented a car for a one way trip back to Nebraska. They stopped at Dorothy's first. They were to stay only a day or two and then move on to do a final check of the horse before it was transported to their home state. They would follow behind the trailer and the hired professionals all the way back home. It would be a long tedious drive, especially for Izzy, and Ruth knew it. Terry would be in the front seat next to her mother, the view would be the back end of the new horse and Ruth was sure Terry would never take her eyes off of it.

Izzy would ride in the back seat, from experience Ruth knew that Izzy would spend hours writing in her journals and pressing her face against the backseat window, taking in every bit of scenery and daydreaming ideas for stories to write in her journals. She would softly hum while she watched the world outside and never complain or ask for anything.

Ruth knew that Izzy would love California, Izzy wanted to see the ocean, she had vivid dreams that she often told her mother of and they always involved the ocean. Her daughter could relay not only the imagery of her dreams, but details one wouldn't expect like the way the air smelled or the taste of the salt. Izzy's dreams were fascinating, she heard music while she dreamt and could describe the smallest details.

Izzy was also interested in Hollywood, she wanted to see how the camera's operated and wanted her Aunt Dorothy to explain how she spliced film together for the studios. She was curious about such an odd eclectic jumble of things that family trips were always difficult with the two girls because there were such vast differences in their interests. Horses took up much of their time because of shows, leaving little time to dedicate to the interests of Izzy. As a result, Ruth often felt guilty even though Izzy didn't complain. This trip would satisfy both of her girls, there was a horse for Terry and Hollywood for her youngest child, Ruth smiled to herself and nodded.

The plan was to spend a couple days with Dorothy. Both of the girls loved their Aunt, although Izzy had always been the closest to her. Dorothy loved to go to garage sales and Izzy liked it too. Izzy liked them because the chances of finding something strange enticed her. Dorothy's house was similar to Izzy's mind, it was full of unique pieces, one of a kind items. An eclectic space full of mismatched items that somehow seemed all connected. Ruth was pleased that Izzy would have things to occupy her on this trip. Terry didn't want to stop at all, not even to visit her Aunt, but Izzy couldn't wait, Izzy and Dorothy had always had a special bond. This trip each of the girls were lost in their own little worlds, Terry could only think of the horse and Izzy could only think of Jack.

Ruth watched her daughter's face grow solemn when Dorothy explained to Izzy that Jack and Keith wouldn't be able to have lunch with them after all. Meeting them had been the thing that Izzy had wanted most since the day her mother mailed the letter. The boys had been in New York at an audition a few days earlier but Ruth had been under the impression that they would make it back in time for the lunch which they had planned. Dorothy had received the call that morning from Jack while Ruth and the girls were on the airplane headed towards California. Jack had been very apologetic and promised that he would try to meet them at the studio instead, their flight home had been delayed, they had made it back to California but the delay had caused some complications that were slowing them down and they wouldn't make it in time for lunch. Not wanting to disappoint Izzy again, Ruth and Dorothy secretly agreed not to tell her that the Enidarracs would try to meet them at the studio, that way if they weren't able to, the little girl wouldn't be further disappointed.

"That's not right." Izzy said, shaking her head when she heard the news. "They are supposed to be here."

"Izzy." Ruth said in a kind voice. "I'm sure that they wanted to, it was their idea to meet you! Your Aunt told you what an actor's life is like. They have to go to these things, they have to go to auditions, it's how they earn a living."

"I know how it works mom." Izzy confirmed. "It just felt like they were here." She said, "They've never not been here."

Ruth was puzzled by what Izzy said, but Izzy didn't always make sense. She believed in what she felt, translating emotions to words didn't always come easy to the child.

Her mother had made a perfume for Izzy that helped her understand her daughter a little better. Ruth and a dear friend who was a chemistry professor, created a perfume recipe that changed with Izzy's moods. Izzy's inability to communicate had been a problem for Ruth when her child was young, so the two of them devised a recipe that would change with the temperature and even the blood pressure of the young girl's body. When she was most excited, she would smell of honeysuckle, when content she smelled of roses, when angry it smelled like sage and when sad it smelled like lilacs with a hint of vanilla.

Ruth's friend had wanted to market the perfume oil, they were going to patent it and planned to reach out to the University of Nebraska and see if anyone could help the two of them find how to best market the product, but Ruth's friend died suddenly from a stroke. After his death, Ruth decided that the recipe should remain a secret and not be sold, it would be Izzy's and she could do what she wanted with it once she was older. As Ruth studied her daughter now, the air smelled of lilac and Ruth's heart ached for her little girl.

Dorothy, seeing the disappointment in her Nieces face, tried her best to make it up to her. She promised to take her to some garage sales and told the little girl that she was going to give her a tour of Hollywood and if time allowed she would even take her to the ocean. Izzy had been to the Gulf of Mexico several times. Ruth's best friend Beth, lived in San Juan Texas and Ruth often took the girls with her when she went to visit. Izzy had always said that the Gulf of Mexico didn't count as an ocean, and of course she was correct. Beth would tell Izzy that oceans looked exactly the same as the gulf did, but it didn't make a difference to Izzy. She wanted to see the ocean. Izzy dreamed of it so often she would salivate remembering the taste of the salty air, so when Dorothy said that Izzy could see the Pacific, she could hardly contain herself and the scent slowly changed from lilac to rose.

Outwardly, Izzy was quiet and calm as always, but inside she was going a million miles an hour. Ruth couldn't tell, the perfume told Ruth that her daughter was content. She gazed at her silent little girl and wondered what she was thinking. Terry would talk non-stop about the horse, about reining, about boys and school, but Izzy just listened intently. Izzy didn't speak until she was two years old, Terry had learned to speak very early. Terry's father had told all of his friends that she could count to ten in Spanish when Terry was only one year old. It was a lie of course, but Terry was very vocal at a young age. Ruth worried about her youngest daughter, she was such an introvert and a strange little girl, her little psychic. Izzy watched everything, nothing went unnoticed by her, but she seldom spoke. Ruth tried to brush it off, telling herself it was because Terry did all the talking, but in all honesty, Ruth knew there was something unusual about her youngest daughter.

There were so many times that Izzy wanted to talk about what she felt. She could look at people and see their colors. Emotions had colors, Izzy could see them. Life had color, Izzy could interpret the colors and understand what the universe wanted from her. After Izzy's father had been killed, Ruth's colors had been dark. Izzy couldn't remember a time when her mother didn't have some dark colors around her. Izzy didn't mind the dark colors, everyone had sadness, but when dark colors turned thick they frightened her.

Ruth's colors were mostly different shades of purple, purple usually meant sadness but even so it was one of Izzy's favorite colors. Izzy liked purple because it was universal, everyone had it. It was a color that was easy to understand. Ruth's colors would brighten when she was teaching. Ruth loved teaching children and she was very good at it. Izzy had toyed with the idea of explaining what she saw to her mother, she wanted to, but Izzy could sense that if she tried to explain the colors to Ruth, her mother would only worry and then her mother's colors would darken and thicken.

Izzy loved her mother very much and never wanted to make her unhappy, as a result, Izzy kept secrets inside, hoping that Ruth's colors would continue to lighten as time passed. The past few months, Ruth's colors had changed drastically. Talking to Jack seemed to bring a lot of yellow and pink hues into Ruth's aura. Izzy knew it was because of Jack, her mother enjoyed his friendship. Jack was like another child to her mother, one that needed her and Ruth loved to feel needed.

Ruth's life had been hard, she had grown up in a strict family during the depression. Her father, George Worthington Nicholas, was a hard man. Everyone who knew him called him Worthy. The world had always been black and white to him. Ruth had three choices as a young woman in choosing a career, she could be a social worker, a nurse or a teacher. Ruth had wanted to nurse, but Worthy wouldn't allow it. He said nursing made a woman hard, so Ruth had gone to the teacher's college in Lincoln Nebraska. It turned out that she was very good at teaching and she had always loved children, but even that hadn't really satisfied her father.

Ruth's mother Aileen, was a kind woman but very needy. Her parents had been quite wealthy and Aileen often wondered if Worthy had only married her for her money. Her insecurities made her difficult for Worthy to live with. He was not a demonstrative man, he never hugged or held hands with his wife and that only added to her insecurities. Aileen was more interested in gaining attention from Worthy than giving attention to her child, often leaving Ruth feeling abandoned. In a lot of ways, Ruth and Jack were very similar although neither of them had realized it.

Ruth's father Worthy was the post office general for Dewitt Nebraska. He also coached sports for the Dewitt highschool. He was a hard man who always wanted perfection from his child. He tired easily of his wife and eventually began an affair with a woman who he worked with at the post office, her name was Birdie. The affair had devastated Aileen. People seldom divorced back then and the wives of cheating husbands were supposed to suffer in silence. Neither of Ruth's parents had ever put the other first or even their child. The two bickered at each other for years, neither ever willing to sacrifice for the other.

Worthy was still cheating with Birdie when Aileen passed away from cancer. Ruth had been in the hospital room when her mother had passed, Aileen had reached for Worthy's hand and he hadn't taken it. Ruth had told her father, "Dad, mom wants you to hold her hand", forcing him to take it in his. That scene had haunted Ruth ever since, she told herself over and over that her father hadn't seen her mother reach for him, but her gut told her that she was wrong.

Ruth had married an incredibly handsome man who was also a coach hoping it would please her father. She had two wonderful sons. The oldest was named John, he had black hair and bright blue eyes. He could teach himself to play any instrument in a day. He was extremely talented, highly intelligent and artistically inclined. The younger boy she named Kent. Kent had sandy colored hair and blue eyes. He was tall and thin. He had the special ability to make his mother laugh no matter what the circumstances. Unfortunately, Ruth's marriage failed and Worthy blamed his daughter. Worthy helped raise the boys, taking them in while Ruth attended the university and she was grateful for her father's help, but he never let her forget that she had failed.

When her father passed away, Ruth was ashamed to admit she felt free for the first time. After his passing, Ruth could take what the world offered her. She loved teaching, but she loved science. Worthy had told her that girls weren't supposed to be good at science so Ruth had studied it secretly. Her friend had been her professor. He was an old man even when Ruth was in school. He had never cared about the norms of society so when Ruth showed a talent for chemistry, he had encouraged it.

Ruth was teaching Kindergarten in Lincoln Nebraska when she met Dorothy's brother Jim. After she married him, John went to live with his father in Colorado but Kent stayed with Ruth. Jim loved that his wife was intelligent, that she understood him when he spoke of lift over drag, accelerated stall, flight plans and the like. Ruth was happy, she had married a pilot who brought her expensive gifts from around the world and didn't care that she was smart. He loved his wife and doted on her. Together they had two beautiful little girls and bought a nice ranch style home in a new development on the East side of Lincoln Nebraska. Her life finally seemed as though it was going to be happy, then her husband was killed, leaving her to raise two toddler's and a teenage boy by herself. Ruth's colors had gone dark again and just never seemed to brighten.

Izzy concentrated on Ruth's colors. She was surprised that they hadn't changed upon learning that the Enidarracs had canceled lunch. She could still see light colors spreading through the darker ones. She knew that her mother was just as excited as she had been about meeting Jack, so she had expected the disappointment would be more obvious. It confused Izzy, but she was grateful for it and so when Dorothy told Izzy about the fun she had in store for the little girl, Izzy was content. She knew that eventually she would meet Jack and Keith, she always did. For now, she could focus on making her mother happy.

The Boulevard was beautiful as Dorothy continued towards the Paramount lot. Each side of the street was lined with incredibly tall palm trees. There were massive homes on either side of the street set back in the rolling hills. Both the girls were eagerly pressed against the car windows as they watched the passing scenery. Dorothy was going to give Ruth and the girls a brief tour, then hopefully Jack and Keith would arrive at the office, if they didn't make it Dorothy would take the girls to the beach instead and Izzy wouldn't be any the wiser.

The tour was amazing, both the girls had been fascinated, Terry was interested in the costumes and sets, Izzy wanted to watch the camera's. After the lot tour, Dorothy brought them up to her office, she explained how she did her work. At 1:00 pm, there was a knock on her office door. Dorothy and Ruth both knew it was Jack but neither had told Izzy that he was coming. Izzy was standing on a chair inspecting a painting on the wall when Dorothy opened the door. Jack and Keith stood in the hall outside, Jack stepped inside and seemed genuinely glad to meet everyone but Keith stood behind him leaning against the door frame with his arms folded across his chest. Both of the men were tall and well built, the two of them in the doorway had created quite a presence. Ruth could suddenly understand why her sister in law was a bit intimidated by them. Ruth tapped Izzy on the shoulder, she turned around from her inspection of the painting and made a slight squeak having recognized Jack. He had crossed the room to say hello and was standing only inches from the chair that Izzy stood upon.

"Grasshopper!" She whispered excitedly.

Jack looked very confused but it didn't deter Izzy, she reached for his face and pulled his forehead down against hers. Ordinarily Jack wouldn't have tolerated anything like that, but he felt such strong emotions emanating from this little girl that it took him completely by surprise. He put his hands against her face and the two held their foreheads against one another for a few moments.

"Elizabeth!" Ruth said.

"It's alright." Jack answered softly without moving away from the girl.

"I'm so sorry Mr. Enidarrac." Dorothy was stammering.

"I said it is alright." Jack answered a bit more tersely, annoyed at having to repeat himself and taking his head away to glare at Dorothy. She stepped back, hesitated, then turned to the younger brother.

"Can I get either of you anything?" She asked. Keith was still standing in the doorway, his arms folded across his chest, but he didn't look angry, in fact he was transfixed on watching the little girl and his brother interacting. Not unlike his brother, he waved a dismissive hand towards Dorothy and entered the tiny office. Ruth, Terry and Dorothy stepped into the hallway.

"Is an hour enough time Jack?" Ruth asked kindly. Jack turned slightly and smiled at Ruth, he nodded. Ruth closed the door leaving her young daughter inside, Dorothy raised her eyebrows at Ruth, then looked at Terry and said, "They are filming a western, want to go watch?" Terry nodded and they all stepped away from Dorothy's office and disappeared down the hallway.

Jack stepped back, still holding the little girl's hands in his. "Why did you call me grasshopper?" He asked her.

"Everyone calls you that." She answered matter of factly. "I'm sorry, I know it irritates you."

"What do you mean everyone calls him that?" Keith asked incredulously. "Why would you say that?"

Jack glanced over his shoulder at Keith, only using his eyes he told Keith to stop talking. Izzy let her eyes rest on Keith for the first time. He was now twenty years old but to Izzy he could have been fifty. She felt strange, a little burning feeling deep inside, a flutter, something she didn't recognize but yet the feeling seemed so familiar to her. She felt like she was blushing, Jack noticed the growing color on her cheeks and stepped between her and his brother, blocking her view.

"It was a curious name to call me." He said to her, she looked down and shrugged, he could see she was going to clam up, so he put his forehead back against hers. He could feel her breathing slow and her manner begin to calm. "I have some questions for you sweetheart, can we talk for a bit?" He felt Izzy nod her head against his, without moving he asked Keith to sit down. "Let's talk about your letter to Keith, would that be alright?"

After a few moments, Keith had taken a chair against the wall, Dorothy had brought in some office chairs the day before in anticipation of the meeting. Jack told Izzy to sit behind the desk, telling the little girl that she should sit in the big leather chair since she was the boss of this conversation. The little girl had giggled in delight, it was an unexpected sound, kind of a low laugh unlike most little girls, it had a raspy hoarse sound to it and Keith thought to himself that it sounded familiar.

Jack didn't sit on a chair but rather sat on the edge of the desk. Izzy starred in admiration while she assessed him, he had a sculpted jawline and sensitive squinty eyes that were hazel, she was pleased with his appearance. She had always loved the way he looked.

Izzy's mother had found a channel that was playing reruns of a western series that Jack had acted in, so that Izzy would know what the man looked like. Izzy had pretended to be interested in the rerun, she didn't know how to explain to her mother that she would recognize Jack anywhere. Looking at Keith on the other hand made her extremely uncomfortable. He too had the same sculpted jawline and she remembered it well. He was tall with long legs. He moved awkwardly like he wasn't at home with himself. His eyes were dark and at times looked angry, she didn't like looking at him and averted her eyes to look only at Jack.

"Can you tell me where you heard Keith's song?" Jack asked.

"I haven't heard it." Izzy giggled again. " Not this time, I was just supposed to send it to you."

Jack picked up a framed photo off Dorothy's desk and pretended to look at it. Without looking at Izzy he asked casually, "Supposed to?"

Izzy nodded, she stood up from the desk chair so she could stand closer to Jack, she tried to look at the picture with him. The corners of his mouth curved but he didn't look at her, instead he set the frame down with the picture facing the top of the desk. He tickled Izzy under her chin and said. "Why don't you tell me the whole story? I think you know a lot more than you're telling me."

Jack had changed his questions from asking for "us" to "Me", he could sense tension between Izzy and his brother, so by removing Keith from the questions, he was putting the little girl at ease. Izzy took a pen off the desk and scribbled a little on a notepad next to it. She considered drawing a picture but she wasn't much of an artist. Even in coloring books Izzy scribbled outside of the lines, she just never liked the idea that colors should be confined inside one space. Jack felt Keith shift in his chair and without looking at his brother, he raised a hand motioning for him to sit still. After a few moments, Izzy looked up at Jack into his beautiful hazel eyes. She liked them because it was as if his eyes couldn't decide what color to be, they were all colors, green, blue, amber, brown. To her, his eyes meant he was like her, he was everything.

"He never liked that part. " She said, scrunching her nose. " Last time he fixed it, but he doesn't always remember to. He wanted me to remind him this time." Izzy said. Jack moved off the desk and sat in a chair beside it. He crossed his leg to rest his ankle on his knee and scratched the side of his face. Keith began to shift in his chair again but Jack held his hand up towards him and Keith stopped fidgeting.

"Last time?" Jack questioned the little girl. "You've said that a couple times now." He held Izzy's gaze in his and smiled kindly at her. Her heart had begun racing again, but his smile instantly calmed her as she looked into his changing eyes. She nodded.

"Yes." she said.

"Tell me about last time." Jack asked her. He put his hand out and took hold of hers as she scribbled. "It's okay, you can tell me, it might help me remember too. "

Izzy looked again into Jack's eyes, they reassured her. She took a deep breath. "You already know." She said, " You always already know. You told me last time to show you this." She looked down and drew a straight line on the paper, on the line she wrote Jack's name, then Keith's and finally Elizabeth, then she crossed it out and drew a circle beside it, writing the same names on the circle and handed it to Jack. At that moment there was a knock on the door and it opened, Dorothy, Ruth and Terry stood outside.

"Jack, I hope you found out what you wanted." Ruth said. "We have quite a drive ahead of us and we need to leave, poor Terry is getting very impatient." Jack smiled at Ruth, then looked at Izzy, he closed his fingers tightly around the piece of paper in his hand.

"Do you want to go to the ranch Izzy, or would you like to spend the afternoon with me?" Jack asked. Izzy's face brightened and Jack smiled even more, his dimples darkened and he smiled beguilingly at Ruth.

"I couldn't leave my daughter with you." Ruth stammered.

"Of course you can." Jack said. "I thought I'd take her to my dad's, we still have a lot to talk about." He turned to Izzy and said,

"Dad has some great danes, huge dogs, have you ever seen one before?" Izzy shook her head.

"She's afraid of dogs." Terry blurted out. "She got bit by the neighbor's dog Rango, he lives down the street from us. Now she's a giant chicken with dogs"

Ruth interrupted. "Terry, that dog is vicious and your sister isn't the only one who is afraid of it, the Humane Society is out there every other week. That dog killed Evelyn Trumble's poodle!" Ruth looked over at the brother's and continued. "It's an Airedale and mean as hell. The gate had been left open and it attacked my little girl. She needed sixteen stitches. She has every right to be frightened of dogs."

Jack took hold of Izzy's hand and led her around to the front of the desk. My dad's dogs are just big goofballs" He said looking into the little girl's dark blue eyes. She seemed so familiar to him. "I think even though you are little, you understand how important memories can be. If the only memory you have of a big dog is a bad memory, I can give you a nicer memory. I'd be with you the whole time sweetheart, you wouldn't be afraid with me there would you?" Jack could sense a bond growing with this little girl, he didn't understand it but he felt it, he was afraid of letting her go. When Ruth had come back to take the child away, it was as if the room had darkened, time felt thick to him. Everything had moved in slow motion. The little voice in his head told him that he needed more time. It had whispered to him from the moment he had awakened that day, it had whispered to him that Izzy was a key to his questions. It was as if he was trying to remember something important and it was almost there. He felt like he needed to hang onto this moment, she was part of a puzzle that he had been trying to put together for years.

"I wouldn't feel right about this Jack." Ruth said.

"My daughter will be there too, the two girls are about the same age. That would be much more fun for her than riding in a car for hours to get a horse for her sister." His words were harsh and struck Ruth where she was weakest. She felt as though she did everything for Terry and didn't pay enough attention to her youngest. Jack knew this from his conversations he had with her on the phone, he used it like a weapon now, stabbing his friend with her own words.

Izzy made it easy to ignore her, she seemed to be in her own little world most of the time. She wasn't interested in horses or sports, she spent most of her time alone in her room. She played with dolls and stuffed toys but also read books on astrology and space. She was a contradiction, half child and half philosopher and because of her quiet nature she was easily overlooked.

All the other children in the neighborhood were older than Izzy, they were Terry's friends. Terry usually invited Izzy to play along with them, but now the neighborhood children were getting older and developing their own interests. Izzy was being left behind. Jack's words stung and Ruth's eyes became a little teary. Jack caught himself as soon as he had said it, he could be such an ass to most people but he never intended to hurt Ruth's feelings, he had actually grown to like her over the past few months. In fact, it was more than liking her, he needed her. Ruth offered sanity to him in an otherwise insane industry. Weaponizing her thoughts to get his way was out of line. He thought about the man that he had become and for the first time that he could remember, he thought maybe he should change.

"I just mean," He corrected. "I can make the trip fun for both of them. It was an unfortunate choice of wording. Clearly you are a wonderful mother to both of your children, but with such different personalities, it must be difficult to plan anything that would please them both. Let me take Izzy for the afternoon, I'll keep her safe for you. You and I have grown to know each other very well, I think you know I wouldn't offer to take her if I didn't want to. When you return you can meet my daughter and my father."

Ruth looked down at her youngest child. Any other child would be pleading, Izzy just stood quietly looking intently at her mother, not so much as a please, but her eyes said it all. Izzy wanted to stay with Jack. Ruth didn't understand why Jack would want to keep her daughter or why Izzy who was quite shy would want to be left with a stranger, but Ruth thought to herself that there could be worse things than her daughter meeting a movie star, maybe this could help bring her little girl out of her shell. She looked at Dorothy who nodded in approvement.

"Jack can call me if anything happens, I can come get her anytime." Dorothy cooed. She had suddenly gone from the formal Mr. Enidarrac to a first name basis. Connections helped even in editing. She smiled to herself.

"I will want your father's phone number and address." Ruth said reluctantly. "I'll also give you the number to the ranch, you have Dorothy's number don't you?"

"I do." Jack confirmed in his soft spoken voice without mentioning it was written on his wall in his home. "May I?" he asked as he took the notepad from Dorothy's desk without waiting for a response. He wrote the address and phone number on the pad, tore the page off and handed it to Ruth. "I'll take good care of her." He promised. Ruth used the same notepad and jotted the ranch number down and handed it to Keith who had just been standing by silently. Jack took Izzy's hand and began to lead her out of the office. Keith was dumbfounded, he had no idea what had just transpired. He folded the paper with the phone number to the ranch in half and stuffed it deep inside his blue jeans back pocket. Nothing had been said to him since the little girl had handed Jack the piece of paper she had scribbled on. What in hell had intrigued his brother so much about this little girl.

Ruth and Terry were both somewhat olive skinned. Ruth stood five foot nine and had long legs and auburn hair. She was in her early fifties but still quite beautiful, high cheekbones and a thin face. Terry was incredibly striking, she wasn't going to be tall like her mother, but she had stunning features, beautiful almond shaped eyes that changed from blue to green depending on the light. Her hair was the color of honey with a few dark brown undertones. Terry had just turned twelve but was already attracting attention from boys and she had an infectious laugh and was very outgoing. Elizabeth was tall and lean, already taller than her older sister. She was pale skinned, her eyes were a very dark blue and her hair was extremely blonde and uncombed. She had long bangs that were uneven and occasionally hid her eyes. Still, when Keith looked at her, there was something familiar about her and even though he was frustrated, he felt almost at home in her presence, maybe that was what interested Jack in her. Lately his brother had been exploring transcendental experiences, trying to see auras and to better understand the non physical realm. Maybe Jack also felt this calming effect that seemed to emanate from the child. Whatever it was, Keith didn't like it. He resented it. He hated that his life was spiraling out of control and he had enough difficult emotions to deal with for the time being. Something about this little girl made him uncomfortable, maybe it was her innocent face, but it made him question the choices he had been making and he was angry with Jack for prolonging the visit.

Before heading to their father's home, Jack had to make two stops. He first stopped to pick up his daughter, he pulled up on the driveway and honked. After waiting patiently for ten minutes he honked again, holding the horn obnoxiously for a few minutes. After the second honk, his daughter Cassie came out the front door, her mother watched from the doorway. Cassie was a pretty girl, creamy brown hair and strong features like her father. She got in the back seat with Izzy and waited for an explanation. Jack backed out of the driveway, his right arm resting on the top of the seat as he looked over his shoulder to see behind the car.

He was driving his brother's car, a green Pontiac sedan. Jack's car was a Ferrari and a two seater, they never would have all fit in Jack's car. Keith's skin began to tingle a bit as he slowly came to the realization that Jack had planned this in advance. His brother had intended on taking the child. Keith shook his head silently to himself, Jack fooled a lot of people. He could be impulsive and self indulgent, few people understood how carefully Jack planned everything.

Jack explained to his daughter as they drove away that Izzy was the daughter of a friend of his and that he was watching her for the afternoon. The two girls eyed one another for a little while but before they arrived at Jack's second stop they were whispering in each other's ears and giggling. Jack pulled the car onto his own driveway behind the bright red Ferrari that was parked in the garage. The garage door had been left open. He put the car in park and turned off the ignition then leaned over the back seat.

"Keith and I need to go inside for a few minutes, the two of you stay in the car." Cassie nodded and watched as her father and uncle exited the car and entered the house. As soon as they were gone the two began to whisper to one another again.

"I don't get it." Keith said. "Are you going to tell me what is going on?" Jack nodded and walked into the kitchen. Aside from a small table and chairs, there was a wooden desk against the back wall next to the patio doors. It partially blocked the arcadia door but it was a small house and not a lot of room for the desk. Jack opened the bottom drawer and pulled out an outline for a script. He handed it to his brother.

"Read this," he said. "It's the television show I told you about."

Keith took the papers and sat down at the table. He read only a few pages before he saw it. "What the fuck?" He said.

"Your lyrics, now my script....there is just no way in hell she could know these things." Jack said to his brother. "But there it is," he said, pointing to a word on the page. "Grasshopper."

Keith ran his hands through his hair, he re-read the pages, then stood up and looked out the patio door. The script gave Jack's character a nickname, it was grasshopper.

"Is this the twilight zone? Could someone have put her up to this?" Keith asked.

"To what end? It would be an elaborate hoax with no purpose. You've watched her for a couple hours now, does she seem like a hoaxer to you? She is a nice little girl, her family is nice. I can't shake the feeling that I'm supposed to know her. There is something so unusual about her."

"You can say that again." Keith mumbled. "Have you noticed how she smells?"

"Smells?" Jack asked. "She smells good."

"Yeah." Keith acknowledged. "But it changes."

"Explain." Jack commanded his younger brother.

"Alright" Keith said while crossing his arms against his chest, "When we first met her at Dorothy's office, she smelled like she had just taken a bath in a Lilac bubble bath. I wondered at first if it was one of the women, you know that sometimes I can be a little sensitive to perfume and you know how older women like to douse themselves in it. Except it wasn't heavy, it was just nice." Keith said. "But the more she talked with you, the scent changed, she smelled more like something wild, I don't know, honeysuckle maybe?. Now in the car it is more like roses, I barely notice it, it's very subtle."

Jack sat down on the kitchen chair and contemplated what his brother had noticed. "Yes, now that you mention it, I notice it too. It is one more intriguing reason I need to know more about this little girl. She is highly unusual, even you have got to see that?" Jack said, smiling sheepishly at his little brother. "She just knows things. I want to know what else she knows."

Jack remembered something he had read about memories, that they can be triggered by scent. He had been curious about her before meeting her, extremely curious, he had even decided beforehand on taking her for the afternoon, but after finally seeing her she felt so familiar to him. He nodded to himself, perhaps it wasn't seeing her, perhaps it was smelling her that made him feel this way. He contemplated his brother's behavior, it too had changed on meeting Izzy. He seemed hostile, behavior that was unusual for his little brother. The more he considered Izzy and the effect she had on both of them, the more curious he became.

Keith nudged him. "Do you have a plan? She isn't exactly forthcoming."

"You've noticed that too?" Jack smirked. "I know a little about kids, mine can be secretive too. We need to gain her trust, how better than a family day with Grandpa?"

Keith didn't look convinced. "I'm willing to give it a shot." He grinned. "At least now we both want answers."

"Do me a favor Keith." Jack requested. "Try to avoid talking directly to her."

"Shouldn't I be the one asking her the questions? I mean, she sent the letter to me." Keith reminded his brother.

"She did," Jack acknowledged. "But clearly you make her uncomfortable. Just try to keep Dad out of my way and let me do the talking."

Keith nodded. He had noticed the little girl didn't seem to like him. He thought it was strange, she had written the letter to him! Maybe he had come off a little aggressive. He didn't really understand kids and wasn't prepared to be a father. Kids were a bit of a sore subject to him at the moment. He would let Jack take over, he actually felt relieved that Jack wanted to.

When the two brothers returned to the car, the girls were missing. Jack slapped the roof of the Pontiac with an open palm but then heard the girls laughing. They were at the neighbors house talking to Braden. Braden was the teenage boy next door. He was about fourteen or fifteen and a terrible flirt, apparently even two girls no older than eight and nine were fair game. Jack opened the car door and honked the horn, the girls immediately ran to the car and climbed into the backseat.

"What part of staying in the car didn't you understand?" He said to his daughter. It wasn't a question. He didn't raise his voice, but both girls instantly knew he was angry. "When I tell you to do something, you do it, do you understand?" Both girls nodded. Jack started the car and backed out of the driveway. Cassie reached over and squeezed Izzy's hand, then they began whispering to each other again.

When the car arrived at their next stop, the boy's father John was in the front yard. He had just watered the bougainvilleas that lined the front doorway and was now kneeling in the damp earth and pulling a few weeds. He was wearing shorts and when he stood up his knees were muddy as were his hands. He used the wrought Iron trellis by the front door to help himself stand all the way up. He wiped sweat from his forehead leaving a muddy streak across his wrinkled brow. John loved his flowers, he loved the smell of the earth and loved nurturing his plants to grow. Jack laughed to himself at the irony.

John's house was pretty simple, most of the family gatherings happened in the backyard. There was a large brick patio, lots of overgrown shrubbery that allowed for privacy and a barbeque pit. The yard was large, extending back quite a bit into the tangled shrubs. It provided ample privacy as well as lots of space for his large black and white great danes. Izzy would have been timid around the dogs, but Cassie was bold. She grabbed hold of one of the hounds and buried her face against it. The dog collapsed on the patio and showed his belly. Before long, both the girls were doting on the dog, scratching his belly and giving him hugs. John was curious about the child Jack had brought with him, but Jack was cautious with the explanation he provided. He simply said he was watching the girl for a friend. John wanted to know what this "friend" looked like, Jack assured him that there was nothing nefarious going on, the mother was an older woman in her fifties and was indeed just a friend. John laughed at the answer "Just making sure I don't have another grandchild," He laughed then dropped the subject completely.

The afternoon was very pleasant. They roasted hot dogs and both Jack and Keith took turns playing the guitar and singing songs. The two girls sat at Jack's feet and watched him wide eyed, begging for more each time he finished a song. Jack's hair would fall over his eyes anytime a strong breeze blew through the yard. He would shake his head to get it off his face only to have it blow back covering his eyes again in a few minutes. Izzy was becoming infatuated with his charm. He would start to smile ever so slowly, his dimples would just start to show, then he would glance sideways at the two girls and the smile would grow. By early evening, Izzy was just part of the crowd, she fit in with the whole family and Jack felt as though she had finally let her guard down,

"Izzy." He said gently, "How about we go inside and talk a little bit?" Izzy nodded then bent down and kissed the dog closest to her on the nose, she then followed Jack inside to the kitchen. They sat down at the table, it was round and covered with a red and white checkered tablecloth. Jack pulled the paper out of his pocket that Izzy had given to him and laid it on the table in front of them. "What does this mean?" He asked her.

Izzy sighed, being eight she wasn't a small child, she could articulate her thoughts quite well and she had a good vocabulary, however, she clearly didn't like explaining things. Even the letter she had mailed to Keith seemed to be forced. Terry was the talker of the two of them, Izzy wasn't used to having to answer. Izzy preferred to put her thoughts on paper and keep them private, she had hoped that giving Jack the drawing would be enough. She took the paper and fiddled with it for a few moments. Jack impatiently considered taking it away from her because he was getting frustrated, but thought better of it.

"Back in the olden days," Izzy finally began looking up into Jack's hazel eyes. She then laughed her hoarse laugh and continued. "They used to think that the world was flat. Isn't that stupid?" She giggled. Jack smiled and nodded to her. "Well, time isn't flat either, this is how you explained it to me the last time." Izzy said simply. She stopped talking and shoved the paper back towards Jack.

"Time isn't linear?" He tried to clarify.

"Yeah, linear." She answered. He looked down at the paper, he understood, it was suddenly very clear to him. That drawing would be exactly how he would have explained it.

"So, you remember." He said. It wasn't a question. Izzy nodded.

"I have a really good memory, my mom says I have a memory like a hawk." Izzy said. She wasn't bragging at all, just providing Jack with information he needed.

Jack stood up and looked outside through the back door window. His father, brother and daughter were all sitting on the woven lawn chairs, Keith had the guitar on his lap but wasn't playing it. He was leaning over it in deep conversation with his father. John was talking about something, demanding attention. Jack looked over his shoulder at Izzy who was still seated at the kitchen table. She was swinging her feet back and forth under the kitchen chair and smiling at Jack. "You remembered the song?" He tried to clarify.

"Um, not really, just that part of it." Izzy said. "Keith wanted me to tell him."

"Keith wanted you to tell him? Were you close to Keith?" He asked her while smiling. He was beginning to understand some of the girl's emotions.

Izzy looked down at the table in front of her. "I suppose," She whispered. "I keep marrying him". She reluctantly admitted while rolling her eyes. "but I'm not going to love him this time." She said determinedly. "He seems meaner than I remember. I should love you instead, you are way nicer."

Jack couldn't hide his grin, he really liked this little girl. "And calling me grasshopper, you remembered that too?" He asked. Izzy nodded. "What else do you remember?" He gently asked the little girl.

3

Ruth couldn't believe she had met the boy's famous father John. Even in his old age, he was a handsome man. He had been so gracious, he seemed pleased to meet her, she had sat on his patio, drank an iced tea and even petted his dog. Izzy apparently had made quite an impression on Jack, the two of them seemed almost inseparable by the evening's end. Terry, Cassie and Keith talked about horses, Terry was impressed with Keith's knowledge about everything western. Keith had explained to Terry that his brother performed in western television shows and had encouraged Keith to ride well so that he could also audition for roles in that genre. He had discovered that he enjoyed riding and was becoming an accomplished horseman. Terry and Keith had spent a good hour talking about horses, Terry had told Keith all about the new mare and dressage. Keith had even told her that he would love to attend one of her shows.

Jack and John spent the hour visiting with Dorothy and Ruth, joking about some of the recent scandals in Hollywood. John told Ruth that Frank Sinatra had his ex-wife Mia Farrow served with divorce papers while she was on the set of Rosemary's baby. The marriage had been a scandal to begin with since Frank was more than twice Mia's age when he had married her and she was barely 21 at the time. They talked about drug use in Hollywood, he confirmed that Judy Garland had been fired from Valley of the Dolls due to her drug addiction. John seemed so sad as he talked, often letting his eyes rest on his son Jack as he spoke. Ruth could feel the disappointment in John's voice. It was a tone she had learned early on from her own father. She understood of course why John would be worried for his son who was developing a reputation of being a drug user, but she also understood how the behavior hurt, that often disappointment instead of love could drive a person to further alienate themselves. She knew this from experience. Ruth let her eyes move towards Jack who she had grown to care deeply for and she realized that he was intently studying her little girl. It dawned on her that his eyes had seldom strayed from Izzy since her arrival and she wondered what the fascination was that he had with her little girl. Whatever it was, she could sense it was positive, Izzy had a calming effect on him and that pleased her.

As Dorothy drove away with Ruth and the children, Ruth said that she hoped they would see Jack again. Izzy smiled softly, "You will mom, he always liked you." Izzy said.

Ruth furrowed her brows and started to ask her youngest daughter what she meant by that, but then changed her mind. Izzy always phrased things oddly, Dorothy had told Ruth a few years ago that her brother Jim had done the same thing as a child. She assured Ruth it was nothing to worry about. Ruth glanced over her shoulder in the back seat at her little girl. Izzy was happier than she had seen her in a long time.

"You and Jack are very similar." She said, "Watching the two of you, I was actually amazed. Even your facial expressions, I told him so before we left." Ruth said. Izzy smiled at her mother.

"We are always a lot alike mom." She replied.

⟶ ᘒᓬ ⟵

"**S**o you're telling me she is reincarnated?" Keith asked incredulously.

"No, that isn't the same thing." Jack said. He was sitting on the couch, he was slouched back and smoking a cigar, grinning ear to ear.

"I don't get it." Keith said. "How can you be so gullible?"

"Keith, settle down." Jack laughed.

"Settle down?, you didn't have an eight year old hitting on you." Keith said.

"Oh god, she wasn't hitting on you, and I told you she thinks that you are mean." Jack laughed.

"Oh well in that case I guess it's fine." Keith said sarcastically, "So you believe her?"

"It makes sense if you think about it." Jack said calmly. "Haven't you ever done something and thought to yourself that you remembered doing it before?"

"Yeah, deja vu." Keith said. "Everyone has moments of deja vu."

"What if it is actually a memory, a memory of time before this life?" Jack asked.

"It's a bunch of crap." Keith said sullenly.

"Little brother, be careful or you will fall off the edge of the earth." Jack laughed. He could just visualize Izzy's adorable little face when she told him people thought the earth was flat back in the olden days.

Keith picked up the paper that Jack had placed on the coffee table in front of them. He knew now what it meant, Jack had explained it all. He laughed and set it back down.

"So you believe we live the same life over and over?" Keith said mockingly.

"I didn't say that." Jack said. "Neither did the girl. What she did say, was time repeated. It's not always the same, but parts can be. You are still the same person, you can make different choices. It makes so much sense if you think about it."

"Jack, it doesn't make any sense at all! What about God?" Keith asked. "I know you believe in God, how would this make sense with the teachings of our church?"

Jack stroked his chin and smiled. "We both know there is a lot about God and the universe that we simply are not capable of understanding. I believe in the girl, I also believe in God."

Keith was perplexed, his brother could be so aggravating. "And in this other timeline, she was the love of my life?" Keith asked.

Jack smiled at his brother, Keith was incensed that a child would speak of him in that manner, circumstances out of Keith's control made Keith uncomfortable with children for the moment. He didn't dislike Izzy, but he disliked all children right now. Keith, not unlike himself, could be bullheaded.

"Eleven years younger than you, seems about right for the perfect Hollywood marriage." Jack winked at his brother. He knew he wasn't going to get through to Keith this time. He smiled to himself realizing that was exactly what Izzy would have done in his place. She would just smile and drop the subject. The little girl seemed to understand the people around her and knew when they would hear her or not. Izzy knew when to talk and when to give up. Ruth was right, he had a lot in common with that little girl.

Jack dismissed Keith without speaking another word and picked up the television script that he had set beside him and began reading it. He hadn't liked it in the beginning, it was just another western, a strange western. After rereading it, his opinion was changing, he liked it now. Izzy had told him that it was going to change his life, now he thumbed through the pages eagerly, he could see how this show could enlighten him. He had been offered the role but hadn't yet accepted, tomorrow he would seal it. He thought about pouring himself a scotch, but he wanted to read this thing with a clear mind.

Keith sat beside his older brother silently for a while, watching him gleefully reading the script. Was he seriously taking the career advice of an eight year old? How could his brother be so reckless? Jack was completely ignoring him, Keith reached over and shoved Jack's leg, Jack just smiled and kept reading. Keith stood up deciding to go to his room, maybe read a little himself. He had just purchased the newest Louis L'amour book Reilly's Luck and wanted to start it. All the talk of westerns from the evening made him feel the need to indulge in the new book.

"Love of my life, whatever." He snorted while heading to his room. Jack didn't even look up.

4

The first time Jack decided to go to Nebraska, he didn't tell anyone. In the airplane, he looked out the window at the forever stretch of endless farming squares below and questioned why he had come, but when he stepped out of the plane and saw the bright blue sky, something whispered "home" to him. The air was humid and it was a little hard to breathe but the sky was clear and the land was lush and green. He rented a car from a booth for Hertz at the bottom of the escalators in the Lincoln Nebraska airport and asked for a map of the city. Sitting behind the wheel of the rental in the airport parking lot, he spread the map out on the passenger seat beside him. Once he found his way to the main street in Lincoln, it appeared he could follow it all the way to the street the Meeks family home was on.

He found that getting to Ruth's house was simple, he probably could have just asked for directions instead of getting a map. Lincoln appeared to be sensibly planned. Lettered streets went East to West, In-between the lettered streets were tree names and Indian tribes. Numbered streets went North to South. In-between numbered streets were last names and descriptive names. It was a sensible grid. The house was just off the main street in town and across from a large shopping mall. He pulled off O street and onto Eastridge Drive, then immediately turned left onto Bruce Drive and headed up a somewhat steep street. The houses were all neat little ranch style homes, all with well watered front lawns and a mailbox at the curb making it feel very rural. He parked in the street and turned off the ignition. The red brick house looked warm and inviting. He stayed in the car for a few minutes, just taking it all in. There were brightly colored rose bushes beneath the kitchen window, evergreen trees on either side of the house. A large picture window on the left front of the house with a wrought iron trellis beneath it. A yellow honeysuckle vine covered most of the trellis and two round evergreen bushes lined the front concrete steps. As he sat in the parked car inspecting the Meeks home, he told himself that he had done crazier things, sometimes he felt as if he had no control over what he did. Something just took over and he lost all reason and all judgment. This time his little voice told him that he needed sanity, he needed help, he needed to reach out to someone sane and the most sane person that he had ever met was Ruth.

Terry and Ruth were listening to music on the stereo in the living room. They were playing one of Jim's old records. It was Eddie Arnold's Cattle Call. Terry hated it but it made her mother happy so she tolerated it. Izzy was tucked away in her room writing a fairy tale. Jack tried to remember how long it had been, was it one or two years? He couldn't quite recall. He and Ruth had remained friends, talking frequently on the phone. He often spoke with Izzy who eagerly waited for her turn to talk to him, then she would hand the phone back to her mother and gallop off to her room.

Jack and Izzy mainly communicated via letter writing. When the girl wanted to express thoughts privately, it was easier to accomplish using letters. Jack felt a little guilty communicating covertly, but it was the only way he had to ask the girl questions about time without her mother knowing. Ruth thought it was cute thinking that the two were pen pals and had no issues mailing letters for her daughter.

Ruth had thanked Jack for helping to bring Izzy out of her shell, the little girl talked non stop now just like her sister. Jack didn't tell Ruth about Izzy's memories or even that he was having them too, it was a secret that he shared with the little girl. She had come out of her shell because it felt good to talk to someone who believed her. Jack hadn't bothered to tell Keith that he still spoke with Izzy for the same reason, he knew that Keith wouldn't believe him but he suspected that his brother knew that he was still in touch with the Meeks family.

Jack had started feeling out of control a few months ago. He had really messed up this time, he needed to hide for a while, keep a low profile. He needed someone to help him find his way back to sanity. Sometimes, Jack went a little crazy. Sometimes he turned to drugs, sometimes he became erratic, sometimes it was a combination of both.

Izzy stumbled out of her room and silently entered the living area. At first Terry and Ruth didn't even notice her, when they did and looked up, they were startled by her face.

"What is it darling?" Ruth asked, growing concerned and turning off the stereo.

"He's here Mom." She answered. "It's starting now."

Terry got up and looked out the large picture window. "Mom, It's Jack." She said.

A moment later the doorbell rang. Ruth looked at her daughter and tilted her head. "He needs you to help him Mom." Izzy said.

Terry opened the door, Jack stood on the front step, holding a bouquet of flowers that he had purchased at the Lincoln airport with the last dollar bill that he had in his pocket. The bouquet wasn't very pretty and had lots of daisies and red carnations. He was smiling and his dimples looked good. His hair was a mess and he looked like he needed sleep. There were dark circles under his eyes, he looked thin.

"Jack!" Ruth exclaimed and told Terry to let him in the door. He took long strides and embraced Ruth holding her tight like a little boy hugging his mother after coming home from camp. Ruth hugged him back and didn't let go until he did. She was good at that, knowing when someone needed help or love. Ruth was good at knowing when someone was reaching out, when they needed someone to take their hand. He let go and handed her the flowers.

"Thank you Jack." She said, "My goodness, what a surprise."

"There wasn't a big selection." Jack said sheepishly. "And everything was red and white."

"Red and white are the football team colors." Terry answered. "The spring game is today."

"Is that a big thing here?" Jack asked.

"You should probably study up on that if you want to continue a friendship with mom." Izzy laughed.

"Or anyone in Nebraska." Terry added.

"Isn't the spring game just a scrimmage?" Jack asked.

"Yes!" Terry confirmed. "Red against white. It's late this year, there was a freak snowstorm earlier and they had to cancel, then the next one was canceled because of hail. I think this is the latest that they ever had one, school is already out."

Jack wasn't sure what to say, he hadn't planned that far ahead. He knew that Ruth loved football and wondered if he was interrupting her plans. He only knew he needed to be there. He stammered a bit but Ruth helped him out. "I'm so glad you are here." She said, "I hope you can stay for a while."

Jack visibly exhaled. He and Ruth had become close friends, talking on the telephone, but they hadn't seen each other since Ruth's trip to California. She thought of him as a boy, almost a son, and he needed that so badly right now and if Ruth was honest, she needed it too.

"I'm sorry I didn't call." He stammered. "I had hoped you would enjoy a surprise. If I'm putting you out at all, I can go to a hotel."

"I wouldn't hear of it." Ruth said. "Did you bring a bag?"

Jack realized that he had come completely unprepared. No luggage whatsoever. He was a little embarrassed, but he also knew that Ruth was aware of some of his problems. Newspapers and gossip magazines had printed a lot of stories about him lately. Doing the television show had got him into thinking different ways, fame had added a great deal of tension to his life. He had never dreamed the show would be as big as it was and he had never planned on staying with it that long. Jack loved the theater, the show trapped him. He acted like any caged animal, sometimes with depression and sometimes with anger. Either option often led to bad behavior and negative press. "No." He said. "I accidentally forgot to put it in the cab. I was so anxious to get on the plane." He lied.

"Terry, can you put the record back in the sleeve for me?" She asked her daughter, " Then please put it away with the others. I would hate for your father's record to get scratched ". Then to Jack she said, "That is no problem sweetie," We can get you everything you need. Are you hungry?" She asked.

Izzy slowly approached Jack and hugged him sweetly. She was eleven now, she had grown quite a bit. Her hair was actually combed and hung in a loose ponytail behind her back. Jack bent down to kiss her cheek. She whispered something in his ear and he looked at Ruth for a moment and seemed as if he might cry. Izzy had seen Ruth's colors begin to glow and she had told him so, Jack felt like he had finally come home.

Ruth and Jack sat at the kitchen table for a few moments, Ruth had poured them both a cup of coffee from the electric percolator, Ruth drank her coffee black, the neighbors had always joked that if you put a spoon in her coffee cup, it would stand straight up. She liked her coffee to be strong. Jack didn't complain, Izzy guessed Jack needed his coffee to be strong too. He had smelled a bit of whiskey when she hugged him.

After a while, Jack and Ruth took their coffee and walked outside. Izzy watched from the window as her mother and Jack strolled in the back flower garden. Terry nudged her sister a little to the side so she could get a better view. The windows were high and they had to stand on the cedar chest in Terry's bedroom to watch, but they managed.

"Why is he here?" Terry asked. Izzy shrugged but Terry wouldn't accept it. "Tell me." She nudged. "I know you know, I'm not mom, you can tell me."

Izzy stepped off the chest and sat on the bed. "Jack gets frightened." She murmured.

"About what?" Terry asked.

"Not having control I think." Izzy answered.

"Who isn't afraid of that?" Terry said. "Men don't deal with stress well. Let them have a period for a few months, that would toughen them up." The girls laughed, Terry with her contagious laugh and Izzy with her hoarse giggle.

"He doesn't have a lot of support and he puts tremendous pressure on himself." Izzy said. "He is really impatient too. His dad gets mad at him."

"I thought you liked his dad?" Terry said.

"It's not that I don't like him, I just wish Jack and his dad could, I don't know, something is broken with them."

Terry nodded. "You and I are fairly lucky, none of my friends have a mom like ours. Granted, she can drive me crazy. I mean my God, Eddie Arnold? Really? But, she is always there for us and she gives us privacy. She has no clue what's in your little letters that you and Jack keep sending to each other." Terry got off the chest and sat next to her little sister on her bed. "I wonder sometimes about fate." Terry said. Izzy looked at her and waited. "Like, is there a God, did God bring us to Jack? Is there a reason for everything?"

"Stop it". Izzy said. "It's too deep. My brain will stop developing."

"Your brain has already stopped developing, you are a mutant." Terry teased her sister. "Besides, I am not Mom, I have read a few of your letters."

"Terry!." Izzy raised her voice.

"Settle down, the ones that I read are boring as hell. The point is, I know you think about things like that." Terry began. "So don't play stupid. You have all those weird ideas in your head. Don't you think fate is why you wrote to Jack in the first place?"

Izzy shook her head. She had already shared some of her thoughts with her sister over the years, but not all of them. The little voice in Izzy's head had always cautioned her not to speak of her memories and she still felt she needed to proceed with caution.

"First of all, Miss Snoopy Pants." Izzy began, "I didn't write that first letter to Jack, I wrote it to his brother. Second, there is no such thing as fate, destiny, anything like that Terry, there is only time."

"You are a weird little girl Izzy." Terry said. "If there is only time then why can't you learn to stop acting so strangely? Seems to me you would have plenty of time practicing to be normal by now." Terry paused. She and her sister talked a lot about what Izzy felt, how she was different, yet Terry knew that Izzy still kept a lot inside. She had read some of the letters, but not to be snoopy, it was out of hope for a better understanding of her little sister. Terry was protective of Izzy but she enjoyed teasing her if the opportunity presented itself. "So mutant," she continued, "I still think it's cool that Mom and Jack are such good friends. It drives Aunt Dorothy nuts! It will be hilarious when Dorothy finds out he came to visit her!"

Izzy nodded in agreement. She loved her aunt Dorothy but she agreed, Dorothy was a little jealous that Ruth and Jack had become such good friends. Ruth had never told anyone of the friendship, neither had the girls. For some reason, it had just seemed like a private thing to each of them. Izzy was wondering about what response if any Jack's appearance would cause in the neighborhood.

"Girls." Ruth called from the kitchen door. "I'm taking Jack to Sears, do you want to come?" Terry and Izzy left the bedroom and joined their mother and Jack in the kitchen. They stepped out into the garage and they all climbed into their mother's blue impala and drove down the street towards the mall.

Sears was connected to the mall with a long ugly walkway. Inside the walkway it was carpeted with orange carpet and lined with other stores. There was a jewelry store, a toy store, a western store and on the other end was Montgomery Wards. Jack wasn't worried about being recognized, he just kept his head down and followed Ruth and the girls. Ruth bought him everything he needed, jeans and t-shirts and even underwear. He was ashamed to admit it, but he enjoyed it. After Sears they walked into the sky walk and went to the western store. Gateway Western had everything from hoof picks to wrangler jeans. Jack picked out some western shirts and found a black leather cowboy hat that he loved. Ruth bought it all, she hesitated a little at the cowboy hat, but when Jack put it back, she took it off the shelf and brought it up to the counter. Terry bought a new pair of Wrangler bootcut jeans. Izzy just watched and smiled.

Jack had come without cash and only one credit card which was almost maxed out. He hadn't brought any luggage and didn't even have a change of clothes with him. Ruth seemed to enjoy having an opportunity to take care of him. After the western store they continued on to Kinney's shoes. She bought him a pair of tennis shoes but ended up going back to the western store for some boots. Jack's face had gone from looking sullen and pale to bright and cheerful. He was smiling and laughing, he flirted with the young girl who helped him try on a pair of boots, winking at her when she tried to slip the boot on his foot. She didn't recognize him at all, it was almost like he was playing a part of an unidentified man. He was so good at acting like he was no one, Izzy thought that he was amazing.

After the mall, Ruth drove to a drive thru restaurant that Jack had never heard of. It was a strange building, you ordered on the drivers side and then pulled up to be handed your order through the passenger side window. It was called Tastee's. Ruth ordered for everyone and they brought it all home. The sandwiches were like sloppy joes and the side was deep fried onion chips with a creamy dip. The sandwiches had mustard and pickles. Jack loved them! "I need to come to Nebraska more often!" he exclaimed. "These are delicious!"

"I would love for you to come more often!" Ruth said and she meant it. "Jack, you are working yourself to the bone. You need to take better care of yourself."

So this is what a real family feels like, Jack thought to himself. He kicked off his shoes and the girls pretended to faint at the smell. He fanned his feet towards them and they screamed. Jack belched loudly and Terry copied him. Ruth rolled her eyes. He could get used to this, he thought to himself, maybe he should get married again. He had a serious girlfriend now, she made him happy. He wanted this, he wanted what Ruth had, he was glad she was letting him be a part of it.

Ruth placed their purchases in the guest room for Jack, then she went to the basement and rummaged through some boxes. After a while she came back upstairs with a handful of shirts, sweaters and blue jeans. She handed them to Jack.

"You can try these things on and see if they fit. You are welcome to any of them." She told him.

Jack held a brown and white ski sweater from the pile to just under his chin and nodded approval judging the size. The mornings were still brisk in Nebraska this time of year, by noon the day would be hot. It would have been senseless to buy warm clothing that would only be worn a few times in the morning.

"I didn't realize that your husband and I were so similar in size." Jack said, sitting down at the kitchen table and placing the pile of clothes in front of him.

Ruth laughed. "He wasn't." She said, "These are Kent's"

"Who is Kent?" Jack asked her suspiciously.

"My youngest son." Ruth answered.

"Youngest son? Youngest implies more than one. I wasn't aware you had any sons." Jack said.

"I guess I've never really told you about them." Ruth answered, taking a chair next to Jack. "They were from my first marriage. John is married and living in Alaska with his wife at Elmendorf Air force base. He is a dentist!"

"Where is Kent?" Jack asked. He could sense a sadness in Ruth.

"He is in Vietnam." Terry said as she entered the kitchen. "Mom doesn't like to talk about it."

"I had no idea Ruth." Jack responded. He was at a loss for words.

"Why would you?" Ruth said cheerfully. "I guess I kept it from you. If I pretend it isn't real, I don't worry as much."

"I told you mom, Kent is alright, he will be fine. He is always alright." Izzy said from the doorway of the kitchen. She was watching her mother intently.

A new thought crept into Jack's mind, there was more to Izzy than her memories. Izzy could do more than simply remember, she felt things. She had been drawn into the kitchen just now by her senses, he was sure of it. He had suspected there was more to her for a while, her letters betrayed her. She seemed to sense when to write to him, to know in advance when he was upset or sad. He had suspected for a while, but now he was sure, Izzy was an empath. It explained so much more to him, he was surprised that he had missed it.

He reflected on this new perception of the young girl. It explained the colors that she saw when she studied people, the colors were a reflection of emotions, her brain interpreted the emotions into colors. He had been reading about auras, he had studied them for years. People perceive aura's when a chemical or electrical wave moves across the visual cortex of their brain. People, any living thing actually, produces energy and energy can be transformed into electricity. He played with this new thought, if a person were somehow able to perceive that energy, then transform it electrically in their brain, then their colors would be visible. He nodded to himself, this new thought brought him clarity. He wondered if it was something that Izzy could teach him to do.

Then his mind wandered again. It could be chemical. Just like Izzy's perfume, the oil reacted to her personal chemistry. Perhaps she could "see" the chemical reaction in other people? Either way, the result would be the same, or would it? Would seeing someone's colors be the same thing as feeling someone's colors? He was confusing himself. Jack smiled at the girl and reached for her hand. When she took hold of him, for a moment he felt what she felt. He wasn't surprised, the connection between the two of them had grown even stronger over the last few years.

Holding Izzy's hand, Jack felt there was a heavy darkness surrounding Ruth, he could feel it through Izzy. The sadness was almost unbearable. Was this what it was like for the girl? Did she feel everything around her? Just this brief moment was more than Jack could stand, he couldn't imagine taking on everyone's pain. No wonder why she spent so much time alone, why she avoided conversation. How incredibly brave she must be.

Izzy's eyes connected with Jack's. He knew! She was sure that he knew. She remembered the times before, before this lifetime. Jack and she had always shared a connection. His ability was different from hers, but he could see the colors and he could feel emotions. Izzy understood that Jack didn't randomly decide to get on a plane, his subconscious had been planning this for a while. Jack planned everything, sometimes he fooled himself into thinking he was acting spontaneously, but he wasn't. Jack planned every spoken word, every action. Jack needed to be able to reach inside himself, he was ready to start his journey, his little voice had led him here. Everything was connected, he needed to learn to be happy before his brother Keith could be happy. Izzy thought about Keith, she knew that the universe was still driving her towards him, in the past her happiness had always depended upon Keith's. They were a trio, a trio that always started with Jack. It was time for Jack to learn and it was time for Izzy to decide her future. She still wasn't sure if the life she had always had was the one that she wanted now. She nodded to herself, their connection was impossible to define, but it was time for Jack to start his journey and it was also time for Izzy. The future lay ahead of them both and the choices they made now would lead the way.

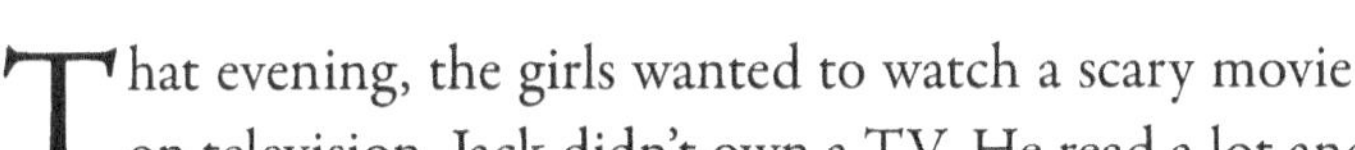

That evening, the girls wanted to watch a scary movie that was on television. Jack didn't own a TV. He read a lot and worked out, he had always thought television was a waste of time, but at this moment, with the two girls he felt so happy that maybe he would reconsider his thoughts about owning a television.

"Do you believe in God?" Terry asked Jack while they settled down in front of the television. When Terry was focused on a subject it was always difficult for her to think of anything else. She always put her whole self into learning. Izzy smiled at her sister knowing that was why she was so smart and did so well in school. Terry would never let it go until she decided for herself or until she fully understood. Terry loved to be challenged.

Izzy turned the channel to station 10, Creature Feature was about to start. Terry kept her eyes fixed on Jack while she grabbed a small handful of popcorn from the big yellow bowl in front of them.

"Terry Leigh!" Ruth said in a raised voice. Jack smiled and tossed a piece of popcorn up in the air and caught it with his open mouth.

"It's quite alright Ruth," Jack said, crunching the popcorn and smiling.

"I only ask because Izzy doesn't and I'm still trying to decide." Terry said.

"I didn't say that," Izzy said quietly. "What I said was I didn't believe in church."

Jack choked on a piece of popcorn. "What do you mean you don't believe in church?" He asked incredulously. "It's there, how can you not believe in it?"

"I don't mean I don't believe that they exist." Izzy laughed. "Of course churches exist. My point is churches are man made. They are controlled by men, and people, especially men, and churches always have an agenda."

Jack considered her words as he popped another corn kernel into his mouth. Izzy had certainly matured. She was much more forthcoming now, he was certainly grateful for that. He had a lot of questions to ask and he remembered how hard he had to work at getting answers from her the last time. Her letters were more open, but Izzy had always been more comfortable putting her thoughts on paper.

Ruth stood up and said, "I leave you to the children and the creature feature. If you get frightened by either, lock your door tonight." She left the three alone snickering as she went.

"How old are you?" He asked Terry. "I'm sure you are much too young to be asking questions like that."

"Jesus." Terry said. "I would think someone like you of all people would be more open minded. I'm almost fourteen and all my friends have conversations like this. Izzy is eleven years old, did she sound immature to you just now? She says there is no God, only time, whatever that means."

"Wrong again Terry, I said there is no fate, only time. Fate and God are two entirely different things." Izzy defended herself.

"So you believe in God?" Terry asked.

"I didn't say that either, just that I never said that there is no God." Izzy laughed.

"Why can't you just answer my question?" Terry argued. "It's a yes or no question, you don't even have to work at the answer. Jesus Izzy, why do you make everything so freaking hard?"

"Maybe I'm just trying to be diplomatic Terry, you know how everyone is. If I say something against Jack's beliefs, it might make him mad, if I say something negative about God in front of mom she will get upset. She gets worried enough about Kent, she doesn't need to worry about my soul. If I say something you disagree with, you will argue with me for hours about it. I'm not making it hard, I'm being diplomatic." Izzy answered.

"That has always been your problem." Terry responded. "Stop trying to please everyone else. Just be yourself damn it!"

"Settle down girls." Jack said. He knew they weren't fighting, they were just finding out who they were, and by the sound of things, they conversed like this between themselves often, but they were getting loud and he didn't want to upset Ruth.

"If you're worried about Mom, don't be." Terry said. "Mom can't hear us when we are down here. This is where I have all my parties. Dad sound-proofed it when he finished it."

The family room was in the basement. The basement was split in half, the first half was finished with knotty pine walls and a bookshelf that separated the family room from a small bedroom. It was carpeted throughout with a brightly colored berber carpet. There was an electric fireplace for heat, two green recliners and a plaid sofa that Ruth had purchased at a garage sale. Above the sofa was an egyptian tapestry that Jim had bought on one of his flights. It had a velvety feel to it and depicted a lion and lioness resting in a forest. At the end near the television was a hammered copper and oak bar with a brass foot rail. It had an oak counter and a cutout copper cowboy on the front of the bar riding a bucking bronco. There were cowhide bar stools and above it was an oak shelf with matching copper mugs and a half wooden barrel for a beer keg. Kent had thrown a few keggers using that bar, it was another of Jim's elaborate purchases from overseas. The rest of the basement was unfinished and hidden behind a well constructed interior wall that hid the laundry room, the furnace, shelves and shelves of school supplies and family keepsakes. There was a dresser that was filled with boxes and boxes of buttons. Ruth loved buttons. As a young girl growing up in the depression, she played with buttons instead of dolls because that was what they had. Ruth never learned to sew, but continued to buy buttons. It was her only quirk.

"Why don't you girls, turn the lights off and sit here on the floor with me?" Jack asked them while sitting on the floor in front of the plaid sofa. "I will tell you both a little about what I have learned while working on the set. I think you will both find it enlightening."

Terry turned off the lights and the room was only illuminated by Dr. Sanguinary. The girls gathered around Jack and he began telling them about Shaolin monks and what he had learned about eastern culture. It was close to one in the morning before the girls went to bed. Jack couldn't remember having so much fun, they were like little sponges, soaking in everything he told them. They were such a captive audience, he couldn't wait for tomorrow.

By the time Jack was settled in bed, It was late. He looked at the electric clock next to the bed with its glowing green numbers, the movie had ended at midnight, the clock said it was two am. He was very relaxed. He lay back on the pillows, his arms crossed behind his head. The girls had answered some questions that he had been struggling with. He had always attended church, this television show had changed his views a bit. He had been struggling, Izzy had told him it was going to change his life, he hadn't realized how much it would influence him. Eastern culture had some fascinating ideas which made a lot of sense to him, but after spending more time with Izzy, he realized there might not be just one answer. Why should there be?

Jack had been trying to remember the conversation that he had with Izzy that night in his father's kitchen. He had more questions for her now and tried to formulate them in his mind. He lit a cigarette, the end glowed in the dark room. Ruth had given him one of her packs. She bought them in bulk at the Air Force commissary in Omaha Nebraska at the Audit Air Force Base because the Lincoln base had closed. Shopping at the commissary was one of the perks of being a military widow. The cigarettes were PalMal, unfiltered. He laughed as he smoked, thinking of Ruth's coffee and fingering the unfiltered cigarette. If Ruth had been a drug user, she would have been hard core. Jack's eyes had adjusted enough that he could make out the bedroom in the dark.

He laid on a comfortable standard size bed, there was one high window that looked into the back yard. He had the window open and was surprised at how much wind there was. The closet had two sliding doors that bounced just a little with the breeze from the open window, enough to make a slight bumping sound as they bounced against the door frame; he found it peaceful. There was a large dresser underneath the window. Most of the items that Ruth had purchased for him she had put in the drawers. His shoes remained in the boxes and had been set on the floor inside the closet. The clothes he had been wearing lay in a pile at the foot of the bed where he had stripped. He took a drag from the cigarette then set it on the ashtray beside him on the nightstand.

Jack had been doing the television show now for a couple years, he enjoyed it more than he ever believed that he would have. He loved learning, and he had been introduced into an entirely new way of thinking. At the same time, the show had made him restless. He hated television, he wanted more than that. It was a source of contention between his father and himself. It paid the bills, but it made him feel as though he were a prostitute. He missed the theater and he wanted to do film, but television provided a steady income. It was when he couldn't come to terms with himself that he acted out. This last time was bad and he had been arrested. He had experimented with a new drug, Peyote. Some had claimed the drug could connect him to God and so he tried it. Jack hadn't found God and had actually run naked in the streets before the police were able to catch him. The arrest had made the papers, he was sure Ruth had read about it. Aside from that, Jack had also been fighting with his girlfriend, he needed help. He really loved his girlfriend and didn't want to blow this relationship like he had all the others in his life. All he could think of was Ruth, she had a way of talking to him that helped him get his head on straight. She was a true friend, she expected nothing from their friendship, she never wanted anything in return, she was genuine. She had never used her friendship with him, she hadn't even told anyone about him. As he lay in the dark, he realized that was just who she was. She kept a lot inside. He didn't even know she had been married more than once. He didn't know about her sons. He wondered what her childhood had been like, why she had learned to keep secrets. He thought of Izzy, much like her mother, Izzy hid who she was. Jack knew without asking that Izzy had never told her mother of her abilities, she hadn't told Jack everything either. He discovered that just today. He wondered what else she had kept from him. Yes, he had more questions for the little girl. He rolled on his side and put the cigarette out in the ashtray. He laid still for a moment, listening to the closet door softly bump with the breeze, then closed his eyes and fell asleep, dreaming of nothing.

5

Jack woke up early, there were Jays outside his bedroom window arguing loudly about something. The wind had died down but the air was crisp. He pulled the blanket up around his chin and inspected the room in the daylight. The walls were a mint green, the bedspread was a yellow chanelle and the blanket was a soft fluffy lavender with yellow flowers on it. There were no pictures on the walls, it was clearly a guest room. The bedroom in the basement behind the knotty pine wall must have been Kent's.

Jack propped himself up with his elbows behind him on the mattress to take in the rest of the room. The floor was hardwood oak and a braided yellow rug was placed between the bed and the dresser. The dresser and nightstand were both white, the lamp on the nightstand had a glass yellow base and a white light shade. The ashtray was a heavy glass orange thing that now had three cigarette butts in it.

Jack sat up and stepped onto the rug, he was naked, Jack slept nude. He opened the dresser drawer and pulled out a package of underwear, he tore open the plastic, pulled out a pair and put it on. They were the fruit of the loom and very soft. Jack put on a pair of soft gray sweatpants that had been Kent's. Ruth had stacked her son's things next to the dresser so that Jack could try them on. They fit him nicely. He picked up the ski sweater that had been neatly folded on top of other clothes that had belonged to Kent and pulled it over his head. He smiled softly to himself, the dresser was full of brand new clothes that Ruth had purchased just for him, there was a pile of her son's clothes next to the dresser which she had also given to him. He had new clothes hanging in the closet, new cowboy boots and tennis shoes , all just for him! She was a kind person, he was glad she was part of his life, he had never known anyone like her. He wasn't sure how much Ruth had spent on him, but he did intend to pay her back. He thought he might ask her if he could leave everything here so if he did this again, things would be here waiting for him. When Kent returned, he would be welcome to any of it.

After dressing he opened the bedroom door and walked down the hall, upon entering the kitchen he found Ruth already at the kitchen table reading the newspaper and drinking coffee. "I don't usually eat breakfast, but you need to." She commanded. "Why don't you put some bread in the toaster and I'll fry you an egg or two. If you would like to go to church with me, I bet we could find you a nice girl." She joked.

"I was hoping you could help me straighten up, so I can save the relationship I have with Barbara." Jack laughed.

"Is she a nice girl?" Ruth asked.

"The nicest I've had yet." Jack said softly. "I should probably call her and let her know where I am."

"My God in heaven Jack." Ruth blurted out. "You haven't told her? She must be worried sick!"

"May I use your phone?" Jack asked, laughing softly.

"Yes!" Ruth scolded. "You jolly well better."

"Keep it up my love." Jack whispered to her and hugged her gently with one arm. "I knew you would be good for me."

He lifted the receiver off the cradle of the phone that hung on the kitchen wall and called Barbara. The cord was long enough that he could step into the dining room for a little privacy.

"Tell her you are sorry!" Ruth called to him. "Tell her that I'll try to get you to church so you can repent." Ruth could hear Jack laugh softly as he spoke to his girlfriend and shook her head silently.

When Jack came back into the kitchen and hung up the phone, Ruth shook her finger at him. "I hope you told her that I would have made you call yesterday if I had known!" She scolded.

"Sadly," Jack said, "I don't think she was too worried. I'm hoping that is more of a commentary on my repeatedly bad behavior rather than on her feelings or lack of feelings towards me."

"I'm sure she had to have some sense that you were struggling." Ruth assured him. "Sometimes no news is good news. Did you want to join me at church?"

"Are the girls going?" Jack asked her.

"They never go to church with me." She laughed. "To tell you the truth, I never made them. I liked having some time to myself. I guess I used God and am going straight to hell." She said, "After last night's conversation I think I probably should have made them attend church with me, clearly I failed in that area."

Jack shook his head. "Your girls are wonderful, you haven't failed them. My family made me go to church every Sunday and look how I turned out! You could sell lessons on how to raise children, you could teach most of Hollywood that's for sure."

Ruth got up and opened the refrigerator, she took out the butter and a carton of eggs. She set the eggs and butter on the counter beside the stove. The stove was electric and was built in above the counter. Beneath it she opened the cupboard door and pulled out a cast iron skillet. Jack popped a slice of bread in the toaster and pushed the lever down, it was set on dark so he dialed it back to light. Ruth dropped a large spoonful of butter on the skillet and waited for it to melt, then she cracked the eggs one at a time and dropped them into the butter. As they cooked she kept spooning the hot butter over the eggs until the yellow yolk was covered with a pretty white top, she sprinkled salt and pepper on them just as Jack's toast popped up. He took the butter and put a thin layer on top of the toast. Ruth laughed and said, "You need to gain weight Jack, you should use more butter." Then she opened another cupboard and pulled out a small plate. She took a metal spatula and scooped the eggs up and put them on the plate and handed it to Jack.

"I don't think a fat kung fu artist would please my fans." He teased. "And it's a good thing too, your son must be long and lanky." He said tugging at the waist to show her the fit. The two returned to the kitchen table and sat down. Jack dunked his toast in the eggs and ate it. Then with a fork he ate the remainder of the eggs. "Thank you." He said. "Other than the drive thru yesterday, I don't think I've had anything to eat in a few days."

"You stay for a while." She said, her face was worried. "I want you to think of this as your home too." She said, "The girls will be up in a bit, they know how to fend for themselves, don't let them bully you." She laughed. "I'll be home around noon. You're safe here Jack."

Jack nodded his acknowledgement, out of all the descriptive words Ruth could have chosen, safe was the word he most needed to hear. Perhaps Ruth was a bit of an empath herself.

After Ruth backed out of the driveway and headed off to church, Jack sat in her chair. He picked up the Journal Star newspaper and read the local headlines while sipping his coffee. It seemed that the red team had won the scrimmage. He laughed out loud that it had made the front page of the newspaper. He thought about pouring a little milk into his coffee, but then decided he could get used to it being this strong. After about an hour the girls wandered into the kitchen. Terry got out a bowl and some captain crunch cereal. She got the milk from the refrigerator and poured some into her bowl. She took the bowl and a spoon and went out into the living room to eat in front of the picture window. Izzy had taken the milk from her and poured herself a tall glass, she put the milk back in the refrigerator then opened another cupboard and took out a box of chocolate chip cookies. She took about five from the box then joined Jack at the table.

"Cookies?" He asked, raising one eyebrow.

Izzy shrugged, "You like to drink your caffeine, I like to chew mine." She said, she took a bite of one of the cookies and then drank some milk "Besides," Izzy continued. "They are good for you."

Jack laughed. "Alright, I'll bite." He smiled. "Explain how chocolate chip cookies are good for you at breakfast."

"Cocoa beans," She stated. "They are vegetable chip cookies."

Jack laughed out loud, then stood up taking his plate to the sink. He rinsed off the egg goo so it wouldn't stick, then joined Izzy back at the table.

"You don't dunk them?" He asked watching her eat a cookie then wash it down with a drink from the glass of milk.

"Gross." Izzy answered. "I can't think of anything worse than a soggy cookie."

Jack laughed some more. "It's good to see you again. You've gotten bigger."

Izzy eyed her friend carefully. She knew that he needed her mother, but she also knew that he needed her. She could feel him questioning who he was. Jack was a Sagittarius, he was a fire sign. He was loyal and honest and valued truth, but he was adventurous, a risk taker. There was no fooling him, his mind was sharp but like most fire signs, he was self centered and had an unquenchable desire to create and be in control. He had powerful colors that gave heat, reds, orange and bright yellow.

"It's starting isn't it?" Izzy asked. She had always been very direct, but the abruptness shocked him. Jack looked deeply into her eyes.

"I'm not sure," he answered truthfully. "I was going to ask you."

Izzy had told him of all the things she could remember that evening in his father's kitchen. Things that she knew would be the same. She had told Jack about the television show, about his fame, but had also warned him. Jack would have problems. When the problems started, he would need to be very careful or he could destroy himself. She had explained that everything was connected and that his choices would profoundly affect his brother.

"I've been thinking a lot about what you told me, back in Dad's kitchen." He continued. Looking up at her he asked, "Do you know what selective hearing is?"

"Of course." Izzy laughed. "We have a cat."

Jack smiled softly, yes, she was easier to talk to this time and he still felt connected to her.

"I think that I might have had selective hearing that night." He waited but Izzy was silent. He nodded to her. "I think, I heard you talk about fame and stopped listening, I need to hear it again, all of it." Izzy nodded.

"Did Keith have his baby yet?" She asked. It was an awkward question, just blurted out, but Jack was used to the way her mind worked, she judged time by milestones.

"Yes." He answered. "Shortly after your visit to California. You might have noticed at the time that he wanted nothing to do with children."

Izzy smiled softly to herself, she was doing some calculations in her head. She closed her eyes and imagined a timeline, placing herself on it when she had first met Jack. She put the birth of Keith's daughter on it and Jack's television show, piece by piece she put together the timeline.

Jack watched the girl closely. He wondered how she knew about the baby. The story hadn't been leaked anywhere. He wondered if she remembered it. She had said the point of living was to learn from your mistakes. Was the child a mistake? Had Keith not learned? He studied the girl in front of him, her eyes closed, piecing together a timeline. He wondered how she could know what is supposed to happen, what is a mistake and what is not. He was a grown man and he had no idea.

"It's starting." She said, "You need to control how you take control." Then she laughed, her laugh still had the hoarseness to it that Jack remembered. "That sounds ridiculous doesn't it?" She laughed again.

Two years ago, in John's kitchen Izzy had tried to explain. She had been direct, she had told him that the television show would change his life, but that at times he would be troubled. She had warned him that he would need help and when it started, he needed to ask for it because the choices that he made could harm other people. She had told him that he needed to be careful and take control of his life. The timing was important, if Jack took too long to fix his problems, he would be ruined but if he solved them too quickly, Keith's life would be ruined. Everything was connected.

Jack remembered those words from the night in his father's kitchen, that he could take control. He thought she had meant he could control what happened in each life, but now he realized she simply meant that he could control only how he chose to deal with it. Each life provided an opportunity to improve, but there was still a lot to learn. She had tried to explain how the world is all connected and that one change can cause a totally different outcome. Izzy had warned him that he needed to be careful, to think everything through, be less impulsive and then when trouble popped up on his timeline he could ask for help.

"That night what I heard was that a television show would change my life." Jack said. "I assumed that you meant it in a good way. That wasn't how it was intended, was it?"

Izzy wrinkled her brow and closed her eyes, concentrating. "It was neither Jack." Izzy explained. "Change can be good or bad, it depends on how you handle it, how you control it. That's what I wanted you to understand. I'm sorry, I was only eight and I'm still not the best at explaining things."

He loved how direct she was with him. The implication was clear, she wasn't judging him but she wasn't pretending either. He had made some bad decisions already and she wasn't tiptoeing around them.

"I think," Jack said softly. "That it didn't dawn on me that I could learn anything from a little girl. I took what you told me and thought that I could use it. Manipulate everything."

"You've always had control issues." Izzy giggled. "I guess we all do. Even me." Izzy said.

"If we all want the same thing, why does it turn out badly for some and better for others?" He laughed.

"It's the way you go about it." Izzy assured him. "Sometimes, you have to trust that the universe knows what it is doing. You used to trust the universe, but you changed when you saved Keith."

"You're talking about a different timeline now aren't you?" He asked. "I don't remember ever saving my little brother."

"Maybe you have already saved him." Izzy said. "Maybe you just don't know it."

Jack remained silent for a while. He knew this girl was trying to help him. She had reached out to them as a total stranger. She was fascinating. He wanted to be more like this girl. He remembered that Ruth had told him that they were very similar, in some ways he could see it, but other ways not at all. This girl was compassionate and kind and as far as he could tell, very truthful. Jack didn't think he was any of those things.

He considered how just the other night he was grateful that he couldn't feel as she did, but now he realized it was a gift. Yes, she felt some bad things when she took the emotions of others into her head, but her mind was so clear. He considered what she had said, that the outcome of things depended on how you used your knowledge.

"How can I use change to make things better?" He asked.

"Well," Izzy said softly, "I remember that you always do better when you are trying to help someone else. It's hard, because you are kind of a selfish person." Izzy answered.

"Ouch!" Jack said, a slight smile on his face. She was right of course.

"If I'm such a terrible person, why do you like me?" He laughed.

"Terrible?" Izzy said, choking. "You're the best person I know!"

"Really?" He said, teasing the girl in front of him. "You just said I was selfish."

"You are." Izzy said, "But you are also loyal and when you love someone, you love them completely."

"What else?" He asked. He couldn't help but grin, Izzy had a great command of the English language. In that respect she reminded him of Keith. She had told Jack that all she wanted to do was write, listening to her carry on a conversation with him now, he was convinced she would be good at it.

Izzy took a deep breath. "Sometimes you can be too open minded."

"How is that bad?" He asked her.

"Searching for meaning, I mean it's cool but you get awfully reckless about it." She said, "If other people can't see things like you do, well you get mad about it."

Jack stroked his chin. He hadn't shaved in days and the stubble was rough to his touch. She was right, he needed to talk to her, he needed to talk to Ruth, but instead of patiently calling and planning a trip, he just hopped on a plane and showed up unannounced. He was conflicted in his beliefs, he believed Izzy without a doubt but Keith made him question his faith. He had turned to drugs once again, hoping to see God. If someone had tried to talk him out of either of those choices, he would have been angry.

Izzy nudged him with her shoulder and smiled. "I get it." She said, "I just want to feel free too. I guess we both just need to understand what makes us free."

"How about we go outside?" He asked. The day was already warming up, cool nights and hot days, typical for May in Nebraska. Summer was just starting, soon even the nights would be hot. He was still barefoot and he wiggled his toes at her. "I always feel free when my feet aren't in shoes." Izzy rolled her eyes and giggled, then led him out the kitchen door and walked through the empty garage, through the side door and around back to the pool. The crabapple trees had just finished blooming but her mother's Iris were still going strong. The rose bushes were exploding in all kinds of colors by the patio just like those in the front yard. There were cedar lawn chairs on the patio and a small matching table. The chairs had white cushions with big yellow sunflowers and were fairly comfortable. Jack sat sideways on a lounge chair facing Izzy who laid back on hers. It was shady against the house but the humidity was something new for Jack and he was already sweating.

Jack waited for Izzy to get settled in, she no longer was afraid to tell Jack what she was thinking. She adjusted her position a few times on the cushion until she found the sweet spot, then turned her face towards Jack. "First off." She said, "I should tell you that I don't know all the answers. You have actually been around longer than I have. I'm a newcomer to the universe. I make mistakes too. I shouldn't have told you about Keith for one thing, I'm completely undecided if that is the right answer for me or not."

Jack chuckled softly. He was certain his brother and this girl would end up together one day. He couldn't put his finger on it, she was still a child, but something felt perfect in his mind when he pictured both of them. When he thought of one, the other always popped into his thoughts as well.

"Okay." He answered. "I accept that you don't know everything and I honor your ability to choose whomever you want for your future partner."

"Are you sure?" Izzy asked him. Her eyes narrowed a bit.

"Why would you question me?" Jack chuckled.

"I seem to recall you meddling a lot last time." She answered.

Jack laughed out loud. "I meddled?" He questioned her.

"Goes back to control issues." Izzy confirmed.

"I'm not sure I can change then." Jack said while grinning. "I do like to have things my own way. I'm usually right anyway."

Izzy laughed. "You do have brilliant ideas." She confirmed.

"Alright then, how can I use my brilliant ideas? How can I learn what you know? That is probably the answer don't you think? Learn what you know, understand how it all works and stop trying to run the world?"

"Hmmm." Izzy thought out loud. "What I do is channel."

"Channel?" Jack asked.

"Yes." Izzy said. "Find something to focus on, something you enjoy. It helps you empty your mind, de-clutter sort of, and makes it easier to see."

"Okay." Jack agreed. "I enjoy drugs. I don't think that has helped me yet."

"Jack!" Izzy said firmly. "If you aren't going to be serious..."

"I'm sorry kid." Jack said and he meant it. "Give me an idea, a method for channeling."

"You need to teach." She suggested, "It helps you focus. Teach your brother, teach aspiring actors. You are a lot like me, even my mom knew that."

"Yeah, I see it too." He confirmed. "But teach?"

"Yes, Grasshopper." She said, "You need diversion. You have too much energy and curiosity. Focusing on someone else will help you cope."

"Not a bad idea." Jack mused. "I quite enjoyed taking Keith under my wing. You're right, when I play the part of the big brother, older and wiser, I seem to get into less trouble. Will that let me learn the things you know?"

"You already know them!" Izzy said. "You've just forgotten."

"So we are back to your memory." Jack stated. "Your memory is the key. You can help me remember, maybe help me remember more next time? I'm feeling a little desperate here."

Izzy closed her eyes and took in his colors. They were becoming more subtle, more muted. Izzy was an earth sign, her colors were browns and rusts and greens. Jack's colors were softening, blending more easily with hers. She smiled softly, he was learning, he was remembering. If he was taking on her colors, then he was taking on her essence.

Jack nodded to himself, he could almost feel Izzy reaching into his mind. He wanted to be more like her. He had always liked helping, offering advice to Keith. It seemed very logical. He looked at Izzy, he could help her too, she loved writing, he could help her with that and explore more of what she knew at the same time. "I think I would enjoy teaching." He said softly. "In fact, I would like to teach you."

"Me?" she asked incredulously. "Teach me?"

"Yeah. Think about it. You could come out during summer vacations and school breaks. I could help you with writing, learning about television. You could come to the set with me. We could explore your memory with writing exercises and you could begin to learn the business. Remember your Aunt Dorothy, building contacts is a fantastic way to get your foot in the door!"

Izzy sat up, clearly excited by the prospect. Jack was already learning and he didn't even know it. Dorothy hadn't said that out loud, she had thought it. Clearly Jack had heard it in his head. Jack's colors were getting bright again, she knew it was because he thought that he was taking control. He still thought that he could manipulate the universe. Izzy shrugged, maybe he could, he had managed to do it before. She also considered what she could do for him, Izzy had a positive effect on Jack and she loved helping people. It might also help her make up her mind about what direction she wanted to take.

"That would be soooooo cool!" She said, "Summers here are so boring, one horse show after another."

"We have to figure out how to get your mother to agree." Jack laughed. "You could come out with me for the rest of the summer, then we can plan how to handle the future. Barbara would be there to help with girl stuff and you are old enough you don't need a babysitter. I think we could do this!"

"You know," Izzy said. "Terry can have really busy summers. Sometimes mom seems frazzled. I am usually just in the way and with mom worrying about Kent and having to drag me along with her and Terry everywhere they go, if you present it right, she might even welcome the idea."

Jack smiled and nodded. He leaned back into the cushions and closed his eyes. He thought about how the universe spoke to him. He thought this was a completely unplanned trip, yet the timing was perfect. The school year had just ended, Terry's shows were soon to begin. Keith was still living with him and was perhaps a little more open minded and had just broken up with his current girlfriend so he would be around a little more. Everything was falling into place. Izzy could help him know which were the right decisions. He needed to feel as though he was part of this family, he needed it. He decided to stay a week, then leave and he wasn't leaving without Izzy. This was the time where everything would begin to come to a head, he needed her for the next few years, he could already sense the changes coming.

6

When Ruth came home from church, she found Jack in the front yard; he was shirtless and still in his sweatpants. There were three of the neighborhood boys and of course Terry with him. Izzy was watching from the front step. All of them were following Jack as he appeared to be teaching them kung fu moves. A few of the neighbors were watching in lawn chairs which they had brought outside onto their driveways. Jack looked so happy and the children were having a blast.

Ruth pulled into the open garage and Jack waived. The next door neighbor, Jan, came into the garage and waited for Ruth to get out of the car. "Ruth!" She exclaimed, "Why didn't you tell us that Jack Enidarrac was a family friend?"

Ruth smiled at her neighbor and friend. "All the Enidarracs are private people Jan, I just kept their secret. Jack is especially close to Izzy, he has a daughter the same age as her." At that moment Jan's son Kent came into the garage. Kent had dark hair and blue eyes, most of the neighborhood girls had a crush on him.

"Mom, is it okay with you if Jack comes over? Kent Heidtbrink too? We want to play guitars." Kent Heidtbrink was an older boy, a good looking young man that lived down the street. He and Jan's son Kent often played guitars together. Some years ago the neighborhood distinguished between the three Kents by calling Ruth's son, Big Kent, Kent Heidtbrink, Middle Kent and calling Jan's son Little Kent. Big Kent had moved to a college dorm before he went to Vietnam so that just left middle and little Kent. Little Kent was now just Kent having outgrown the prefix and Middle Kent was now Kent Heidtbrink. Jan really didn't like kids in her home. She had some nervous issues and preferred her home tidy and quiet but it was difficult to say no to a television star coming into her home. She was just going to agree when Ruth chimed in, "Kent, you boys are welcome to set up in my garage, I can park on the street."

Jan nodded to Ruth in appreciation. She knew it would end up with all the neighborhood children in her home, not just the two Kent's. "Ruth, you can park your car in my driveway if you would like." She offered. Jack's rental car was still parked in front of Ruth's house and was taking up most of the space in front of her home. Jack had just entered the garage and had heard the conversation.

"Allow me Ruth." He said. He took the car keys from her hand and kissed her cheek and flashed her one of his most charming smiles. A moment later he had parked the car on the opposite side of the street and was jaunting up the driveway. Kent was headed towards the garage carrying two guitars and The Kent Heidtbrink was already headed down the sidewalk with a bass guitar in hand. For the next few hours the boys played guitar in the garage, the acoustics were great and everyone on the block had stopped to listen. Jack was surprised at the talent the two boys had, neither of them sang so Jack performed the vocals, Terry who had an amazing voice joined in towards the end. When they were finished, the crowd of neighbors gave a hearty round of applause.

By evening, Jack wanted to see the stars. The sky was so clear in Nebraska and quite honestly he had forgotten how many stars were in the heavens. He went outside and sat on the driveway, it was still warm from the heat of the day. He leaned back with his arms propped up behind him and stared into the blackness above him. Izzy came out and sat beside him on the driveway. Soon the two Kents and a few other children were also stretched out on the drive.

Ruth came outside with a brown paper grocery bag. She had popped corn and filled the bag with it, she had melted butter and poured it on the popped corn inside the bag and then added salt. She was shaking the bag as she stepped out onto the drive. Craig, the middle boy in the Heitbrink family stood up from his sitting position on the driveway. "Yum, popcorn." He said as he took the bag from Ruth. Jack realized this was something that Ruth must have done often, he could tell how loved she was in the neighborhood and was so happy to be a part of it. The air was beginning to chill a bit, Izzy scooted over closer to Jack and leaned up against him. He pulled her in against his side and placed his hand on the side of her head. He wasn't sure if it seemed familiar or just natural, but the sky above him and all those stars, he swore he remembered this moment from before.

7

When Jack stepped off the plane, he had Izzy with him. Keith didn't recognize her at first. Jack of course hadn't told Keith he was bringing her or even where he was coming from. He had just called and said that he needed a ride home from LAX and had given him the time that his flight would arrive, he had explained that he had left his wallet at home and couldn't buy a cab. Keith felt a little awkward greeting her. Izzy had a small duffel bag in her hands and told Keith she had no other luggage. Jack assured Keith he didn't have any either. The only thing Jack had with him was a shoebox that held a pair of really nice black cowboy boots. Keith was still living with Jack, it wasn't a large house, just two bedrooms. Jack and his girlfriend in one and Keith in the other. He imagined that meant that he was now sleeping on the sofa. He didn't mind, but it would have been nice to have been informed prior to picking them up from the airport.

On the way home, Jack told Keith that he had been in Nebraska. He didn't go into a lot of detail but Keith could tell Jack was much more relaxed. He told Keith about his plans to coach Izzy, help her with her writing and introduce her to his television set. They were going to start filming again soon and Jack was going to bring her along. Keith imagined if anyone could get away with it, it would be Jack. He had a way of getting what he wanted, even after behaving badly.

Keith glanced in the rear view mirror at Izzy who was blissfully watching the traffic on the freeway. He wished that she didn't annoy him, he wasn't even sure why she did. Sometimes, Keith wanted to be like his brother. Jack took everything in stride, he seemed to understand exactly who he was. Keith was still trying to figure himself out. Jack was brilliant and accomplished but then there were times like this, where he had just disappeared, not telling anyone where he was going, not even his girlfriend. He wasn't even sure if Jack's girlfriend Barbara was aware he was coming home and bringing a little girl with him. When Jack acted like this, Keith was grateful that he wasn't like his brother, that he was more conventional. Jack made a lot of mistakes and Keith paid attention, he learned from them.

Izzy remembered the house. It didn't seem so long ago that she sat on the driveway in Jack's car with his daughter Cassie. She had never been inside of it, but entering the house she knew where she was. Coming in the front door, the living area was to the right and the kitchen straight ahead. The bedrooms were down the hall to the left and straight out of the kitchen was the backyard. When Izzy walked in she immediately began looking around, her eyes searching. Then she giggled and dropped her duffel bag and headed towards the cat. Jerome eagerly approached her and rubbed against her legs.

"Now that's weird." Keith said. "That cat hates everyone."

Jack shook his finger at Keith. "That is just not true, the cat only hates you." Jack laughed.

The two watched as Izzy stroked the cat. "Seriously," Jack whispered, his eyes twinkling at his younger brother. "It's like he knows her."

"Starting that up again are we?" Keith asked. "She is just a cat person." He said glibly. Izzy picked up her duffel bag and headed down the hall, taking the first room on the left without getting any instruction. Jerome galloped behind her and jumped on the bed. Jack just looked at his brother and laughed.

Izzy made a difference in everyone's life almost immediately and Barbara was grateful for the help. Izzy picked up the dirty laundry and had it washed, folded and even ironed on day one. Izzy instinctively knew that Jack needed order to clear his mind. She cleaned the house constantly, dusting and vacuuming and even took 409 to the windows. Barbara didn't understand the relationship, but was grateful to have someone else pick up after Jack. Although Keith had been right, Jack had not told Barbara about bringing Izzy home with him, Ruth had been thoughtful enough to call her and give her a heads up prior to Jack's return. Keith begrudgingly appreciated his laundry being clean and folded but being stubborn, refused to give in. He continued to think of Izzy as a strange anomaly in life that for some reason his brother had become fascinated with.

Izzy made sure they were all well fed, she cooked mainly healthy foods for Jack, but occasionally she would sneak in home-made mac n cheese, lasagne or a chocolate cake. The cake was the most moist cake either Jack or Keith had ever tasted and was covered with at least an inch of chocolate frosting. They had watched in amazement everytime she cooked for them, never referring to a recipe. She helped Jack with lines, she screened his calls and organized his desk for him. She made it her duty to make sure that he had enough time for Barbara and Barbara noticed and appreciated it. Jack was resolved to try harder with his girlfriend and Izzy was trying to make that happen. Izzy understood Jack's weaknesses, so she reassured him constantly, about his talent, his decisions and kept him grounded.

Jack took lots of vitamins, he had a vitamin for everything. Izzy always had them ready for him and along with providing him good meals, Jack seemed to look healthier each day. She learned everything he taught her eagerly. The crew on the set had been impressed with her, she did every errand they asked her without complaint and she was always very quiet while they worked. She even noticed where some gaffer's tape was missing and quietly pointed it out. In truth, Jack had grown dependent on her and at summer's end when she left each year, it killed him.

There was another side to Izzy however, it was the side that really intrigued Jack. It was her intuitive side, her empathetic side. She would sit on the floor in front of his coffee table for hours, playing with a deck of cards. At first he just thought it was because he didn't own a television set, but as the time went on, he watched her more closely. She would sit in front of the table and flip the cards over, making two different piles. He tried to figure out the game she was playing but it didn't make any sense.

On Izzy's third summer with Jack, she was now thirteen. He sat beside her on the floor while she played her game.

"Tell me what you're doing." He asked in a gentle tone. Izzy looked at him, then shrugged.

"I just make two piles." She said, "The ones I get right go in this pile, the ones I miss go in the other."

"Little grasshopper," He nudged. "You are being vague again." Jack had begun calling her his little grasshopper shortly after his visit to Nebraska and Izzy really liked it.

Izzy smiled. "Alright." She laughed. "I just do this." She looked at the deck of cards in front of her, concentrating on the deck. "Red." she said, then flipped it over. It was the Jack of hearts. "So this one goes in the pile I got right." She explained.

Jack looked at the cards on the table. Her pile of cards that she guessed correctly was about two thirds bigger than the other pile.

"Sometimes, I try it differently." She said, "Like this." She picked up a card from the top of the deck and closed her eyes. She moved her fingers around, touching both sides of the card, then laughed and said. "Black." She opened her eyes and it was the Ace of Spades. She added it to the correct pile.

Jack was intrigued. She consistently guessed about two thirds correctly. "How are you doing that?" He asked.

Izzy shrugged. " I don't know, I'm good at the game of concentration too." She laughed. "When I touch them, the black ones don't feel like anything, the red ones have heat." She said, "It's kind of the same way when I just think about them, but the heat feels different, because it's in my brain, not on my fingers. It's like a tugging sensation" She said, "Once I get tired, I can't do it, also sometimes I second guess myself, like I turn over six red ones in a row and my head wants to go with the odds and say the next one is black, it's like when you don't listen to that little voice."

Jack sat beside her and tried to turn some over, he didn't even get fifty percent correct. He leaned back against the sofa and watched her again. He wanted to be able to feel what she felt, it was fascinating. He had hoped that by now he would be able to, but he hadn't remembered how to do it yet.

"It helps me." Izzy was saying. "I told you once that I had a coping mechanism, this is it! I get all confused about things in my head, if I just focus on nothing but the cards, I get better." She shrugged. "It would help you too."

"Ah yes, the channel method. I have tried to teach a little." Jack said, "I admit, I've relied more on your intuition than my own devices." He let his body bump Izzy against her shoulder and she laughed. "Is it too late? Can I learn to do that?"

Izzy looked at her mentor and smiled. "You already can do it." She said, "How many times do I have to tell you that? You just need to trust yourself and remember how, and you are teaching, you're teaching me!"

After a while Izzy set the cards down and went out to the back patio. She wasn't out there long before Braden heard her and leaned over the fence to flirt with her.

Keith had broken up with another girlfriend and had been staying at Jack's until his living arrangements were settled. When Keith entered the house it was apparent he had been drinking. He wasn't drunk, but he was acting a bit belligerent. He glanced over at Izzy leaning against the fence outside then noticed what she was wearing. "Uriah Heap?" He said loudly. "Who listens to that garbage?" He asked his brother.

Jack motioned to Izzy to come inside. He had moved to the kitchen table when Izzy had gone to the patio and was watching the two kids through the glass door. Braden was about 20 years old now and Jack didn't entirely trust him around the girl. Izzy said goodbye to Braden and hurried through the patio doors. Keith scoffed at her. "I hate your shirt." He said.

Izzy adjusted the black t-shirt with the band name on the front, pulling the bottom hem downward. She didn't like confrontation and was never sure how to respond. She had known the shirt would provoke him and wore it on purpose, but she hadn't prepared how to respond to him when it did. "Jack doesn't mind if I wear this." She pointed out.

"Oh good, well if Jack doesn't mind, then it must be okay." Keith responded.

Jack, listening to the conversation, got up to intervene. "Keith, what's going on?" Jack asked, his voice was soft and kind. Keith pushed past him, opening a cupboard above the refrigerator. There were several bottles of liquor there, he took one out and he poured himself a scotch and sat at the table. Jack followed him over and sat down next to him. He didn't say anything, he just waited for Keith to talk. Jack was trying to be more like Izzy, be more empathetic but it wasn't natural for him.

Izzy had settled down in front of her cards that she had left on the living room coffee table. Her heart raced and she tried to remain calm as she flipped the cards over revealing the color of the suit. Outwardly, she seemed at ease but inside she was frantic. She felt as though her skin was the only thing that prevented her from dissolving into the universe. The stereo was on and the music was a bit loud, it was a rock station that Izzy had found earlier, for some reason it was really bothering Keith. It was soft rock, Dan Folgelberg, Carly Simon, nothing Keith should find offensive, but the music clearly irritated him.

"I don't know what it is about that kid." Keith said to his brother. "She just makes me feel uncomfortable. Why do you keep wanting her around, Jack, it's weird." Keith said. "I don't get why Barbara puts up with it either."

Jack took the drink from Keith and finished it. "It's alright," Keith said sarcastically. "I didn't want the rest of it."

Jack smirked, then motioned for his brother to follow him. They walked behind the sofa and leaned against the wall so Jack could show Keith what Izzy was doing. Keeping behind her, she wasn't aware of them. Keith looked at his brother and shrugged his shoulders to let him know he didn't understand what they were watching. Jack leaned over and whispered in Keith's ear, then they turned and watched some more. Keith was clearly unimpressed.

The sun had set, Jack flipped on a light switch and the kitchen lit up. Izzy turned around from her place on the floor and Jack beckoned her to follow him with his finger. Izzy set the cards down on the table and got up and followed Jack down the hallway. "Keith has had a bit to drink tonight, why don't you go read in your room for a while." He said.

"I think I'll just go to bed if it's okay with you." Izzy said.

"Are you alright?" He asked. "It's still early."

"Yeah, my head is just cluttered, the cards weren't helping." Izzy replied. "I'm confused."

Izzy went to her room and got a nightgown from her duffel bag, then went across the hall and brushed her teeth. She closed the door and put on the nightgown, then brushed her hair, picked up her clothes and went back to her room. Jack was waiting in the hallway and followed her to her room. He waited for her to crawl under the covers and then sat beside her on the bed.

"What are you confused about?" He asked.

"It's Keith I think." Izzy said. "He makes me feel weird."

"Weird how?" Jack asked, smiling to himself because both Izzy and Keith had used the same adjective when describing the other. "About the t-shirt?"

"Nah." Izzy smiled. "I wore that to vex him. I don't even know who Uriah Heap is, it was my sister's shirt."

"Now why, would you want to vex my brother? Good use of vocabulary by the way." He said. "Didn't you tell me that the two of you are supposed to love one another? Vexing him seems a strange way to start a romance."

"Romance." Izzy softly laughed. "I'm too young for romance."

"What about a crush then?" Jack said, smiling at her.

Izzy shrugged. "I don't know. I remember so much about you, but just bits and pieces when I try to remember Keith. I see his face all the time in my head. Mainly his eyes. Sometimes at night it's like he is on top of me." Jack grinned.

"Jack, ewe, not like that." Izzy continued, crinkling her nose. "It's frightening, not primal. I feel weird, I get hot, sometimes even angry. I don't understand what my brain is telling me. It's stupid. I don't know what it means or why I get mad. It's almost like I'm testing him, trying to make sure he matches his colors. I wish I could explain it better, I know it has something to do with you."

"I suspect that you are supposed to forget some things." Jack mused, "I've never really asked you about the colors." He continued. "I don't know if I actually see them, They are kind of like that weird perfume of yours aren't they? I can't see them, but I feel them." Jack said.

"Makes sense." Izzy replied.

"How so?" Jack asked, he was intrigued.

"Well," Izzy continued, "Think of it like art. A good artist uses color to invoke certain emotions."

"Same with film." Jack confirmed. "Red and green lighting for example is a classic combination in suspense, horror, and even sci-fi. The right color can make or break a film."

"Now that is interesting." Izzy said. "Did you know the most common color blindness is not being able to distinguish the difference between those two colors?"

"You're making that up." Jack laughed.

"No, I'm not. If you take a black and white picture of a red cardinal in a green tree, you won't see it." Jack smiled at Izzy clearly not believing her. "It's true. I learned it in my photography class" Izzy said, "regardless if you believe me or not, it does make sense. Color can stimulate emotion, then if you feel emotion, it must also make you perceive the color. If red and green colors create suspense, maybe those are the colors Keith gives off and I'm color blind to them."

"But you aren't color blind." Jack whispered.

"No, but those aren't real colors are they? They are perceived colors. Also, sometimes we are blind with people we care about. You know, like when they catch a serial killer and then they show on the news an interview with his wife or girlfriend and the woman is always so shocked."

"Are you implying that Keith might be a serial killer?" Jack laughed.

"No." Izzy giggled her hoarse laugh. "But maybe the key to evolving, to being better, is distinguishing the colors. Maybe the universe is telling me I shouldn't be blind when it comes to Keith." Izzy thought quietly for a moment. "Or maybe," she continued, "maybe the universe doesn't want me to see his colors, maybe I'm supposed to decide how I feel without crib notes."

Jack loved the way this girl's mind worked. What an unusual ability she had to think in so many different directions all at once. He tried to not laugh at her analogy of seeing colors as being crib notes.

"Maybe you aren't supposed to think about it at all?" Jack said to her softly. "You aren't supposed to plan feelings."

"I'm a Capricorn. I overthink, I calculate, I like to be sure." Izzy replied.

"Love isn't something that adds up Izzy. It is something that comes from deep inside of you, sometimes against all reason." Jack spoke softly, thinking about red and green. "An interesting thought, going back to your crib notes though," He continued, "If you are an earth sign, then green must be one of your colors, Keith is a fire sign so Red is one of his….I find it strange that you can't distinguish between the two of them. At least when it involves my brother."

Izzy nodded. She knew that Jack was right. She did love Keith, she had felt it for some time, but there was a battle going on inside of him. She could feel his anger. Izzy couldn't remember what had caused it, but she remembered it from their lives before. She knew the anger had carried over, she knew that people became who they were from their own experiences, there was an experience somewhere that made Keith angry yet that wasn't who he was. She felt as though she were on a precipice, that somehow cause and effect would be determined by her actions. She felt as Jack so often did, she felt caged. Izzy knew that in the past she had made a choice, she had chosen to love Keith despite the anger, maybe even because of it. She just wished that she better understood it. If what Jack had just expressed to her was true, she was overthinking it. Their colors, although different, were the same. It was like they were one person. It was an interesting thought.

Was she also angry? She continued to think to herself. She constantly tried to provoke him. She thought about it and knew that she had deliberately left the stereo playing louder than Keith liked, then she left it on while she went to see Braden. She reflected on the first time she had laid eyes on Keith, she had told Jack that she thought Keith was mean, she knew that Jack would tell him that she said that. Maybe they both carried anger with them. She wondered why.

Izzy considered things that made her feel angry. She hated feeling helpless, that always made her angry. She often felt anger when trust was broken. When Jack didn't trust his instincts, it made her a little angry. Maybe Keith's reluctance to trust the universe had been an issue. She thought about the word good, she could visualize the word in her head. She considered its meaning. Without bad, good wouldn't exist. Everything needed an opposite to be real. If that were true, then to have love you would also need anger. She wondered if two opposing forces made things stronger. She thought about scars, flesh came together and formed scars, sealing a wound and making the skin stronger. Yet, sometimes even after a wound is healed, the scar is painful to touch.

Izzy hated it when her mind did this. She knew it would go on and on all night long. She smiled softly and wondered if she could sneak quietly into the kitchen cupboard and drink enough of one of those bottles so that she could shut her brain off and manage to sleep.

Jack stroked his unshaven chin as he watched the young girl struggle with thoughts that were above even his head. He had almost convinced himself that he was teaching her, almost forgetting why he wanted her with him in the first place. This girl held secrets to the workings of the universe. She had told him on so many occasions that he already had the ability, that he just needed to remember it. Now more than anything, Jack wanted to remember. He brushed her hair out of her face and tucked it behind her ear.

"So if Keith has colors that you can't tell apart, is that something new?" Jack asked her.

"I don't think so." Izzy said. "I'm just trying to remember what started it. I think that it is important to know the best part and the worst part of someone. If you know the worst thing about them, and love them anyway, then your love must be true. If I have brought this love with me, over and over, then it endures so I must already know the worst part of him. I'm just trying to remember it."

"What's it matter if the worst part is from a different time? I think you are overcomplicating things" Jack laughed. He leaned down and put his forehead against hers. "I want to crawl inside of your brain and see and feel what you are thinking." Jack said.

Izzy laughed, "There isn't enough room in there for you. I'd have to kick out some of the voices."

Jack laughed out loud. He loved this girl. He tried to remember his life before he knew her, it was getting harder for him to do. It was as if he had known her forever. The smile slowly ebbed away, forever, was that crazy? He needed this girl, just like air to breathe. He needed her mother. It was more than it seemed, they had become part of him, if he lost them now his brain would hemorrhage and his thoughts would all bleed out, leaving nothing inside.

"What colors do you see in my brother?" He asked. He was curious why this young girl would want to test his brother. It was clear once again that Izzy hadn't told him the complete story. It was evident that there was more to be revealed. Why did she question the colors that she saw in him? Izzy always seemed so sure about everything else.

Izzy shrugged. "Depends on what I'm remembering." She said, "I'm assuming that you mean other than the red, his fire color. There are lots of yellows, but sometimes lots of purples too. Purple alone isn't bad, purple is sad and everyone has sadness. I like purple, you have to have sadness to recognize happiness, but when it gets thick it's never good. Sometimes when I think of him, and I see just his eyes hovering over me, I feel the purple and it is so thick I can't breathe, but I figured out something a few years ago, the thick purple I see is my purple. I'm seeing mine and not his. It's also just a memory, it isn't really thick. Maybe it isn't even a memory, maybe it is a reminder. It's telling me something but I don't understand it. So, I study him, I try to figure out why, why are my colors getting thick because his colors aren't. So I try to make him mad, it usually works too, but even then his colors don't change. Maybe I'm just afraid of the unknown."

"Izzy Meeks!" Jack said, "You are not afraid of anything."

She rolled over on her stomach, folding her hands in front of her and rested her chin on top of them. "I know you were teasing me earlier when I said I see him on top of me, maybe you are partly right. I'm just a kid, too young for thoughts like that, maybe I am having them and that is what scares me. Even now while he is being a dick to me, his colors aren't thick. I don't know why I feel the need to test him."

"The colors really have texture?" Jack asked.

"I guess so." Izzy continued. "Like a heavy perfume, it's thicker, it has more weight to it. It's difficult to explain."

"You aren't too young, you know." Jack whispered softly. "I mean to think about it. Believe me boys start thinking about it at your age. I suspect Keith is letting his mind wonder a bit about you too. He behaves quite differently when you aren't around."

"I wanted to provoke him," Izzy confessed. "I wanted to see the colors but then I got mad when it worked. Almost as if I was angry that his colors weren't thick. I should be glad they were just dark colors and not thick colors. I had no reason to be angry."

"I don't think he had a reason to get mad at you." Jack said. "Maybe, he feels emotions that he also doesn't understand." Izzy nodded. Jack didn't know it, but he was learning. He was feeling what she felt and what Keith felt, she had helped him avoid some of the bad decisions that he feared, most of the challenging situations that she could recall from the past had been resolved. Jack would be tested a few times yet, but his colors were balancing out. She put her hand on his cheek and wondered if he would still want her around once he was sure he could control his future.

He leaned down and rested his forehead against hers once more. "Of course I will." He whispered.

Izzy closed her eyes and smiled, Jack got up and left her room. She wondered if he had even been aware that she hadn't asked the question out loud. Yes, Jack was learning and Izzy was very happy for him. After he left the room Jack found Keith drinking another scotch in the kitchen.

"I don't buy it." Keith slurred.

"Drunk? The choir boy is drunk?" Jack goaded.

"Stop calling me that." Keith pouted.

"I don't think that card game is one you can cheat at." Jack said.

"The girl is weird." Keith said. "I need to get some of my clothes. Why do you always put her in my room? She's old enough, she could sleep on the couch for once."

"First, it isn't your room, it's my room." Jack said sternly. "Second, she is my guest, you are my family."

Keith sat quietly at the table, he swirled the scotch around in circles in the glass, contemplating the liquid.

"I keep messing up my relationships." He said. "What's wrong with me?"

Jack pulled out the kitchen chair beside his brother and sat down. "There is nothing wrong with you." Jack assured him. "You just haven't found the right one."

"What if I never do?" Keith asked. "I want to get married, I want a family. Maybe no one wants that with me."

"Want to tell me what happened?" Jack asked softly.

"Same thing that always happens." Keith mumbled. "She wanted a commitment, I couldn't give it to her."

Jack took the glass away from Keith. He opened the refrigerator and took out a ginger ale. He popped the can open and handed it to Keith. "Sober up." He said. "If she wanted something you weren't prepared to give her, that's on her."

"What if you're right?" Keith asked.

"About?" Jack responded.

"What if the person I'm supposed to be with is sleeping in my old room?"

Jack smiled, his right dimple more pronounced than the left. "Only time will tell little brother."

"It would be just my luck." Keith said. "Falling in love with a kid."

"Maybe you will someday Keith, but by the time that happens my guess is she won't be a kid anymore. Why don't you just focus on your career for a while. You've always taken a long time when deciding what you want. As I recall it was only a few years ago you wanted to be a forest ranger."

"Enidarrac trait." Keith said. "Never being satisfied. I need to get my things."

"She is asleep." Jack warned. "Please be quiet when you go in there." Jack really enjoyed having Izzy stay. He only got to have his daughter stay with him once in a while. He liked parenting. He had grown protective over this little girl and it felt good.

Keith walked in the open bedroom door, Izzy was on her back, one arm up beside her head on the pillow. He wasn't sure why he resented her so much. Something about her made him want to be better than he was, maybe he was angry because he felt flawed when he was around her. He went to his dresser and pulled out a pair of clean blue jeans, underwear and a clean white t-shirt. Everything had been neatly folded and put in the correct drawers. He guessed she was good for at least that. Keith hated folding clothes.

He turned around to leave but saw that Izzy was awake and looking at him. "Sorry, kid, I didn't mean to wake you up." He said.

"I'm sorry I made you mad." She said earnestly, "I wasn't asleep. I don't sleep a lot. I'll be heading back home pretty soon. Then you can have your room back if you still need it"

She was just a young kid, but Keith was suddenly surprised at how pretty she looked. It must have been the scotch he told himself. He sat next to her on the bed and moved a long strand of hair from her face just as his brother had done earlier. "I can be a real ass." He assured her. "I'm glad you are here, you make my brother much saner." He laughed. "Plus it's nice to have toilet paper on the roller, Jack never puts it on." He noticed she smelled like Lilacs tonight. It was a nice scent, but made him sad and he wasn't sure why.

Izzy just gave him a look, she had a very expressive face. He knew instantly that she didn't believe him.

"Cross my heart." Keith said to her while motioning a cross against his chest. She gave him a closed mouth smile, clearly not convinced.

"Am I the reason you can't sleep?" Keith asked. "Because I really am sorry."

"No." Izzy affirmed. "I've always had this problem."

"You need to learn to relax." Keith joked, he lightly shook her by the shoulder with one hand. "You're here to learn right? Have Jack teach you, he can fall asleep any time, anywhere."

Izzy softly chuckled to herself but Keith heard her. He was surprised how good it made him feel.

"A truce?" He asked.

Jerome jumped up on the opposite side of the bed and strolled across the covers to Izzy. He lay halfway on top of her legs, staring at Keith and swishing his tail back and forth.

"I'll talk to Jerome about it and let you know what we decide." Izzy giggled. It was the hoarse giggle that Keith had grown strangely accustomed to.

"I'm not sure I like those odds." Keith laughed as he got up from the side of the bed. Izzy laughed again and rolled over on her side facing away from Keith, dismissing him and petting the cat. He was surprised to notice the curve of her hips and how much he appreciated it. Maybe he needed to stop drinking when she was in town.

Something about her made him want to be better, better than he was. Maybe that was why he resented her. He realized that ever since he had met her, even when she was eight years old, his behaviors had changed. He had been reckless in the past, he slept with women, drank and even smoked a little weed. If his brother hadn't been such a mess with drug addiction, Keith probably would have followed suit. In fact, he had been considering it the summer they met the girl.

It had been a combination of witnessing Jack's horrendous struggle with drug addiction and Izzy's innocent blue eyes that gave him resolve not to try the harder drugs. Something about those dark blue eyes, the sweetness, the innocence, he just wanted to be better than he was. Izzy seemed to correct the behaviors of others too. Jack had stopped using hard drugs almost completely ever since his visit in Nebraska, he had only relapsed a few times and had immediately regretted it, largely because of Izzy's influence. Keith nodded to himself, he should probably be grateful to her instead of being mean. She changed his behaviors just as she had improved his brothers. He laughed to himself as he carried his clothing and set it on the green chair beside the sofa, Izzy had told Jack that she thought Keith looked mean, she had been right.

The next morning at breakfast, Jack sipped on a cup of hot coffee, Keith sat beside him at the table, staring out the patio doors. Izzy was outside on a lawn chair enjoying the morning sun, her back was to the house and her long hair softly blowing in the morning breeze. The toaster popped and Keith got up to retrieve the toast. He lightly buttered it and then sprinkled some cinnamon sugar that

Izzy had mixed together on top of the toast. He had always liked cinnamon toast but never bothered to make it. He poured himself a cup of coffee, he left it black, then rejoined Jack at the table.

"You really believe she feels colors?" Keith asked.

"You saw it yourself." Jack asserted.

"Lucky guess was all I saw." Keith mumbled back to his brother.

"Why can't you just accept there are things in the universe that we don't understand?" Jack asked. "Izzy is one of those things."

"Jack." Keith said. "I don't believe in psychics, fortune tellers or time travelers."

Jack smiled slightly at his brother. "Good." He said. "Because she is none of those things."

"Look." Keith said. "She is a weird little girl, I'll give you that. I also realize that I have behaved badly, that she isn't all bad, I admit, I was the problem." he noticed that the corner of Jack's mouth was beginning to curl upwards, it slightly annoyed him. "She isn't magical Jack. She just has a knack for bringing out the best in people. She is good at reading people, what she does is she zeros in on a person's weakness and bam! Makes you feel guilty about it."

"Keith." Jack said, muffling a laugh. "She doesn't do that."

"Hey, I'm trying here." Keith said.

"And how would that explain the message she brought to you about your song?" Jack asked. "Doesn't really align with that does it?"

Keith shrugged, he didn't have an answer but he wasn't going to give in. Jack took the morning paper and began to doodle on it. He drew a clown holding a balloon but was struggling making the balloon round enough. He leaned sideways in his chair and looked at Izzy. "Izzy!" He hollered through the open patio door. Izzy immediately got up and came inside.

"Do me a favor?" Jack asked her. "Could you bring me the checkers bag?"

Izzy nodded and hurried to the living room, she opened a drawer in the end table beside the couch and took out a red velvet bag, then hurried back to the kitchen. She started to hand the bag to Jack but he waved her off saying, "Hand me a red checker please."

Izzy nodded, curious what Jack was doing. She reached inside of the bag without looking and brought out a red checker. Jack took it from her hand, then traced the checker making a round circle, he handed it back to Izzy then finished the circle by turning it into a balloon on a string. Without looking back at Izzy, he asked her to please get him a black one. Izzy again reached into the bag and without looking handed him a black checker and then sat down on the chair opposite Jack in order to watch him finish his clown.

"That is so good." Izzy said, clearly impressed with his artwork. "I didn't know you could draw. Can I have that?" She asked giggling. Jack nodded and tore the doodle from the newspaper, most of the clown was on the classified ads, but there was a little space in between two car dealership ads and his face was free of print. Izzy took the drawing, stood up and kissed the top of Jack's head, then hurried to her room to put her prize away.

Keith didn't say a word, he looked at his brother's smug smile and took his coffee outside, eating the last bite of his toast before doing so. Jack stood up and picked up the velvet bag that held the checkers and carried them back out to the living room. Before putting them away he reached into the bag feeling them, he felt their rough edges and held several, searching his mind to feel any difference between them. "Red." He said, and pulled one out. He kept his eyes closed and put it in his pocket. He thought it felt different, but he was afraid to look, he would check tonight before he went to bed. Izzy had told him that anyone could learn how to do it, they just needed to open their minds. Jack wanted to learn this, Jack needed to learn this, Izzy might not have all the answers to the questions that he had, but she held the key for him to find them.

Izzy was all packed, everything she had brought with her had been stuffed neatly into her duffel bag. She always hated saying goodbye to Jack, they had developed a strong bond over the years and it broke her heart when she had to leave. Jack felt the same way. This was her third summer with Jack. She was thirteen, not quite a little girl but still new to being a teenager.

Sometimes Jack felt like a real cad, the way he let her do all the cooking and cleaning while she was with him, but Izzy told him she liked to do it. She did more than that, she took messages for him, organized his desk and even managed some of his appointments. Each year she visited him he grew more reliant on her. She helped keep him sane and she challenged him, she made him explore new possibilities. She taught him nothing was black and white and made him feel as though he could finally find answers to questions he had had his whole life. He was still thinking about what she did for him while she was boarding the airplane. He saw her turn around and leave the line of people, running towards him and reaching into her bluejeans pocket.

"Oh my gosh." She said, "I almost forgot." She pulled out a red checker and placed it onto his palm. "This was in your pants pocket. I almost washed it. I meant to put it away last night and forgot" She laughed.

Jack looked at the red checker she had pressed into his hand and felt a new emotion he didn't recognize wash over him. He felt powerful. Izzy noticed the change in expression and smiled knowingly.

"I told you." She whispered. Then she turned around not waiting for a reply and hurried back in line to board the plane. Jack watched until the plane taxied down the runway and disappeared from sight, he actually cried, this little girl had changed his life.

8

In 1974, Keith began working on the film on location in Tennessee. He had played some of his music at a party and it led to an idea for the movie. His song had become the centerpiece for the film. He vaguely remembered Izzy's letter; he had since changed the lyrics to match those that Izzy had mailed to him. They clearly had not been her words and he had brushed the memory aside as coincidence. Jack had stopped talking about Izzy's predictions, she had just blended into the family, no one really knew why she was there so often, it was just the way it was. She had a calming effect on Jack and the family was happy about it.

That summer at Jack's, Izzy was a little lonely. Although she and Keith barely spoke, she was surprised at how much she missed seeing him around. Keith had moved into his own place some time ago but had always managed to stop for visits when Izzy was in town. This time, Keith was in Tennessee filming and there would be no visits. Izzy was surprised at how disappointed she was that he was gone.

Barbara, Izzy and Jack were all sitting cross legged on the living room floor. Although she had always been curious, Barbara had never asked.

"How did you two meet?" She finally managed to get the question out. She looked at Izzy and laughed. "Did you answer an ad in the paper, wanted, young slave who will idolize me and do my bidding?" She had expected Jack to quietly laugh as he usually did,

97

but his expression was reflective. "I was only kidding, babe." She said softly.

"It's alright." He said. "It occurred to me the other day you weren't here when it all happened and that I should share this with you, provided Izzy is okay with it?" He asked, focusing on Izzy's face. Izzy smiled, put her hand on the side of Jack's cheek and nodded. Jack leaned over and touched his forehead to the girl, then turned to Barbara. "It all started so long ago, I actually hardly think of it anymore, she is just part of me." He said. Barbara scooted back against the sofa and got comfortable. She took a throw pillow from the couch and placed it in her lap and leaned forward on it. Jack was an excellent storyteller, but he spoke softly, often avoiding eye contact and she didn't want to miss any of this story. She listened to every word without interruption, Jack had always found her to be open minded but even he was surprised at how willingly she accepted the story.

Afterwards, they all sat quietly, taking it all in. It had been a long time since even Jack and Izzy had spoken of it, now it was all out there again and all three of them were a bit overwhelmed,

"Wow." Barbara finally managed. "That explains so much."

Jack seemed confused by her words. "What does it explain?" He asked.

Barbara put the toss pillow back on the sofa behind her and pulled herself up. She stretched her legs, then walked behind the sofa and leaned over on it, looking at the two of them. "Everything." She said simply. She clasped her hands together and concentrated on her fingers. "For one thing, it explains the feelings I sense everytime you and Keith are in the same room." She said, looking up at Izzy.

"What?" Izzy said somewhat startled. "Keith doesn't even like me."

"Honey," Barbara said, smiling. "He can't take his eyes off of you."

Jack got up and sat on the arm of the sofa and reached for Barbara's hand. "Tell me what you see." He asked. "Clearly, we both." He said, motioning to his ward. "Need a set of fresh eyes."

"For one thing, everytime the two of them are alone, he has to leave the room." Barbara pointed out.

"Because he can't stand me." Izzy stated.

"Oh no sweet girl." Barbara smiled. "He leaves because he is afraid of giving himself away." She let her words sink in a bit. "He follows you from room to room but as soon as it is just the two of you, he splits, those are the actions of a man in love and who is afraid of what he might say or do."

"Oh that's nonsense." Izzy said, clearly flabbergasted. "I would know if he felt anything other than contempt towards me." She laughed. She focused on Jack's face now who oddly, wasn't nodding in agreement with her.

"He is around quite a bit when the girl is here whether it is her summer stays or just short visits." Jack mused. "Finding an excuse to spend the night or just stopping by unannounced." He smiled and gazed at Izzy, playing with the unshaven stubble on his face. "This time he seems to be calling here frequently, for no reason really." Jack confirmed. "When I answer the phone, he never wants anything and gets off the call fairly quickly, could he be hoping Izzy would answer the call?"

Barbara was smiling and nodding. "Of course he is." She said, "I'm sure he just wants to hear her voice. If everything you have told me is true, Keith is conflicted, it might have started out with him being annoyed having her around, but has obviously progressed to some pretty strong feelings. I'm sure he doesn't know how to admit it to himself or anyone else after behaving the way he has over the years. Men never know how to express themselves, especially when they are wrong." She laughed looking at Jack. "Also, she is young. What he needs is some time alone with her. He needs time to see that she has grown up" Barbara said.

Jack remembered his conversation he had with Keith that last summer. Keith had questioned then if it could be possible Izzy was the one. Jack nodded to Barabara, still fingering his unshaved face.

At that moment, the conversation was interrupted by the ringing of the phone. All three of the conspirators jumped, and then laughed. Jack waived to Izzy to answer the phone. "It might be Keith." He said. "Let's see what happens." It wasn't Keith, it was someone for Barbara. Izzy handed her the phone in relief and went outside on the patio, Jack followed her and said, "Tell me what you are thinking."

Izzy didn't face him. "Oh god." She said, "Part of me is going a hundred miles an hour, hoping it's true, the other part is terrified that it is true. It doesn't make any sense." She whispered. "To Keith I'm just a baby, I can't imagine him thinking of me as anything else. It's probably for the best, I don't know what I'm even doing around him." She said, "I swear to god I have a little voice in my head, it tells me to get him to notice me, then tells me to make him mad. I really hate that little voice!"

Jack sat down on the lawn chair beside Izzy and pulled her hand so that she sat beside him. "I understand that little voice." He said. "I wish I listened to it more often, before you taught me about it I never did. " Jack had such a soft way of speaking, it always made Izzy lean in and listen. " You want to hear something funny?" He asked. "I threw your letter away, that first letter you sent to Keith so many years ago." Izzy's face looked shocked. "It's true." He continued, "Well crumpled it up in a ball anyway. That little voice told me to uncrumple it and read it again, that little voice told me!" He said. Izzy leaned into Jack's shoulder and closed her eyes. They hadn't spoken of any of this in years. They had focused on feeling colors and listening to the universe, other than the one night that they had discussed Keith's colors her feelings about him had been forgotten. She was exhausted but exhilarated, Jack had always believed in her and it felt so good.

Barbara came out on the patio and sat on the chair across from them. She really liked Izzy, there had been times she was jealous of Jack and the girl, but now it all made sense to her. Jack was taking hold of fate, he had always been a control freak. If he had a chance to know the future, of course he would take it and try to control it, it was who he was. Now there was a sense of relief as she realized there was no competition for Jack between the two of them. She could see plainly now, Izzy and Keith were destined to be together and she would help in any way that she possibly could.

Summer was wrapping up, Izzy was preparing mentally for her last year in middle school. Her brother Kent had come home safe from Vietnam. He had two purple hearts and still had shrapnel in his leg but he survived and her mother's colors were finally bright. Izzy had finished writing a short story for Jack to review, he was so helpful, giving her insight on how to improve and how to make words just a little more enticing. She was leaving tomorrow. She set the story down on the kitchen table, Jack and Barbara were off doing something and Izzy had the house to herself. She made one last round looking for dirty laundry and found a few things in Jack's room. She tossed them a laundry basket and carried it to the kitchen. The washer and dryer were in a small cubby hole at the far end of the kitchen next to Jack's desk and the glass patio doors. There was enough in the basket for a small load, she poured a little Oxydol powder into a cup, started the washer, dumped in the clothes and soap then stepped outside the patio doors. Braden heard her come out and came to the fence. "Hey girl." He said and waved to her.

Izzy was always happy to see Braden. His face was always smiling, his voice always cheerful. "Hi Bray!" She answered and walked over to the fence.

"You leave tomorrow don't you?" He asked.

"Yeah, bright and early." She sighed. "I wish I didn't have to." She confided.

"I wish you didn't either." Braden smiled. "You're the prettiest scenery here. Maybe I could take you to the airport?" Braden asked. Right then the phone rang. Izzy looked over her shoulder at the patio doors.

"I better get that." She said, "It could be important."

"I can wait." Braden laughed. Izzy waved him off but noticed he was still standing there when she looked out the patio doors as she picked up the phone.

"Hello?" Izzy answered.

"Hi Iz." Keith said. "You must be getting ready to leave huh?"

"Keith! Hey, how is filming? Anything cool in Nashville? Too bad it's all country music there!" Izzy teased.

"Sure, make fun of my music." Keith replied. "Besides, this song is actually soft rock."

"Well, even if it was a pure country song, I'm sure that yours would stink less than most." Izzy said. Then giggled that course laugh that Keith had grown to crave.

"Gee, thanks." Keith said. "Maybe you should try being nice to me once in a while." Then he laughed. He always found himself laughing when he talked to Izzy, Jack accused Keith of not having a sense of humor from time to time, but he did laugh a lot when he talked to Izzy. He was surprised at how his opinion of her had changed over time, he now actually liked the kid, she had grown on him. She made him laugh, but he also got so angry with her and that confused him, never had anyone caused him to have so many intense feelings at once as this little girl did.

"Are you all packed?" He asked.

"Duffel bag loaded sir!" She said then saluted the phone with her free hand.

"One of these times, you really should bring a few things with you." Keith said.

"I have everything I need, I really don't need much." Izzy confirmed.

For as long as the brothers had known the girl, she crammed everything she needed into a small green duffel bag. Most girls that Keith knew, carried bag after bag with them when they traveled. Some girls had a separate bag just for makeup. Izzy never did, he actually liked that, she just never seemed to want "things".

"Have you been sleeping better?" Keith asked.

"It comes and goes." Izzy giggled.

"I worry about you, you know?" Keith said softly. "It's a proven fact that you can have all kinds of health issues if you don't get enough sleep."

"Then Jack will outlive me." Izzy teased.

The front door opened and Jack and Barbara walked in, Jerome dashed in the open door and almost knocked Jack over. Izzy waved silently to Barbara and mouthed "Keith" to her. She gave Izzy a thumbs up.

"Your brother just walked in." Izzy said to him. "Hang on and I'll give him the phone."

"Wait." Keith said. He paused for a few moments, searching for something else to say. "Have a safe trip. Be careful at the airport too, that place is dangerous."

"Braden might take me." Izzy said. She looked outside and Braden was still leaning over the top of the fence. "I think he wants me to ride on his new motorcycle. " Izzy said.

Keith snapped at her. "You tell him no!" He said. "Your mother wouldn't want you riding a motorcycle to LAX. I mean it Izzy, Jack might not have enough sense to tell you no, but I do."

"And speeding down the freeway in a Ferrari with the top down is better?" Izzy laughed.

Keith was incensed, what was wrong with his brother. "Put Jack on the phone and you go tell Braden I said no!"

"Whatever." Izzy said, but was careful to hold the phone away from her mouth as she said it. She liked this new side of Keith. Provoking him had become second nature to her over the years but this time, she thought better of it and only a little part of her wanted him to hear it.

"Grasshopper, Keith wants to yell at you." She said handing Jack the phone and skipping outside to talk to Braden. Barbara sat at the kitchen table and smiled.

When Jack got off the phone fifteen minutes later, he was still smiling. "Thank you my dear." He said to his girlfriend. A week ago, I wouldn't have understood, I would have thought he was just being a dick. He's jealous." Barbara nodded in agreement. "I have got to find a way to get these two alone." Jack smiled. "Can I borrow your car tomorrow? Seems Keith wants the package delivered safely to the airport and not by motorcycle or Ferrari, kind of takes the fun out of it doesn't it?"

At the end of 1975 Jack's television show was coming to an end, he was glad, but also on edge. Keith's song had been nominated for an Oscar, best original song. Jack wondered what would have changed if Keith hadn't fixed the lyrics. Izzy had missed their usual summer visit, there had just been too much to do preparing for highschool. In the beginning of 1976 Jack was starting to fall apart. The Oscars were just around the corner and Jack needed to be strong. He felt as though his career was flailing wildly out of control. He needed Izzy, he knew that this was the final test Izzy had told him was coming. He reached out to Ruth to ask if Izzy could come out for winter break, imploring her that he needed Izzy there and couldn't wait for the coming summer. Ruth said it would be alright and Izzy packed a few things and got on a plane.

Izzy showed up with her usual small green duffel bag. Jack greeted her at the airport and she flung her arms around his neck. A few people stopped and stared, a little whispering could be heard but neither Izzy or Jack cared.

When they got to Jack's, it wasn't long before Izzy could tell things weren't right with him. Arriving at the house she saw that he had left the front door wide open. Jack had always behaved a bit like a hippy, but leaving the front door wide open while Barbara was still in bed, that was a problem. Jack had left the garage door open again too. Izzy closed the garage door herself then followed Jack into the house. It was cluttered, papers were scattered across the coffee table and the kitchen table as well. Izzy leaned into the kitchen and glanced at his desk and sighed. She had her work cut out for her and only had a couple of weeks before school started back up. She would do what she could to help declutter his living space and hopefully his mind; she had learned a long time ago that when he let his house go, his mind would usually follow.

Keith having his own place now, might have been part of the problem. Jack needed an anchor. Izzy was great for him, but she was only part time. Things hadn't been going well with Jack and Barbara again either. Barbara had got her own place and now traveled back and forth between the two. Emotionally it was good for her especially when Jack's life was creating chaos but the chaos got worse when Jack was alone so it was an endless cycle. The first thing Izzy needed to do was get to the store. Jack reluctantly took her in his Ferrari because Barbara would need her car when she woke up. Jack used his car as an excuse and argued about everything that Izzy put in the shopping cart saying, there was no room for that many groceries in his car. Izzy ignored him. She bought lots of fresh vegetables and fruit, lots of high protein red meat which Jack balked at and some odds and ends that she would use during her visit. Jack begrudgingly paid the cashier and carried the sacks to his car. They managed to find room for all the brown paper sacks and returned home to an empty house. Barbara had left shortly after waking up.

Together Jack and Izzy both put away most of the groceries, Izzy kept out a package of hamburger, garlic, green pepper and onion. She also left out tomato paste, sauce and a can of italian style plum tomatoes. She browned some hamburger, chopped up the vegetables and dumped it in with the meat. Jack didn't want to admit it, but as the meat simmered with the vegetables, his mouth watered. Izzy opened the cans of tomato and Jerome ran into the kitchen. Izzy laughed and also opened a can of Purina cat food for him and spooned some into his bowl. She then emptied the canned tomatoes into a large saucepan, added some red wine and brewed coffee from Jack's coffee pot. She didn't measure any of it. Last she added some fresh basil and some powdered oregano and then dumped the meat into the sauce and turned it on low. On a different burner she boiled some water and took some angel hair pasta and dumped it into the boiling water and while that cooked, made a big salad.

"Sit," She commanded Jack. He sat down at the table acting as if he were put out, but one of his dimples was beginning to show. She took a lemon from a basket on the counter and sliced it, Jack didn't like salad dressing. Izzy dished up some salad onto a paper plate, noticing most of the dishes in the house were dirty and in the sink. She set the salad on the table in front of him and handed him the lemon. He squeezed it so the juice landed on the salad. While he ate his salad, she drained and rinsed the spaghetti and put some on another paper plate. She slathered butter on top of the noodles when Jack wasn't looking and then put a big ladle of sauce on top of it. She set it in front of Jack and commanded him to eat. His vitamin bottles were a mess and all over the kitchen counter. Izzy began to organize the bottles while filling the kitchen sink with hot water, after squirting a little Palmolive under the running faucet. She shook a few of the pills out into her hand, a multivitamin, a vitamin C and a Biotin, then placed them beside Jack's plate.

"I can't believe you poured coffee in this." He said while twirling his pasta on a fork. He tried to sound irritated with her but Izzy knew that he wasn't. He tasted the spaghetti and had to pinch himself to stop from making a yummy sound. It was delicious. Jack picked up the vitamins and washed them down with a glass of milk that Izzy had poured for him. He took another bite of spaghetti and smiled. Izzy watched him as he did so, he opened his eyes wide and nodded approval to her, indicating that it was good. Jack had squinty eyes, so when he opened them wide it really changed his appearance. "This is fantastic!" He said.

"It smells good." Came a voice from the hallway. Keith stood in the hallway, leaning on the wall near the phone.

"Keith!" Izzy whispered.

"You left the door unlocked again Jack." Keith said. "I was hoping to borrow this ring from you for good luck." Keith said, holding up a gold ring with a cross on it. Jack nodded.

Izzy had learned over the years that both the brothers were a little superstitious when it came to auditions or performances. They had to follow a certain ritual or wear a certain color. She knew that neither really believed what they did mattered or would change an outcome, but they found solace in handing their fate over to something other than themselves. It wasn't really any different than her mother leaving the room when the Cornhuskers had a big play, she always said the team would lose if she watched.

"How long have you been here?" Jack asked.

"Since the two of you carried in the groceries." Keith answered. "I could have been anyone, you really need to lock your door." He chastised.

"Sit down, I'll feed you too." Izzy laughed, trying not to make fun of the ring. It was a ring that their father John had worn in his earlier years and had given to Jack as a token of appreciation when Jack followed his father on to the stage. Keith caught his breath when he heard Izzy laugh, it had been a couple years since he had seen or heard her and it dawned on him how much he had missed her. "I'm glad you came." Keith continued as he took a place at the table. "Jack needs some help organizing."

"I noticed." Izzy laughed again. Keith watched her intently while she ladeled sauce on his pasta and carried it to him.

"No salad?" He teased.

"Ah, sorry, of course, let me get you a plate." Izzy blushed.

"Aren't you joining us?" Keith asked.

"Nah, I'm not hungry. I'm going to start some laundry, then maybe go see Bray." Izzy said. Keith tensed up at the mention of Jack's neighbor, and pursed his lips. Jack noticed the change on his brother's face but didn't let on. Izzy took a laundry basket off the top of the dryer and went down the hall towards Jack's room.

"You think she should be hanging out with that guy?" Keith asked.

"There's no harm in it." Jack answered, both of his dimples on full display. Keith looked at his plate and spun some more spaghetti around his fork.

"I don't like it." He said, then put the fork in his mouth. "She does makes a mean spaghetti." He said. "What, took her like fifteen minutes?"

Jack nodded. Izzy came out with a basket full of clothes and dropped it in front of the washer. She pulled out the whites and dropped them in, then poured some Oxydol into a cup, looked at the whites that she had just dumped in the washer and then poured in a little chlorine bleach. "You were walking outside in your stocking feet again weren't you?" She said to Jack not looking at him and not waiting for an answer "You know, you could just take off the socks if you want to feel foot freedom." She started the washer and then kissed the top of Jack's head. "I'll be back in a few." She said then hurried out the front door.

Keith pushed his plate away and took a carrot strip out of the salad and chewed it. Jack studied his brother for a few moments. "Do you think you can help?" He asked. "About what we talked about earlier. I know it is a lot to ask, I shouldn't be but a few days. I want to get that film out, we wrapped three years ago, I don't know, it's like the last nice thing I can do for Barbara, I've really destroyed a nice thing."

Keith stretched back in the chair and nodded. "Of course." He answered. "The Enidarrac curse. Making bad decisions when it comes to women."

"Single again?" Jack asked his brother. He already knew the answer, their father John had told him about the breakup a few weeks earlier, the breakup had inspired Barbara and Jack's timing to release the film.

"Not single, free." Keith laughed. "I hope Izzy is wrong about time repeating, I don't want to relive this break-up."

"I swear, if we really do come back," Jack said softly. "I'm not doing this again. The stress is unreal. Next time, I'm choosing a different path."

"Nonsense." Keith said. "The world needs you. You would die without the theater in your life"

"Ha!" Jack laughed in response.

"Seriously, what would you choose if you could do it over again?" Keith asked.

Jack stroked his chin. "Maybe I would buy a little community playhouse somewhere. I could do my own productions and also teach."

Keith studied his brother's face, then nodded. "It would be more peaceful, I'll give you that. Maybe I could join you."

"My life isn't what I imagined it would be." Jack confessed to his brother. "I'm going to be typecast forever because of that show. I'll be like Bob Denver, I'll never find work again unless it is for a B list movie just like dad." Jack picked out a piece of lettuce from the salad and ate it. "You know it kills me, to say I'm like dad."

"First, you have so much more talent than Bob Denver ever had and everyone knows it. Second, you will find work again, you just need to behave. You and I both know it. It is not lack of talent that gets in your way, it's your need to control everything. Third, Dad did B movies but had a brilliant stage career. Between you and me, I think he wanted to do the B movies. He thought they were fun. Dad is complicated, so are you."

"Complicated." Jack repeated the word. "That's a fair assessment."

Keith didn't answer but smiled. He also leaned back in his chair and looked out the front door. "She's really changed." He stated. "Hell, I barely recognized her." He looked at the salad and fished out another carrot. "Does she know?" He asked.

"No, not yet." Jack said. "I don't think she will mind, like I said, it should only be for a few days. I just wanted to make sure I could count on you"

" Of course you can." Keith said. "I'm curious why you would tell Ruth you could take her if you had to finish this project."

Jack averted his eyes from Keith's and hoped he wouldn't be found out. He had told Keith that Ruth had needed him to watch Izzy, he and Barbara both had determined telling Keith this white lie was the answer. Izzy didn't know either, Jack and Barbara had scattered papers around the house in a desperate attempt to make Izzy believe she was needed. She was needed, Jack was falling apart, but he hid it well. This trip was planned for Izzy. He and Barbara had been planning it for some time, waiting for the right opportunity.

"She will be all alone on Oscar night, I can't be in two places at once." Keith continued, oblivious to the meticulous planning his brother had gone to. Keith turned and looked out the front door again. "At least I hope she is alone. How old is that guy now?" Jack didn't answer but silently laughed. Barbara had been right, his brother had it bad.

9

The house looked great and smelled like lemon pledge. The laundry was done, the papers that had been scattered around the house had been neatly organized. The kitchen had been swept and mopped and the finger prints that were all over the wall by the telephone had been wiped away with 409. Izzy's mother's number and Dorothy's number remained on the wall. Izzy never wiped them off, she thought it was funny. The bathroom was clean, Izzy had scrubbed the tub for an hour and she had even washed the shower curtain. The bathroom was green, avocado green. The tile was green and black but the toilet and tub were white. She changed the blade in Jack's razor and put some fresh bar soap on the dish by the sink. Dial soap, she liked the smell of it.

Izzy went to the kitchen and opened the refrigerator door, she took out a bottle of coke, closed the door and opened the coke using the bottle opener on the side of the refrigerator. She found Jack outside, barefoot, sitting in the grass and smoking a cigar. He looked much better than when she had first arrived, his color was better, he had bathed thank God and he seemed more eager to smile. Jack greeted her by holding his bare feet in the air and wiggling his toes, then he winked at her.

"Better?" He asked.

"Yes." Izzy nodded in approval. It was really too cold for him to be barefoot but Izzy didn't have the heart to reprimand him.

"I know I shouldn't be jealous of him." Jack said without looking up. "I should be proud of him. And I am, I'm both." Jack said.

"Of course you are." Izzy said. "And you should be both."

Jack looked at her. He picked a dandelion from the grass and twirled it. "You're the only one that I could ever confide that to." He stated simply. "Including Barbara."

Izzy plopped next to him in the grass and bumped her shoulder against his. "Nothing wrong with being human." Izzy said. "You know, I feel the same way about my sister, and have less motive to feel that way. I didn't teach her about horses, she learned it all on her own, I didn't teach her to draw, or to sing, but she is better at all those things than me. I get jealous. Keith isn't better than you, you have way more talent, and you taught him most of what he knows." Izzy paused. She looked at the man sitting barefoot in the grass. He had so much pride, it had to be hard for him to admit he was jealous. "I'm so very proud of you." Izzy continued. "You opened up a whole new world to people, you embraced your role. I know it wasn't easy, but you made it famous. It was you! No one else could have created the success that you did for that show. Plus, you are very cute!"

Jack leaned over and pulled her close and kissed the top of her head. "Sometimes," He said. "I'm even jealous because of you. I'm not sure that he deserves you to love him. If I were fifteen years younger, I'd put up a fight."

Izzy giggled. "Only fifteen?"

"That really stings." Jack laughed. "You shouldn't hit a man when he is down."

Part of him meant it, he was forty one years old, his career was at a stand still and he was afraid of losing Barbara. It was his own doing and she wasn't gone yet, but he suspected that it was inevitable. Part of him would love to just bend over and kiss Izzy, it would be so easy, she knew him better than anyone else and loved him anyway. It was just like she had explained to him, if you can see the worst in someone and still love them, it is real. He played with the idea for a few minutes, she was very pretty, but he was listening to his little voice for once, and it was saying no. He remembered Izzy warning him of this very thing. Jack could be blunt, judgemental and careless, when it came to relationships he was selfish. This girl in front of him, he cherished, he had to follow through with what he knew was right. This girl was meant for Keith.

"So, I'm going to be gone for a few days." He said. Izzy looked up, clearly surprised. Jack handed her the dandylion and she accepted it. "I know this is awkward, I mean I asked you to come out."

"Do you want me to leave?" She asked.

"Oh God no, I wish you never had to leave." Jack answered truthfully. "I'd adopt you if your mother would let me, I'm trying to finish up some details on a film, nothing big but Barbara and I have some loose ends we need to tie up. I'm just going to disappear for a few days so I can concentrate on what needs to be done and so you know, I've asked Keith to come stay here with you while I'm gone." He watched her face for a tell of some kind. When he first met her, he could read her every thought. Over the years she had become more adept at hiding them. Now she was as good as he was at hiding her thoughts with a smile. At least from him. "You'll be alone on Oscar night, I'm buying a television so you can watch it."

Izzy stood up and looked around, she cupped her eyes and looked at the sky. "What are you doing?" Jack asked, smiling.

"Looking for locusts, some sort of warning that the world is ending." She laughed.

"Ha ha." Jack said. "I might even keep it for your future visits."

Izzy sat back down and shoved Jack in the shoulder. "I don't need a babysitter." She said, "But I'll take the television."

"He isn't a babysitter." Jack answered. "Your mother wouldn't want you to be alone, and, since you can't drive, I didn't want you to get bored."

Izzy nodded. She knew he was lying of course, but he had allowed her a way to not be embarrassed. "I'm not folding his underwear." She laughed. "Chauffeur or not!"

"I wouldn't expect you to." Jack smiled. "Try not to give him a heart attack will you? I've grown to love him a bit over the years."

"Leave the hard rock T's in my duffel bag?" She asked.

"Please." He said. "Give the kid a break."

Keith arrived at the house as planned. Jack was getting ready to disappear for a few days, figure out the film, get it ready to release. He had directed it and Barbara had done a fantastic job acting in it, but Jack had never done anything with it. Now that the television show was over combined with the problems he was having in his personal life, it seemed like a good time to get the film out there.

Keith had pulled up on the driveway and let himself in, the front door was unlocked again. Keith entered and walked past a blue suitcase on the tile near the front closet door. The closet was on the left and a few steps after that was a stunning carved mahogany entry table. He noted that car keys were in a small green dish on the table, above the table was a large mirror with a carved mahogany frame. Keith was carrying a black tuxedo with a very ruffled shirt that was wrapped in plastic. He had a small bag with some other clothing and toiletries in his other hand and was balancing a shoe box on his arm. He didn't open the closet door, but hung the tux on a hook that was placed on the outside of it. He set his shoebox on the entry table next to the keys then glanced at his reflection in the mirror. Keith ran his fingers through his thinning hair then muttered to his image shaking his head at himself and then proceeded on into the house. There were lots of mementos from some of Jack's many journeys that he had made around the world, but it was sparsely decorated, still, leaving the door wide open was asking for someone to steal and he knew Jack would miss some of those items if they were to disappear. He set his other things on the chair that Jerome was stretched across the back of. Jerome gave him a half-hearted hiss, barely opening his eyes. Jack was in the backyard, kicking back on the green and white woven lawn chair and smoking a cigar. Jack had assured Keith that Izzy would be no trouble. On the night of the awards Keith promised to call and check on her. Jack was going to call her as well.

"You know, " Keith said. "If you're so concerned for her safety, maybe you should lock your front door," Keith confronted his brother. Jack smiled at him then waved his hand as if brushing the suggestion away. Keith sat beside him in another woven chair, but he didn't lay back on it, instead he sat on it sideways, facing his brother.

"So, on the big night, will the Limo pick you up here?" Jack asked.

"Yeah, then on to Dad's house." Keith answered.

"Keith." Jack was laughing, "You're a good looking guy, you're going to win an Oscar and you're bringing your dad as your date?"

Keith tried not to take the bait. Jack had been drinking and his eyes were a little bloodshot. Keith wasn't sure how long he had been drinking but he knew the signs well enough to avoid any conversation about their shared father. Still, he had to make a minor attempt or Jack would continue to goad him. Keith had been down this path with his brother before.

"I know you have issues with him," Keith responded. He shrugged simply and said. "I love him. You know he is getting older, Jack, who knows how much longer he will be around."

"Maybe he was different when he was with you," Jack was saying. "I'm not saying he is all bad, but the word absent comes to mind." He inhaled a few times from the cigar, then smiled and said, " I can think of a few other adjectives as well."

Keith waited, counting to five in his head. He wished his father and Jack would get along. They were actually so very much alike. Maybe that was why they fought. They were both arrogant, both immensely talented, both underrated and both so sure they were right. He decided to drop the subject.

" So, where is she now?' Keith asked, changing the subject from their father to Izzy. Jack waved towards the house and smiled that damn knowing smile of his.

"She's in there somewhere." he smirked. "Why don't you go find her. You can make sure no one came in the open door and took her." He said, slurring his words a little as he spoke. "I need to give her a few instructions before I leave". He picked up a drink that was sitting on the table beside the chair. The ice cubes made a rattling sound against the glass. He swirled the drink around in the glass, then set it down beside him without taking a sip. Instead he put the cigar to his lips and inhaled deeply.

Keith reluctantly headed back inside the kitchen. The Hallway was to the right, one bathroom on the right, a small bedroom on the left and the larger bedroom at the end of the hall on the right. As he walked down the hall he could hear movement in the bathroom, he looked in and saw Izzy there. She was straddled over the bathtub, one leg in and the other out. She was wearing a soft earthy colored sundress. One strap had fallen carelessly down the shoulder towards him, revealing a light tan line and a sprinkle of freckles. He leaned against the door frame and watched her for a minute, she was lathering up her leg in the tub. He smiled, then caught himself and tried to look stern, then cleared his throat.

Izzy turned her head and looked over the strapless shoulder at him. She softly smiled, then motioned her head for him to enter. It was a small bathroom, it was a small house. The only place for him to sit was on the toilet. He put the seat cover down and sat on it. She laughed softly, then brought her leg up and rested it on the edge of the tub, the skirt of her dress slid carelessly down her leg but she either didn't notice or more likely didn't care. Keith took it in, her slim leg and shapely ankle. He watched as she made long slow strokes with the razor all the way up to her knee. It seemed like a lifetime ago when she had been a kid playing a guessing game with a deck of cards. He remembered that even then, she was strangely attractive and suddenly he felt kind of awkward, she wasn't little anymore and his view was right up her skirt and he knew he shouldn't be looking. Damn it, why did he always feel so intense around her, she might be growing up but she wasn't there yet. He had to stop thinking of her like that, a scandal could ruin his career. He had worked too hard to let a kid ruin it.

"Almost done". She said, then laughed again like she might know what he was thinking. He was about to leave when she put her leg back in the tub, turned on the faucet and bent over to rinse off the soap. When she did so, she playfully put her hand under the running water and then flicked water off her long fingers towards Keith.

"Quit it brat." he quipped. She laughed and did it again. He rolled his eyes. "You're really asking for it." He said.

"Ha!" Izzy laughed. "Promises promises."

Keith felt a little burning sensation start at the top of his head and ears. Adrenaline rush. He thought to himself. Stop it now Keith. "Jack summons you." He managed to say his voice cracked a bit and he hoped it didn't give him away.

She had stopped laughing and was intently gazing at him. Her eyes were dark blue, the darkest blue eyes he had ever seen. She had fair skin but it was slightly tanned. Her hair was very blonde but he noticed there were slight streaks of red in it. Izzy was Irish and although she was a natural blonde, there was a reddish sheen to it. She had high Irish cheekbones and a straight nose with just a few freckles across the bridge of it. Her hair had grown even longer, it now reached just above her waist, but it was smooth and tapered, clearly trimmed by a professional. He thought about her when he had first laid eyes on her, messy blonde hair and crooked bangs. He imagined how hard it must have been to get her to hold still long enough to cut those bangs. Yes, she was growing up. He snapped himself out of the memories of the past and found her looking intently at his face. She had just finished drying her leg with a hand towel.

"What are you looking at?" he asked.

She was noticing just how good looking he was, it had been a while since she had really noticed. He was so tall, sitting on the toilet his knees almost touched her. He still had the long hair and beard from the movie, she wasn't sure if she liked it. She remembered him with his sculpted chin and kind of missed it. He had full lips and a high brow, when he smiled he had a toothy grin.

"Just looking." she said. "It's been a while since I've seen you." She swung her leg over the edge of the tub and stood up, placing the hand towel back on the towel rack, then she squeezed past Keith and stood before the vanity mirror. There was a small pink case on the counter, she opened it up and took out a brown tortoise shell comb, starting at the ends she slowly combed through her hair. She put the comb back in the case and then removed a small black tube. She twisted it and pulled out a thin mascara brush and leaned forward towards the mirror.

"Wait a minute." Keith said. "Is that mascara?"

Izzy paused and looked at Keith. "Yes, it's mascara." She replied, trying not to smile.

"Give that to me." He demanded but in a quiet tone.

Izzy continued to look at Keith, fighting the urge to smile. "You don't need mascara." She quipped. "Your lashes are long and dark." She turned around and leaned her butt against the bathroom counter top. "I have often wondered why so many men have thick dark lashes, it really isn't fair. She said, then turned to the mirror again. Keith snatched the mascara brush out of her hand.

"I said to give me that."

"You are not my boss." Izzy fumed. "Give it back."

Keith used his other hand and picked up the rest of the mascara container. He put the brush end back in the tube and screwed it shut. "I think I'll keep it." He answered. "You don't need it. Women look better naturally, trust me I know. Men like women who aren't made up." Keith stood up and put the mascara in his pocket. Izzy narrowed her eyes. This was a direct challenge. She shrugged and said, "I'm not giving up my lip gloss." She reached into the pink bag and pulled out a small round container and twisted the lid open. She scooted out of reach from Keith's long arms just in case, then she dipped one finger into the container and then gently applied the gloss to her lips. It was clear and made her lips look soft and moist. She smiled at her reflection, then turned and faced Keith making a popping sound with her mouth as she did so.

"Cute," Keith said. Izzy just smiled, still calculating to herself how to regain custody of the mascara. Keith couldn't take his eyes off her lips, she really was beautiful. Izzy put the lid back on the gloss then dropped it back into the pink bag.

"Fine?" She asked. He nodded and stood up from the toilet seat. He tried to step around her, as he did she made a grab at his pocket. Keith was anticipating the move, she had been far too submissive and he was ready for the ambush. He was faster than she was and he caught her hand. She laughed.

"Give it back." She pouted.

"Does your mother let you wear that?" He asked.

"Please." She said, "Mom bought it for me."

He remembered Jack mentioning once to him that Izzy's Aunt Dorothy had criticized how Ruth was raising the girls. If she was his daughter he wouldn't have allowed them to wear make-up at all, but in all fairness, Izzy had turned out remarkably well and looking at her beautiful eyes, he was very grateful that she wasn't his daughter.

"Well you aren't wearing it here. You really are beautiful the way you are. " He was still holding her arm in his hand. He tried to swing around towards the door but brought Izzy with him, her back now against the door Keith towered over her. It was a cramped bathroom and as he pulled her arm to the side, he ended up pulling her closer to him. They stood in the doorway, tangled together for a few moments before Keith released her arm and stepped out into the hallway. Together they both went out to the backyard, Jack had his eyes shut and one arm up with his hand behind his head, the other to his side still holding the cigar. The corner of his mouth curved upward as they approached him but he didn't open his eyes.

Izzy caught Keith's hand and pulled him down to her level. "He's been drinking a lot this time. " She whispered in Keith's ear. He nodded to let her know he was aware and squeezed her hand.

"Keith, Izzy is going to a party with Braden tonight," Jack said, then opened his eyes and looked intently at Izzy.

"What?" Keith asked, clearly taken aback.

"Yeah, I should have called you." Jack slurred. "I think I'll stay here one more night just to make sure she is okay. You can go back home tonight if you want, come back tomorrow morning."

"I'll stay." Keith said. "One of us should be sober. I wouldn't have let her go."

Jack's eyes were hazy, he smiled at Keith and Izzy. "I'm trusting you, don't let me down."

"I won't, grasshopper!" She whispered as she leaned down and kissed his cheek. Keith just didn't get their connection, she was the only one Jack smiled like that for.

"I know you didn't want to come, I'm sure you would rather be living your life in Nebraska than being pawned off to stay with some old guys in California." Jack mumbled.

"Old guys?" Keith said, "Speak for yourself brother!"

"What?" Izzy laughed. "Of course I wanted to come, I always want to come. There is no one that I would rather be with and you aren't old!." Izzy answered truthfully. Jack nodded then looked at Keith.

"I think I'm going to close my eyes for a bit, take care of my baby grasshopper." Jack said to Keith. Izzy smiled and looked down.

"Maybe she shouldn't go out." Keith said, he took the glass off the table next to the chair.

"She'll be fine." Jack said, not opening his eyes.

Keith looked at Izzy and shrugged. Jack would always be Jack, he was used to it but Izzy hadn't really seen this side of him. She was aware of it of course and he had traveled to the Meeks house to recover a few times, but she hadn't seen him spiral downward before, he hoped they would have a chance to talk about it.

"You're wearing a sweater, I insist." Keith said. Izzy smiled at him and nodded sweetly.

"Hey Izzy!" A voice bellowed over the privacy fence.

"Bray!" Izzy answered. Suddenly she was grabbing a pair of white tennis shoes that she had left outside and slipping them on. The left one wouldn't slide on and she had to bend over and pull the back of it with her fingers. Keith tried not to look at her ass but deep down he thought Jack who had opened his eyes had probably noticed that he had.

"Grab a sweater!" He yelled after her. He saw her open the closet door and take out one of Jack's sweaters from it. It was a soft beige cashmere cardigan and It was too big for her. The creamy color accentuated her hair and because it was too big it kept sliding down her arms exposing her soft shoulders, making her look even more enticing and he was sorry he told her to take it. She closed the closet door and Keith's tuxedo nearly fell off the hook, then Izzy skipped out the front door slamming it behind her as she went.

"What the hell?" Keith asked Jack who was now sitting up, facing sideways on the lounge chair. "Seriously Jack, Braden has got to be 22 years old! Do you really think Ruth would approve of a party with this guy?"

"He's 23." Jack answered, still slightly smiling at his brother. Jack didn't really like the idea either but letting her go with Braden had been a calculated move.

"That girl has you completely wrapped around her finger, she is 15! I just had to take make-up away from her."

Jack's eyes narrowed just a bit. He could see the struggle in his brother's face, he hoped this didn't backfire on him, but he and Barbara had carefully laid this plan out, he had to trust in it.

"She seems to attract the interest of many different types, little brother." He looked for his drink but Keith was still holding it in his hand. "Especially older ones." He laid back down and closed his eyes, determined to let the night play out. He couldn't control this, all he could do was set it in action.

Keith stood up, taking Jack's drink with him and walked into the house. He looked out the living room window. The window was covered with heavy beige drapes that helped block the afternoon sun. Red oriental birds were embroidered on the outer fabric. They were quite beautiful, but Keith didn't notice, all he could do was watch Izzy. She was getting on the motorcycle behind Braden, She wrapped her arms around his waist and a minute later they were gone. Keith let go of the living room curtain in disgust. His brother was sleeping, Izzy was gone, he was alone. He looked at the new television sitting awkwardly in the living area, but didn't turn it on, instead he picked up a newspaper and thumbed through it. He knew he wouldn't get rest until Izzy was home, he was so sorry he had agreed to watch her for his brother.

It was a little past midnight. Keith dozed off and on, thinking he heard a motorcycle in the distance, but he never did. He lay on the sofa, wondering if he should turn on the front door light, if nothing else it might make Braden more careful when he brought the girl home. He heard the doorknob turning and sat up. He hadn't heard the motorcycle, maybe a burglar was going to actually walk in like Keith had warned his brother might happen so many times in the past.

It was Izzy, he could see her silhouette against the street light as she entered the house. She pushed the door open and closed it silently behind her. She tried to focus her eyes but the room was darker than usual so she had to pause and let her eyes focus, Keith had pulled the heavy living room curtains shut, Jack never did. She tried to walk silently past the sofa, but Keith was awake and sitting up. "I didn't hear the motorcycle." Keith said.

"I didn't ride home." Izzy said bluntly. "Sorry if I woke you up, I was trying to be quiet."

"Did it break down?" Keith asked.

"No." Izzy replied. "I walked home."

Keith swung his legs to the floor, he reached over and turned on a lamp. "Walked?" He asked. "Where was this party?"

"I don't know." Izzy answered. " A few blocks away, no biggie."

"Wait, you mean you walked alone?" Keith asked. "At this hour?"

At this point Jack entered the house, he had fallen asleep outside but had awoken shortly before Izzy had come home. He had a cigarette in his hand as he entered the living room.

"Did I hear you say you walked home?" He asked, flipping the light switch on in the kitchen.

"Yes." Izzy said. "What's the big deal, I walk everywhere in Nebraska."

"There is a big difference in walking the streets at midnight in California than there is in Nebraska." Keith said. "A young girl isn't safe acting that way here."

"Why did you leave?" Jack asked.

"Braden was being a jerk." Izzy said. "He was drunk."

"Did he try something?" Keith asked. He was getting entirely too worked up.

Izzy rolled her eyes and headed towards her bedroom. Keith put his hands on his hips and glared at Jack. Jack nodded and followed Izzy to her room. Jack entered and sat on her bed while Izzy rummaged in her duffel bag for her nightgown.

"Izzy." He began.

"Just stop." Izzy commanded. "You can't do that."

"Do what?" Jack asked.

"What you're doing." She said, "The hypocrisy is insane."

"What hypocrisy, we are worried for your safety." Jack said gently. Keith was listening from down the hallway. Jack was so kind and gentle with her, as far as he was aware, this was the only time that they had ever argued.

"You can't warn me about his intentions, then get angry when I put a stop to them!" Izzy said. Keith smiled at this, knowing that Jack had in fact actually said something to her about Braden. The guy only wanted one thing, he had been chasing Izzy since that first day he saw her so many years ago. Good for Jack, Keith thought to himself.

"It wasn't that far away." Izzy continued. "You walk all the time. I have a basket of dirty socks on the washer to prove it" Izzy stormed into the bathroom across the hall, carrying her nightgown with her. She peeled the cardigan off and tossed it on the floor then began to pull her sundress up over her head.

"Close the door." Jack shouted. Izzy used the back of her foot and loudly kicked the door closed behind her. "You could just not watch." She mumbled to herself, not quite loud enough for anyone to hear. "But by all means, let me close the door."

She faced herself in the mirror and ran a comb through her hair. She knew no one heard her mumbling but still felt a little guilty for having said it.

Keith worked his way down the hall and peeked his head in the doorway at his brother who was still seated on her bed. "Wow." He said, I don't think I've ever heard her angry before.

"It doesn't happen often." Jack confirmed, he was smiling just a little.

A moment later Izzy left the bathroom, her clothing in a ball in her arms. She shoved past Keith and tossed her clothes on a chair by the bedroom door. She walked past Jack and pulled the covers back just enough so she could climb in underneath them. She smelled like Sage.

"Look Izzy." Jack said gently. "There is a big difference between me walking around at night, I'm forty one years old. You are a young beautiful girl who shouldn't be, that's all we are saying."

"Male gender bias." Izzy stated flatly.

"It is." Jack said. "But it is also true."

Keith stepped out of the room but stood outside in the hallway, out of sight from the both of them. He leaned against the wall, his back towards Izzy's room and wondered what exactly Braden had done. God he hated that guy.

Izzy sat up and smiled at Jack, she couldn't stay angry with him for long. She had already forgiven him before she opened the bathroom door. "I'm sorry," She said. "Next time, I'll call."

Keith heard her say it and thought to himself that there wouldn't be a next time. His teeth were clenched and his jaw muscle twitched.

"I'm glad you didn't put up with anything." Jack said. "What exactly did he do?"

"Nothing outrageous Jack." She said, "He was just getting more familiar than I wanted, tongue and hands in the wrong places. When he got up to get another beer, I split." She grinned.

Keith grimaced and his jaw twitched a little more. The thought of that guy touching Izzy made his skin crawl.

"Why didn't you just call?" There are payphones all over the place that you could have used."

"Honestly," She said. "Partly because I can take care of myself, I didn't need one of you coming to rescue me, I knew the way home." Izzy said. "And partly," she admitted, Lowering her voice. "because I didn't want Keith to know he was right." As she confirmed this, she glanced up and saw Keith was back in the doorway. "How long have you been standing there?" She asked.

"Long enough to know you think I was right." Keith smiled at her.

"Both or you, get out." Izzy said in her sweetest tone she could muster. Then she took her pillow in her hand, let herself fall backwards on the bed and covered her face with it. Jack stood up and headed towards the door, he flipped off the light switch as he left, Keith stood in the doorway for a few minutes and smiled, his jaw muscle loosened a little, for some reason her admitting he was right really gave him some satisfaction. After a few moments he followed Jack and headed to the patio to have a drink in the dark.

"I told you that guy was bad news." Keith said to his brother. Jack had a drink in one hand and a cigarette in the other. He didn't reply but smiled kindly at his brother. He and Barbara couldn't have planned it any better, he couldn't wait to tell her about Braden.

"Seriously," Keith continued, not noticing the smug smile on his brother's face. "The more I think of that jerk trying to put his hands on her, the angrier I get." Keith continued.

Jack took a drag of the cigarette and inhaled deeply. He set the drink down on the patio floor and took another drag. "I think Izzy handled it well." He said. "She shouldn't have walked home alone, but she did alright."

"I'd like to kill him." Keith said.

"I don't think I've ever seen you like this before, choir boy." Jack said.

"I wish you would stop calling me that." He said to Jack. "You and I both know that isn't true." Keith reached over and took Jack's cigarette from his hand. He took a drag and handed it back to him.

"Now you smoke?" Jack asked, the dimples on the sides of his face were forming. "If she is bad for your health, maybe you shouldn't watch her for me. She is old enough to be left alone, you know."

"After tonight you would leave her alone?" Keith asked indignantly. "I don't think so."

"She is a pretty brave kid." Jack beamed.

"God, you're proud of her." Keith muttered.

"Yeah, I am." Jack grinned.

It was about 2:40 am, the brothers were still up. It had been a while since the two had talked like this. They were enjoying the time together, they discussed Izzy and her willfulness, they talked about Keith's ambitions and the Oscars. Jerome came outside and sat beside Jack as the two discussed parenthood. They barely heard the motorcycle but the pounding on the door made them both jump. There was a second knock before they made it to the front room. Opening the door they found Braden swaying back on forth on the front step,

"I lost Izzy." Braden said, clearly upset.

"She is safe." Jack said. "She got home around midnight."

"Man, I am so sorry." Braden said. "I've been looking everywhere for her."

"Sounds like maybe she had enough." Keith interjected.

"Enough of what?" Braden asked.

"Enough of you," Keith said. "What gives you the right to.."

"To what?" Braden interrupted. "Izzy and I like each other, she went to the party with me."

"She's just a baby." Keith blurted out.

"She doesn't kiss like a baby." Braden argued, clearly trying to provoke Keith. His breath smelled like beer.

Keith was enraged. He could feel the hair on his neck bristol and the adrenaline rush behind his ears. "Keep your mouth off my girl." Keith hissed.

"Your girl?" Braden replied, stepping closer to Keith.

"You know what I meant by that!" Keith said, not backing away.

"Yeah," Braden said. "That's the thing, I know exactly what you meant by that."

Jack stepped between the two. "Braden, go home." He said. "Trust me, you do not want to get into a fight with my brother, you wouldn't stand a chance against him."

Braden eyed Keith up and down. He was tall, but not gangly and had some good biceps on him. Keith worked out with weights and it had paid off. He probably could hold his own in a fight. Eyeing Keith, Braden could tell Keith was tough. Keith hadn't even raised his voice, in fact Keith seemed to become quieter when he was angry. The softness of his voice sounded deadly. Braden hadn't really ever thought of Keith as a threat before, mainly Keith was just good at making him feel stupid. Keith's command of the English language was incredible. Whenever Keith spoke to Braden, he made him feel like an idiot, a simpleton. Braden was realizing for the first time that Keith had more than a quick wit to battle with and it gave him pause to think. Braden backed away slowly, "Tell her that I stopped by." He said. "And that I'll see her tomorrow."

Jack pulled his brother inside and closed the door behind him. This time he remembered to lock it.

"Tomorrow?" Keith asked. "I don't think so." He said. Jack patted his brother on the back and headed towards his room, flipping the kitchen light off before he left. "You can ignore me, but we are talking more about this tomorrow." He said firmly to Jack as the man headed towards his room. Keith counted to ten in his head before taking some cleansing breaths and laying down on the sofa. He laid on his back and tried to think of ways to prevent

Izzy and Braden from seeing one another. He had every intention of distracting Izzy the next couple of days, that guy and his thick dark hair really rubbed Keith the wrong way.

The next morning, Jack decided to leave. He was in a better mood, and he had sobered up. He went outside with a cup of coffee and a cigarette to enjoy the morning. Keith followed him out. "I called a cab." Jack said. "Should be here anytime."

"I'm not sure if I'm up for this." Keith confided. "Is it like this all the time? I should have gotten to know her better over the years. You are so good with her. She does whatever you want her to do."

"She will for you too and no, she isn't like this all the time." Jack laughed. "I think she was embarrassed," he said to Keith. He stood up and headed towards the house. "I trust her, you can too." A cab honked from the driveway. He walked towards the front door and picked up the small blue suitcase. "Just rein in the leash when you think she has gone too far." he said to Keith who had followed him inside. "I appreciate it, you wish you had got to know her better, well now is your chance and good luck Oscar night, you're going to win and I'm already jealous." Jack nodded to the car keys in the green dish.

"I saw them." Keith said. "I'll be driving my own car."

"I want to tell you something Keith." Jack said, leaning in towards his brother. "I want you to listen, this is important. You have horrible taste in cars."

Keith smiled, he also had dimples but they were hidden under his beard at the moment.

"Take good care of my girl." Jack commanded. "Have you noticed she is a young woman now? Protect her Keith." Jack said, then took hold of the suitcase by the handle and headed towards the cab. Keith hadn't asked where Jack was going, Jack did what Jack wanted to do, there was really no point in asking.

Keith followed Jack to the cab, Braden and Izzy were out in the yard. She was still in her nightgown and that really pissed Keith off. Braden was whispering something in Izzy's ear while holding her close to him with one hand on her shoulder. Keith felt a flash of hot on his cheeks and the hair on his neck felt as though it was bristling.

"That girl has no shame." He said to Jack. "She parades around the house half naked, she doesn't close the door when she changes her clothes and now just look at her." He continued. "She's out in the front yard in her nightgown!"

"Have her come in, she won't hate you." Jack said, then winked at his brother and got into the cab, sliding his suitcase onto the seat beside him. He turned and waved to Izzy who smiled and waved back. Jack pulled the cab door shut and it took off, in a few seconds, he was gone. Keith was left alone, standing on the empty drive and watching Braden continue to whisper in Izzy's ear while she giggled.

Keith counted to 5 inside his head, then said, "Hey Iz, Jack wanted you inside now." It was a cowardly move, but it felt to him like it was the safest way. He certainly didn't want to say HE wanted her inside. Izzy and Braden both walked towards him, Keith straightened his back and felt even taller. Braden had dark thick hair and a mustache. If he hadn't been standing next to Keith he probably would have seemed tall himself. He was a friendly guy with an eager smile. Keith hated him.

"Talk to you later little girl." Braden said. It made Keith's skin crawl, just the way he said it, it sounded dirty. Without acknowledging Braden or even looking at him, Keith closed the front door and locked it. Izzy had galloped inside ahead of him when he had opened the door. He looked at himself in the mirror above the entry table and ran his fingers through the beard, then decided to take a shower. Keith looked in the back yard expecting Izzy to be there, he imagined he would find her whispering to Braden over the fence, but she wasn't in the back. He closed the arcadia doors and locked them too, then went to the living room. It was decorated with a bit of an eastern flair to it. Jack's time on the tv series had certainly influenced his taste. The front windows had a sheer curtain and then a heavier curtain with a embroidered brocade of oriental birds in red thread. He walked to the window and looked out, then pulled the cord closing the curtains. Next he headed down the hall to check Izzy's room. He was sure the curtains would be wide open. He could just picture her parading around the room in next to nothing in front of the open windows. Not on his watch. When he peered in her doorway, Izzy was lying on her stomach on the bed with her nose in a book. The curtains were pulled shut. Her knees were bent, her feet in the air behind her head, a lock of hair in her mouth as she greedily read the book. He stepped back out of the doorway so she wouldn't see him. He leaned his back against the wall and took deep breaths counting again to five but this time, he was giving himself time, time to clear his head.

Keith stepped out of the shower, the mirror was fogged from the steam. He wiped it away but it fogged back up. He gave it a few minutes, opened the window above the shower with the crank handle, then he put on a lot of deodorant while he waited. The mirror slowly cleared and he looked at his image. He took the scissors and slowly started cutting away the beard and the mustache. He sprayed a ball of shaving cream into his hand and applied it to his face. Carefully he shaved away the signature facial hair from the movie. He turned on the faucet and cupped warm water into his hands and washed away the remaining shaving cream. It had been some time since he had seen that face in his reflection. It was good to see it again. He really didn't like the guy that he had played in the movie and although Keith liked growing beards and thought he looked good with facial hair, he was glad to get rid of that image. He had planned on keeping the look for the Oscars, but decided at the last minute to shave, ending his relationship with his character.

He thought about his character and how similar it was to Braden. Shaving the beard and mustache was almost a sweet revenge, one that only Keith would know of but it still felt good.

He slid his fingers through his towel dried hair, it was really starting to get thin. It bothered him more than he cared to admit. He wrapped a towel around his waist and left the bathroom. He had laid some clothes out on Jack's bed and dropped the towel. After putting on his briefs he pulled on a pair of dark gray jeans and an army green t-shirt. After dressing he picked the wet towel up off the floor so Izzy wouldn't have to. He carried it to the kitchen and dropped it in the basket on top of the dryer with Jack's dirty socks, then he remembered he had left his own dirty clothes in the bathroom and went back to get them. Izzy was already there, picking them up off the floor. "Where is your towel?" She asked.

"You don't need to pick up after me." Keith assured her. "I was just coming to get them."

"I don't mind, it gives me something to do." Izzy smiled. Keith was blocking her exit again so she sat on the closed toilet holding the laundry in her lap.

"You could turn on the television, Jack bought it just for you." Keith replied.

"Nah." Izzy said. "I've grown used to not watching it."

"But you'll watch the awards?" Keith asked.

"Of course." She giggled. "I want to hear your speech."

"I probably won't win." He said. "I think Mahogany will take it."

"You of little faith." Izzy replied.

"I'm sorry about last night." Keith said.

"Don't worry about it." Izzy said. "I actually like that you are so protective of me, it makes me feel safe. I reacted badly."

Keith liked hearing her say that, he did feel protective of her. He wasn't sure when he started feeling that way, but lately he had thought more and more about how men might take advantage of her. "I was supposed to tell you Braden stopped by to make sure you made it home." Keith smirked.

"I gathered as much talking to him this morning." Izzy smiled.

"What do you see in that guy?" Keith asked. He picked up a comb from the bathroom counter and combed his wet hair. He was waiting for Izzy to say something about the beard but she just looked at him with a smirk on her face. He finished combing, set the comb on the counter and looked at her. "It's too late now, you're laughing, do I look stupid?"

Izzy tilted her head and looked him over. "Turn sideways." She commanded.

"Forget it." Keith said exasperated.

"Keith," Izzy laughed playfully. "You look great. You are a very handsome man. Incredibly handsome really" Izzy said honestly. "Probably the best looking man I've ever known but we do need to get you out in the sun today."

Keith looked in the mirror, Izzy was right, the lower half of his face needed some sun. "Alright." He said. "Let's go to the beach."

"Really?" Izzy asked, hardly able to contain her excitement.

"Yes." Keith laughed. "I don't know of a better place to get some sun."

Izzy threw on a sweater and a pair of long shorts. She tied her hair back in a high ponytail and pulled on her white sneakers. Keith couldn't help but notice the curves under her black sweater, she looked effortlessly stunning. He took her hand and led her out of the house, warning her that she might be cold in shorts. He made sure to lock the front door behind him then took her hand again and led her to his car, he no longer drove the green Pontiac but had a blue Chevrolet Impala, very similar to her mothers car but it was newer. Keith was more frugal with his money than his older brother and made practical purchases. He opened the door for Izzy and she slid onto the front seat trying to disguise her enthusiasm with a polite smile. Keith walked around and got in behind the wheel. As he backed out of the driveway, Braden was in the front yard of his parents home watering some potted plants. He waved to Izzy who smiled eagerly and waved back. "God, the guy is like a stalker, he is always there." Keith said between closed teeth.

"He lives there." Izzy laughed.

"That's another thing I don't like about him, he is like what, twenty five?" Keith asked.

"Um, twenty three I think." Izzy answered.

"Regardless, he should be on his own now. I was out of the house at eighteen." Keith said.

Izzy smiled softly to herself and didn't point out how many times she had come to visit Jack only to find that Keith was living with his brother.

"He helps his parents out, I think they like him there." Izzy said.

"Does he even work?" Keith asked,

"I don't want to talk about Bray, you always get all riled up when we talk about Bray." Izzy said.

"Bray?" Keith asked. "You call him Bray? Appropriate I suppose since he is an ass."

"Keith." Izzy said gently.

"Alright." Keith said. "Let's just relax at the beach. He is too old for you though." He added as a second thought.

"Age shouldn't matter to anyone." Izzy replied. "You can't help who you fall in love with. The heart wants what it wants."

Keith's shoulders immediately tensed. "Are you in love with him?" Keith asked incredulously

"Of course not." Izzy laughed with her raspy laugh that made Keith weak at the knees. "I was making a point, if I fall in love with someone older or younger than I am, it shouldn't matter at all. Love is love."

"Hmmm, how old is too old for you?" Keith asked. He was teasing her but he also wanted to hear her answer.

"Jack is pushing it." Izzy laughed. "But, I could still visualize myself with someone like him, making wild passionate love."

"Quit it." Keith said. Izzy laughed again.

"Now I'll never unsee that." Keith said. "You and my brother."

"I said someone like your brother." Izzy corrected. "Besides, that wouldn't be awful. Jack is passionate and brilliant and charming and has the cutest dimples ever!"

"I'm going to be sick." Keith said. "I'd ask you to turn on the radio but God only knows what station you would pick."

"I bet we could find a station playing your song!" Izzy said.

"I don't want to hear it." Keith mumbled.

Izzy turned on the car radio. It was tuned to a country station. Willie Nelson was singing Blue Eyes Crying in the Rain. "Oh man, I love this song." Izzy said. Keith took his eyes from the road long enough to give Izzy a shocked look. "What?" Izzy responded, her eyes wide and innocent.

"It's country, you realize it is country don't you?" Keith asked her.

"Well, kind of country." Izzy smiled. "Willie Nelson is to country like Bob Dylan is to Rock."

"Just when I think I have you figured out." Keith mumbled. "So you do have a little taste in music." He laughed.

"I like your music." Izzy said.

Keith smiled softly and wished he still had his facial hair to hide it from her. He was going to enjoy getting to know this young lady.

The beach was cold and pretty empty. Izzy still wanted some ice cream. They had stopped at a Dairy Queen, Izzy wanted vanilla but when he ordered her a cone she interjected and asked for it in a dish. "You don't like cones?" Keith asked as he licked his strawberry cone.

"No," Izzy answered. "Cones are gross." Jack had told his brother about his Nebraska visits. Izzy wouldn't eat cereal with milk on it or dunk her cookies either, he guessed she just didn't like the feel of soggy things in her mouth. It made him laugh out loud, she was certainly a unique person. Person, he thought, a day earlier he would have thought kid, now he had aged her to a person. He wondered if thinking of her being manhandled by Braden had done the trick. Today he had graduated her in his mind to being a young lady and now a person.

It was a partially cloudy day, every so often the sun would come out from behind a gray cloud and shine on Izzy just long enough so her hair seemed to almost glow against her black sweater. Yes, she was a young lady now, there was no question about it.

The two sat on a metal bench that faced the ocean. It was anchored in concrete and had a trash receptacle on the end. Izzy took her shoes off and buried her toes in the white sand and ate a spoonful of vanilla.

"You know," Keith said to her, "I had you pegged as a chocolate girl."

"Nah." Izzy said. "I do like Hershey syrup on my vanilla though."

"Doesn't that make it chocolate?" Keith asked her.

"Not at all." Izzy answered. "It makes it vanilla with chocolate syrup."

"Explain to me how that is different." He demanded.

"I don't know." Izzy continued, "But it is different. Even if you stir it all together. It tastes sweeter I think."

"You know, the cones are pure sugar, how come you don't like cones?" He asked her.

Izzy just shrugged and smiled at him. He popped the end of his cone, which was beginning to leak, into his mouth and smiled back, wiggling his eyebrows at her. Izzy laughed and tossed what was left of her ice cream in the trash container beside the bench, then picked up her tennis shoes and waited for Keith. He didn't stand up, but instead patted the bench beside him, asking her to sit back down. "It occurred to me, little grasshopper, that after last night, I realized I really don't know you. Oddly, that really bothers me. You have been in my life for the past seven years and I don't know a thing about you. Jack suggested we use this time to get to know each other a little better, would you mind?"

Izzy nodded and smiled and sat down beside him. "You want to know me?" She asked, then continued. "The first thing you need to know is little grasshopper is a term of endearment reserved strictly for your brother, you, Mr. Enidarrac, may not call me that." She said firmly.

"I can't?" Keith answered pretending to be hurt. "Then we must come to an agreement as to what I may call you." He continued. "Would pain in the ass be alright with you?" He asked.

"Hmmm, I think not." Izzy laughed. The hoarseness of her laugh was intoxicating, her eyes reflected the blue of the sky and the darkness of the sea that stretched in front of them. Keith shifted uncomfortably on the metal bench.

"You may call me, my Goddess." Izzy giggled. "And you may kiss my hand," she stretched her dainty hand outward towards Keith. He smiled, took it, kissed the back of it and then said that hell would freeze over before he ever called her his Goddess. Izzy laughed and pretended to pout, Keith noted that today she smelled of roses.

She had soft hands and long slim fingers, her nails were painted with clear polish, they weren't long at all, just nice nails. He always disliked women who grew their nails long and especially hated red polish. Izzy's nails were perfect. He almost forgot to let go of her hand as he inspected it. Izzy didn't mind, she liked the feel of his flesh against hers, his hand felt strong. She closed her eyes to feel his colors, they were yellow and lavender, just as they always were. Keith was consistent. She let the colors wash over her until she felt him let go of her hand.

"If not my Goddess, what will you call me?" She asked as she opened her eyes.

"I'll just stick with Iz if that's alright with you." He replied.

"I've always liked that," Izzy said shyly, looking down at her feet in the sand.

"So it's settled. Now, let me get to know you."

"Why now?" Izzy questioned him.

"Well," Keith said. "I had hoped that you were just a phase that my brother was going through. When it became clear that wasn't the case, I hoped he would tire of his new toy. When that didn't happen I figured I could just avoid you, but now it is apparent you are never going away so I'm throwing in the towel. Better late than never."

"Thanks." Izzy said in a monotone voice.

Keith chuckled softly, "I've been a bit of an ass the past few years." He confessed.

"A bit?" Izzy questioned him.

"I wasn't that bad was I?" He asked, feigning surprise.

"Hmmm, let me start a list." Izzy said.

"Nah." Keith replied. "I've seen the error of my ways, let's stop wasting time. I have questions."

Izzy smiled and nodded. She liked this side of Keith. He was playful and witty. He was finally beginning to feel very familiar to her. She wished that he would touch her again, she wondered if some of her memories of him were finally creeping back into her mind. She had strong memories of her friendship with Jack, but only a vague primal feeling about Keith. He stirred thoughts inside of her that she couldn't speak of outloud. When she pictured him in her head, she felt heat. He was a fire sign just like his brother, heat made sense but it was more than that. When Izzy was with him, she wanted to just let herself go, act on instinct. She wanted to brush her lips against his, run her fingers down his back and biceps. She wanted to know what he tasted like. When he asked if they could get to know each other better, answering questions wasn't the solution that had first popped into her head. She swallowed and tried to just concentrate on his voice so as not to reveal her thoughts.

"Ask away." She said smiling and adjusted herself a bit on the cold metal bench. She noticed she had to squeeze her thighs together a bit to stop from squirming.

"The first question that comes to my mind, while trying to get to know you, is how can you stand Jack?" He asked.

Izzy laughed somewhat relieved. He clearly didn't see the effect he was having on her. "What do you mean? I love Jack!"

"Well I know he is mentoring you, but he is so demanding." Keith said, watching her face for answers.

"I know that a lot of people think that." Izzy confided. "The truth is Jack doesn't demand much at all. He is a perfectionist, but he doesn't expect perfection, he just demands one hundred percent."

Keith nodded, she had that correct. He hadn't really thought of Jack like that. How could she understand his brother so much better than he did? Izzy pulled her knees up to her chest and wrapped her arms around her legs. Her legs were beautiful. Keith tried not to look at them. He knew she had just shaved them so they would feel smooth and silky. He thought about what it would feel like, having those silky legs wrapped around his waist. He cleared his throat and tried to picture her with her crooked bangs and messy hair. "So what kind of things does Izzy like?" Keith asked.

"Too broad of a question." Izzy answered while smiling at him softly.

Keith knew she was probably cold, he had warned her about wearing shorts but God he was glad that she did! He looked out at the sea in front of him, the waves looked cold and the water was choppy. "Alright." He said without looking at her. "Tell me about your faith. Do you attend church?" He asked.

"Not really." Izzy said cautiously. "My mom goes to church, but I think it is really just for social reasons. She uses it as an excuse to have time away from us. I mean think about it, no break from two obnoxious kids" Izzy paused, studying Keith's face. "I can't even imagine how difficult it was for her, raising me and my sister alone and by herself. Sometimes I go to church with my Aunt. She goes to the Episcopal church, I quite enjoy it, it is like being Catholic except without all the rules. " Izzy laughed. "Sometimes I even genuflect."

"I know what Episcopal is." Keith said while laughing at the thought of Izzy genuflecting.

"A lot of people don't." Izzy said.

"So do you believe in God?" Keith asked, his curiosity peaked.

"I do? I don't?." Izzy answered somewhat hesitantly.

"Sounds like an answer John Lennon might give." Keith said.

"Hmm, yeah, it kind of does, doesn't it?" She offered no further explanation. Keith didn't know her well, but he had seen her end conversations before. He knew that Izzy had finished with this subject.

"You don't ride horses, I know your family spends a lot of time with horses. Why don't you like to ride?" He asked. He had taken a hold of her hand on the last question. His touch was driving her crazy, putting thoughts in her head that made her blush.

"I like to ride." She answered. "I even have a horse. It's just that when I ride my horse, I want to enjoy it. If I ride horses because I have to, it kind of takes the joy out of it."

Keith understood what she meant. He had loved theater in Highschool and thought that acting would be a lot of fun. It came easily to him and he had learned a great deal from his father and brother, but when it became his profession, suddenly it was a business. He could truthfully say that although there were a lot of times that he loved what he did, there were more times that he didn't.

"What do you enjoy other than horses?" He asked her.

Izzy shifted again on the bench. His touch and his eyes were driving her crazy. She considered pulling her hand away but for some reason she couldn't. She wanted his colors to penetrate her mind, she wanted his essence inside of her. No one had ever asked her what she liked to do, not even Jack. Izzy just followed what other people wanted, she would go along with it. This was new territory for her and she wasn't sure if she wanted to open up, but on the other hand, it felt good hearing him ask.

"Other than writing, I like photography." Izzy said. "Sometimes I go to the cemetery and take pictures. I like the way the light comes through the trees and shines on the statues. I like to take pictures of playgrounds and spider webs. Those waves are beautiful, it would be cool to walk out there and take pictures inside of the waves."

"Those all sound like lonely pictures," Keith said. He was seeing a new side to this girl, one he hadn't considered before. If she really believed that time repeats, it must be very lonely. She had to know about sad events that lay in wait for her in the future. She must feel helpless at times. It would take nerves of steel to tell anyone about it and to face things head on, he thought about her as an eight year old, explaining the future to his brother. He wasn't sure if he believed her story yet, but he admired the strength she had to tell it.

"I suppose to some people they are lonely pictures." Izzy responded, referring to the photographs. "There is beauty in everything. It's all perspective. I took one picture from inside the jungle gym, looking at my old elementary school. My mom says it looks like something from a prison, but I think it is cool. To me, it's a view from a child who is free for the moment, knowing that the happiness he feels at that moment is only temporary, soon he will go back inside the school, but at that moment in time, he is happy and free."

"So inside the school will make him unhappy?" Keith asked.

"It might, it depends on the kid. I personally don't like school as an institution, but knowledge is power so I endure it. I want to learn everything. School provides me an opportunity" Izzy explained.

Jack had told Keith on so many occasions that Izzy thought in many different ways at once. He hadn't understood what Jack meant, he had chalked it up to hyperbole, but suddenly now he was beginning to understand. When she said it was all just perspective, she could see from all sides. She had different perspectives on everything. He was intrigued.

"Tell me more about your photographs." He encouraged her.

"That particular day it had just rained and there were still rain drops pooling on the metal bars. In front of the school doors, the colored chalk from the hopscotch squares were running together. I don't know, I thought it was beautiful. It was like seeing the inside of a thinking mind, I had to take pictures of it. I took another picture of the basketball hoop that day too, it is a chain hoop because the other ones kept getting vandalized. I thought it was beautiful with the rain dripping off of it." Izzy told him, getting lost in the memories.

"They have vandals in Lincoln, Nebraska?" Keith asked.

"One or two." Izzy answered. "I'm sure they have since been caught and are at the reformatory in Kearney."

Keith laughed. Just like Jack she could say something softly and with a straight face making it difficult to know if she was joking. She was a lot like his brother, intuitive and independent but she didn't seem reckless at all, Keith was secretly grateful for that. He was finally getting a clear picture of who she was. She didn't feel like she was part of anything, she was a loner, a lot like himself. He still wasn't sure who he was and he was twentyseven years old. There was a voice inside Keith that told him he was going to be special, but he hadn't found his way yet. He did feel like an outsider, always looking in. He understood this lonely feeling Izzy had. Her description of the jungle gym picture sounded like thoughts he had as a boy.

"I love reading about ancient Egypt." Izzy confessed. "Cleopatra was amazing! Such an intelligent and strong woman, fluent in many languages. She is the one that got me interested in perfume."

"Perfume?" Keith asked. His thoughts moved from the lonely pictures she had described to ancient egypt.

"Yeah." She replied. "My mom and I made this recipe." She said, waiving the air around her with her free hand towards Keith.

"You make your own perfume?" He asked incredulously.

Izzy nodded. "I thought Jack must have told you. Mom and a friend of hers made this when I was like six years old. Mom taught school, her friend was her chemistry professor. They worked with me and scents that I liked and created an oil that would react with different temperatures. They figured out how our body temperature and blood pressure changes with our moods and wa-la, mood perfume!"

"You mean it's always the same perfume that you have on?" Keith asked.

"Actually, it's body oil." She answered. "We found that oil holds the scent more. When I'm excited it smells like honeysuckle, content or at peace it smells like roses, when I'm sad it is lilacs and angry it is sage. I think it's cool."

"You could make a fortune selling it." Keith said.

"Yeah, but then everyone would have it, I like it being my own perfume." Izzy said.

"And your mother's." Keith corrected.

"Nope, just mine." Izzy said. "Mom prefers her Channel number 5."

Keith contemplated everything that she had told him but he still wanted to know more. "What makes you happy Iz?" He asked. "What do you want from life, or are you too young to know?" He teased, then he squeezed her hand playfully.

"Hmmm," Izzy smiled. "I'm too young." She tried to pull her hand away but Keith held on firmly.

"Nope." He said. "Answer the question."

Izzy stopped pulling her hand. She turned sideways and studied Keith's face. He looked kind, for once she didn't think he looked arrogant, she wanted to touch his face and might have if he hadn't been holding onto her hand. "I don't know." She shrugged. "I'd like to feel like I'm part of something. I'd like to feel free. I'm not sure if you can be both."

Keith understood that feeling too. Every decision he made, he weighed the consequences, the possible outcomes. At times it was overwhelming. Sometimes he felt trapped, like even though he was in charge of his own career, he was bound by behaviors that others wanted him to follow. He thought about Jack and slowly realized why Jack acted out, perhaps he and Jack had more in common than he had been willing to admit. Izzy wasn't much different. She behaved in a manner that worked for her family, her dedication to her mother was admirable, perhaps visiting Jack gave Izzy the opportunity she desired most, to be herself. Keith nodded to her.

"What makes you feel free?" He asked.

"Honest answer?" She asked. Keith nodded. "Following my own heart." She said, "I know that sounds hoaky, but it is really difficult to do. My mom wants my life to be one way, I think my teachers try to direct me another way, Jack wants something else for me," She paused and looked out at the horizon beyond the sea, then continued. "I feel trapped sometimes. I feel as though I can't make my own decisions. I don't know how else to describe it. I want to make people happy, but sometimes in doing so, it makes me sad."

"I guess we are both trapped in a way." He said. "I always try to be the good guy, you know? There are times that I wish I could be the black sheep of the family. Jack just does what he wants to, I wish I could too" Keith also looked out at the horizon, some gulls appeared almost motionless in the air a few feet away. "

"The most outrageous thing that I've ever done was to change my last name. I didn't even make one up on my own, I copied Jack." He continued to watch the gulls for a few minutes silently, then he smiled softly. "It did make me feel free though." He laughed.

Izzy smiled softly at him watching his profile as he stared out at the sea. If she could keep any memory forever, life after life, it would be this one. His chiseled good looks, his tenderness, his vulnerability and the smell of the sea. Most of her dreams involved the sea, ever since she was a little girl. Perhaps this was a memory she kept deep inside of her heart, tucked away for safekeeping. She had some very naughty urges towards this handsome man, perhaps her mind had kept this memory hidden on purpose, protecting her while she was too young.

"So, let's talk about happier thoughts, what type of music do you like? Jack told me you don't really like Uriah Heep." Keith said, turning to face the girl beside him. "By the way, why do you like to make me mad?"

Izzy smiled a long slow smile on one side of her mouth. "He told you?" She asked.

"He is my brother, you know." Keith confirmed. "You aren't the only one he confides in."

"Hmmmm." Izzy said. "I'll have to be more careful of what I tell him in the future."

"I'm waiting for an answer." Keith said. "Why do you try to provoke me?"

"It's fun." Izzy laughed. Keith shook his head and sighed.

"You aren't getting out of this question." He chided.

" Really, no hidden agenda." Izzy said. "I just know you don't like me very much"

"I don't dislike you." Keith said while carefully watching her face. "I think maybe I was a little jealous of the bond you had built with my brother. You bring out a lot of good qualities in him."

Izzy returned his contemplative look. She hadn't considered that he could have been jealous of her relationship with Jack. She still questioned his sincerity about his feelings towards her but she was willing to take him at his word for now.

"Music?" He asked.

"I like James Taylor, Joni Mitchell, Carol King.... Oh and I love love love Dan Folgelberg!" Izzy said.

"Okay, so folk music?" Keith asked.

"Oh yes," Izzy confirmed.

"What do you love so much about Dan Folgelberg?" Keith asked. He was getting extremely curious.

"His music speaks to me." Izzy said. "I guess it is a little like my pictures."

Keith nodded, he understood what she meant. This musician had a lonely sound to his voice, Keith liked him too. His songs were lonely, but invited the listener into them.

"And he is sooooo sexy!" Izzy said. "All that dark hair and when he sings, it is like he is singing to just you. There is nothing sexier than a man who sings to a girl."

"You seem to have a thing for dark hair." Keith commented, thinking of Braden with his head of dark wavy hair.

"I do like it." Izzy confirmed. "But a man's eyes are more important than his hair."

"Okay, now I'm intrigued. Lets say I dyed my hair black, would I be sexy?" Keith teased.

"You would look stupid with black hair." Izzy laughed.

"Well that's hurtful." Keith replied putting his hand on his chest.

Izzy continued to giggle. "You don't need to have dark hair." She said, "You have beautiful eyes."

"You like my eyes?" He asked. "You said you like eyes more than hair?"

"I'm done, you're just fishing for compliments. You promised me a beach." Izzy laughed. "You know all the times I've stayed with your brother and we never once went to the beach!"

"Not even once?" He asked her. He was actually surprised. While waiting for a reply they stood up and Keith led her onto the sand.

"I think he was always busy." Izzy stated. "Your brother always has a lot going on."

Keith nodded in agreement, then waved his hand forward towards the oncoming waves. "I give you the beach my Goddess." He said then made a low bow.

Keith and Izzy spent most of the rest of the day there. She was fascinated that a beach could be so cold. In her mind, she had always pictured California like a Caribbean island, it hadn't dawned on her that California could be seasonally cold. Most of her visits had been in the summer and the few times that they weren't it was still much warmer than Nebraska.

The wind came in off the ocean and wrapped around her like long cold fingers, she loved it. She had set her tennis shoes down and ran barefoot in the sand. The waves stretched towards her and lapped at her feet. She screamed lightly when the cold water touched her, then giggled with delight. She ran after the wave when it retreated to the sea, only to scream and giggle and run back to shore when the next wave raced towards her. Keith sat on the beach and watched, his long legs crossed indian style, his elbows on his knees, his hands clasped together. He watched her chasing the waves then running from them, laughing the whole time. She was always such a solemn girl, this was a new side to her. She looked up and waved to him then screamed again as a wave hit her legs from behind. He decided maybe the shorts hadn't been a bad idea after all, she would have been drenched by now had she worn anything else. A group of young men in wetsuits approached carrying surfboards. He guessed them to be late teens or early twenties. Keith wasn't oblivious to the fact that they lingered a while watching her. He wasn't jealous he told himself, it was just like Izzy had said, he had grown protective of her.

Izzy stopped and watched the boys as they entered the sea and then paddled out. She held her right hand over her eyes, shading them from the sun as she watched. Another wave hit her from behind, Keith noticed this one got her wet, it was then he noticed how far out she had waded and he felt himself panic. He stood up and called to her but she didn't hear him, his voice was out of her range, the water was hitting her at her waist, she knew nothing about undercurrents, he wasn't even sure if she knew how to swim. He took off his shoes and ran towards the waves calling her name and waving. She had felt the sand under her feet pulling outwards from beneath her feet, it was such a weird sensation. When the waves splashed and the foam hit her face, the taste of salt was amazing and delicious. She started walking backwards towards the shore but she didn't want to take her eyes off the boys, she had never seen surfing before and was so excited. She didn't even hear Keith before he grabbed her by the shoulders. This time she screamed but it wasn't out of fun. Izzy had never liked being grabbed from behind, it terrified her. He spun her around, he was standing thigh deep, his jeans were soaked but he had such a worried look on his face that she was startled into silence. He let go of her shoulders and took her hand, leading her back to the shore.

"You were getting too far out." He whispered. "It can trick you into thinking you haven't gone far." His voice cracked just a little, he wasn't angry, it was something else. His jeans were soaked past his thighs but he didn't care. Izzy was shivering but she wasn't cold, they stopped and picked up their shoes and then he led her back to the car in silence. She was surprised when he opened her door for her again. She slid in and he gently closed it. A moment later he was seated behind the wheel. He put his forehead on the steering wheel for just a few seconds, then turned on the ignition, shifted into gear and headed back to Jack's house. They didn't talk, he was deep in thought, she was trying to understand. They walked in the house just as silently, Keith headed towards Jack's room. He stripped off his wet jeans and pulled on a pair of sweatpants. He was cold, he was shaking, he yanked off the green t-shirt and pulled a gray sweatshirt over his head. He sat on the bed for a few minutes and closed his eyes, then stood up and walked out of the bedroom and headed towards the kitchen. He opened the fridge and pulled out a beer. He used the bottle opener on the side of the fridge, and then he took a long cold drink.

What would he have done, he asked himself. What if he had taken his eyes off of her and she had slipped under the waves. The thoughts spun around his head and the pit in his stomach grew. He felt a little nauseous just thinking about it. It was in that moment that he realized she meant more to him than he was letting on. He had fought off any desires he had felt towards her for such a long time, but in truth, he did want her. He thought about her all the time and had done so for a few years now. He knew that he was too old for her, he knew it, but God he wanted to hold her, to taste her. This was going to be harder than he thought, being alone with her, but he didn't want Jack to come back home either.

Izzy wasn't sure what to make of Keith's behavior. She wished Barbara was around so she could ask her what it meant and what to do. Sometimes, Izzy felt like such an idiot, an older woman would know what it meant but she was baffled. Was he angry at her, had she done something wrong? Was he just worried and if so, was that a good sign or was it because he thought of her as a child? She pulled her wet shorts off and slipped on a pair of pajama bottoms. She pulled off the sweater and unhooked her bra, then put on the matching top to her pajamas. They were silky and felt good against her skin. She balled the wet clothes up in a bundle then went into Jack's room and found the clothes Keith had taken off. She added them to her pile in her arms but as she carried them out, she buried her face into them. The green t-shirt smelled so good, it made her happy. She paused in the hallway, then went back into her room. She set the damp clothes on the bed and lifted the t-shirt off the pile, then stuffed it into her duffel bag. After a moment, she wickedly smiled to herself and picked the remaining clothes up and carried them out to the kitchen. Keith was sitting at the table drinking a beer. She dropped the clothes on top of the laundry basket. She reached into the refrigerator and helped herself to a beer and opened it, then she walked out onto the patio, leaving the door open behind her.

Keith had heard her open the beer and figured she was testing him. Hell, Jack and her mother both let her drink, he wasn't her parent, if it was okay with both of them, who was he to interfere? Besides, wasn't he just thinking of her himself in a very grown up way? He still had the cap to his beer in his right hand. He squeezed it, leaving little indentations in the palm of his hand. He set the cap on the table and spun it around with his index finger. After a few minutes he picked up his beer and joined Izzy outside leaving the cap on the kitchen table.

It was too cold out for her to be dressed like that. The sun was setting and the temperature was dropping fast. She had on silky pink pajamas and the cold was bringing attention to her in ways he didn't like. He tried not to look at her growing nipples and tried to look her directly into her eyes. He felt like an eight year old boy.

"What did you think of the beach?" He asked, sounding as if nothing was wrong. Izzy took his que.

"I can't imagine having an ocean so close, I would be there every day!" She answered. "Have you ever surfed?"

"Every man who has ever lived in California has surfed at least once." He joked. "Listen Iz." He said gently.

Izzy loved it when he called her that. She tilted her head up and looked into his dark eyes. "How do you get into one of those wetsuits?" She asked. "A tight rubber suit, I can't even imagine how anyone could pull it up."

"I just need you to listen to me for a minute okay?" He asked. I don't want to talk about wetsuits, I'm trying to say something to you."

"Okay." Izzy said and looked him in the eyes. He had such beautiful eyes, they were soulful and dark. Izzy was pretty sure she could remember his eyes from before, when she looked into them she felt his colors and hers exploding inside her head, like a well choreographed fireworks display.

"I'm really sorry that I frightened you. I don't want to sound pathetic, but I really don't know what I would do if something happened to you. I panicked. I know you think I was angry, I really wasn't, I was terrified."

Izzy tilted her head a little more. "What could have happened? Like a shark?" She asked.

Keith laughed, "No, not a shark although now that you mention it, you have seen Jaws right?"

Izzy smiled and looked down. She set her beer on the patio floor next to her chair but kept a hold of it. Lowering her arm Keith had a clear view of her now. Her hard nipples protruded against the dark pink satin of her pajama top. Keith was grateful the light was fading because he felt a bit of a blush growing on his cheeks. He took a seat on the lawn chair next to her.

"There is an undertow in the ocean, it can pull you out." Keith said.

"I think I felt it!" Izzy said, she made a little sound of excitement.

"It can drown the most experienced swimmers, Izzy. It's really my fault, I didn't prepare you and I didn't notice how far out you had gone. Forgive me for scaring you?"

Izzy let go of her beer and stood up. "There's nothing to forgive." She said, "You're my protector!" She bent down and hugged him. She smelled like honeysuckle, it was intoxicating. Keith patted her arm in an attempt to make her release him. It worked. She bent down and picked up the bottle of beer then turned to him and said, "Unless you want the rest?"

Keith nodded and took it. Izzy went inside, completely unaware of what she had done to him. He downed the last of her beer then laid back in the chair for a few minutes, restless he sat back up. He couldn't believe the feelings that he was having. He was being drawn towards this girl, like a moth to a flame. He hated it, but he liked it.

Jerome rubbed softly against his legs, at first Keith didn't even notice the cat. It must have climbed over the fence without him seeing, the cat could be silent and sneaky just like his brother.

"What?" Keith asked the cat and bent down to stroke it's back. The cat head butted his hand and purred. "Now you like me?" He asked. "I don't trust you Jerome, you are up to something." Keith laughed. He got up and headed towards the sliding glass door, as he opened it Jerome dashed in and ran down the hallway towards Izzy's room. Keith followed the cat, he just wanted to check on the girl before returning to the patio. Looking in the open door, he saw that Izzy was still awake and stroking Jerome in long smooth strokes. She looked up at the silhouette in the doorway.

"You can come in if you want." She said, "I'm obviously still awake."

"One of those sleepless nights again?" He asked.

"Of course." Izzy laughed. "Come in, I think Jerome wants you to."

"Fickle cat." Keith said, then entered the room. He sat on the edge of the bed and Jerome head butted him again. "Seriously," Keith continued, "That cat is demonic! He is up to something!"

"Keith." Izzy laughed. "He is not. He is just a nice cat. Sometimes, he comes in here when I can't sleep and his purring helps me." Izzy confessed.

"Purring is relaxing." Keith whispered to her. "That is what you need. Your mind goes a million ways at once doesn't it?"

"Doesn't everyones?" Izzy asked.

"No." Keith laughed. "Most people can shut it off."

"Teach me." Izzy pouted.

"Alright." Keith said softly. "I'll try. Why don't you roll over."

Izzy obediently rolled onto her stomach, placing her head in her folded arms.

"Move stupid cat." Keith said, shoving Jerome out of the way. Surprisingly the cat moved and curled up in a ball on the pillow beside Izzy.

"I want you to think about something peaceful, but something you love." Keith said quietly. Izzy nodded and her thoughts immediately went to Keith's profile on the beach. She could hear the waves and smell the salt.

Gently Keith stroked her back, moving her hair to the side as he did so. The satin pajamas felt smooth to his touch, his fingers gliding smoothly down her spine. It took discipline for him not to bend down and kiss her neck, he told himself that any man would have issues resisting her.

"Don't speak." He said to her, "Just nod. Are you someplace that makes you content in your head?"

Izzy nodded. The image in her head made her happier than she had been in a long time.

"Breathe." Keith said. "Slow deep breaths. Think only of the image in your head. Let your muscles relax."

He gently stroked her back, then let his fingers move upward to her shoulders and neck. He applied gentle pressure, slowly working the knots from her tense muscles. He softly hummed the Willy Nelson tune until he felt her breathing change. He lightened his touch and ran his fingers through her hair. The fragrance of roses surrounded him and he smiled softly.

When Keith was sure that she was asleep, he lingered momentarily in the twilight. His eyes had adjusted to the dark, he could see the cat fast asleep on the pillow beside the girl. He could see the side of Izzy's face, still resting quietly on her folded arms. He could just make out a soft smile on her lips and wondered which memory she had selected for her happy place. He was well aware of the hard on in between his legs and was grateful she had fallen asleep unaware of how she had affected him. He remembered the cool air on the patio and decided that maybe he would get another beer and sleep outside. Jack's room seemed too close to Izzy's for the time being.

Keith awoke to the morning sun warming his face. It was cold, sometime in the night he had had enough sense to go get a blanket, but he had in fact slept on the lounge chair in the backyard. He stretched in the early light and pulled the blanket up around his neck. He tried to close his eyes but he was awake, so he stood up, folded the blanket and carried it with him into the house. He set the blanket on the table then popped a couple slices of bread in the toaster. He plugged in the coffee pot and let it percolate. When the toaster popped, he buttered his bread and slathered it with apricot preserves. Keith still remembered the feelings which he had the night before and was determined to put them behind him. Izzy found him reading the paper with coffee and toast in the living room, his feet on the coffee table.

"Is Jerome in?" She asked. Jerome had left the pillow when Keith entered the house and had asked to be let out the front door.

Keith didn't answer her or look up but shook his head. Izzy went to the front door and opened it. "Jerome, kitty kitty kitty." She called. A second later the cat came darting inside. Jerome was getting old now, he had a few scars on his nose from some nasty cat fights and his face looked a bit more aged, but he still had a good appetite. He followed her to the kitchen where she filled his bowl with some kibble and set it on the floor by the washing machine. She picked up his water dish and rinsed it out and refilled it. After a while the cat had his fill and strolled off towards Jack's room. Izzy found a few beer bottle caps on the kitchen table, she picked them up and tossed them in the trash can. Then she rinsed out the bottles that Keith had left in the sink and set them in the dish strainer to dry.

"What should we do today?" Keith asked as he sipped his coffee but was still hesitant to look directly at Izzy. "I need to be distracted." He said.

Izzy poured herself some milk and dropped a spoonful of Nestle's quick into it and stirred it up. She came out of the Kitchen with glass in hand. "That's your breakfast?" He asked after finally looking at the girl.

Izzy just smiled and shrugged. "Let's make cookies!" She said, Keith nodded in agreement thinking it would be a fine distraction.

Izzy downed the last of her milk and walked into the kitchen, Keith following behind her. She rinsed her glass out and set it in the strainer next to the bottles. Keith looked at the bottles and grinned. Izzy had already dressed, she had on the same black sweater from yesterday but a pair of pale blue jeans instead of shorts. She retrieved a stepping stool from beside the washer and began getting ingredients out of the cupboard. Keith stood beneath her and took them from her as she got them out. As she backed down the stepping stool, Keith put his hand on the small of her back, she realized he was still feeling protective of her and it made her blush a bit. She thought about his touch and how she had fallen asleep to it and blushed a little more.

"I need the mixer and two bowls." She said, hoping to change the subject inside of her head. While Keith looked for her supplies, she turned the oven on to 375. In a small bowl she combined sugar, baking soda and flour and salt. On the stove she melted butter then poured it into another bowl where she had put brown sugar and vanilla extract. Then she cracked a couple eggs and dropped them in and turned on the mixer. After it was smooth she began adding the flour mixture a little at a time. Once it was all well stirred, she dropped in chocolate chips and mixed it all together. It made about three cookie sheets. Keith helped himself to the batter in the bowl that was left over. Izzy put her finger in it and put some on the end of his nose. He walked around with it there for a few minutes making Izzy laugh so hard she nearly cried.

After all the cookies were baked, they both had to have a couple. "And you just know this recipe by heart?" Keith asked.

"Well yeah, it's for chocolate chip cookies." Izzy said. "Any female should know it." Keith laughed, he was really starting to appreciate her matter of fact humor. "What should we do now, how can I distract you?" Izzy asked.

"Come here." Keith said. "You have chocolate on the side of your mouth and that's distracting me."

Izzy took a paper towel from the dispenser beside the sink and carried it over to Keith. He licked the end and brought it up to the corner of her mouth and wiped the chocolate off. Her lips were so beautiful, young and soft, she had no idea what she did to him.

"Better?" She asked. Keith nodded. "I know," Izzy continued. "Let's go to a pawn shop!"

"What? A pawn shop? Why would you want to go to a pawn shop?" He asked, rather indulgently. Of all the things he thought she might ask for, this was not one of them.

"I love pawn shops. They are a great source for albums, tapes, guns and jewelry!" She giggled.

"Guns?" he asked.

"Keith, I'm from Nebraska. I could shoot before I could ride a bicycle." She replied matter of factly. She was telling the truth. Her father, an avid hunter, could shoot a moving rabbit in the eye. He had died before she was three years old, but her uncles had taught both her and her sister how to shoot and how to hunt and she had found it a bonding experience with her father even though he was no longer on earth. She had been determined to shoot as well as he did, and she had become quite a marksman. She refused to hunt large game, but she was an excellent pheasant hunter and felt her father was proud of her.

Keith hadn't really considered that possibility. Of course, he hadn't really bothered to learn much about her. Most of what he knew of her, Jack had told him. Listening to her talk now, he realized he should have not been so distant. He could see why Jack loved her so much, she was a contradiction just like his brother. She was pretty and quiet and reserved but she was direct and sincere and apparently knew how to carry a gun. She had a very interesting past and such an odd outlook on life. He was going to use these few days to try to get to know her better, learn what made her tick. Oddly, he thought it would even help him better understand his brother.

"I'll take you." He said. "There is a nice one not too far from here."

Izzy lit up. Clearly excited at the possibilities. Keith loved the way her face was revealing her every thought today, usually he couldn't read her at all. He laughed out loud realizing that she could never lie to him, at least not today or he would know instantly. He wasn't sure why he could suddenly read her so clearly, maybe it was just today, maybe she was letting her guard down but right now he wished more people were like that and it was very refreshing. "No guns." He quipped.

Izzy nodded and smiled. "I have enough at home." She answered slyly. Keith had finished his toast, he handed her his plate. She took the dishes to the sink and rinsed them off with hot water. Then she filled the sink with soapy water and placed them in it. She took a sponge out of a ceramic frog that was sitting beside the sink and carefully washed the dishes, making sure she rinsed off the soap using cold water. For some reason Jack liked dishes rinsed off with cold water, he believed it removed the soap better than hot water and Izzy always did what Jack asked of her.

"I should change, my sweater smells a little like fish." she said to Keith after she finished the dishes.

When Izzy emerged from the bedroom, she was wearing a blue jean skirt that Keith thought was a little too short for his liking. She had on a plain navy blue t-shirt and her white tennis shoes. Her hair was pulled over in a side ponytail. He could tell she just threw something on without taking any care about her appearance, yet he found her strikingly beautiful. This thin fifteen year old girl was blossoming before his eyes. Her legs were shapely and long, her waist was thin, she was developing a curvaceous silhouette, and her hair and skin popped in the dark blue clothing she had selected. He wanted to tell her to go back to her room and change, but he refrained. What would he have said to her, to change her clothes because she was too pretty, or change because he couldn't stop looking at her legs? She was fifteen and he needed to come to terms with it, there were women everywhere that he was attracted to, he just needed to deal with this. He told himself that he was just curious, allowing himself to finally get to know her. Recognizing her physical attributes was just part of the process.

He was glad that he didn't drive a flashy car like Jack did. Keith liked being anonymous. If he won the Oscar, he might not be able to enjoy anonymity again for a while. He was good at blending in. His agent had wanted him to keep the beard and mustache for the awards and he was going to, but when he looked at himself in the mirror, it disgusted him. His character was loathsome and treated women badly. Keith couldn't stand men like that, there were a few things that Keith couldn't tolerate and men who treated women as a possession was one of them. He was freshly shaved, his skin now had some color and he was pretty sure that no one would recognize him.

Izzy leaned against the car seat and turned her head towards Keith. She loved his sculpted face, he had great cheekbones and a chiseled chin. He had a toothy grin but she found it charming. The windows were down in the car and his thinning hair was being blown about his face, Jack's hair did the same thing and she loved it.

They pulled into the parking lot, it wasn't a bad area, Izzy looked around. There was a Mexican restaurant next door and what looked to be a hardware store on the other side. Keith got out of the car leaving the window rolled down. Izzy opened her door and stepped out. The parking lot was gravel and she could feel it under the rubber soles of her tennis shoes. Keith headed towards the pawnshop door, his long legs put him several steps ahead of her. She had to hurry to keep up. Before opening the door he looked over his shoulder to make sure she was coming. He did not hold the door for her but made sure he didn't shut it on her either. They stepped inside, it was fairly crowded, a few men were at the counter bargaining over something, the store seemed cluttered. It smelled of grease and cigarette smoke. There were several customers milling around looking at items on shelves and one other female in the store looking in the glass cabinet of jewelry. It was fairly clean for a pawnshop, at least the floors and the shelves appeared to be free of grime. Keith had already wandered away and was looking through some albums on one of the shelves, no one seemed to know who he was or that he was going to be sitting in a theater full of movie stars in just a few days. He looked perfectly at ease and happy. Izzy looked briefly at the albums Keith was inspecting from behind his shoulder but nothing appealed to her. She wandered deeper into the bowels of the store, she admired the guns but didn't stop to really look at them. She found some cassette tapes and flipped through them. There was Chicago and The Eagles but nothing really stood out for her. Izzy looked over her shoulder at Keith, he was pulling an album out of the sleeve, looking for scratches. It looked like Farewell Andromeda by John Denver. She moved over to the counter beside the other lone female in the store and began looking at jewelry. There were lots of pretty things, earrings, bracelets and of course tons of rings. Lots of diamonds which the woman was looking at. They were pretty, Izzy agreed with that, but Izzy was fixated on a tiny little gold ring. It was very delicate, it was filigree with diamonds so small that you could barely see them. They formed a tiny star inside a Celtic knot. Izzy thought it was the most beautiful thing she had ever seen, it was unique and dainty. She wasn't sure how long she had been staring at it but was very startled when Keith put his hand on her shoulder.

"Are you finished?" He asked. She had jumped a little when he touched her, she had been lost in her daydreams and oblivious to anything going on around her. She was a little embarrassed.

"Yeah, I'm finished. Nothing here." She whispered. Keith led her out of the store, this time he held the door for her. He strode to the vehicle and opened that car door for her too. She looked up at him under her bangs and grinned. "Thank you kind sir." she said then made a quick courtesy to him. He smiled, she slid inside and then he closed the door and stood there for a second thinking to himself. He placed his palm on the roof of the car and said to her through the open window, "Stay here, I think I will get an album I was looking at. Roll the windows up a bit and lock the doors okay?"

"I'll be fine, you don't need to be so overprotective." She responded.

"Just pretend Jack asked you ok? Don't argue, just do it, I'll be right back." He said, then slapped the top of the car.

Izzy did as she was asked and rolled up both hers and Keith's windows. She gazed out the now slightly cracked window, watching the traffic from the parking lot. She closed her eyes and wondered what Jack was doing and hoped he wasn't drinking. She understood a little about what was bothering him and wished she could do more to help. Jack had worked so hard to help Keith, he had paid for acting lessons, helped him with auditions, he had managed to get him small roles on his show. Jack was responsible for Keith entering the industry but Jack ended up doing a silly western on TV while Keith was up for an academy award. It would be difficult. She knew he was so proud of his brother, but there was a very human side to Jack. He had demons, weaknesses, in some ways he was very fragile and she knew he was struggling. He and Barbara were fighting again too.

Keith opened the back door of the car and laid the bag with his album on the seat. He closed the door and then got into the car behind the steering wheel. He turned his head towards Izzy and said rather sarcastically, "You didn't lock the doors."

"Oops." She laughed. "Jack is rubbing off on me."

"Iz, what if something had happened?" He seemed so sincere.

"I forgot, I'm sorry. I was worrying about Jack. You know, I think you are just a tad over protective, maybe a little sister would have helped you with that."

"Maybe some brothers would have given you a little common sense." He retorted. He started the car and pulled out of the parking lot.

Izzy waited a few minutes until they were driving down the road. "I have some." She responded.

"Have what?" Keith asked while flipping the blinker on to signal a right hand turn.

"Brothers." Izzy answered.

"What?" Keith asked. He stopped paying attention to the road and a car honked at him from behind. He realized he was supposed to turn so he gave the car some gas. He pulled over carefully into the next parking lot and shifted the car into park.

"Can you answer a question for me?" Izzy asked, then continued without waiting for an answer. "Why do men always want a stick shift?"

"Huh?" Keith asked. He hated when she did that, changing the subject with a lame question that had nothing to do with the conversation.

"I mean, it is kind of a phallic thing, the gear shift." Izzy continued. "Seems strange to me that men would want one in their hands."

"Izzy!" Keith said, clearly exasperated.

"What?" Izzy asked. "It's a perfectly sensible observation."

"You shouldn't talk like that." Keith said.

"Again, I feel I must point out to you that I'm from Nebraska. Not just any town in Nebraska. I'm from Lincoln." Izzy said.

"What does that have to do with anything?" Keith asked, he was getting flustered.

"The state capital." Izzy said. Keith shrugged. "Home of the penis of the plains."

"What in the hell are you talking about?" Keith asked

"That's what they call our state capital building. Doesn't Jack tell you anything?" Izzy said.

Keith turned off the ignition and started counting to ten in his head. Izzy stopped talking, she thought that this time she might have gone a bit too far. Keith could be kind of a stuffed shirt.

Keith finished counting then took a deep breath and counted again. Izzy could really get under his skin. When he finished, he managed to ask her about her brothers.

"You have two brothers and never thought that you needed to mention it to me?" Keith asked. He was envisioning being pummeled by them both if he had let Izzy get swept out to sea.

"I didn't think I needed to tell you." Izzy answered. "Jack knows."

"Of course he knows." Keith mumbled.

Izzy told him briefly about her brothers before he started the car and shifted to reverse, then looked at his hand and wanted to wash it. Izzy smiled impishly to herself. She could feel what he was thinking.

"Gross isn't it?" She giggled. Keith shook his head and rolled his eyes. It made more sense now, of course she had brothers. Ruth would never talk like that but men would. He had learned that her brothers were similar in age to him and Jack. Everything made sense now. She really didn't think of them as old, she saw them as she did her own brothers. She saw both Jack and Keith as peers. She could talk to Jack and him the way she did because she probably had similar conversations with her brothers.

Keith considered this news carefully. Ruth might not object to Keith if he pursued her daughter, it would be like rejecting one of her sons! What was he thinking, Izzy was only fifteen, he needed to say it in his head over and over, it would be his new mantra.

Keith spent the rest of the next day getting to know Izzy even better and with each new piece of information she seemed more enticing to him. He reminded himself of her age at least once an hour, usually more. She made a delicious meal for him each night, but he learned that she herself was a picky eater. She had made a wonderful potato casserole with cheese and Campbell's cream of chicken soup. The main course was barbecued meatballs. He was well into the meal before he realized she was just picking at her food.

"Eat." He coaxed. "This is delicious! "

"I'm really not very hungry." Izzy replied.

Keith had observed Izzy earlier outside, she had been reading and snacking on Corn nuts, "You have to eat healthy food." Keith said. He got up from the kitchen table and looked in the trash can, then pulled out the empty Corn Nut bag and shook it at her.

"Corn nuts are healthy." Izzy stated in a deadpan tone.

"In what world are Corn Nuts considered healthy?" Keith laughed.

"It's corn, so it's a vegetable." Izzy replied dryly.

"Next you will try to convince me chocolate is healthy." Keith retorted.

"It is." Izzy smiled. "Chocolate is a vegetable too."

Keith sat back down at the table and took another bite of food. He pointed to her plate, commanding her to eat. Izzy sighed and took a small bite of the casserole. Ever since Keith had taken over, Izzy couldn't think clearly. The truth was she wasn't hungry, not because she had filled up on snacks, but because she couldn't chase visions of Keith out of her thoughts. They were consuming her.

"Explain to me," Keith said, setting his fork down on his plate. "How is chocolate a vegetable?"

"Cocoa BEANS," Izzy laughed, "I had to explain the same thing to Jack"

Keith laughed, picked up his fork and took another bite. The food was really good. "Okay," He said, "explain away all the sugar."

"Sugar comes from sugar cane." Izzy smirked. "So if sugar grows from the ground, it is organic and must be a vegetable too."

Keith laughed so hard he choked. He truly was enjoying learning how this girl's mind worked. He wished he hadn't wasted so many years avoiding her. She made him laugh and as Jack so often had pointed out to him, he needed to lighten up and laugh more.

Keith was a wreck, he couldn't remember ever being so jittery. "I'm glad I've never been nominated before, or for that matter will ever be again." Keith confided to Izzy. Izzy was just heading out the front door, Keith knew where she intended on going. He maneuvered himself in front of her, taking his tux from the hook on the front closet door.

"Listen Iz." He said. "I'd prefer for you not to hang out with Braden tonight." Izzy scowled but let him continue. "It's true I don't like him, I'm not going to lie to you about that." He confessed. "But it's because I don't trust him. You can't blame me for that, he has proven that much to you and he knows you will be alone tonight. I'm so nervous Izzy, I don't need one more thing to worry about and I would worry about you all night long. Please, just this once, humor me?" He begged. "I won't be able to function, I'll trip or say something stupid if I'm worried about you."

Izzy stopped at the door, she hadn't considered Keith's side at all. She nodded to him submissively and took his Tux from his hands. He took the shoe box from the entry table and followed her towards Jack's room, a little surprised that she had obeyed him. Jack had assured him that Izzy would do as he asked, but until this moment he hadn't been convinced. She took the tux out of the plastic and laid it on the bed for him. "Better hop in the shower." She said, "It's almost time."

"Are you going to watch?" He asked.

"Of course, Jack bought the television just so I could." She laughed.

After Keith showered and applied extra deodorant, he wrapped a towel around his waist and walked into Jack's room to see Jack's cat, laying on the tux. The cat raised its head then stretched and curled on its back as if saying "look at me shedding all over your good clothes." Keith just sighed, "And why not?" he asked himself.

Keith closed the bedroom door trapping Jerome in the room with him. The cat didn't move.

"You know Jerome, if you had a brain you would be terrified." Keith said softly to the cat. Jerome sat up and stretched one hind leg in the air while licking his butt. "Same to you buddy." Keith said and gently shoved the cat off of his clothes. He thought about snapping the towel at the cat but thought better of it and tossed the towel into the empty hamper instead. He put on his underwear, then took the trousers off the bed. He sat on the edge of the bed and pulled them on, then he pulled on his socks. He removed the shoes from the box which he had set on the bed and put them on too. He stood up and pulled the shirt over his bare chest. He was just buttoning it up when there was a knock at the door.

"Are you decent?"

"Come on in." Izzy came in as he finished buttoning the shirt. Jerome darted out the door into the hallway. Keith picked the tie up off of the bed and went to the large vanity against the wall. Izzy sat on the edge of the bed and watched as Keith struggled with the tie.

"Damn it." He said as he tried again.

"Let me." Izzy stood up and stood on her toes trying to reach Keith's neck. He rolled his eyes and bent over.

"I'm not that tall." He said. "You're just short."

"There." She said and patted his chest. "It's perfect." Then she ran her hands up and down his shirt and said, "That's a lot of ruffles."

"Does it look bad?" Keith asked her, he was getting nervous.

Izzy stepped back to inspect him. She smiled at him, admiring his chiseled good looks. "Keith, you look really good."

She handed him his jacket, then picked up a lint brush from the vanity. After the jacket was on, she cleaned the cat hair from the lapel and then had him turn a few times, inspecting for any more cat hair she might have missed.

"Good?" He asked. Izzy nodded. "Okay, I'm going to go. The Limo is here. Now you are going to lock the door behind me right?" Izzy nodded.

Keith stood outside the door until he heard the latch turn. The limousine was waiting, the driver got out and opened the door for

Keith. He got in and they headed out, they would pick up his father and then it would start. Keith closed his eyes and swallowed. He felt anxious and

nervous and excited. He could feel he was on the cusp of change, something big was coming, he knew his life would never be the same after tonight. He just wasn't sure if it was because of the awards or because of Izzy.

Izzy had to screw around a bit with the television antennas to get a clear picture. She laughed knowing this was probably the only time the set would be used, unless Keith came over and used it. She loved watching all the movie stars on the red carpet, the dresses were amazing. She had put on her white cotton nightgown and curled up on the couch under the same blanket Keith had used on the patio. She had seen him sleeping out there, she had questioned if she should wake him, but he looked so peaceful that she just couldn't do it. She had a couple cookies and a glass of milk earlier, but didn't make any dinner. She was too excited to be hungry. Braden had asked if she wanted to watch the awards with him, but she had politely declined remembering her promise to Keith.

Angie Dickenson and Burt Bacharach read the nominee's. Angie's dress was stunning, Izzy couldn't quite tell if it was pink or gold, everything always kind of looked pink to Izzy, but it was low cut and sparkled like the stars. Keith accepted the award graciously in a very short speech. He thanked the director saying that he had helped him more than anyone, Izzy kind of cringed. She hoped Jack wouldn't feel slighted. In any case, Keith looked amazing and she was happy for him. She turned off the television, folded the blanket and headed towards her room. She laid there for a few minutes, wondering when the last time was that Keith had laid in that bed. The thoughts in her head made her restless, she closed her eyes tight but knew sleep was going to play its elusive game with her tonight.

She wished Keith was across the hall from her again, she wondered what he would be doing tonight.

10

It was 3:40 in the morning. He shouldn't stop by, he should have called after the awards like they had planned. He could have made sure she was safe, the doors were locked and she hadn't let Braden come over. He could still be at a party, having a good time, savoring the moment and probably getting laid. The women were throwing themselves at him, hell he could have had more than one. Why was he in a cab on this wet morning heading to Jack's to check on a little girl.

The cab driver was saying something about the Oscar Keith was holding in his lap, he wasn't sure what he said but he smiled and nodded, then continued to look out the cab window. Droplets of mist were dripping down the glass, obscuring the view, but he wasn't really looking out, his eyes weren't focused on anything outside the cab, he was lost in thought.

Yesterday seemed so long ago. He wondered if Izzy had let Braden in after he had left. What was he going to find when he stopped by unannounced? What would he do if he found them in bed together, would he react? The thought was making him physically ill, or maybe he simply had too much to drink. Regardless, he was beginning to think he had made a mistake in coming, but the cab was already on Jack's drive. He paid the guy and nodded again at the driver as he babbled something at Keith. He tipped him $100, it was an outrageous tip and Keith really couldn't afford it, but he had to keep up the appearance.

The cab drove off and Keith stood in front of the house. It was dark inside, what did he expect? It was almost 4:00 am. He pulled the keys out of his pocket with his right hand, holding the Oscar in a firm grip in his left. Quietly he inserted the key and turned the knob and entered into the darkness. Closing the door softly behind him he listened. He didn't hear anything, but what did he expect he would hear? He had only taken a few steps inside when a light came on down the hallway. Izzy entered the room not seeing him and reached for the phone just before it rang. The sound made Keith jump and his movement made Izzy shriek. He hurried towards her and flipped on the kitchen light. "It's just me." He said pulling her towards him.

Her heart was pounding and the phone kept ringing. She smiled awkwardly at Keith and lifted the phone off the cradle.

"Hello?" Izzy said, Her voice cracked a bit. "Jack. Is everything going ok?"

She was winding the cord around her arm as she spoke to him. She was wearing a simple white nightgown, clingy cotton fabric and smelled like roses.

"Yeah I watched!" she was saying. "Thank you for getting the television. Yeah he is standing right here. I hope he lets me hold it! Do you want to talk to him? Ok, I love you." she said then stretched her arm with the phone towards Keith. He took the phone, still hanging on to the Oscar. Izzy reached out and touched the gold statue. A strange look came over her face and she jerked her hand back like it had burned her. Something stirred deep inside of her, a forgotten memory that she didn't want to feel. She sighed softly and left the kitchen, leaving Keith alone while he spoke to his brother.

Keith explained to Jack that he hadn't had a chance to call and thought he would just stop by to make sure everything was alright. He was too wound up to sleep and thought he might as well come over. Jack was in one of his creative moods, he seldom slept when in these phases and probably didn't even notice the time when he called. The talk was brief but felt good. They hadn't grown up together, but they had a strong bond. Jack was intense, demanding and opinionated, but he had always been kind to Keith and had helped him so many times. Hearing his voice and his congratulations meant more to Keith than he had realized that it would. He had had a great night, his father had come with him to the ceremony, he was holding an Oscar in his left hand and felt his career was on track. He hung up the phone on the wall in the kitchen and turned off the light. As he went down the hall, he saw Izzy was in the bathroom. She must have just washed her face because her hair was in a ponytail on top of her head. She smiled at him and then hung up the washclothe that she had been holding in her right hand. She pulled the rubber band out of her hair and it fell around her shoulders and down her back.

"I'm surprised you came over." She said softly to him.

"Well I said I would check on you and I never called." Keith responded.

"No, you didn't call," Izzy said. "You sure scared the crap out of me."

"I should have called, I lost track of time." Keith confessed.

"I'm sure you were busy, you didn't need to call or come over. I wasn't waiting for you to call or anything. We have gotten along a lot better than before, but I'm still not convinced you actually like me." Izzy said. Her scent was changing from roses to honeysuckle and Keith noticed it and smiled. Izzy tried to leave the bathroom but Keith blocked the door with his arm. He thought about the mascara, here they were again in the same place. Izzy took a step backwards and bumped up against the door. She looked down at the floor to avoid his gaze. Keith lifted her face up towards him with one finger under her chin.

"I like you." He said.

"Really?." she asked in a coarse whisper. "I want you to like me, but not because Jack forced you to." She tried to get through again but Keith wasn't moving.

"I said that I like you." He said. He smiled at her. "Hasn't the last couple days proven that to you?" He asked.

"We did have fun." She agreed, "But you never want to be here when I am here," Izzy said. "You only came this time because Jack made you. I always make you angry. Even this trip. I'm not little anymore and I still make you angry. Braden, the party, the beach. I really don't mean to."

"Now that's a lie." Keith said calmly. "You confessed to me that you like to make me angry."

Izzy looked down. "That was before," Izzy said, "I haven't tried to rile you up in a long time."

"You're lying again." Keith said softly. "Have you forgotten the gear shift?"

Izzy laughed.

"You never did say why you liked to do that." Keith whispered. She was pinned in, her back against the bathroom door. She smelled more and more like a honeysuckle vine. She decided to just answer his question so he would let her by.

"It is fun." Izzy said truthfully. "But in all honesty, I just wanted you to pay attention to me. I don't want you to dislike me. I don't know, I can't help myself, I see you and I provoke you because then you have to talk to me."

Keith considered her words carefully, she was right. It was true what she said, he thought he would avoid her but everytime she made him angry, instead of avoiding her, he engaged. Ever since that first encounter. She made him crazy and he didn't like it. He wanted to have control, she was a little girl but when he was near her, he couldn't think straight. He did pay attention to her when he was angry. He hadn't really thought about it, but he enjoyed being angry, having the opportunity to pay attention to her. He might have been angrier with her over little things than he should have been, it gave him a reason to interact with her. He looked down at her and noticed how shapely she had become, the white nightgown clung to her breasts and he could see she was breathing quickly. He was getting aroused again, he could feel himself getting hard. He said his new mantra quietly in his head over and over "she's 15, she's 15, she's 15 " but his body was betraying him and was telling him something different. Maybe if he explained.

"I like you Iz," he began, "maybe too much. You're smart and a fast learner. You bring out something in my brother that no one else ever has. You make me laugh without even trying. You bring out something in me too, you make me want to be a better person than I am. I just have to be careful, I'm not Braden, you are an underage girl and I can ruin my career before it gets started. You don't make me angry, I make myself angry. You make me crazy, I have to keep telling myself that you're 15." There was a pause, a silence.

"I'm 16" She whispered, her back still against the bathroom door.

"What? Keith said. "Jack would have told me."

" Why? " Izzy asked, her voice still soft. "He doesn't know, my birthday is in January."

Keith hesitated. It was still young, too young and he knew it, but somehow it seemed different. It was probably the champagne or just the high from winning, but he felt invincible. Without even thinking he bent down and kissed her. She hesitated for a moment as he leaned into her and the bathroom door, then she responded. She put her hands on his face and pulled him closer to hers. Her lips were soft like velvet. Her breath was fresh, her skin was dewey and she smelled so good. He pressed forward, his tongue brushed against her lips and she parted them eagerly. At first he barely entered her mouth, then his tongue went deeper in. She accepted all that he gave her. He cupped her face with one hand and dropped the other that had been supporting him on the bathroom door. He slid it down her side, feeling the side of her breast and the curve of her waist. He pulled her even closer, his hand now on her hip, he dropped it beneath her nightgown and let his fingers seek her warmth. She wasn't wearing any panties, he found the place he sought easily. She moaned just slightly, and he slid his fingers against her. She was wet and swollen and warm. He ran his fingers back and forth and she became even wetter. She threw her head back and it hit the bathroom door. He bent down and picked her up and carried her into the room she used as hers. The covers were thrown back from when she had left the warmth of her bed to answer the phone. He laid her on it and pulled off his already loose tie. His shirt was partially unbuttoned but he just pulled it over his head. She sat up just a bit and unfastened his belt. Then she lifted the nightgown over her head and laid down. Her eyes glistened and she watched him remove his pants and briefs.

He bent down and kissed her neck, then he moved down and kissed her breasts. She held his head as he kissed her stomach. His fingers found her again and moved back and forth and went in a little deeper. She threw her head back against the pillows but made no noise, she was trying to hold it in, and he wondered if she liked what he was doing. He spread her legs apart and got between them and thrust himself inside. He realized then, when he felt the barrier, she whimpered just slightly but pulled him closer to her. He was losing control, he felt the barrier break and the blood flow, she hadn't slept with Braden, she hadn't slept with anyone. What was he thinking, he wasn't thinking, she was warm and wet and tight and he lost himself inside of her. Izzy's back arched and she cried out a bit, she wasn't sure what was happening. She had never felt anything like it. She squeezed her pelvic muscles as tight as she could, thinking it would help but Keith moved inside of her and nothing stopped the contractions. She brought her legs up and wrapped them around his waist, using the leverage to pull him deeper inside of her.

Colors exploded in her head. She could feel Keith inside of her as he ejaculated, the sensation was incredible. She turned her head into her pillow to muffle her cries. Her muscles continued to contract and tighten. She didn't want him to ever leave her body. She remembered him now, she remembered this. She remembered feeling what he felt and feeling herself as well, she remembered coming together body and soul as one person. All her questions about his colors were gone, she could feel his colors and they were the same as hers. There was no difference between her greens and his reds.

Keith's heart felt as though it was going to pound out of his chest. He dropped to the pillow beside Izzy and lay facing her. She was breathing hard and her face was sweating. She rolled on her side and put her hand on the side of his face. Keith put his hand atop of hers, then moved it down and pressed it against his chest. "Feel my heart," He whispered. "Feel what you do to me."

He noticed a tear on her cheek and released her hand and wiped it off. "I'm so sorry." He said.

"Please." She whispered. "Don't be sorry. I couldn't bear it if you were sorry."

Keith pulled her close to him and kissed the top of her head. "I'm not sorry." He said. "Not about that, just sorry if I hurt you."

"You didn't hurt me." She whispered.

"Then why the tears?" He asked.

"I'm just so happy." Izzy said. "I feel so free."

Keith felt free too. He had denied his feelings for so long. He had chosen not to believe her story, he had questioned his brother's intentions. Making love to Izzy stirred something deep inside of him. It was like a long forgotten memory. Everything seemed familiar to him now, her scent, her touch, her voice. Part of him questioned the validity of his own memories and fought off the others, another part of him called to them. He was almost sure now that Izzy's story was true and accepting it gave him the most incredible sense of freedom that he had ever felt.

The two fell asleep in each other's arms and awoke a few hours later, long after the sun had risen. Keith woke first, he was still cradling her in his arms, the one underneath her had fallen asleep but he didn't care. He gazed at her perfect face, she still looked so innocent. Part of him really hated himself for taking that from her, but mostly, he was glad it was him. He loved her, he studied her face, her lashes, the freckles across the bridge of her nose and she made him feel good. He pulled her close and she opened her eyes, he kissed her gently on the lips then ran his fingers through her hair.

"I should ask you how you feel." Keith murmured. "Are you in pain?"

Izzy shook her head. She started to sit up and winced just a bit. "Stay here." Keith commanded. "I shouldn't have been so rough with you. I didn't know, I should have known. When I realized, God, I had no control, I shouldn't have pumped you so hard, I should have been gentle, I've never lost control like that before."

"I think I was the one that lost control." Izzy said softly. "I think I drooled on the pillow."

Keith tried to hide his smile and walked across the hallway and ran a warm bath and poured some of Izzy's bubblebath under the facet. After it was full he went back to Izzy and gently lifted her into his arms, he carried her across the hall into the bathroom and then set her down. She stepped into the bath and lowered herself in. Keith stepped in and sat down in front of her. "I forgot a washcloth." Keith said.

"It's okay, we don't need one." Izzy laughed. She took the bar of soap and lathered up her hands, then washed Keith's neck, shoulders and chest. Keith took the soap from Izzy and did the same. He bent over and kissed her neck, her shoulder then moved to her mouth. He pulled her up on top of him and she let out a gasp. She hadn't noticed his erection under the bubbles and was surprised when he slid her down on top of it. This time, she was in control, she wasn't sure what to do but Keith helped her. He placed his hands around her waist and pulled her up just a little, then pulled her down. She understood what he wanted and obeyed, the feel of him inside of her sent sparks of color in her brain. She let her body take over her mind, she simply did what felt good.

Keith could barely stop from exploding immediately. He had wondered if the night before excited him because she was a novelty, but this time made it clear that wasn't the case. Izzy was a sensual being, she let her body take over trusting that if it felt good, it was what she should do. He had moved his hands down to her thighs and had stopped guiding her completely. Watching the pleasure on her face made him harder, hearing the soft moans drove him to a frenzy. Water spilled over the edge of the tub with the waves the two created. He slid his body backwards so he could rest his back against the tub and when they finished she let herself fall against his chest, in no hurry to pull off of him.

"We need to stop." Izzy was laughing now. "I'm not going to be able to walk."

"I don't want to stop." Keith said. "I want to do this over and over until I die."

"Until you die?" Izzy asked. "I hope that isn't anytime soon. Besides, I leave in a few days." Izzy chided.

"I don't want you to leave, ever." Keith said and he meant it. He sat up and kissed her, gently on the lips. She loved the smell of him, the taste of him, she swore she could still taste the ocean breeze from the day before."

"I'm not sure what I should be doing for you." Keith said, "I've never been anyone's first". Izzy could feel herself blushing. She was embarrassed, she wondered if her inexperience had amused him.

Keith saw the blush and realized what she must have been thinking. He pulled her in against his chest and held her tightly. "It was beautiful." He whispered to her. "I feel like we belong to each other. Izzy, I believe you. I think I remember this."

"This?" Izzy asked, motioning to the bathtub.

"No," Keith answered softly. "By this, I mean loving you. Everything about you seems so familiar. It really is special, I feel it."

"I wonder what Jack will think." Izzy whispered.

"Oh God, Jack, I forgot, what are we going to tell him?" Keith mused out loud.

"Yes, what are you going to tell Jack?" Jack said from the hallway. He stood in the open doorway, his arms folded and a look on his face that Keith didn't recognize.

"Crap." Izzy said.

Keith lifted himself out of the tub and pulled the shower curtain shut. He took a towel from the towel bar and wrapped it around his waist. He guided his brother out of the bathroom and closed the door behind him. Jack motioned to the bed they had occupied where a large red stain was on the white sheet. Keith acknowledged it with a nod, then went to Jack's room and pulled on some pants. Jack motioned with his head for Keith to follow him and he led the way to the patio.

"I just thought you would be a little smarter about it." Jack was saying. "I'm not going to lie, I think the two of you were destined to be together, and I'm not talking about Izzy's memories, you are perfect for one another. But Keith, I hoped you would ease into it. You have avoided her for years, I thought you would get to know her. I didn't think you would just pounce on her. Clearly she was unprepared, did you use a condom?"

Keith didn't answer but looked down. "Jesus Keith!" Jack put his head in his hands. "A Enidarrac trait I suppose, we leave a trail of children everywhere we go."

"I'll marry her." Keith said. "I want to."

"Ruth will never let her fifteen year old daughter get married." Jack said.

"Sixteen." Keith corrected.

"When did that happen?" Jack laughed.

"On her birthday." Keith answered.

"Thanks." Jack said. "I had that much figured out on my own."

"January." Keith said.

Jack had poured himself a scotch before stepping out on the patio. He drank some of it now. He shoved Keith in the shoulder and laughed, "Well at least she can drive now." He said. He took another sip from his drink then rubbed the glass between the palms of both hands.

"I'm not sure I appreciate your humor." Keith said.

Izzy came out on the patio. She was wearing cuffed jeans and a cranberry colored blouse. She was barefoot, the patio was cold but she didn't care. Keith watched her approach and was surprised at how confidently she walked towards them. He noted she smelled like roses, she was content. He nodded in approvement, she didn't regret it either.

She sat on the patio between the two men and stretched out so the sun could hit her face. It shone on her blonde hair which still hung loosely around her waist. She had combed it and the fine strands blew behind her in the gentle breeze. Jack smiled at her, he loved that little girl. He and Barbara had brought the two together, it just hadn't quite worked the way they had planned. Jack had no doubt it was going to happen, he just thought it would take a little more time.

"Here's the thing, tiny grasshopper." He said to the breeze, not looking at either Keith or Izzy. "You are only fifteen." He began.

"Sixteen." Keith and Izzy said in unison. Jack smiled but still didn't look at either one of them.

"Okay, sixteen." Jack said. "It's still too young." He held up a hand before either Keith or Izzy could interrupt him. "Izzy, you just started highschool. Keith and I both, want you to have a normal childhood" He looked at them now. "I wanted you two together, I just wanted you to take your time, bond a little. Keith started to say something but Jack held up his hand stopping him. "Keith, you just won an Oscar, you are going to be a hot commodity soon. If you were me, no one would think a thing about it, but you aren't me and the public would never let you live this down, your career would be ruined." Jack let his words sink in. Both Izzy and Keith were looking downward, not at each other and not at him.

"Jack." Keith said, "I'm prepared for what might come, I never want to be parted from her."

Izzy studied her lover's face carefully, she knew if she made him hang on to her, that it would ruin him. She hadn't thought about it, she hadn't thought at all, it had been instinct, a primal instinct. His only chance at freedom was to not tie himself down with her. He had told her doing what he thought was right, stopped him from being free. She didn't want to be the cause of him being unhappy. She wondered if she remembered this, touching his Oscar last night had almost been painful. She knew it had a memory with it and she let go, not wanting to remember. She looked over at Jack and nodded to him. Jack smiled his sweet gentle smile and nodded back to her. Jack always knew that Izzy was strong. She understood what had to be done and would go along with it. This slim, pale young woman would do what it took, calling on all the strength she had inside of her. He was so proud of her.

Jack loved them both. He didn't want either of them to be hurt. He carefully considered his options then smiled. Keith and Izzy both noticed the smile and looked at one another perplexed by the expression.

"Keith, go put on a shirt." He commanded.

"What? Why?" Keith asked.

"We are going to Tijuana!" Jack laughed.

11

So, the plan was Keith and Izzy would get married that day in Tijuana. They would have one more day together then Izzy must be sent home. If, God forbid Izzy did become pregnant, they could admit they had been married and try to salvage what they could. It would be scandalous but would at least save Izzy's reputation and redeem Keith's a little. They wouldn't worry about it unless it happened.

The ceremony certainly wasn't the marriage either of them had dreamed of, Jack wore a sombrero and shook maracas. Izzy thought he looked darling, but didn't want to admit it. Keith and Izzy didn't dress any differently, they were keeping a low profile and hoping no one would recognize him. The drive home took forever, Keith and Jack sat in the front, Izzy sat in the back. They had taken Keith's car, again so as not to draw attention to themselves. It was dark as they pulled up on the driveway. Izzy had fallen asleep on the backseat.

"Poor kid." Jack said aloud. "She must be exhausted."

"I don't want her to leave Jack." Keith said.

"It's not just about you kid, you know that." Jack answered. "Neither of us had anything close to a nice childhood, she only has a few years left. Give that to her brother." Jack said. "I know patience doesn't exactly run in our family, but you have to wait a few years." Keith nodded, he got out of the car and opened the back door quietly gently placing his hand on her shoulder. She opened her eyes and smiled at Keith. "We're back?" She asked.

Keith nodded and stepped aside so Izzy could get out of the car. She had bought a mexican blanket while she was there. It reminded her of Keith, it was purple, yellow and black. She picked it up off the back seat and held it close to her heart. Even in the dark she could see the look of sadness on Keith's face and felt tremendous guilt. She should have been stronger.

"Did you guys go to Mexico?" Braden asked. He had silently walked up behind the car and was watching Izzy pull the blanket from the backseat. Keith started to say something but Izzy stepped between them.

"Yeah, I leave for Nebraska in the morning and we wanted to do something different before I left." Izzy smiled.

"Hey Keith, congratulations old man!" Braden said. "An Oscar, man that is so cool."

Keith was about to come unglued, but Jack also stepped in between them, shoving Keith towards the house. "It is cool, Braden." He said. "Excuse Keith, he hasn't eaten and he is a little grumpy."

"Ah, that's alright." Braden said. He was smiling smugly at Keith.

"Old man!" Keith muttered to himself. Jack continued to shove Keith towards the front door, ushering him inside. He hadn't locked the door again. "I'm not leaving her alone out there with that guy." Keith said.

"He is her childhood friend Keith, clearly there is no competition now. Let her be." Jack reassured him. "Stop being possessive, remember Izzy is a friend of the family, not your wife."

Keith sat down on the brown sofa and shook his head. "My wife," he said. "Jack, I'm married."

Jack slapped him on the back. "You sure are, at least in Mexico. I want to tell Barbara, but I think the less people that know, the better." Jack said.

Keith nodded. "We can't tell anyone I suppose." Keith confirmed. "All these years, it seems like every woman I dated wanted this, I never did. Now it is all I want, I have it, but I can't speak of it. It's like the universe is slapping me in the face."

"Or maybe," Jack said, "Maybe the universe has opened a new world up to you, and you just need to be patient."

Ketih shook his head at his brother. "It's going to be hard on her." Keith said, looking towards the front door. Jack rested his hand on Keith's shoulder, he knew Keith was right, it was going to be very hard on his little grasshopper.

"I wouldn't worry too much about her little brother." Jack said, "That little girl is the toughest person that I have ever known."

"Do me a favor, would you Jack?" Keith asked. "Please stop calling her a little girl."

When Izzy came into the house a half an hour later, she headed straight to her room and shoved her things into her duffel bag. She stripped the bloodied sheets off the bed and the mattress pad. She carried them to the kitchen, and soaked one at a time with dish soap and cold water rubbing the fabric together until the blood slowly disappeared. Once that was done she tossed them in the laundry basket on top of the washing machine. The two men watched in silence as Izzy laundered the sheets, then she headed back down the hall. She planned on wearing the same clothes she was wearing that evening when she went to the airport in the morning. To save time she decided to copy Jack and just sleep in the nude.

Izzy felt confined, caged, she didn't like feeling as though she had no choices. For the first time on any of her trips to California, she no longer felt free. Izzy unfolded the Mexican blanket, laying it down upon the bed. She crawled underneath it and closed her eyes. She tried to absorb the soft colors from the blanket that she associated with Keith, into her mind. She wanted them to blend with her own colors, she wanted to feel him inside of her one last time.

Keith and Jack had made themselves some eggs and toast for dinner. Keith popped his head in the doorway and flipped on the light, asking if Izzy was hungry. She smiled at him but shook her head. He carried in a plate with toast and scrambled eggs anyway and sat beside her on the bed.

"It will work out." He said. Izzy nodded at him, but she didn't believe it. How could it possibly work out? Jack had been right, they should have eased into it slowly. Now instead of building a relationship, they were hiding one. She looked at his profile, he was eating the egg he had offered to her, while sitting beside her. He looked so strong, she knew that he would probably miss her for a while, but he was a grown man, he would move on and she really couldn't blame him. He would wait to make sure that she wasn't pregnant, praying to God that she wasn't so he wouldn't have to do the right thing and once that was verified, he would be free. Free, she hated that word right now, but Keith had told her what had always stopped him from feeling free and she would be damned if she was the cause this time. She watched the man she loved, eating the last bite of her scrambled eggs and she knew in her heart that she would never love another man. He was everything to her. If you really love anyone, you put the needs, desires and well being of that person before your own. She nodded to herself and held onto the blanket as tightly as she could. Keith would find his happiness, Keith would find his freedom. She was determined that this man she loved would be happy. Keith leaned over and kissed her on the cheek, oblivious to the dark thoughts inside of her head. "I'll be back in a few minutes." He said.

He took the plate to the kitchen, Jack was still at the table. "She ate?" He asked. Keith shook his head. "You ate it?" Keith smiled and nodded. He put the plate in the sink, ordinarily Izzy would have washed everything by now. He thought about washing them himself but then turned to his brother and said, "I'll wash these in the morning. I just kind of think she shouldn't be alone right now."

He said. Jack nodded approval. Keith started to leave, then looked at his brother. "Thank you." He said.

"You're welcome," Jack answered. " I guess, it's nice to know you still need me."

"I'm realizing," Keith confessed. "That I need a lot of things. I've always needed you Jack, you've shown me the way in more ways than you will ever know. I should have thanked you at the Oscars. You are the reason I am who I am." Keith leaned his back against the wall next to the phone. The numbers Jack had written there so many years ago were just above his left shoulder.

"You never need to thank me Keith." Jack said, the lines on his face had softened, he looked very young. "I love you, I know I don't say the words very often, but I really do love you."

"I used to think," Keith continued, "That to be free, to really feel free, I needed to stop doing the right thing all the time. I wanted to be more like you."

"Thanks." Jack laughed. "I'm reconsidering the love thing."

"I didn't mean that the way it sounded." Keith laughed. "On the outside, I mean to anyone who doesn't really know you, it might seem like you don't give a shit about how anyone else feels, but you do don't you?"

Jack didn't answer but the dimples on the sides of his face became a bit more obvious.

"You've always cared about me. I mean, I didn't see it, but you put me first so many times. I know that you hated doing the television show, you kept it for income. I thought it was because Dad told you to, I thought that was part of the reason the two of you fought, but looking back on it, every time I was in trouble and needed a place to stay, or needed stability in my life, you kept working the job. You worked, provided income, supported me all the while doing something that you didn't want to do."

Jack's dimples faded a bit, he shifted uncomfortably in his chair.

"The point that I'm making, and rather badly, is that you are the freest person that I have ever known. You want something, you go after it. Nothing stops you, yet you sacrifice for others too. You do the right thing, it just isn't as obvious to everyone else because, well, you also are who you are."

"I'm not entirely sure you should continue talking." Jack said, but the dimples had returned fully to his face.

"Jack," Keith said. "I just did the right thing and I have never felt so free. That girl in there," He continued, motioning his head towards the hallway. "She inspires me. She makes me want to be better than I am."

"She has that effect on people." Jack said softly. "You once told me she zero'd in a person's worst quality and made them feel guilty about it."

"I was such an ass." Keith confessed. "But I was right. My worst quality was that I hated doing the right thing. I resented doing the right thing. I thought that doing what I should, would limit me from doing what I wanted. You have shown me how to do both, do the right thing but also do what you want."

Jack grinned at his little brother, he had longed for Keith to recognize how hard he had tried to help him, it felt good that the boy could finally see it. He nodded slightly to himself, sometimes Izzy worked miracles.

"Sometimes." Jack said, thinking about conversations he had with Izzy, "Sometimes doing the right thing, and doing what you want, even though they are entirely different things, can actually be the same thing."

"I'm not sure I follow." Keith said.

"It's like being color blind." Jack laughed. "Red and green look the same in black and white pictures but they are two different colors. It is all perspective."

"Now you're just being weird." Keith laughed.

"Okay, look at it this way." Jack continued. "You never wanted to be forced to do anything, assuming being forced was making you do the right thing. Maybe it was, I don't know, but this time, what you wanted was also the right thing. They were two different colors, but they were the same thing. You wanted to marry Izzy, and marrying her was the right thing."

"Bam!, I'm free." Keith said.

"Yes, Bam!" Jack agreed.

"Do you think, in the past, doing the right thing would have felt the same?" Keith asked hesitantly.

"I think, little brother," Jack said softly, knowing very well what his brother was referring to. "That was similar to this situation. You were a child, she gave you time to grow up. That leads us back to doing the right thing again. It might hurt, but I suspect you will feel very free letting her go. You know in your heart, it's just distance and distance is just geography. Nothing will change true love and you will be giving her a gift. A three year gift, she can be a cheerleader, prom queen, whatever, and then she can be your wife."

"There is that unspoken fear." Keith whispered.

"What fear is that?" Jack asked.

"That she will change her mind." Keith said so softly Jack had to lean forward to hear.

"Fat chance." Jack said. He knew his brother's greatest weakness was the fear of not being loved. "Have you forgotten that girl traveled through time to be with you?"

"I thought you said she wasn't a time traveler?" Keith reminded him.

"My mistake, she isn't." Jack said. "But she loved you before, she loves you now. She brought the love with her." Jack chuckled out loud.

"What could you possibly find so amusing?" Keith asked his brother.

"I was just thinking about Izzy and that stupid green duffel bag." Jack said.

"What about it?" Keith asked.

"She has always said she has everything that she needs. That she travels light." Jack said.

"Yeah." Keith agreed, "Go on."

"I just realized what she meant." Jack said, then winked at his brother. "She brought with her the love, love doesn't take up a lot of room." Jack said. He noticed Keith's face changed a bit at this new thought, he looked very happy. "Actually," Jack continued, "I take that back, the love she brought with her, it is huge and it fills up the whole house."

Keith nodded and left the room, still smiling. Jerome followed him down the hallway and darted into Izzy's room. He jumped on the bed and purred. "So you like me now?" Keith asked the cat. He pulled off his shirt and pants, leaving them on the floor and crawled into bed beside his young wife. She was already asleep, one hand lay against her head on her pillow. He watched her sleep for a long time. He had thought about waking her, making love to her, even consoling her but she looked so peaceful that he didn't have the heart to do it. He could make love to her again in the morning, he lay back on the pillow in anticipation. He moved closer to her and smiled, feeling her flesh against his. He noticed she smelled a little like roses and a little like lilacs, he told himself it was to be expected. He was really growing to appreciate that perfume. After a while he closed his own eyes and fell into a deep sleep. After making love to her in the morning, he would let her know this was only temporary and that everything was going to be alright.

When Keith awoke the next morning, he could tell by the sun that he had overslept. Izzy usually was up at the crack of dawn and always woke Jack up, Keith had assumed she would also wake him. He heard Braden's motorcycle pull into the driveway next door. He rolled over and looked at the clock, it was ten am. Izzy's flight was in thirty minutes. He shot out of bed but Izzy wasn't beside him. He pulled on his pants and shirt that he had left on the floor and stumbled out of the bedroom. Jack came out of his bedroom looking very disheveled. "What time is it?" He asked.

"It's ten o'clock!" Keith answered.

"How did we oversleep? Get Izzy, if she isn't on that plane her mother will skin us alive!" Jack bellowed.

Keith hurried to the kitchen, she wasn't there, he looked out on the patio but she wasn't there either. Jack came down the hallway pulling on a pair of loafers. "Where the fuck is she?" He asked. Keith opened the front door and the cat ran inside.

"The cat was inside last night, it slept with us." Keith said. "Jack, did you forget to lock the door again?"

Just then Braden cut across the grass to the front door. "Hi guys." He said. "I took Izzy to the airport, she said you two were sleeping too hard and she didn't want to wake you up."

"Fuck" Keith said. Jack grabbed his keys from the green dish and commanded Keith to run. They sped in the Ferrari down the highway, in and out of traffic and pulled up in front of the terminal blocking the way for all the other cars. "Run!" Jack commanded. Keith flew from the car and ran to the terminal, he was out of breath by the time he found the correct dock. The plane was already taxing onto the runway and all Keith could do was lean against the glass and watch. Jack showed up a few minutes later out of breath and leaned against the glass next to his brother. They watched the plane take off and stayed until it was out of sight.

"Women," Jack said, then slapped his brother's back and laughed.

"That is so not funny." Keith said. "Why would she do that?"

"They are a whole different species Keith. She probably just couldn't say goodbye." Jack said. He was almost confident when he said it.

"I can't believe she would do this." Keith said, his hands on the glass.

Jack put his hand on Keith's shoulder. "She is a sensitive woman." He said,

"Woman." Keith mumbled. "Yeah, I guess she is. I think I liked her better as a kid."

"Those days are gone, I think our obedient little girl has flown the coop." Jack mused.

"Literally." Keith said. "And I can't believe she let Braden take her."

12

Over time, Keith became angry. Jack had kept in touch with Izzy, speaking in code about what had happened between her and Keith. He was relieved when she mentioned she had cramps, taking it as confirmation that no little Enidarracs were on the way. When he told his brother, he was surprised by his reaction. He thought Keith would be relieved, but the boy seemed downright disappointed about it.

Jack would tell Keith every time he planned on calling Ruth, expecting Keith to show up so he could speak with Izzy, but Keith never did. He sadly grew to realize that his plan had fallen apart, Izzy and Keith were farther apart now than they ever had been.

Jack's life had fallen apart too. There had been more arrests, Barbara had left him for good. Jack found love again the next year and she moved into the house. He didn't invite Izzy out after that. His new girlfriend wouldn't have understood. Izzy was practically a grown woman, he wouldn't have been able to explain her away and Izzy's marriage was secret so he couldn't say she was family. He missed his little grasshopper, but he felt good knowing she was having a more normal life than either he or his brother had in highschool.

Keith was in and out of relationships but everytime they started to become intimate, Keith would break it off. He told his family he just wasn't ready to settle down. He threw himself into his work, doing movie after movie. By the end of 1978 a new movie was going to be released. He worried about it, he had lost a lot of his Hollywood sparkle since his Oscar. His insecurities were resurfacing, he questioned if he had any talent. The Oscar had been for his music, not his acting ability. To prove himself he began choosing controversial parts. They were difficult roles, he played a lot of characters that just weren't likable. The critics often panned him, implying he was washed up. Keith thought his good looks were fading a bit too, his hair was thinner and when he looked in the mirror, his eyes always looked depressed.

Keith questioned if he was choosing unappealing roles on purpose, avoiding being a Hollywood crush so it wouldn't be a big deal if word got out that he had married a sixteen year old. The thought of it pissed him off. He still couldn't believe that she had left the house as she did. That the last person she had seen in California was Braden. He thought about how she had told him that she liked to make him angry, she liked the attention. He wondered if this was another game. He hated feeling as though he was being manipulated so he had waited for her to call or write, she was the one that had sneaked out of the house, she didn't even leave him a note. Izzy never contacted him so instead of reaching out to her, he ignored her.

In any case, Keith had taken another unappealing role, this one his character married an underage prostitute. Jack had a lot of practice with bad press. Keith knew this movie was going to give him some. He wanted to ask his brother for advice on how to handle it so he found himself driving over unannounced to Jack's. When Keith entered Jack's house, he found him curled up on the sofa submersed in a typed manuscript. Jack nodded towards Keith but didn't look up. Keith sat on a green chair across from the sofa and waited as Jack slowly lifted one page after another stacking them facedown on the coffee table in front of him. Keith adjusted his weight and leaned forward, resting his forearms on his legs. Jack continued to read without so much as looking at his brother.

"A screenplay?" Keith asked. He knew he was interrupting his brother's concentration but he really needed for Jack to listen to him. His brother and his new girlfriend had become interested in discovering new material for the theater. Jack had wanted to buy a little playhouse somewhere but ended up renting one instead. He liked to put on new plays and musicals and discover new local talent. Keith assumed this was one in contention. Jack didn't stop or look up. Keith stood and moved to the sofa, he sat down and lifted the pages up that Jack had stacked and turned them over. "Before I remembered him" by Eli Nicholas." Keith read. "It sounds delightful." Jack finally looked up at his brother.

"Read some of it." Jack said. "I think I'm going to produce it, the title needs work but the content is riveting."

Keith began reading, it was well written. It was a story of a young girl who was raped by a stranger, a heroine addict. The imagery was vivid, the words understated, he had to admit after reading only a few pages he was intrigued.

"Eli Nicholas? One of your students?" Again Jack didn't look up or acknowledge his brother's question, he just kept intently reading page after page. Keith picked up the new stack of pages from the table and placed his stack underneath them so as to keep it all in order. He sat back for a minute and watched Jack read for a while. He ran his fingers through his hair in impatience and stood up. He walked to the kitchen and opened the refrigerator, then closed it without taking anything out of it. He walked back to the sofa but didn't sit down, then went back to the kitchen. He looked out the patio doors and stared at the empty yard, he remembered Izzy in her sundress, pulling on her white tennis shoes and then kissing his brother on his forehead. He knew Jack missed her, she had brought sanity to his life, she gave him some stability and a channel for his endless energy. Jack had loved teaching her and she had instructed him to channel his energy that way. Jack's new found happiness of producing new material on the stage was all because of Izzy.

He remembered how Jack had taken him under his wing, he had paid for voice lessons, he had helped him find an agent and he had worked with him on perfecting his skills. Jack was a teacher in so many ways and Keith felt such guilt having contributed to ending his time with Izzy. Keith put one hand on the glass door and closed his eyes, he could hear Izzy and her raspy voice, he could see that one sided smile of hers, he hated himself right now. He opened his eyes and pushed off from the door, he walked back out to the sofa, Jack had finished the manuscript and was sitting cross legged on the sofa deep in concentration.

"So what happens?" Keith asked. "She is raped in the first pages, what is left after that?"

Jack looked intently at his brother. "It's a story of recovery and forgiveness." He said. "It turns out her rapist, the addict, becomes her pen pal without knowing who she is or vice versa. They fall in love through phone calls and love letters only to discover their true identities at the end.

"Ok, it has some meat to it." Keith said.

"The twist is at the end, he finds out she had known all along who he was." Jack said. "She ends up loving him anyway. It's really well written."

"It read well, the first few pages." Keith agreed. "You never answered, Eli, is he someone you have known for a while?"

Jack sat still for a few minutes, then he began rolling the back of his thumb across the inside of his fingers, it was Jack's tell. He worked his fingers like that when he was anxious, excited, Keith knew there was something about this screenplay that had given Jack something new to be excited about. He was grateful and relieved. Jack's new girlfriend helped ground him but she didn't challenge him, not like Izzy had always done.

"Eli, yes I've known Eli for quite some time." Jack smiled.

"I'm surprised I've never met him, or heard you speak of him." Keith responded.

Jack uncrossed his legs and swung his bare feet onto the floor. He wiggled his toes in the brown carpet and then looked at his brother and grinned. Keith sat back down on the sofa, he was trying to formulate his thoughts, he needed his brother's advice.

"My movie is going to be released soon." Keith said, looking down at his folded hands.

"Great! So what is the issue?" Jack asked, he could read his brother and Keith was struggling with something.

Keith looked at his brother. "I'm going to catch a lot of crap over it." He said.

"Why?" Jack asked.

"My character is a washed up unhappy alcoholic who marries an underage prostitute." Keith confirmed.

"Sounds like a dark movie." Jack said. "Why have you been taking these kinds of roles?"

"I don't know, self loathing maybe." Keith said softly. "In any case, even though the girl is a prostitute, I can just imagine what children's advocate groups are going to say. Hell, there will probably be protests outside the theaters."

Jack leaned back and closed his eyes, formulating questions carefully in his head. It had been nearly three years since Keith had spoken Izzy's name, yet Jack knew her name was always there, unspoken. He wasn't sure why Keith had abandoned her but Jack knew his brother still loved her. A curious thought began to ebb its way into Jack's mind. He smiled wickedly and opened his eyes.

Jack slapped his brother on the back. He laughed, a loud cackle. "So you have met Eli." Jack said, then slapped Keith's back again. Keith was annoyed, he was begging his brother for advice, for his perspective and he wasn't listening.

"Jack," Keith began but Jack interrupted him again.

"Eli isn't a he." Jack blurted out. Keith didn't care, he wanted Jack to listen but Jack just continued on. "Eli can be short for all kinds of things." He smiled.

Keith was trying to be patient, he ran his fingers through his hair, getting it out of his face. It had started to get long again and was driving him crazy. "Okay, short for what? Just tell me, clearly you are dying too."

Jack laughed again and continued running his thumb under his fingers over and over. "What if telling you something could fix all your problems Keith, would you accept it or make it over complicated as usual?"

Keith stood up and paced behind the sofa, Jack brought his legs back up onto the cushions and crossed his legs again. Keith paced back to the front of the sofa and looked down at his brother. "Go for it." He said. "Fix my life."

"Eli can be short for Elizabeth." He said. Jack watched his brother but didn't see a connection in his face. "You know what else can be short for Elizabeth? Beth, Liz, Lizzy or even Izzy." He stopped talking and let his words sink in. His brother's face slowly changed as he realized the implication.

"This is by Izzy?" He asked. He bent down and picked up the manuscript and frantically began reading through it. "Is she implying I raped her?" He gasped.

"Settle down there bro." Jack laughed, "Not everything's about you. no, she is not implying that. Why would you even think that? Are you a heroin addict? Are you pen pals?. She is just drawing from her feelings like I've taught her, using her real emotions, it makes it raw."

Keith sat down again on the sofa beside his brother. Some of the words on the papers burned into his brain. Rape, innocence, advantage, helpless, lost, numb.....he kept seeing the words and her face and those sweet tears she shed the first night he made love to her.

"So you've been in contact with her? I thought we agreed not to." He said.

"I never agreed to anything like that." Jack continued. "I just didn't tell you about it when I realized you dumped her."

"I didn't dump her." Keith said, sitting beside his brother. "I'm pretty sure that she dumped me and I'm not sure how this whole thing got so messed up. How does this fix my life?' Keith put his head in his hands, seemingly exhausted. "This makes it worse." Jack laughed again and slapped his brother's back.

"Own it little brother." He laughed. "Own it, embrace it. I'm assuming you are asking me because I have some expertise on the subject?" Keith looked at his brother and nodded. "Then use it!, it's perfect."

Keith looked at his brother perplexed. Jack just laughed louder. "I don't know what you are talking about." Keith said.

"It's not difficult." Jack said. "You do still love her don't you? Isn't that your problem? I wasn't sure until just now, but I'm right aren't I?"

Yes, Keith loved her. She was the first thing he thought of in the mornings and the last thing he thought of before he went to sleep. When he made love to another woman, he could only see Izzy's face. He couldn't keep any relationship going because none of them were Izzy. He loved her alright, but she was just a kid back then and he was sure she had moved on.

"Call her." Jack said and motioned with his head towards the phone on the wall. Keith could still visualize Izzy standing in that very spot, wearing her white nightgown. He closed his eyes and remembered the feel of her skin against his, the sound of her breath, he could still feel her heart racing as he held her against his chest.

He opened his eyes but didn't look at his brother. "Why would I call her?" He asked. "How could that possibly help anything? I'm going to get raked over the coals for this role and you're encouraging me to call Izzy. Have you forgotten her age? Have you listened to a word I've said?"" As he asked this, he turned to look at Jack, the last part of his sentence slowed and a look of revelation began to ebb on his face. "Okay, I'm beginning to see where you're going with this." He said.

Jack laughed again, a devious laugh. "Use it little brother. Three years ago you were the good Enidarrac, those unpleasant roles that you have taken since have moved you to my level. Take advice from an expert on negative press. You are going to get negative and positive publicity, you can't control it, but you can use it. Show them a love story, go get your girl, the timing is perfect and this time, don't hide it, flaunt it. Stop being a choir boy, be a black sheep, be a Enidarrac".

Keith let the words sink in. Jack could be so devious. Keith knew that Jack was correct, he was going to be slammed by both sides. Why not show everyone that it was possible, why not let everyone know love is love. He remembered Izzy saying that very thing to him while on the beach.

"Get dirty," Jack Smirked.

"Be like you". Keith mumbled.

"No, you'll never be like me Keith, I'm like the Anti-Keith, but you can let a little of the devil in. You can be happy, I'm telling you, the publicity alone will make the movie!"

Keith quietly thought it over, Jack was right, it would bring more people to the film, a younger audience too. The publicity could be amazing. It was a well done film. It was filmed on location in Ireland, and was about a lonely washed up alcoholic boxer who slowly fell in love with a young prostitute. Jack was right about him too. Keith was too careful at times, always overthinking, always trying to do the right thing. He lifted his face up from his hands and turned to look at Jack who was still smiling like a Cheshire cat.

"Jack, how can I call her? After all this time, she must hate me." Keith said.

"Maybe she does. Call her and find out." Jack looked slyly at his younger brother and motioned his head again towards the phone. Keith thought of all the tabloid pictures there had been of him with various women. The public break ups, the stories of broken hearts. How could he possibly call her? She was smart too, if he somehow managed to get her back, she would see what he was working on and see right through it. Jack seemed to know the doubts his brother was feeling and stopped smiling. He shifted on the sofa, leaning in a little closer to Keith. He picked the script up off the table and handed it to Keith.

"This is a testament to her feelings." He said. "It is about forgiveness, about growth of the human soul. This character in the book starts out angry, hurt in the worst way that a woman can be hurt, but she forgives because she loves him. Call her."

Keith stood up and went to the phone. The wall still bore the phone numbers Jack had written on it so many years ago. Keith smiled when he looked at it, remembering his messy haired little blonde and how she had matured over the years. He ran his fingers gently over the phone numbers on the wall and he took a deep breath and exhaled between his teeth. Lifting the phone off its cradle, he dialed the number for Ruth that was written on the wall but paused on the last digit.

"Be brave man." Jack whispered softly. Keith jumped, he hadn't even noticed that Jack had followed him to the phone.

"How often have the two of you been in contact?" Keith asked.

"Off and on." Jack smirked. Keith narrowed his eyes. Jack had led him to believe that he had cut ties with the family but the manuscript told him otherwise. "Finish dialing." He nudged.

Keith dialed the last number and took a deep breath. He closed his eyes as the phone rang. A woman answered, it was Ruth. A flood of emotion overtook him, but he managed to say hello.

"Ruth!" Keith said, trying to sound as cheerful as possible. It's Keith Enidarrac."

"Well hello Keith, how are you?" Her voice sounded so happy. He always liked Ruth, there had been times he had longed to have a mother just like her. She was friendly, eager to smile and very kind.

"I'm well, thank you for asking. I have a new movie coming out soon" Keith confirmed.

"Oh that's wonderful Keith." Ruth was saying. She was so genuine, so happy to hear he was doing well. Clearly Izzy had kept her word and never told her mother. A wave of guilt rushed through him, how could he have ever asked or expected Izzy to keep such a secret. It must have been so hard on her, god he was such a selfish man!

" I was wondering if I could speak with Izzy for a few moments?"

"Oh I'm so sorry Keith, Izzy isn't home, she is actually with one of her friends she met in California, he stopped by earlier today and they have been out ever since. I'm sure she will be sick because she missed your call." Ruth cooed.

Jack was watching his brother's face, he knew something was upsetting him. "A friend from California? " He asked, his voice cracked a bit.

"Yes, Braden? I guess he is a neighbor of Jacks?"

Keith went a little pale. "Yes, he is. Well Ruth, don't tell her I called, I wanted to surprise her, I'll try again another time. Yes yes, it was nice talking to you too."

"What?" Jack asked. Keith placed the phone back in the cradle. He turned around and rested his back against the wall.

"You knew didn't you?" Keith asked. "You gave him her address? Why would you do that? Braden? Why?"

Jack walked past his brother and pulled out a kitchen chair from the table. He eased into it, he bent one knee and brought his bare foot up to rest on the other leg. He leaned back a bit in the chair and said, "Well, I thought he was just going to write to her at first, but he told me he was going to visit her a few days ago. Took off on his bike, all that glorious hair blowing in the wind." Jack pretended to pick something off his toe, giving his brother a few minutes to process. "So, the question is little brother, do you love her enough to fight for her?"

Keith stood up from his stance against the wall and also pulled out a kitchen chair to sit on. He put one leg over the side and straddled it, his arms resting on the back of the chair while he faced his brother. The two sat silent for a few moments, then they both grinned. Jack got up and got out a phone book from a kitchen drawer. He looked up a number in the yellow pages then went to the phone and dialed. "Yes, I need to book a flight for two to Lincoln Nebraska, what is the earliest flight you have?"

13

"I've never been to Nebraska." Keith was saying to his brother as they boarded the 747. "It's flat isn't it?" Jack had been a few times back when he was working with Izzy. He and Ruth were very close. She treated Jack like a member of the family, he was always welcome. She didn't fuss over him, she never made him feel like a guest. Jack had told Keith that he was more comfortable there than he had ever felt anywhere else. He always came back clean, relaxed and happy, Keith had often been jealous of it.

"The air is clear, the sky is big, the grass is green." Jack laughed. He was excited to go, Keith could tell. Keith was terrified. He refused to let his brother know, he was an Enidarrac, he would hold himself high, he would not be afraid of a teenage girl. He could offer her an exciting life, they wouldn't be rich, but she could work in the industry if she chose to and they would never be bored. He was sure she could get a job writing for just about any television show on the air. Keith could offer her anything she wanted and she would surely remember how good the sex was. What did Braden have to offer? Braden could offer her fresh pot, a hippie lifestyle and a full head of hair. Big deal, he told himself. Keith was going to win this battle.

They boarded the plane and stuffed their bags in the overhead compartment. Neither of them had packed much, they barely had time to pack at all. Keith had run to his place and stuffed a few things into a small suitcase and then drove back to Jack's. Jack packed even less and was just going to stuff it all in a grocery sack, Keith talked him out of that. They left in a hurry and almost forgot the manuscript but remembered before he walked out the door. Jack started to squeeze into the seat but Keith took his arm.

"Hey, I want the window."

"You can have it on the way back," Jack winked.

"You're just going to fall asleep, let me have it, I've never seen Nebraska." Keith said.

"What are you, twelve?' Jack laughed then continued on into the seat. Keith rolled his eyes and sat beside his brother, the seats were dark blue and close together, Keith's knees touched the seat in front of him. Jack laughed again and said, "It's only four and a half hours, you'll be fine." Then in a move Keith was sure was designed just to irritate him, Jack stretched his legs under the seat in front of him and closed his eyes. The plane taxied out to the runway, lined up and then accelerated and in seconds Keith felt the wheels leave the ground. He leaned over Jack and looked out the tiny window until all he could see was the sky. Four hours, it was going to seem like ten, he felt like he was coming out of his skin. How were they going to pull this off? He turned to ask Jack but his brother was already fast asleep. How did he do that? The man didn't have a care in the world.

The flight was uneventful. The seatbelt sign stayed off the whole flight. Jack woke up long enough to drink a couple drinks. The flight attendants recognized Jack and flirted with him, no one seemed to recognize Keith or maybe they did and he had just grown used to it. There were some young boys a few rows down that kept leaning over and looking at Jack while he slept. The stewardess stopped by frequently, asking if Jack needed anything and Keith would have to answer for him that he was fine. The flight would get in at 8:25 pm, Keith and Jack both thought they should get a hotel room and then get Izzy the next day but Keith kept dreading waiting. It was Sunday he thought, Braden couldn't keep her out too late, Izzy had school tomorrow. God, School, what was he doing? He closed his eyes but only had thoughts of Catholic school girls in their little school uniforms. He opened his eyes and ran one hand through his hair. Maybe he was a pediphile? No, he wasn't, it was only Izzy, but did she want him? He felt an elbow jab his ribs and turned to see Jack awake and laughing at him again "Your face is betraying your thoughts little brother." Jack said.

"This is nuts, I can't believe you talked me into this." Keith whispered. "She hates me. Rightfully so. I've never even got a letter from her."

Jack reached inside his coat and handed him an envelope. "I forgot to give you this." He said. Then pressed the call button. The stewardess was there in seconds, smiling and flirting, Jack ordered another Scotch. Keith waited until she was gone then looked at the envelope. It was a letter and it was from Izzy and it had been opened. He furrowed his brows into a frown and looked accusingly at Jack. Jack just laughed again and swirled his ice cubes around in his drink, then drank it all.

"How long have you had this? You opened it." Keith said

"I got it a couple years ago. I'm your brother, I had to protect you." he laughed. Jack was clearly loving every minute of this, it was like he had orchestrated the whole thing. Keith opened the letter, it wasn't very long.

Hi Keith,

What a stupid way to start a letter. I hope you are well. I want you to know that I think of you all the time, I know, laughable right? I'm sorry I snuck out of the house, I just thought my heart would burst if I had to actually say goodbye to you. Upon reflection I realize sneaking out might have provoked you again, please know it wasn't my intent. I understand and agree we are doing the right thing. (please note the pronoun) I remember our conversation, the one about feeling trapped and all you wanted was to feel free. You told me as long as you had to do the right thing instead of what you wanted, that you would never really be free. I never wanted that. You know that stupid saying, the one that says if you love something to set it free, if it doesn't come back it was never really yours or some such garbage, well, I'm letting you be free. I hope your career is everything you want. Until we meet again,

Iz

"Why in the hell wouldn't you have given me this?" Keith whispered. His voice was angry but his words were softly spoken.

"You would have gone to her." Jack answered simply, then shrugged his shoulders. "The point is, she did write to you. Clearly she doesn't hate you either."

"You crossed a line Jack."

Jack laughed loudly, the scotch was getting to him. "Do you really want to talk about crossing lines?" Jack said loudly. People were starting to stare. Keith really didn't want a scene on board a 747 and he knew Jack was going to start talking about everything. Keith put his hand on his brother's knee. "No, I don't want to talk about it. Thank you for watching out for me." he closed his eyes, pretending to sleep. He could hear Jack rattle his ice cubes and he knew he was finishing the last of his drink. Even with his eyes closed, Keith was aware of everything, he could feel the plane dropping altitude then level off a little at a time, he felt it even before the seatbelt light came on. He could feel the pressure in the cabin change, he could feel the excitement of people around him. He took deep breaths and exhaled slowly. The intercom came on, it was the same stewardess that had been flirting with Jack the whole flight. "Ladies and gentlemen, the plane has started its gradual descent towards Lincoln Nebraska. We ask that you put your trays in the upright position and fasten your seat belts. We should be arriving on time in about fifteen minutes and hope you enjoyed your flight with United Airlines."

It was after ten by the time they got a couple rooms at the Cornhusker Hotel. Jack had insisted on a sports car for a rental, he had wanted a Ferrari but they didn't even have those to rent in Omaha. The rental company had brought two flashy cars up from Omaha for him to choose from, a Chevrolet Camaro or a Porsche 928. The Camaro was green and the Porsche was Silver, Jack didn't like either color and bickered for thirty minutes and then took another thirty to read and sign the paperwork. He settled on the Porsche, Keith was grateful they didn't pack much because there was no place they could have put luggage.

The time difference meant they were still wired, Keith went to his room and turned on the television, Jack went to the bar. Keith laid on the bed, and put both pillows under his head, the bed wasn't too hard which surprised him. The room felt stuffy, then the air conditioner switched on and it became instantly freezing. He got up and found the control and adjusted it. The bedspread was orange and brown, he wondered who had picked it out and if they had thought it was pretty. The room had textured wallpaper, similar to burlap on one wall, the others were painted a light tan. There were plenty of clean, fresh towels in the bathroom and on the dresser there was an ice bucket and several glasses wrapped up in cornhusker tissue paper. He picked up the menu by the bedside table, it said he could order room service until 11:30 pm. He thought he was hungry but looking at the menu made him queasy, he couldn't believe he was so nervous. There was an old black and white movie on the television, Fred Astaire was dancing, he made dancing look so easy. Keith laid back down and took out Izzy's letter and re-read it, it was so like her. It was kind, tender and well meaning and it pissed him off. He had been an ass, at the first test of love he had failed. He had let his anger control him and had ignored her just like he had so many times in the past. Maybe if she had written him an angry letter he would have felt better, forgiving him just made him feel all the more selfish. He fell asleep with Izzy's heart in his hand and Fred Astaire dancing in his head.

At 8:00 am the phone rang loudly, Keith almost fell off the bed. The television was still on and he was laying on top of the ugly orange and brown bedspread still in the clothes he had worn on the plane. He picked up the phone. "Hello?" He said, the voice on the other end told him the time and that this was his wake up call. He thanked the girl and hung up the phone.

Izzy's letter lay on the floor where he had dropped it after falling asleep. He leaned off the bed and picked it up, he read it one more time, still angry with Jack for not giving it to him. "What must she think of me, I never even wrote her back." He said out loud to the empty room. "I'm going to kill Jack." He said. "It won't solve anything, but I'll feel better,"

He sat on the bed and counted to five. "Let it go." He said through his teeth. He raised his butt off the bed and reached into his back pocket, pulling his wallet out. He had to fold the letter several times in order to get it to lay correctly inside, then he got off the bed, set the wallet on the nightstand and undressed. He folded his clothes, laid them on the ugly bedspread and walked into the bathroom. After unwrapping a bar of soap he turned the shower on and tested the water, when it was warm enough he stepped in and let the shower pour on his face then turned and let it pound on his neck and shoulders. After a few moments he took a washcloth and began to lather it up, remembering California, the morning after he had first made love to Izzy. He thought about the bathtub with the two of them in it. The thought made him become aroused and he quickly turned the water to cold. It helped a little, he turned and faced the shower, he put one arm forward, bracing himself against the shower wall and bowed his head under the water. He was drowning in thoughts of his future with Izzy and for the first time in a long time, let himself think of her as a woman and not a child.

He had to knock for five minutes on Jack's door before it opened. Jack did not fall asleep in his clothes, Jack was naked and unashamed to open the door that way. "Nice." Keith said as he pushed his way into Jack's room.

"I hate mornings." Jack mumbled. He went into the bathroom, filled the sink up with water and put his head in the sink. Keith shook his head then sat on the edge of the bed. Jack's bedspread was the same design but was blue and brown, it was equally ugly. Keith noticed the phone was off the hook and placed it back in the cradle. Jack came back into the room toweling his hair dry. He put some deodorant on, then smelled his shirt that he picked up off the floor where he had thrown it the night before. "Does this stink?" He asked, shoving the shirt towards Keith's nose.

"Jack just put on a clean shirt."

"Someone's in a hurry." Jack teased.

"How long were you in the bar?" Keith asked.

"They close down at 11: 00 pm here it was Sunday." He answered.

"You're kidding?" Keith seemed surprised

"You're in the bible belt now." Jack answered. "I raided the mini fridge." Jack confessed. He looked at the phone. "I think I fell asleep talking to Julie. Did you hang up on her?"

"What? She was on the phone?" Keith asked.

"We left without telling her, I try not to do that kind of thing anymore. I called her, we wanted to feel like we were together, we needed to hear each other breathe." Jack said softly.

Keith smiled, his brother was a lot of things, but when he loved someone, he really loved them. He hoped that his own future could be like that, he remembered laying next to Izzy, listening to her breathe, breathing with her, feeling like they shared a heartbeat. He loved his brother, for making so many sacrifices for him, for being with him now. He was a good man, imperfect, but good.

14

"So this is East High School. There aren't any windows! Now that is depressing." Jack said as he slowly drove the Porsche towards the front of the building. It was a large, modern red brick building, there were some windows but they were long straight windows that appeared to be only in the hallways. The only other glass they could see was the glass walkway in what appeared to be the front doors. There were three levels on the west side of the building that attached the rest of the school with a glass and brick corridor, the school stretched eastward housing classrooms and the gymnasium. The school sat in a large grassy park, the parking lot was set far away from the building to the south and was a shared parking lot with Seacrest Field, the highschool football stadium.

Jack followed the winding road up towards the windowless building. There was a small parking lot in front but it was full. "Must be the teacher's parking, huh?" Jack asked out loud. He pulled close to the front door and looked out the window on Keith's side of the car. "Oh my god that poor kid." He said. He put the car in reverse, backed up a few feet, then put it in gear and drove forward, up the curb and to the front door. The car left tire treads in the soft earth, he left the car partially on the sidewalk and partially in the grass and turned off the ignition. "Let's spring her." He said, wiggling his eyebrows at Keith.

"I don't think you can park here." Keith said as Jack got out of the car. "Jack!" Keith said again.

"What?" Jack asked.

"Look what you did to the grass!" Keith said, pointing at the tire marks in the soft earth.

"And your point is?" Jack asked his brother.

"You aren't supposed to park here." Keith answered.

"Sometimes you just have to be bold." Jack laughed.

"I think you should move it, I'm just saying." Keith retorted.

Jack ignored him and just walked inside and Keith silently followed him.

The school office was easy to find, it was just to the right of the main entry. Office staff were already headed towards the door, having seen Jack tear into the grass. Many students were in the glass breezeway that the main doors led into, staring dumbfounded at the Porsche parked hap-hazardly in front of the door. They stared open mouthed and a buzz of whispers resounded as Jack followed by Keith boldly entered the building. They were met with admonishment by a tall man with gray hair and glasses perched halfway down his nose as they entered the building, Jack greeted him with a broad smile, shaking his hand.

"Hello." He smiled. "Jack Enidarrac, loudly dropping his well known name so everyone could hear him."

The man hesitated as the name registered with him and he realized who the men were that were standing in front of him. Jack continued to shake his hand and smile with charisma that had served him well over his lifetime.

"Jeff Martin." The man was saying, clearly at a loss as to whether he should smile or reprimand. "School principal." He stammered using one finger to push his glasses back up to the bridge of his nose. Jack held his gaze and smiled even broader.

"I have heard great things about your school." He continued to charm. "Don't worry about the grass, I will see it is replaced. Forgive me Mr. Martin, or can I call you Jeff?" He continued. "This is my brother Keith, is there a place where we can speak privately?"

Mr. Martin nodded, he was certainly star struck. A crowd of students that had continued to grow in the breezeway was slowly moving closer to the three men. He motioned with his head towards the growing crowd of students to the woman who was standing beside him. She was a short woman, short brown hair with excessive highlights. She was dressed in a low cut, clingy teal dress that Keith found wholly inappropriate for a high school, Jack didn't seem to mind. Keith noticed immediately that Jack's eyes slowly moved over the woman's silhouette and silently he shook his head at his brother.

"Mrs. Pitchka, can you see these students find their way back to their class or study hall?' He asked, then didn't give the woman another thought. "Please come this way." He softly said to the Enidarrac brothers motioning towards office.

Mrs. Pitchka could be heard directing the students to leave in a very unpleasant voice. It was nasal in tone and had a child-like quality that sounded as if she was trying to sound younger than she was. It made Keith's skin crawl.

The front of the office was floor to ceiling glass, lined by shelves that displayed school trophies and photographs of athletes so that those passing the office could be impressed. The front desk was directly behind the window and a maze of desks were scattered behind it. Right in front was a large desk with a name plate that read Geraldine Pitchka. Keith noted to himself that she would be the woman who was largely in charge. To the right of the front desk were two offices. One was quite large, the other about half the size. The large office bore the name Mr. Martin on the door. Jeff opened the door and held it open as both Jack and Keith walked in. Jeff closed the door softly behind him, taking note that everyone in the office was loitering by the counter, staring as the three of them walked by. This was Jeff's fifteen minutes of fame, two movie stars at East High and in his office.

Jack waived Keith past him so that he would sit in the chair furthest from the door. The two sat down and Jeff sat behind his massive desk. Jack, taking in the decor, assessed that Jeff thought highly of himself, and his post. He grinned at the principal, commenting on how grand the school was and how well they had been doing in sports that year. Keith was astonished yet not surprised at his brother's knowledge. Jack did thorough research on every job he took on when acting, why would this have been any different. In a way, it made Keith feel completely inferior. Keith didn't know anything about the school Izzy had been attending, Jack seemed to know it all. Jeff and Jack were talking about the basketball team and how they had taken the state championship. Jack even seemed to know the players names.

"Your school was quite lucky to have Derek and Paul on the team." Jack said.

Then Jack moved on to the theater department. He knew the drama teacher's name, Dan Farling. He transitioned to how he would like to help in some way, possibly a donation and a conversation with Mr. Farling, he was hooking Jeff in. It was staggering how smooth his brother

could be. Jack could start a fight with anyone, he was stubborn and at times self indulgent, but he could also win anyone over. His charm was unstoppable, if he wanted something from someone, he got it. Jack had Mr. Martin in the palm of his hand.

"We will have to work something out." Jack was saying. "I would be very interested in working with you to build the program in whatever way you think would be best. You should talk with Mr. Farling and get his opinion."

"Yes, yes!" Jeff Martin stuttered. He was thinking of the headlines that would be in the local paper, Jack Enidarrac working with East High Theater Department, opening doors for East High Students. Jeff smiled deviously to himself, his fifteen minutes were suddenly expanding, his career was taking off.

"Well I'm sure you are wondering why we intruded in your school," Jack was saying. "There is a student here who I have worked with quite often. My brother and I need to speak with her. I believe her mother has probably called already to give permission for us to take her away for the rest of the day. I am so sorry to have disrupted your school and again I apologize for the lawn and assure you, I will have it repaired. It's just that it is urgent we see the girl right away."

"Which student is it?" Mr. Martin asked, He was intrigued, he wasn't aware that any of his students had ties to Hollywood, and he usually knew all the gossip because Mrs. Pitchka told him everything. She had a daughter of her own in the school, so Geraldine had a direct line of communication with the student body.

"Izzy Meeks." Jack answered. "We have been friends with the family for years."

"Really?" Mr Martin stated more than asked. "I wasn't aware of the relationship. Her mother taught kindergarten at Meadowlane elementary. I would think I would have heard something about it at board meetings. She must keep the friendship secret? "

"Ruth understands we like our privacy." Jack nodded.

"Izzy." Jeff murmured. "She is a beautiful young lady. Always quiet, even more so this year. I've always said that still waters run deep."

Jack stood up and opened the office door, Mrs. Pitchka almost fell in. There was a small crowd outside Jeff's door. Keith silently laughed and stood up, turning to shake Mr. Martin's hand. Jack had taken Geraldine by the arm to steady her, her face reddened a bit but neither Jack or Keith acknowledged they were aware of her eavesdropping. She giggled that obnoxious laugh and handed Jack a small piece of paper with a room number on it.

"She is in English class with Mr. Holojak, I'll take you there." She crooned. Jack glanced at the number and walked out into the hallway, there were signs pointing which direction to go with room numbers on the wall. He left suddenly before Mrs. Pitchka could stop him but Keith gently took the woman's arm.

"I would be happy for you to walk with me." Keith said softly. Looking at the woman made his skin crawl, but he was an actor and Jack had to get to Izzy first. Keith was grateful, he wasn't sure how Izzy would receive him, but he knew Jack could work his magic with her. Geraldine eagerly accepted the young actor's arm and willingly strolled down the hallway with him.

"Mr. Enidarrac." Mrs Pitchka crooned.

"You must call me Keith." He crooned back.

"I just love your movies." She said, "It must be such a glamorous life, my daughter Kerrie is a very talented actress herself, you should hear her singing voice."

"I hope I have the chance to." Keith smiled. The woman made him feel nauseous.

The school hallways were red brick and lined with tan lockers. There were a few students in the halls, he noticed that the young girls wore a lot of eye make-up, he had always hated that look. He supposed they thought that they believed it made them appear older. He remembered taking the mascara away from Izzy and wondered if she now caked it on. He hoped not.

Most of the girls in the hallway wore blue jeans, some girls had on dresses, the boys were all in jeans. There was a young couple by a locker, a tall boy with blonde curly hair, his arms around the girls waist. She was a cheerleader, a royal blue and white outfit, short skirt, white tennis shoes and no socks. Keith noticed she had full thighs, he thought about Izzy and her long slender legs, he wondered how much she might have changed since the last time he saw her. The cheerleader had auburn hair, a nice build and the blonde boy had his tongue halfway down her throat.

"Mr. Vergmin, I'm sure you can find a more appropriate place for your hands." Geraldine was saying to the couple. The two laughed and nodded, then closed the locker door. The cheerleader stared at Keith, she recognized him, he knew the look. As soon as they passed he could hear the two whispering. Geraldine heard it too and seemed thrilled, she held onto Keith's arm just a little tighter, clearly loving the secondary attention.

Keith wondered how Izzy would receive him. He slowed his pace a little more, stopping to ask Geraldine questions. "I can see you have a great relationship with the students in the school." He lied.

"Oh yes," She giggled. "My daughter is a senior here, so I get to know all the students. Kerrie, my daughter is such a kind girl, she is just friends with everyone here." She bragged. Keith stopped walking, grateful for a chance to slow down even more.

"You must be so proud." He said. "Does she know Izzy?"

"Of course she does!" She giggled. "Why, I believe they are good friends."

Keith could tell it was a lie. Something about her tone. "Izzy is such a quiet girl, not nearly as outgoing as most of the other girls in the class, Kerrie is so patient with her."

There it was, a tone of superiority, she was so condescending, Keith really wanted to peel her hand from his arm, but he smiled and let her continue.

"We were all so worried about poor Izzy this year, but she managed just fine. A lot of the time those quiet ones are so strong willed." She said,

Keith wasn't sure what the woman was talking about and he really didn't care, he was purposely dragging out his walk to the classroom and hoping he was providing Jack with enough time to prepare Izzy.

"Here it is." The woman was saying. Keith thanked the obnoxious woman and peered in the open door.

Jack had got to her English class quickly. He moved like a cat, silently, elegantly and with purpose.

Izzy hadn't been listening. She loved Holojak's English class, but her heart just wasn't in it today. He was in one of his moods, mocking the illiteracy of his students. Izzy was daydreaming, she was writing a new book in her head. Walking Charlie, it would be about a pet store manager being stalked by a lunatic, the hero would look like Keith, all her heroes did.

She began writing the new story in her head. Maybe this one would follow the same characters as her last book, just a different timeline. She smiled softly to herself, she had a lot of timelines to choose from.

She had been thinking of Keith even more than usual lately, she missed him. She had never stopped thinking of him but she tried to. Sometimes when she let her mind go blank, his colors would fill her thoughts. They seemed darker than they had been, she wondered if she really saw them when he was so far away or if she imagined it. She missed everything, she had finally felt like she belonged, then she went and screwed it up. Keith had never even bothered to write her back.

The classroom was awkwardly shaped, when you entered the room you were staring directly at a wall, the room went towards the right. Mr. Holojak had the room divided in two with an aisle in between that led to his desk and the chalkboard. On the outside wall, there were three rows of desks, they were all occupied by athletes who seemed to like to sit together, probably so they could cheat more easily on exams. The inside wall had five rows of desks. Izzy sat two rows back right in the middle. The other desks were occupied mainly by girls and a few young men who didn't belong with the jocks. There was one lone cheerleader in the front row. She spent most of her time flirting with Mr. Holojak and giggling when one of the athletes made a snide comment.

"Well miss Meeks?" Damn, Mr. Holojak caught her daydreaming again.

"I'm sorry, what was the question?" Izzy asked, refusing to be embarrassed. The jocks on the other side of the room snickered. Izzy let her eyes glance at the boys but then locked her eyes on her teacher.

"I asked if anyone knew who wrote the Rubaiyat and I'm sorry to say you must not know either" Her teacher said to her.

Izzy was pissed. Mr. Holojak knew Izzy didn't like being called on, she did her assignments, she was an A student, why was he trying to humiliate her? She reacted on instinct, doing something she would have never thought she would have done. Instead of shyly answering the question, she stood up and cleared her throat.

"Awake for morning in the bowl of night, has flung the stone that puts the stars to flight, and low the hunter of the east, has caught the sultan's turret in a noose of light. It's the Rubaiyat of Omar Khayyam, it's incorrect to call it the Rubaiyat. Because of that, it took me a few minutes to know what you were talking about." Izzy lied. She hadn't been paying attention and her teacher knew it. She quietly sat down, not being sure why she had done what she did, but secretly rejoiced in her behavior. The room erupted with applause from the jock side of the room. Mr. Holojak smiled and applauded too.

"You never let me down, Miss. Meeks." He smiled. Then there was more clapping from the doorway, everyone turned to look. Jack was leaning against the door frame, a slight smile on one corner of his mouth. It took a minute for Izzy to register who she saw, she almost fainted, then she leapt out of her desk unable to contain herself and ran to the door.

"Grasshopper!" She gleefully shouted and threw her arms around his neck, she put her hands on either side of his face and pulled his forehead down to touch hers. He laughed and hugged her tight. "What are you doing here?" She asked.

It had been nearly three years, she had thought at first, her heart would literally break. She had gone from telling Jack everything to suddenly having no one. At first his phone calls were painful, she wanted to hear Keith's voice but each call Jack would make an excuse as to why Keith wasn't there. She had finally asked Jack to please stop calling her.

As time passed, she realized more and more that Keith didn't want her in his life. She wrote to him once, but it went unanswered. She had become very depressed. She missed their summers together, she missed Jack's face and his sweet smile, she even missed his clutter and laundering his dirty white socks. She wasn't stupid, she had known that things would change after what had happened, she just hadn't been prepared for how much things would change. She had thought in a childish way that they could continue as they had in the past, and they would just keep the relationship with herself and Keith a secret. Of course as time progressed, she realized that would have been impossible, even if they managed to avoid each other, Izzy knew she wouldn't be able to hide the emotions on her face. Everyone would guess her feelings just by the way she looked at Keith. The only way to keep the secret was to stay apart, the situation was hopeless and Izzy had accepted that nothing would ever come of it.

The first time she saw Keith's picture in a Globe magazine with a beautiful woman on his arm, she felt sick. It broke her heart but she had no one to blame but herself. Almost instinctively, Jack had reached out to her. They had always been connected so she wasn't surprised. Enough time had passed that his calls no longer hurt, but she still asked that they communicate mostly via mail. He reluctantly agreed. He had given her something new to focus on. Instead of guessing the suit or color in her deck of cards game, he made her write stories for him. Jack had a way of forcing her to obey him, she never really understood why, but she could never say no to him. It was as if she felt like she owed him a great debt, some sort of self sacrifice. Whatever the reason, she didn't remember it, it had to have happened many many lives ago. All she knew was that she just loved him for it and could never refuse to do what he asked.

At first, it was just an occasional story, her heart wasn't in it. The heart wants what the heart wants and mailing Jack stories was a sorry substitute. After her accident, she had more time to think things through clearly. Her anger had prevented her from seeing all perspectives. Jack missed her too, by sending him her work she was letting him back into her life. He must have wanted that, or he wouldn't have pressured her like he had.

Jack squeezed Izzy tightly. God he had missed her so much. He knew she still loved his brother, she wouldn't even let Jack call her anymore, she was probably afraid that Keith would walk in and hear them. Jack knew that she would be angry, her Irish temper could be formidable. He needed to prepare her, let her know that Keith was here and that finally everything was going to be alright. He leaned forward and whispered in her ear. "I'm here to be the best man at my brother's wedding."

Izzy stepped back, she felt sick, she refused to cry, she just refused, but Keith was getting married? Jack realized too late what she thought and pulled her in quickly. "Use your head Iz, think, I'm here, I'm in your highschool."

Izzy stepped back and looked into Jack's eyes, her own eyes narrowed. He laughed, then pulled her close again. She inhaled, she loved the way he smelled of cigar smoke, cologne, a hint of incense. When she had spent her summers with him, she had always liked to do his laundry, just so she could bury her face in his clothes. At this moment, even his scent failed to soothe her. Her heart was beating so loudly she was sure everyone in the classroom could hear it. She was blushing, she buried her face in the front of Jack's shirt. She could feel all the eyes in the classroom on her and it made her blush even more, even Mr. Holojak had stopped talking. She was trying to make sense of what Jack had just said, as it sunk in, she became angry and her Irish temper began to flair.

Jack could read every thought on her face, she had lost her ability to hide her thoughts, too much time apart from him he guessed. He could feel her emotions through her body. He loved how well he knew her and he could feel what she was thinking. Her colors were turning red, he remembered the feel of the checker in his hands, there was no doubt, Izzies color was red. Izzy had taught him to feel a lot of things. He and Izzy just had a connection, he couldn't remember a time that he didn't understand her. He knew she was going into defense mode, he could feel her body stiffen and the color flush on her cheeks. It reminded him so much of when he had first met her. Her eyes narrowed and if they could, they would spit fire. He pulled her in tight and whispered gently against her neck,

"Don't make a scene, he's coming, I want you to talk to him.' He felt her muscles tighten even more and he gave her a quick squeeze. He stepped back, looked her in the eyes and raised his eyebrows, the smile was still at the corners of his mouth, but he was commanding her to do his bidding. He leaned forward and whispered in her ear, "Leave with us, don't give your friends any more to talk about then they already have"

It had been a long time since Jack told her what to do. She looked at his face and knew she was still powerless to disobey him. She loved that man with all her heart, but when she was out of earshot of her classmates, well she was going to give him a piece of her mind.

In the hallway Mrs. Pitchka was giggling and hanging on Keith's arm. She had stepped into the room with Keith a few minutes after

Jack. "Mr. Enidarrac, that was very naughty of you to sneak off to this room without approval." She drawled out in her nasal voice directing her comment to Jack. He had let go of Izzy and stepped towards her empty desk. Izzy was standing in the middle of the classroom alone, she felt very awkward and everyone was staring at her. "Izzy your mother wants you to leave with these gentlemen, you are excused for the rest of the day."

"Is this all you have?" Jack asked. He was holding a Dracula novel and one notebook with no notes on it. Izzy nodded. The classroom was no longer silent, the whispers sounded like the humming of a hundred bees on a hot summer day.

"I travel light." Izzy answered.

"I remember." He smiled. The sound of the whispering grew louder through-out all the class room, Jack and Keith pretended not to hear it, the two of them had enjoyed years of practice, but Izzy wanted to run far far away. Jack picked up her things from the desk and took care to get her purse that was hanging on the desk chair. Keith was in the room now, he took Izzy by the hand and pulled her close. She dug her feet into the floor but he still managed to pull her in. He hugged her with one arm, taking care not to embarrass her. He noticed a strong scent of sage and smiled, preparing for what he knew was to come. Mrs. Pitchka was standing in the doorway, her arm outstretched wiggling her fingers at the three of them in an attempt to hurry them along. As they left, the room erupted with talking.

"Dude, that was the Kung Fu guy." "Those were the Enidarracs!" "How the fuck does she know them?" "That was fucking Jack Enidarrac"

Keith put his hand on Izzy's shoulder and wasn't too surprised to feel it tighten and a slight attempt to shrug his hand away. He leaned down and said, "Your secret is out." Izzy shot him a look, he wasn't sure if it was a dangerous look, but he knew to not let his guard down. He kept a hold of her shoulder, instinctively knowing not to let go.

When they stepped out the front door, there was a crowd of students around the Porsche that Jack had hap-hazzardly parked on the grass near the sidewalk. "Nice parking." Izzy mumbled aloud. The crowd broke up a bit but there were a lot of whispers. Everyone was looking at Izzy, the Enidarracs, the Porsche, Izzy could feel the blush spreading up her cheeks, even her ears felt hot. "It's a two seater, you'll have to sit on Keith's lap." Jack smirked.

Izzy shook her head. "I don't think so, I drove, I'll just meet you at home." Izzy blurted out, planning on making a quick getaway. She tried to walk away from the crowd. But Keith held firmly on to her shoulder, applying just enough pressure so she knew that he wasn't letting her go anywhere.

"We will take you to your car." He said, instinctively he knew if he let her get away, she would drive the opposite direction. This was everything Izzy hated and she would never live this down. She probably hated him now if she didn't already. Jack got in the Porsche behind the wheel, Keith hung onto Izzy as he sat down, he pulled the lever and scooted his seat back as far as it could go, then pulled Izzy onto his lap. She hid her face from the onlooking crowd for just a minute, then stopped fighting it and smiled and waved at them all as Jack put the car in reverse and backed off the sidewalk.

"How do I get to the parking lot from here?' Jack asked.

"You have to drive down to that road and then take it back that way to Seacrest field." Izzy instructed him, pointing to a road to the west of them.

"Why can't I go back that way?" Jack asked, pointing east towards the Gym.

"It's one way." Izzy said, clearly frustrated.

"Bullshit. I'm just heading straight for it." Jack put the car in gear and went over the curb, into the field and across the grass.

Keith expected Izzy to be mad, but she giggled. She put her head out the window and screamed. Jack yelled out the other window and suddenly Keith felt like the only grown up in the room. They drove across the field and off another curb and into the parking lot. "Where are you parked?" Jack asked.

"Right there! Front row! Mine is the Gold Duster, Kent bought it for me!" Jack pulled up behind a 1972 Duster Plymouth. Keith had forgotten about her brothers. He wondered if Kent still lived in Lincoln, he wondered how big he was and if he would pummel him once he heard Izzy's story.

Izzy opened the door and stepped out, Keith got out too, this time holding firmly onto Izzy's hand. She tried to peel it off but he was too strong. He closed the car door and continued to hold on to Izzy's hand. Leaning in the window of Porsche he took from Jack Izzy's car keys which Jack had removed from her purse. Keith nodded and waved to Jack. Jack peeled out of the parking lot leaving a trail of white gravel dust behind him.

"What are you doing?" Izzy asked.

"I'm riding with you." Keith answered His face looked soft and kind, but his eyes looked stern. All she wanted to do was get in her car and drive far away, he must have sensed it and she could tell he was going to stop her.

"What the hell Keith?" She asked, surprised by her own tone. He moved in closer to her, she stepped back but bumped into her car door. He moved forward, lightly pinning her against the door. She was in blue jeans that were too long so she had rolled the ends in cuffs. She had on a plain white t-shirt, her hair was in a loose ponytail and of course her white tennis shoes. She was adorable, and shapely. He put his hands on the car on either side of Izzy's shoulders and leaned in so she was trapped. He bent down and kissed her forehead. She squirmed and tried to get away, he stepped a little closer. He could see her breathing faster, he knew she was feeling it too, he bent down and kissed the side of her head, she moved it away but not as adamantly as before. With his left hand, he took a hold of her shoulder and pulled her up closer to him, he kissed her neck and felt her gasp. She smelled like vanilla, or cinnamon and also of honeysuckle. He closed his eyes and inhaled and slowly kissed her neck again. He could feel himself getting hard and he could feel her succumbing to his touch. He kissed her neck one more time and this time she turned her face towards him, she put her hands on either side of his face drawing their lips closer together. This time she kissed him, her lips felt like butter against his, she kissed his lips again and again, he parted her lips with his tongue and she eagerly accepted, then she returned his kiss. He was surprised, she had learned a little. He suddenly thought of Braden and kissed her angrily and rougher.

"Meeks! You go girl!" Someone yelled as they walked past her car. She came to her senses and pushed him away. More students were headed towards the cars, it was early yet but many left campus on free periods or early lunch. Keith felt her stiffen as the crowd called her name and walked past, he knew the moment was gone.

"Let me drive somewhere quiet where we can have a talk," he said. Izzy looked down at the gravel parking lot and her white shoes. She paused for a few moments, gathering her thoughts..

"No." She answered firmly. "It's my car. My brother Kent bought it for me. Only I drive it."

He smiled softly at her. He tried to do the math, was she eighteen, nineteen? Giving her the car keys could be a mistake, she was still angry. He knew if he did she would probably peel out of the parking lot and leave him behind. He was keeping control, there was not a chance in hell that he would hand her the keys.

"Not going to happen." He said.

"Because I'm a girl?" Izzy asked, prepared to argue over male gender bias.

"I have no issue with a woman driving me anywhere." He said. "I just don't think I should trust an angry woman. I'll let you drive, but I'll hang on to the keys until we are both in the car."

He opened her unlocked car door for her and then went to the otherside of the car climbing in beside her. Once inside he fastened his seatbelt and then handed the keys to Izzy. She snatched the keys from his open palm rather angrily and then she turned on the ignition. She took a couple breaths, then headed out of the parking lot. She turned east down A street and drove straight until it became a gravel road. Keith was amazed how quickly the scenery changed from city to corn fields. She drove a mile or so down the road then turned on another and then another. Keith had a good sense of direction but he was completely lost in this countryside. No wonder why Stephen King thought Nebraska was terrifying. A short while later Izzy pulled into a field and drove behind a small glade of trees. It was completely hidden from any road. "How did you find this place?" Keith asked, amazed at the solitude.

"It's a good place to hide and drink." Izzy shrugged. "Cops can never find it. Plus it is for seniors only. Now talk." She demanded.

He had almost forgotten how direct she was, no beating around the bush. He liked that, she didn't play games or make anyone guess. He should have known when she let Braden take her to LAX, that she had done so for a good reason. He should have known he told himself.

"Want to get out, walk a bit?" He asked.

"We can." She answered simply. "Where we talk won't change anything."

Keith understood her meaning but he wasn't taking no for an answer. He got out of the car and walked to her side. He opened her door for her and she stepped out. She had changed a bit, she was still lean but had fuller curves. Her hair was shorter and only came to about her mid back.

When everything had come to a head three summers ago, Izzy was angry. She was mad at Keith of course, but she was mostly mad at herself. She had locked herself in the bathroom one evening with her mother's scissors and cut her hair. She had cut it fairly short, it was level with the bottom of her ears. It made her feel good, it was as if she was severing all ties with the person she had been before, the person she was angry with. It had grown out quite a bit since then, but she refused to let it get long again. Keeping it shorter made her feel lighter, she told herself it was like losing the weight of the ill fated secret.

Keith had always liked her long hair, there was something sensual about it. He noticed the length and wondered why she had cut it but he was still impressed with her simple beauty. She had grown her bangs out, they hit about ear length now and framed her face. He was curious what it would look like loose instead of in the ponytail. She was pale, but he thought it was due to the moment and suspected her face would warm up a bit once they spoke. She was a little taller now, he noticed how well she fit when he had pulled her close to him earlier. He wanted to take her hand but he thought this time he should go a little slower. She had fought him in the parking lot, he didn't want to force her, he wanted her to want him.

She led him down a path and to a little brook. There were some rustic benches there that someone had nailed together from some cut firewood. There was a fire pit and a few empty beer cans laying nearby in the dirt. Izzy picked up a stick and sat on one of the benches. She took the stick and began drawing in the dirt. It reminded Keith of the first time he met her, she had drawn on Dorothy's notepad, he realized now she did it to avoid eye contact and fight nerves. Keith moved closer to see what she was writing but she took the stick and scribbled it out with the loose earth around her. "Talk." she commanded again.

Keith sat on the bench across from her, he leaned forward, his forearms on his legs, his hands folded in front of him. He made sure to look her in the eyes, he had one chance at this and he realized he wanted it more than he had ever wanted anything. He looked into her dark blue eyes, she was wearing eyeliner and probably mascara, it annoyed him a bit. She had beautiful eyes and didn't need to embellish or enhance them, but compared to the other girls he had seen in the school, she was barely made up. He never moved his gaze from her eyes, he told her straight up, there was a movie, he was already catching negative publicity because it was controversial. It involved prostitution and his character falling in love with an underage girl. He told her the complete story, including how Jack had said the publicity he would gain from a real marriage to Izzy would drive movie ticket sales and help his career. He told her his career was floundering, he needed a hit. He didn't hold back, she deserved to know the whole truth. When he finished, he continued to look into her eyes, he wanted to coax her to speak, but he held his words and waited, he could see her working every scenario through. Her face was transparent, she was easy to read, but he liked that. She was struggling, but she was considering everything that he had told her.

"So let me understand, just to be clear." She finally said out loud, Her eyes were fixed on his deep brown irises but she refused to get lost in them. "You couldn't stay with me, because of your career. Now, you need me because it would be advantageous to your career. Is that what you are saying?"

"Yes." He flatly stated. "And no. We both know it isn't that simple. I know you are mad, and rightly so....."

"I'm not angry with you Keith." She lied, then stood up and paced around the wooden bench. "I'm not angry at all. I barely think about you." She lied again.

Keith stood up and approached her, she backed away. He wasn't going to weasel his way back into her life. She had let her guard down in the parking lot, but she wasn't doing it again.

"You seem angry." Keith smiled. He had seen her like this once before, her temper completely loose. He remembered it didn't last long, a red Irish storm that passed quickly, but he was still cautious. The last time her temper flared, he had Jack there. Jack had a way with her, an ability to see through her and an ability to listen to her, he knew what she felt without her saying it. Keith hoped that he could learn to be more like Jack.

Izzy stepped to the other side of the bench, putting it between the two of them "I've never stopped wanting you," He said softly, He knew it wasn't the type of proposal a young girl would dream of, but he had to explain everything to her. She had to know it all or there would never be trust between them.

" God I was so mad at you. I woke up in the morning and reached for you but you were gone. Jack and I panicked. Braden came over and told me that he had taken you to the airport. Braden!" Keith kept his voice soft, but it was a bit raspy as he grappled with the emotions that he thought he had left behind him. He could see that Izzy's face had begun to soften, she always hated hurting anyone.

"Not even a note was left for me." He continued. His voice became a little more hoarse. "Jack and I must have gone 90 miles an hour racing to the airport. I've never run as fast as I did when I ran to that terminal. I watched your plane take off and felt empty, I don't know how else to describe it. You always speak of a person's colors, I can tell you that at that moment I didn't have any, I had nothing. You had left me colorless."

Izzy tried not to let his words convince her. He was an actor, he was a talented actor.

"I need you to understand what you would be getting into. I started taking these awful roles because I hated myself, I didn't want to be anything but despicable. What I have discovered is I like these types of roles, I like to be challenged artistically. I guess I'm trying to prove to myself that I'm a good actor. This won't be the last time there is controversy, and you know very well what my life is like, sometimes I'm riding high and sometimes I starve. It's not glamorous, I live like everyone else in the world. I want my wife to know what she is in for."

"Wife?" Izzy asked incredulously. "Wife, are you not hearing me? I don't even think about you!" She stuttered. She knew now that she had hurt him, it was something that she hadn't considered before, but it didn't make up for him completely ignoring her for nearly three years.

"Not angry? You sound pretty angry." He reached over the bench and snatched her hand so she couldn't get away and stepped around the bench to her side of it.

Izzy made a growling sound. "I'm not angry! I just hate you." She blurted out. She knew it was childish but she didn't care. She kicked the wooden bench in front of her, it made her wince. "God damn it!' She said, Keith immediately let go of her hand and spun her to face him.

"Are you okay?" He asked, clearly concerned.

If she hadn't been so mad she might have calmed down. His tone reminded her of how he had tried to protect her so many times, the pawn shop, Jack's open door, Braden and of course the beach. She heard it again in his voice and wanted to give in, but her pride wouldn't let her give in so easily. "I'm fine." she said cursley, barely opening her mouth. She wanted to believe his story but she had written to him and he hadn't answered.

"Why are you rubbing your hip for god's sake? Shouldn't your foot be what hurts?" Keith asked.

Izzy straightened up, she limped just a little but walked it out. She was hiding something, Keith was sure of it. Maybe she and

Braden were together now. Maybe she really did hate him. He let his thoughts go back to the kiss in the parking lot and tried to chase the thoughts of Braden out of his head.

"I know that you don't hate me." He said.

"And how would you know that?" She whispered to him. "I haven't spoken to you in nearly three years. How could you possibly know anything about me or know what I feel?"

"For one thing," Keith said, "I'm getting waves of honeysuckle along with the sage scent." He laughed.

"It reacts to heat." Izzy said tersely. "It's hot out here."

Keith took both her hands and stood in front of her. She wouldn't look at him, but her voice was softer now.

"I shouldn't have been angry." He said softly to her. She still refused to look up. "It was more than that. I wanted to protect you. You saw what happened at your school just now, can you even imagine what it would have been like for you at sixteen?" Izzy slowly raised her chin up and looked into his eyes. He had hoped to see the kindness he knew she had in her, but her eyes were still angry. " You say you've not thought of me in years? Well guess what? You are all that I think of, I can't get your image out of my mind. Your eyes, your hair, your scent, your kindness and even that god awful sense of humor. I know you don't hate me, I know it. You aren't the kind of person that changes her feelings."

"I was abandoned.' She stated simply.

She was breaking his heart, she was right, they had welcomed her into the Enidarrac clan, and then just closed the door and shut her out. He had thought it would be easier for her, but now in hindsight, he knew it had been wrong. Izzy was so sensitive, probably why she could do her little trick, how she could know card colors and sense what other people were thinking. He felt her grip soften and he looked into her eyes, there were tears, but they weren't falling yet. In all the years he had known her, he had only seen her cry one time.

That was his way in, she knew what he was feeling, He just had to get her to let herself feel. Relief ran through his entire body, he pulled her closer to him. "So help me God Iz, I thought it would be less painful for you that way. I was robbed of a happy childhood, I couldn't take a happy childhood from you."

Izzy continued to return his gaze. "Say it." She said "I need to hear you say it."

"I'm sorry." He said. "I am truly sorry. I want to marry you again, legally, in front of your mother." He said simply. "Is that what you want to hear?"

Izzy didn't move for several minutes, she returned his gaze but with no indication of her answer, not one tell. He shifted his weight but kept his eyes on her face.

Izzy let herself into his head. She had been so angry, so hurt that even in the school parking lot she could only feel her own colors. Holding his hands now calmed her. She took a deep breath and could smell an ocean breeze. She could see him in her mind's eye, thigh deep in the waves, terrified for her safety. She could feel his colors leaving his fingertips and entering her soul. She had let herself be colorblind, she was like a cat. They both had been in pain but she could only recognize her own. Red and green, his or hers, she had to see it all in order to grow. She played back what he had said to her over and over in her head. He hadn't told her that he loved her. She had asked him to, but he hadn't said it. She closed her eyes tighter, reaching inward and outward. The red and the green were the same, she loved him so she knew he loved her. She placed her hands on either side of his face and pulled it towards her. She kissed him, lightly then put her forehead against his just as she had always done with Jack. She let go of his face, turning as she walked towards the stream.

Keith had sensed the change in her, he was relieved but not jumping to conclusions. Izzy was complicated, she was never black and white. He watched as she walked away and noticed she limped a bit. He was beginning to get worried about her foot, he hoped she hadn't broken a toe, she had kicked that bench hard. He had kissed a lot of women in his time, he wasn't sure what this one tasted like, was it a yes? Was it a goodbye? He honestly wasn't sure.

Keith sat down on the bench, giving her space to work through her emotions. He kept watching her as she approached the brook that was nestled in the trees. It was shady where she stood under the cluster of river-birch that had grown around the little stream. Sunlight still broke through the branches and he could see the streaks of red in her hair, reminding him of her Irish temper and cautioning him to choose his words and actions carefully. She picked up another stick and wrote in the dry dirt with it. It was so different here than the lush watered lawn of the school. He took a deep breath, the air was hot, Nebraska was hot.

The sun was beating on his neck. Something in the air was making him feel congested and a wasp of some sort was making circles around his bench. He wasn't sure he liked Nebraska, he wasn't sure at all. Izzy wasn't moving, she continued to stand frozen in front of the brook. The sun was straight above his head, burning his scalp, he figured it was around noon, only Izzy was in the shade and he really wanted to go somewhere with air conditioning. Finally he stood up, he followed Izzy to the brook. She heard him coming and dropped the stick but didn't turn to face him. Keith bent down to pick up the stick that Izzy had tossed to her side, then he saw what she had written in the dirt, it was one word. A slow smile grew on his face, suddenly the air seemed lighter and the sun less hot. He came up behind her and wrapped his arms around her, he kissed the side of her neck and she reached behind her and put her hand on the side of his face.

"Come on." He whispered. Slowly she turned to face him and he held her against his chest for a moment, then took her hand and led her towards the car being careful to step over the word "probably" that she had written in the dirt.

She stopped briefly at the car, without looking at him she said, "If I do, I'm keeping my cat" Keith let out a loud laugh, then leaned in and kissed her hard on the mouth. "I mean it." She said, "I know you don't like cats."

"I like cats." Keith said softly. "I don't like Jerome. He has been mad at me ever since you left. He blames me, you know."

"Smart cat." Izzy said, she paused at the car door, then turned to Keith with a troubled look on her face. "Where did Jack go?" She asked.

"He went to meet your mother." Keith responded.

"He's telling her?" She asked.

"We thought maybe it would be best, let him soften her up." Keith answered. "For some unknown reason, your mother likes Jack." Keith laughed. Izzy began to pace back and forth.

"He's telling my mother, oh God!'

"Izzy, it's alright, we are going to be married for real. You're a grown woman now."

"She's going to hate me." She groaned. "And I didn't say yes, I said maybe."

"She won't hate you." Keith said. "And you didn't say maybe, you said probably."

"I lied to her, oh God." Izzy fell forward on the hood of the car and covered her face with her hands. Keith wiped the sweat off his face, his back was wet, his deodorant had failed, he really wanted out of the hot Nebraska sun.

"Come on," He whispered, leaning towards her ear. "She will be alright."

Izzy laughed. "You don't really know my mother. How can I face her? Oh God, what am I doing, what am I feeling? I don't know what to do. I've already put her through so much!"

Keith moved closer, he gently moved her ponytail to one side and sweetly kissed her neck. "Everything is going to be alright." He promised her.

She rolled her head sideways and accepted the kiss, her shoulders stopped shaking and she took a deep breath. Keith gently ran his fingers down her side, strumming her ribs like the strings of his guitar. He let his hand continue downward and rested his grip on her hip, then he leaned in and kissed her neck again, more eagerly this time. He felt Izzy succumbing to his touch. She was giving in completely to her desires, no thoughts, just pure emotion, just as she had in California. He gave in too, he reached around in front of her and unfastened her jeans while continuing to kiss her neck. She sucked in a gasp but didn't fight him. He eagerly tugged her jeans downward towards her knees, then unfastened his own pants and pulled them down. Driving her forward against the hood of her car, he took her, she bent forward, leaning over the car and made a soft noise. Keith didn't last long, he couldn't believe what he had just done and smiled to himself as he realized he always seemed to lose complete control of himself when he was with izzy. He knew in his heart that all these years, she had been right, they were meant to be together. He wanted nothing else.

Izzy continued to lay across the hood of the car for a few moments. Then she inhaled deeply and without turning around, pulled her pants back up and fastened them. Keith was fastening his own pants when she turned around to face him. "I can't believe we just did that." She laughed.

"I'm a little surprised by it myself," Keith answered. "But I have to admit it was like coming home."

"God, home." Izzy said. She let herself fall backwards this time against the car and looked down at her white shoes.

"I can't wait to see your mother again." Keith teased. Izzy looked up from her shoes and turned her gaze towards Keith.

"I'm personally terrified for both of us." Izzy said. Keith smiled and brought her chin up with his hand and then bent down and kissed her.

"Do I have an answer yet?" He asked. Izzy shrugged. "Are you leaning towards yes, can you give me a breadcrumb?" Keith smiled and asked.

"I thought I just did." Izzy laughed. "I need some time though, not to sound corny, but this is all very sudden." She laughed again.

Keith nodded and smiled and then opened the passenger door for Izzy. "I'll drive," he said to her. "I'm worried about your foot, you're limping a bit."

Izzy nodded and got in the car, Keith walked to the other side and climbed in. He started the car then reached for the air conditioning switch. Izzy stopped him. "It's broken." She told him.

Keith wiped his face with the sleeve of his shirt. He was wearing a long sleeved gray and white striped button shirt. He unbuttoned the cuffs and rolled up the sleeves, then took hold of the front of the shirt, tenting it and shaking the fabric, trying to air his sweaty chest.

"You should roll the sleeves a bit higher." Izzy smirked. "You've got to look like a farmer."

"Just tell me how to get out of here before I melt" He commanded. The temperature inside the car was at least twenty degrees higher than it had been outside. Keith rolled down his window with the hand crank, Izzy did the same.

Izzy guided him out of the field and onto the road. "Go slow." She commanded. He drove down the sweltering dirt road and then another, dust from the road flew in the open window and he could feel it sticking to his sweaty face. The car fishtailed once and Izzy reminded him to slow down. "You've got to be careful on dirt roads if you don't know what you're doing." She chided softly.

It wasn't long before they were back on the paved road. They drove past the highschool, cars were pulling out of the parking lot causing a bit of a traffic jam. Keith pulled up behind them and waited patiently. "Must be lunch time." Izzy commented. "Let's get something to eat."

"I could use a cold drink." Keith agreed, his face was still glistening from the sweat and he looked like he might pass out. Izzy smiled. After moving past the school, Izzy directed Keith towards a drive-thru of a local Dairy Queen. She asked Keith to order her a dish of vanilla ice-cream. He ordered a large iced tea. They pulled into the parking lot and he turned off the car. He managed to park under a large Elm tree so that they were in the shade. Izzy slowly took spoonfuls of Vanilla ice cream and licked it off the spoon. Keith knew it was deliberate, but it still drove him crazy. He took some long sips of his tea from the red straw and smiled as Izzy continued to tease him.

"Still prefer plain vanilla?" He asked. He remembered the time they had spent on the beach, she beguiled him then and she beguiled him now, he could tell she was still angry, but at least they were talking and she was no longer trying to get away.

"Vanilla is the best." She stated simply, "I just wish they had Hersey's syrup." She held the spoon in front of her mouth vertically and licked it off. "You look hot. Is the tea helping?" She asked, batting her eyes at him.

"A bit." He answered. "I know you are stalling, but we better head towards your mom's now." Keith said. He started the car and backed out of the parking spot, leaving the respite of the shade. "Which way?" He asked.

Izzy pointed and Keith obliged. When he pulled into the street Izzy rolled up her window and leaned forward and turned on the air conditioner. Keith took his eyes off the road and glared at her. She just smiled and aimed a vent at her face.

"Broken huh?" Keith asked. Izzy just smiled and looked out the window. "Not mad huh?" Keith asked, not expecting a reply.

15

When Jack met Ruth at the house, she had run down the driveway to meet him. Ruth threw her arms around him and hugged him tightly. Jack loved Ruth for so many reasons. She had taken him on like a son, he was always welcome in her home. She had been kind to each of his girlfriends he had introduced her to and never judged him. She laughed at his jokes, loved to hear him sing and most of all, she never let go first. Hugging Ruth made Jack feel like he belonged to her family, he loved that.

"Jack, where have you been? My god it has been so long! I have so missed your face!' she said and then kissed his cheek. "Why have you been such a stranger?"

Jack held her hands and kissed her back on the cheek. "My visit is long overdue." He said. He let go of her hands and looked towards the house. Ruth stood beside him, looking at his face. "Why do I have a feeling you don't have good news? Where is my daughter and where is Keith?"

Jack didn't answer or look at Ruth. She nodded to herself. "Why don't we go sit by the pool." Ruth said.

"Would you mind if I pulled the car into the garage? Jack asked.

"Of course not. Pull it in, I'll be waiting out back." Ruth said, she squeezed Jack's hand and then strolled up the drive and disappeared around the side of the house. Jack got back in the car and pulled it into the garage. He was grateful it was the middle of the day, no neighbors had witnessed his arrival and he needed privacy. After turning off the ignition and exiting the car, he left the garage and walked around the side of the house. There were climbing roses on a trellis that stood next to the garbage cans. They were covered with dark red blooms. There was a concrete sidewalk that led to the back patio, he found Ruth waiting there on the cedar lounge chair with the sun flower cushion. Jack pulled up a matching chair and sat sideways on it, his arms on his legs, his hands folded.

"What did Izzy tell you about her last visit with me?" Jack asked.

"Izzy wouldn't speak of it to tell you the truth Jack." Ruth reached for a pack of cigarettes on the table beside her chair. She took one out, lit it and inhaled deeply. Jack motioned to her, she handed him the cigarette and he also took a drag, then he handed it back to Ruth.

"I wish it was something stronger." Jack said. "You've switched to filtered tips."

Ruth smiled. "Not in my house Jack." He nodded and knew she was not speaking of cigarettes. She gave him a stern look and then she offered the cigarette back which he accepted and took another deep drag. "So tell me what is going on." Ruth said. "I knew something had happened. She came back different. I asked her for months what had happened, she insisted it was nothing."

"It was something." Jack replied. He handed the cigarette back to Ruth. "You aren't going to like it."

"I'm pretty sure I already don't." She answered.

"Let's talk about Izzy." He began. "You are aware of her differences." Jack watched Ruth closely. She nodded. Jack continued. "You know that first day, I knew she was special." He smiled, picturing the memory of the little blonde girl climbing all over him. "Did she ever tell you why she wanted to meet us?"

Ruth shook her head. "Even then Izzy kept things to herself."

Jack shifted uncomfortably in his chair. He looked around the yard, it was beautiful. Flowers were blooming everywhere, the grass had just been mowed and the pool was an inviting blue in the afternoon heat. He held his head up and looked directly into his old friend's eyes.

"She has an unusual gift, Ruth." He said.

"Yes." Ruth agreed. "She is my little psychic."

Jack inhaled another drag then handed the cigarette back to Ruth. "She is a little psychic." Jack agreed, "But there is more to it than that."

"I'm listening." Ruth said, stubbing the cigarette out in the ashtray on the table beside the lounge chair. "Will I need another?" She asked picking up the package beside the ashtray.

"You might." Jack said. "She believes, and I do too, that we live many times. She carries some of those memories with her." He let it sink in. Ruth pulled out a new cigarette from the pack and lit it, but didn't interrupt. "The truth is Ruth, Izzy believes time isn't linear, it is circular, so it repeats. The letter that she sent to Keith was a correction to Keith's Oscar song."

"A song he hadn't written yet?" Ruth asked incredulously.

"That's the thing Ruth, he had written it. Izzy told him that last time, Keith wanted to make sure she gave him the correction."

"Last time? What are you talking about Jack."

Jack paused. It was a bizarre story, hearing himself say it out loud, he knew it sounded nuts. "Izzy believes she has lived this life before. It's never exact, but some things remain the same. Izzy remembered his song, she wrote it down and corrected it. Ruth, she said she and Keith were married, they had a beautiful life."

Ruth put her cigarette out in the ashtray on the side table, leaving the half smoked cigarette next to the butt of the other. Her auburn hair was almost silver now, her face was worn. She had aged a lot in the past few years, Jack wondered why.

"I know she knows things. She knows them before they happen. It used to scare the crap out of me Jack." Ruth sat up taking another cigarette from the pack of PallMalls on the table. It was a nervous habit, it would probably be snubbed out after one or two drags just like the other. "But living the same life over and over? That is what she believes?"

"Something like that. She believes we learn and grow, we become better." He said.

"Okay," Ruth said. "I know she has never been traditional. Are you going to tell me about what changed her and why it matters that she thought she had been married to Keith?"

This time Jack laid back on his chair. He looked at the sky and admired how blue it was. "The sky doesn't look like that in California." He said.

Ruth lit the third cigarette. "I'm waiting Jack." Ruth said sternly.

"From the time I first met your daughter, she revealed more and more to me. The one constant was how much she loved my brother. I guess I was so used to it, I didn't see that she was growing up in front of me." He rolled over on his side and met Ruth's worried gaze. "It's my fault, " he said. "I should have seen, I shouldn't have left them alone."

Ruth began to see what Jack was talking about. Her face seemed stoic, her eyes narrowed. "I hope to God you aren't saying what I think you are saying, she was fifteen!" She blurted out.

"Sixteen." Jack corrected.

Ruth looked up at the sky and made a guttural sound. "What in the hell is wrong with your brother?" She whispered.

"Here is the thing Ruth. They were both so happy. I came home and they were like one person. Izzy was outgoing and giggly and Keith, well I've never seen him so content. Keith has never been what I would call happy. Life has always been a business to him, he enjoyed some of it but he was always focused on what was next. When I realized what had happened, well I reminded them both of the consequences. The scandal might have ruined Keith's career and Izzy's life, at least that was what I thought then."

"So your brother used her and tossed her aside? No wonder she acted the way she did. Where is he Jack? I'm going to kill him. I still have my husband's guns!"

"Then I should tell you the rest before you have a chance to load them." Jack said.

"My God, what more could there be?" Ruth pleaded with her friend.

"First, I feel I should tell you that Keith didn't use her. That boy loved her, he still does. We wanted Izzy to have a normal childhood, that wouldn't happen if she was with Keith. I'm just going to say it, I don't know how else to do it, Ruth, I drove them to Tijuana and made them get married."

"You what?" Ruth stood up. She was livid and Jack suddenly felt very small. He sat up, Ruth was pacing around the chair. He stood up and took hold of her by the shoulders.

"I want you to listen." He said. "I was worried, what if she had been pregnant, they were so in love, they hadn't used any precautions, they just, well I took it upon myself to try to cover their actions, then I put her on a plane and sent her home."

Ruth sat down shaking her head. "That explains so much, my poor baby. I knew she was in pain and she couldn't even talk to me. My God, I'm her mother and she couldn't talk to me. I am so mad at you Jack Enidarrac."

A white cloud passed over the sun sending shadows across the patio, a bluejay was shrieking in the crabapple tree, Ruth wiped an angry tear from her cheek. Jack wasn't sure how to continue, he loved that woman, she was so kind to him, she made him feel like part of her family. He had to continue if the plan was going to work.

"I should have told you." Jack confessed. "I should have handled a lot of things differently. I am so sorry Ruth. I usually ask you for advice in situations like this, but I couldn't ask you this time. The point is, Keith is back, he wants to marry her for real this time and if it causes a scandal it won't matter."

"It won't matter for Keith." Ruth declared, "But it will hurt my daughter."

"No Ruth, it won't." Jack continued. "It's perfect timing, she is about to graduate and she can leave all the highschool gossip behind."

"A girl only has one reputation." Ruth stated.

"No one needs to know about the previous marriage, the gossip will be about Izzy marrying a movie star right after highschool." Jack said, trying to reassure her.

"Married to a man eleven years her senior." Ruth said. "I suppose that isn't a bad thing, Terry also married an older man. Explain to me why the scandal now won't hurt your brother but it would have three years ago." Ruth commanded.

Jack nodded, choosing his words as carefully as he could.

"First, I want you to know that this was my suggestion. I don't want you thinking he has ulterior motives." Ruth acknowledged with a nod of her head. "Three years ago, the only reputation Keith had was that of a clean cut upcoming star. That star has dimmed, he did it himself, on purpose, taking darker roles in darker movies. Keith is now doing a movie, his character marries an underage prostitute. It's a story of a lonely man with some problems in Ireland. The story doesn't matter but he is going to catch a lot of flack regarding the underage girl."

"Rightfully so." Ruth said without blinking.

Jack nodded.

"Ruth, he has been miserable without her. He has tried some other relationships but they never go anywhere. He let your daughter into his heart and has never let her out. I told him now was the time, time to go get her. He could use the marriage as publicity, it will probably help at the box office and everyone loves a love story. We will have to figure out a cover story, no one needs to know the whole thing, but the point is Keith still loves her and I suspect that Izzy feels the same." Jack waited, remembering what Ruth had said about how Izzy had changed. "Am I wrong? You said she has changed?"

Ruth sat back on the lounge chair and Jack sat across from her. She nodded. "When she first came back, she just seemed sad. Now of course it makes sense. Later, she just got reckless. She started hanging out with kids I didn't like. Potheads, drinkers. She cut off her hair and stayed out late at night, she was angry. She argued with me all the time. I thought Terry was a handful, but lord this little girl, so stubborn, I couldn't control her at all."

"Izzy?" Jack asked incredulously.

"Yes, Izzy." Ruth confirmed. "Then about a year ago she had her accident."

"Wait, accident? What accident?" Jack asked.

"She insisted I didn't tell you and since the two of you were different, less close, well I reluctantly agreed." Ruth said. "I guess we both kept secrets from one another."

"Tell me now." Jack softly commanded.

"She was going out with some of her friends. We had fought, I told her she couldn't go, but she just laughed and said nothing mattered and stormed out of the house. I saw her get in the car and it took off. It was about one thirty in the morning when the call came."

"Car wreck?" Jack asked. Ruth nodded. "Tell me everything." Jack asked again.

16

When Keith and Izzy pulled up to the house an hour later, Jack and Ruth were outside admiring the roses in front of the house. They pulled up on the driveway, parking behind her mother's car that was inside the garage the Porsche Jack had insisted on renting was parked next to it.

Keith assessed the house that he was seeing for the first time. Roses were planted in front of the house under what appeared to be the kitchen windows. The front door was to the left and then the house jutted back, beside the front door under the eave was a large picture window. It was a red brick house, one level, a large front yard on a street of neatly manicured lawns. Keith turned his attention to Ruth who he thought looked worried, maybe even angry when she greeted him. She knew the truth, Keith could feel it in her rigid hug. He glanced over at Jack who nodded. He took a deep breath and followed her into the house through a screen door that you entered through the garage. Jack had been to the Meeks house a number of times, Keith had never been there. Even dreading the conversation that he knew was coming, he felt at home.

***

Ruth sat down at the kitchen table, taking the chair closest to the wall that looked out at the roses. She motioned for Keith to join her at the table and he obliged, Izzy stood behind him. Through the kitchen door Keith could see the dining room table and a hallway opening. Jack

sat at the table in the chair nearest the screen door. For the first time in a long time, Keith felt like a little boy, part of him wanted to run out that screen door and not look back. Another part of him had yearned for this very feeling, a real mother that made you have consequences for your actions. He was now facing the consequences and was terrified.

"Well Keith." Ruth was saying. "I'm not sure what I'm supposed to say to you. You took my daughter's innocence when I trusted you. Jack tells me that now after all this time, you can use what you did and help boost your film."

Keith looked down, then looked at Jack, he realized now how much he had depended on Jack over the years to help him with so many things, up until that moment he hadn't realized the depth of his dependencies. Ruth was livid, but she was still gentle. He nodded slightly to himself, realizing now where Izzy had learned her kindness. If a man had behaved this way with a child of his, he would have killed him, yet Ruth invited him into her home and although he knew she was seething, she was holding it in.

"I can't apologize enough Ruth." Keith said. "I assure you that I had every intention of devoting my life to her. I want to make good on those intentions, I want to marry her again, as soon as possible."

"She's 18." Ruth stated. It wasn't an argument, it was a statement. "She was 15 years old, you were 27." She reminded him.

"16 mom." Izzy corrected.

"Yes, 27," Keith said, "and I should have known better, I did know better. All I can say is that it is in the past. I hurt her, I wish I hadn't. I tried to make it right and when I knew she was okay, I stayed away from her."

Keith was looking directly into Ruth's eyes. Her eyes were blue also, but almost a silver blue. Her Auburn hair was turning gray and complimented her eyes and her complexion. She had different skin than her daughter, he remembered that from so many years ago but he had barely paid attention then. Now he looked at her, her face was weathered, but beautiful. She was tanned, she had high cheekbones, short styled hair that brushed to one side in large curls. She had a thin straight nose, long legs and big feet. She looked a little like an older version of Maureen O'hara.

"Making it right? Marrying a child? You tried to make it right by sneaking off to Mexico then putting her on a plane? You broke my daughter's heart!" She whispered loudly.

"I was trying to do what was best." Keith said quietly.

"Best for who?" Ruth asked bluntly. "I could never understand the sadness she had after that trip. She had always loved going to see Jack, but she would never speak of that trip and refused Jack's calls for such a long time."

"I didn't know." Keith said.

" How would you know?" She asked. "Did you ever call her? Did you come to see her? You never answered her letter." Ruth said accusingly.

"That would be my fault too Ruth." Jack answered. "I kept it from him. I thought I was protecting them both."

"What?" Izzy gasped. It was the first time she had uttered a sound since arriving home.

"He has it now." Jack said to Izzy. "I gave it to him on the plane."

Izzy slapped the back of his head with her hand.

"Ouch!" Jack said.

Izzy did it again. Keith had to bite the inside of his lip to stop from smiling.

"Ignorance is no excuse, you should have made a point to know." Ruth had dismissed Jack and was looking directly at Keith. Her blue eyes turned silver and narrowed at him. He looked over Jack's shoulder at the screen door, wondering how fast he could get out of it. "Getting married in Tijuana," Ruth continued. "Like a joke!"

"I assure you Ruth, it wasn't a joke. I took those vows very seriously. I know it wasn't legal but in my heart I thought of myself as married."

Ruth picked up a stack of Globe magazines that she had sitting on the kitchen table. She thumbed through a few until she found a picture of a woman in tears with a headline about Keith Enidarrac breaking the woman's heart and shoved it at him.

"Mom likes crossword puzzles. The globe has some really good ones." Izzy said. She was torn between defending Keith or defending her mother. She suddenly didn't like being grown up.

Keith adjusted himself in the chair, he knew very well that his name had been linked to many beautiful women since that summer. He knew he should continue to explain.

"I've dated a few women since then. Part of me wanted to, I confess I was angry with your daughter. Did she tell you that she left the house without telling anyone? She didn't even leave a note." Keith lifted his chin up and looked directly into Ruth's hardened silver eyes. "I take full responsibility for everything, I know how she felt because I felt the same way. Every single time I tried to be with another woman, I could only think of your daughter. The more women I dated the emptier my heart felt. I need her, only she can make me happy, even when she's mean to me." He laughed, thinking of the airconditioner in the car.

Ruth held Keith's gaze for a long time. "I believe you." She confirmed. She was impressed that Keith never once tried to shift the blame to his brother. She now knew the whole story and that most of it was Jack's doing. Jack could be devious, no question about that, yet Keith accepted the blame, it showed strength of character. She didn't know the younger Enidarrac but he had to be a bit like his brother.

She studied his face, it took guts to come here, it took strength to face her, she thought she could like this young man.

"Jack helped explain things to me and so much makes sense now, my daughter kept all of that inside. Do you know how hard that must have been? A child that can't even tell her mom why her heart is broken."

Keith swallowed. So much of what he had done hadn't dawned on him before. He wanted Ruth to like him. He wanted to be part of this family.

"Please believe me when I tell you that I'm sorry." He whispered.

"Is this really what you want sweetheart?" She asked her youngest child.

Izzy shrugged softly, "I'm not mad anymore but I have a lot to think about. If I learned anything from the experience, it was to think things through more carefully. Izzy said.

Keith let himself smile ever so softly, remembering what had just transpired between the two of them in the cornfield. Izzy was practical, methodical, organized and also completely unable to control her most primal desires. It was an insane juxtaposition. Logic verses lust. She might fool herself into believing she needed to think about it, but Keith knew that she had already decided.

Jack had remained silent, now he reached across the table and took hold of one of Ruth's hands. "Ruth, I'll be there too, your little girl is grown up now. It was a bad situation, but it's in the past, let them decide their future."

Keith was confused. Why was Jack asking for permission? Izzy was eighteen, she could decide for herself. Then he heard Jack continue. "We can get permission from a judge if you say it's okay, I mean if your daughter says yes."

"I'm not sure it is." Ruth was saying. "School isn't over, I want her to finish high school. I wanted her to go to college."

"She has a bright future Ruth. The manuscripts she has been sending are very good, I have contacts to help her. She can continue to write like she loves, she can write plays or even get a job writing for television. I was thinking of producing this last one. I can help her find work if she wants to. She has a lot of talent. She is going to be something, I'll see to it." Jack said.

Still standing beside Keith, Izzy had seen the puzzled look on his face. She leaned down and whispered in his ear. "The age of majority in Nebraska is 19. " Keith stiffened, he was going to have to fight for her in more ways than one, the full meaning of Jack's challenge began to dawn on him. Keith had thought Jack was just talking about Braden, that bushy haired biker was just a small part of what he needed to overcome. He looked at his brother who was still holding Ruth's hand, just how much of this had Jack planned? It was like a supreme orchestration, how long had he been working on this? Keith nodded to himself, he would change Izzy's answer of probably, to a yes, he would get the approval from Ruth, he was determined to have things work out. Keith was an Enidarrac, he could be just as good as Jack was at getting what he wanted.

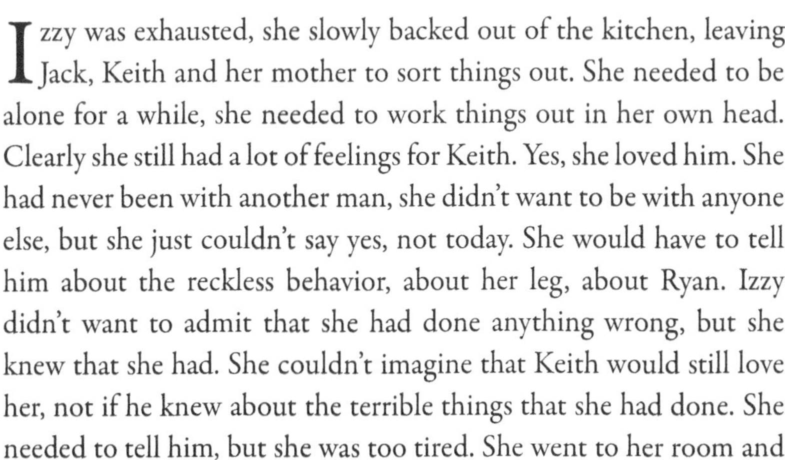

Izzy was exhausted, she slowly backed out of the kitchen, leaving Jack, Keith and her mother to sort things out. She needed to be alone for a while, she needed to work things out in her own head. Clearly she still had a lot of feelings for Keith. Yes, she loved him. She had never been with another man, she didn't want to be with anyone else, but she just couldn't say yes, not today. She would have to tell him about the reckless behavior, about her leg, about Ryan. Izzy didn't want to admit that she had done anything wrong, but she knew that she had. She couldn't imagine that Keith would still love her, not if he knew about the terrible things that she had done. She needed to tell him, but she was too tired. She went to her room and laid down on her bed, reaching under her pillow she pulled out an army green t-shirt and buried her face into it, it still smelled like him. Sea salt and sweat.

17

"The whole school knows about them now, it won't be long before the press starts digging into the relationship. The secret is out, we need to plan a wedding, she won't be able to just live a private life anymore, they will dig deeper and eventually they might learn more. They might learn about her abilities, if they do, they will try to use her. Even I tried that." Jack was saying to Ruth. "You've protected her all these years, give them something else to gossip about Ruth, give them a raunchy relationship with a rising movie star and they will run with it. There is no need to dig deeper, they will think that is the secret. There is no need for them to know more."

Jack was talking about Izzy's abilities. Keith racked his brain, he remembered the words to his song, the eerie life predictions, the time that circled over and over like a planet orbiting the sun. He remembered the deck of cards and the checkers, he remembered the times she got up to answer the phone before it rang, there had been so many times she had presented these "gifts'" and he remembered now the interest she had sparked in Jack. Had he planned this whole thing? Why? Did he leave them alone those days and nights before the Oscars on purpose? Jack had always been intrigued by new ideas about life, religion and the universe.

"Yes Jack, you made sure that the whole school knew." Ruth said. She didn't let go of Jack's hand but the look she shot him was deadly.

My god, Jack had orchestrated the entire thing Keith thought to himself. He gave Izzy's address to Braden, making sure that Keith knew about it. Jack had stoked Keith's jealousy on several occasions. Keith remembered the night Izzy went to the party with Braden, Jack hadn't "forgot" to call Keith and tell him not to come over, Jack wanted Keith there, to make him jealous. At the airport they had both been tired but Jack insisted on renting a flashy sports car. It had taken hours. Jack had parked it on the grass at the highschool so that everyone would see it. He walked into her classroom instead of waiting in the office under the guise of helping prepare Izzy but on reflection, they could have simply had Geraldine go and get her from the classroom. Every step had been calculated, possibly from the very beginning. It was brilliantly devious and Jack had played Keith like a fiddle. He turned all these thoughts around over and over in his head but Keith didn't care, he had a shot at getting Izzy back and that was all that mattered.

Jack smiled a sly smile at Ruth. "Would you expect anything else from me?" He winked at her and even in her anguish, she laughed. How his brother could be so manipulative and still get the woman to smile was beyond Keith. Ruth had always loved Jack, they had developed a relationship quickly and she was never bothered by his demons. She welcomed him as part of her family. He saw the love in her eyes as she smiled at Jack and hoped someday she would feel the same way towards him.

"You win as always Jack. Help her keep her secret. Don't let people use her, promise me." Jack squeezed her hand. "I promise." He said. "Except for me of course." He grinned.

"I need some time with my little girl, I give my permission, but ultimately, it's going to be up to Izzy. She and I are going to have a conversation." Ruth stood up and turned to Keith, "Well Keith, why don't you and Jack go get your things from the hotel. I think I should get to know you, I really don't know anything about you. Once you're back, we can have dinner and a nice long visit."

Keith had never been intimidated by a woman before, but he knew it wasn't a suggestion. He nodded acknowledging the command and left the same way he had come in, through the screen door and out into the garage. Jack stood and kissed the back of Ruth's hand and left without saying a word. A few moments later they were backing the Porsche down the driveway and heading west towards downtown and the Cornhusker hotel. Izzy had come back to the kitchen and had watched them leave through the kitchen windows, feeling sad and excited and embarrassed all at the same time.

When the two men returned to the hotel, Keith had still not said a word to his brother. In a way he was angry, having been manipulated so easily, but he was also in wonder. Was it all just fate, had that little girl been telling the truth all those years ago about everything. Keith had told her that he believed her, but he realized that he really hadn't. He believed that she believed the story. That isn't the same thing. He had thought at the time that she had a wild imagination, he had laughed off the coincidences, the song lyrics, the predictions. He had changed the lyrics to his song, they sounded like his own words. After he won the Oscar, he still told himself it was nothing, when he found himself consumed with thoughts of her, he told himself that any man would feel that way. She was young but beautiful, he had convinced himself that HE was in control, that the universe held no magic, life happened and ended.

Keith believed in God, his beliefs left very little room for any other interpretation. He remembered reading Jonathan Livingston Seagull when he was about 21 years old. It was an allegorical fable written by Richard Bach, he now wondered if life was really like that. He remembered at the time he read it, briefly comparing it to the story Izzy had given to his brother and had wondered if maybe time was just a chance to get things right. He had ultimately dismissed the thought and put it in the back of his mind. He tried to visualize Jack's cluttered desk in the kitchen, wasn't a copy of that novella in one of the letter slots of the desk? He was lost in thought, trying to figure out what the hell was going on.

As they rode the elevator to their rooms, he still hadn't spoken to his brother. Jack took it in stride, he just leaned against the back of the lift, arms folded across his chest, one foot casually crossed over the other. Keith guessed Jack had worked through all these thoughts a long time ago. It made sense, he would have done massive amounts of research on the subject, just as he did for any role or project that he took on. Jack had believed Izzy, he had spent years asking questions and understanding, Keith had acted like a punk. He avoided her at all costs, he chose not to believe and by that choice, he was now totally unprepared.

The Elevator door opened and the brothers stepped out and headed to Jack's room first. Jack opened his door and left it wide open, he grabbed his small bag that he had already packed and closed the door. He motioned to Keith towards his room.

"You're already packed?" Keith asked. Jack just nodded. "You knew she would ask us to her home or did you remember?" He nodded again. Keith rolled his eyes and opened the door to his room and walked inside. Jack stood in the doorway while Keith tossed a few things into his bag. He hadn't brought much so it didn't take him long. He did take time to remove his damp shirt, renew his deodorant and put on a soft yellow t-shirt. The men were headed back to the elevator in a matter of minutes. "Do you know how this ends?" He asked Jack. Jack just smiled and pushed the lobby button, the doors closed and the elevator moved downward.

The kitchen smelled delicious. Ruth had begun cooking dinner, she had pork chops simmering in a frying pan, they were bubbling in tomato soup, there were sliced green peppers and onions on top of them. The walls of the kitchen were covered in wall-paper, it had green vines growing on a trellis. The room was done in light oak, the stove, refrigerator and oven were brown and built into the cabinetry. The flooring was white linoleum and the kitchen countertop was a white acrylic. Keith couldn't explain it, but he felt as if he had been there a million times before.

Izzy was in the dining room setting the table. Keith found her and began to help. She corrected his placement of the silver ware. "The fork goes on the left, knife and spoon on the right." She chastised while smiling. "Who raised you, wolves?"

"Sorry, I was thinking of you, not the silverware." He grinned.

Jack and Ruth came in carrying plates of food. The pork chops were delicious, so tender they could be cut with a fork. There was fresh corn on the cob, cornbread with real butter and a tossed green salad with fresh cucumbers, onion and tomatoes and lots of cheese and croutons. Keith noticed that Ruth and Jack ate slowly, stopping to talk and joke often. He followed his brother's que and tried to ape the same pace. He realized now why Jack loved visiting Ruth, dinner took at least an hour, it was filled with laughter and conversation. It was warm and inviting. After dinner, Ruth brought in a chocolate cake, it was the same recipe Izzy made for Jack. Moist and homemade and covered in chocolate frosting. Keith hadn't eaten so much in a long time.

"I'm going to get fat if I keep eating like this." Keith said.

"You can burn off the calories doing the dishes." Ruth answered. Keith stood up and immediately began clearing the table. He was surprised to see Jack stand and help. Ruth had Jack trained well, he chuckled to himself. The two boys stood at the sink, Keith washed and Jack dried, Izzy took the dry dishes and put them away. He watched his brother and saw that he was smiling and humming, Jack was enjoying himself, it was amazing. When the last dish had been put away, the group joined Ruth on the patio. It was still hot even though the sun was lower in the sky. Hummingbird moths buzzed around the patio, sipping nectar from the honeysuckle vine and swarming the cleomes that grew near the wooden patio privacy fence.

The conversation turned to Izzy. Jack told Keith that Izzy had been a little difficult after they had sent her home. "Well, I guess I don't blame her." Keith replied. " Tell me Just how difficult was she?"

"Let me tell you." Ruth said.

"Mom." Izzy groaned.

"She argued non stop for one thing." Ruth said, smiling at her daughter. "Mostly, she just withdrew."

"Yeah yeah," Izzy said. "Always a problem child. Sulking, arguing, hiding."

"Hiding?" Keith said. "I'm intrigued."

"Oh yes, she wouldn't go to sports games, friends houses, dances..."

"Now wait a minute." Keith said. He looked at Izzy. "I sent you home to have a normal life, are you telling me that you wasted it?"

"Why would I want to do any of those things?" Izzy replied.

"What, you didn't want to dance with any of those dreamy jocks I saw leering at you in your classroom?" Keith asked.

"Who uses the words dreamy and jock in the same sentence?" Izzy said.

Jack snorted then quickly took a sip of iced tea. "What about prom?" He managed to ask after swallowing the tea.

"I'm not going to that." Izzy said.

"Going? You mean your senior prom hasn't happened yet?" Jack inquired, smiling.

"I'm leaving." Izzy grumbled, she stood up and went inside. Jack and Keith looked at Ruth who was smiling.

"It's this weekend." She told them, Jack and Keith looked at eachother and grinned.

"I think we both should take her." Jack said. "I love to dance."

Keith began to wonder if even the timing of this trip had been planned by his brother. He wouldn't put it past him.

Ruth laughed loudly, she had a real laugh and Keith loved it. He remembered Geraldine Pitchka's laugh and shuddered. Even though he wondered if Jack had planned this trip around the prom, he agreed to himself that Izzy should go to it.

"What do you think, Ruth? How can we get her to go?" Keith asked.

"Blackmail or trickery is all I can think of." Ruth answered. "I'd have to get her a dress."

"We have to rent some tuxedos anyway." Jack said, the corner of his mouth slowly turning upward. "Or have you failed getting a yes out of her little brother?"

"I'm working on it." Keith said.

"Better get on it." Jack nudged. "Time is wasting."

Keith decided he should follow Izzy inside, his insecurities were surfacing. He found her alone in the living room, quietly contemplating. She nodded silently to him then stood, he followed her towards the front door and together they stepped outside. The day was finally cooling off, somewhere down the street a blue jay was scolding loudly and a crow was retaliating.

"Why don't you show me around?" Keith asked.

Izzy nodded and stepped off the stoop. "I guess this is new to you, I mean you never came to visit." She said, It was a barb and Keith accepted it.

"Not mad at all." Keith mumbled as they headed up the street. He thought about taking her hand but one look at her profile told him it wasn't a good time. She was still angry and it showed. He decided to pretend he didn't notice. They walked up Bruce drive until the street ended and in front of it lay a red brick school house. It was at the bottom of a steep grassy hill. There were concrete steps with black metal railings leading down to the main doors, then on either end of the school were smaller entrances. Izzy crossed the street and headed down the grassy slope towards the school not using the steps and Keith followed her. She walked around the left side of the building and it led to a playground.

Keith looked around, they stood on a large upper playground directly behind the school but just twenty feet away were more concrete steps leading down to a lower playground that was obviously used for track and baseball. At the very back was a large chain-link fence, at least ten feet tall and beyond that were more houses. To the left of the school grounds was a large open field that sprawled down another slope towards a slightly wooded area.

"Hey!" Keith said, "That's the jungle gym you told me about. I want to see your photos!" He jaunted up to the monkey bars and crinkled his face. "God, was I ever that small?" He said aloud. "I don't think I could even squeeze through those bars now."

He looked over his shoulder at the field and saw the basketball court with the metal baskets that Izzy had described. He nodded at her, letting her know he remembered that as well.

"I've always liked the sound a basketball makes when it hits the backboard." Keith said. "The concrete too, you can hear the ball is hollow. I don't know, it's kind of a neat sound."

Izzy studied him cautiously, she didn't want a repeat of what they had done in the corn field. If she said yes, and it was a big if, she wanted to know it was the right decision. She thought about climbing the monkey bars just to get away from him, he was way too big to squeeze in between the bars, but then she looked into his eyes and just wanted to get closer to him instead. She thought to herself how confused she was. It was very unlike her, she and Jack were so similar, she planned everything but when she was with Keith she couldn't be cautious, her mind and her body behaved separately and she seemed to have no control. She decided to change the subject.

"Come on." She said, and started heading towards the field.

Keith hurried after her and caught up just as she stepped into the tall grass. The field was full of insects, grasshoppers would click and buzz jumping ahead of her as she made her way in the grass. Bees were everywhere, there was clover and vine weed, daisies and goldenrod. As Keith followed her a garter snake darted through the grass in front of him. After a bit, the tall grass disappeared and the area that they walked in had been freshly mowed. There were houses to the left that butted up to the field, ahead was the wooded area and beyond that Keith could see East High in the distance.

"What is this place?" Keith asked.

"It's Taylor park." Izzy answered. "This used to be all corn fields, my brother Kent used to come here and catch salamanders. When old man Taylor died, he left the creek and surrounding area to the city as a park. I've spent a lot of time down here, it's one of my favorite places." She confided in Keith.

Keith took it all in. There were mulberry trees and old willows, and a little creek ran through the center of them. There were cattails and rushes and large blue dragon flies darting between them. He could hear frogs and as he looked towards the creek he saw what appeared to be a muskrat slide into the water.

"I can't believe this is in the city." Keith commented. Izzy just continued walking towards the thicker wooded area. Keith followed her, either side of the park was now surrounded by houses and nestled deeper inside the old willow trees was a swing set. It was really tall and had rubber seats. Izzy sat on one but didn't swing. Keith leaned against the metal frame that held the swings and watched her. She turned in the swing, twisting the chains that held it, then she would lift her legs off the dirt beneath her and the swing would twirl as the chains untwisted.

"When I was little, I couldn't get enough of swinging." Izzy said, "I'd pump my legs as hard as I could, I could never get high enough."

"I liked that feeling too." Keith confided.

"It feels a little like that on the back of Bray's motorcycle." Izzy said. She said it deliberately, then she watched Keith's face closely. She saw his jaw tighten, but was impressed that he kept his tongue. She twisted the swing again then let loose to spin one more time. Izzy was doing what she had always done, testing Keith, making him angry so she could feel his colors. She knew her heart wanted him, it always did. She wasn't sure what she was remembering and why she needed to test him. The universe was speaking to her, telling her to listen to her heart.

He watched her silently for a while. The sun was casting long shadows now against the trees. He saw something in the grass by the creek that caught him by surprise, something glowed off and on. Then suddenly he noticed more of them, they were in the grass and on the willow trees, they were slowly taking flight into the humid darkening evening light. "Oh my god." He said, "Fireflies?"

Izzy laughed, she couldn't help herself. Keith felt a little hope when he heard it.

"I always forget those things aren't everywhere." Izzy giggled. "In the midwest, we call them lightning bugs."

"They are so strange." Keith said, "Do they sting?"

Izzy got up and walked towards the creek, it only took a couple seconds for her to catch one from the tall grass that lined the water's edge on either side. She carried it over to Keith and asked him to open his hand. He did so and she placed the bug on his palm. It crawled around for a few moments, then opened its wings a few times, lit up and took off. Keith held his palm in front of himself for a few minutes then smiled. Izzy thought even in the growing shadows, that he was gorgeous.

It dawned on her that Keith was like a lightning bug. He was a changeling. He could have both lightness and darkness, she had seen both sides. She slowly remembered something, something she had been searching for, she remembered from the time before, that without her Keith was swallowed by darkness. She remembered that Keith needed her. If she compared him to a lighting bug and held Keith in the palm of her hand, with her, he could spread his wings, light up and be free. She hadn't been searching for a bad memory of Keith all this time, she had been searching for a sign that they were better together.

"I held a lightning bug." Keith smirked, sounding proud of himself.

Izzy laughed, it was a different laugh than her usual hoarse giggle. "I'll write it down in my diary." She told him.

"Am I in your diary anywhere else?" He asked.

Izzy didn't answer, she just held his gaze. She had given him his breadcrumb already, she wasn't going to be pushed but she knew her answer now.

"You remind me of a lightning bug." Izzy told him.

"How is that?" Keith asked and then braced himself for the answer.

"Because you are unsure of your colors." Izzy said, "You light up, you go dark, you love me, you don't." She teased.

"Not an accurate description." Keith responded. "My feelings for you have always remained the same." Keith paused. He could feel Izzy turning, she was coming back to him. He tried to push her, coax her to tell him.

Was she disappointed she asked herself? She had left the door wide open for Keith to tell her that he loved her. He said his feelings had remained the same. He hadn't said the words. Her answer was still yes, but she could keep the word inside just as long as he could keep the other word inside of him. Red, green, it didn't matter. They were different words but meant the same thing.

"My brother says you had another visitor from California this week, should I be worried?" Keith asked.

Izzy realized he knew that Braden had come to visit, it was awkward for her but on the other hand, Keith had certainly seen many women in the past three years. Izzy had read a few of those stories in her mother's gossip rags. She had even gone out and purchased a few for herself, making sure that there were photos of Keith inside, just so she could take a black ink pen and block out the teeth of whoever was photographed with him. She smiled mischievously thinking of her artwork. She knew she should reassure him, let him know she did still love him but a lot had happened to her the past few years, she needed to tell him everything.

"We should head back," Izzy said, trying to change the subject. "I still want to swim a little bit tonight."

Keith nodded, they hadn't spoken much but he felt as though they were making progress. She hadn't answered his question, but he could feel her coming back to him. Izzy led him up another grassy slope but this one cut between two residential houses. From there they walked on a tree lined sidewalk up a steep hill. "That's Tom Osborne's house." she commented, pointing to a brown house that butted up against the park.

"Who is Tom Osborne?" Keith asked.

Izzy stopped walking. "Keith." She said, "Never say that in front of my mother." Then she continued up the street until they were in front of the school again without providing him an explanation.

"I always thought Nebraska was flat." Keith said, sounding a bit winded. Izzy just laughed. "At least it is downhill from here." He said to himself as they headed back down Bruce Drive.

When they got to the house, they walked around the side of it to the back yard. Keith was still amazed that there were no fences separating the neighbors yards. There was a small wrought iron fence around the swimming pool, but that fence was required by law. When standing in the back yards, it was like one immense yard spreading behind all the homes on either side of the Meeks house.

Jack and Ruth were still on the back patio. Ruth was telling Jack all about Terry's home in western Nebraska. She had married a wealthy doctor who also loved horses and was living her dream. They had tons of horses, she rode everyday and she was doing very well in shows.

"I wasn't sure if you two were coming back." Ruth said as Izzy and Keith came around the corner.

"I showed him Taylor Park." Izzy replied. "I came back to swim." She bent down and kissed the top of her mother's head then let herself in through the patio doors.

18

When Jack and Keith went inside, Izzy was just coming out. She had her swimsuit on and a towel wrapped around her waist. She walked past them without saying a word, the sun was almost finished setting and the evening sky was changing from a medium blue to purple. Izzy bent down and told her mother she needed to exercise her leg. Ruth nodded and watched her little girl head towards the pool.

A few minutes later Keith and Jack returned, they were wearing swimming trunks and each carried a neatly folded towel. They sat down on the lawn chairs next to Ruth and watched Izzy in the pool. She was under the diving board not facing them. She had a hold of the board above her head while she was slowly lifting her right leg up and down. The pool lights illuminated her body, almost making it glow. Keith couldn't take his eyes off of her, then laughed a bit to himself wondering why she wasn't swimming.

Izzy let go of the board for a moment, then turned and faced the other direction. She looked directly at them, then continued her leg lifts, the front of her leg now visible. Keith's smile slowly faded, there was a long red scar running from under her swimsuit and part way down her leg. His face didn't change but Ruth heard him inhale sharply. She turned to Jack,

"You didn't tell him?" Ruth asked. Jack shook his head.

"Maybe you should." Keith said.

"It seems she was in a car crash." Jack responded.

267

"We almost lost her." Ruth said to Keith.

"And you knew about this?" Keith's voice had gone soft and quiet, a true indication of his anger.

"No Keith, he didn't know until this afternoon. Izzy wouldn't hear of me telling either one of you, and well since she seemed to have lost touch with the both of you, I didn't see any reason not to honor her request. She cracked her pelvis and broke her femur. She needed emergency care and then surgery. Izzy has always been peaceful. I'm sure you know what I mean. So many of her peers turned wild when they hit their teens. Her sister was a handful." Ruth smiled at the memory of Izzy's older sister. Grateful that those years were in the past.

"Terry was headstrong and outspoken. She was driven and always knew what she wanted. When she became a teenager, she was impatient waiting for her life. She aggressively sought it out, crazy nights cruising with her older horse friends. Drinking with the cowboys, the phone constantly ringing with invitations. Izzy was different, Ruth actually worried about her, not that she wanted to go through the same rebellion, but her youngest daughter was so introverted. She was happiest when she was planning her visits with Jack, or when he was going to come see her. She was curious about everything to do with writing and film and stage, but that had all changed when she had returned after that last visit. Izzy wouldn't talk about the trip other than to say it had been nice and they had gone to Mexico. After that, she started behaving recklessly." Ruth said.

"Tell me all of it." Keith said. Ruth nodded.

"Izzy had always been a homebody but after returning from California that changed. She started going to football games and sleep overs. At first I had been pleased, she wasn't being defiant like her older sister, just more adventurous, how could that have been bad? Slowly the adventures began to become more dangerous.

She was hanging out with boys who drank and drove fast cars. Her girlfriends had stopped calling."

Ruth looked over at her daughter, she was resting against the side of the pool, her arms holding on to the ladder behind her. She was kicking her feet out in front of her, it was something her surgeon had told her she could do.

"Maybe the fast cars reminded her of Jack." She said, "Maybe all of it reminded her of Jack, of you, of happier times. I'm wondering now, if she had just stopped caring if she lived or died." Jack nodded, he could connect the dots, Ruth was on to something.

"That evening, she was so restless." Ruth continued. "When her friends pulled up on the driveway, she paced a few moments before she left and when she hugged me goodbye, she hugged me so tight." Ruth looked again at her daughter, her eyes welled with tears and her voice cracked a bit. "I had told her she couldn't go, we fought about it. I couldn't stop her, she went anyway. When the phone rang, I swear I knew." She said, "I think I had been waiting for it."

"The car crash?" Keith asked. Ruth looked at him and nodded.

"The boy who was driving was dead on the scene." Ruth paused, giving herself a moment to compose her thoughts. "The other two had mainly internal injuries, they have both since recovered. Apparently both families sued the family of the driver. I think they won some money. I didn't see any sense in it. Izzy knew it was dangerous, they all did. That's why they did it. Suing for compensation wouldn't heal my daughter's leg and frankly, the leg wasn't what was wrong with her."

She could hear water lapping in the pool and looked over at her daughter again. Izzy was under the diving board, her hands were firmly holding it while she faced the edge of the pool and she was slowly lifting her legs up out of the water and holding them still, then releasing and doing it again and again. Her daughter was showing the same determination now that Terry had when she was that age.

They were working towards different goals, Terry was always working towards a life with horses, Izzy was working at recovery, but it was a sight that made her mother smile.

" It could have been so much worse." Ruth breathed in deeply. "She had surgery that night to repair the leg, stop the bleeding. The pelvis needed time to heal. She couldn't walk for a month. She absolutely refused to use a walker and begrudgingly used crutches."

"I wish you had told me." Jack whispered. He actually seemed hurt. Jack had considered himself part of this family and to be shut out confused him.

"She wouldn't let me honey." Ruth said. She took Jack's hands and held them. He looked up at her and nodded. "I love you like a son and I would keep any secret you told to me, I owed my daughter the same."

"Did she say why she didn't want you to tell us?" Keith asked. Ruth looked at Keith, holding his gaze.

"I think I can guess, I think you can too." She answered. "I'm sure she knew Jack would tell you, and we both know that is why. After knowing what transpired between the two of you, I'm sure she didn't want you to come to her in pity" Ruth paused to see his reaction, he looked very pained. She wasn't sure if she should continue, but knew Izzy would probably never say a word. Part of her thought she should keep it to herself, but part of her wanted Keith to know. She wasn't mad at him, not any longer, but she was finally realizing the pain her daughter had kept to herself and telling Keith was only fair.

"After the accident, Izzy and her surgeon became very close." Ruth said. She let it sink in a bit.

"Close?" Keith asked. His voice had become even softer.

Ruth nodded, never taking her eyes from his face. She saw his jawline tense a bit, his brows furrowed inward.

"He is a young man, freshly graduated, an uprising star." Ruth said. "He was highly recommended and is quite brilliant. He was recommended by his brother, Terry's husband. I'm not telling you this to upset you." She said,

"Go on." Keith prodded.

"His name is Ryan Mckinney. He took special interest in her."

"I bet he did." Keith said between gritted teeth.

Jack sat on the edge of his seat, this was something he hadn't expected nor had he planned for. He saw the anger in his brother's face, it was different than anything that had seen before. The truth was, Jack was also feeling angry, Izzy belonged to him, to them. She was his sister and his student. She was promised to his brother, she always had been. It was an understanding that had never been spoken but the two of them had understood. He had let too much time pass, it was his fault.

"Ryan is a good man." Ruth said. "I can honestly tell you I don't know how far their relationship has gone. They spend a lot of time together, here at the pool, walks in the park, if it wasn't for Ryan I don't know if Izzy would have ever got in a car again. He has been good for her." Ruth said

"You are speaking in the present tense." Jack said to Ruth. She nodded. "Keith?" He looked at his brother and Keith shook his head. Keith stood up and took off his shirt, he was wearing a tan short sleeve shirt that was unbuttoned and dark blue swimming trunks. He laid the shirt on his chair and approached the pool. He didn't test the water, but slid into the pool from the shallow end. It was cold and he took a breath sucking in his stomach.

"I thought maybe you forgot how to swim." Izzy teased from under the diving board. "Or maybe you California boys just can't handle cold water without a wetsuit?"

Ruth and Jack watched silently for a few moments. "Should I have told him?" She asked him.

Jack watched silently for a while, then squeezed Ruth's hand. "Even my brother couldn't expect the world to stand still and wait for him, let's go inside and give them some privacy."

Keith leaned forward into the cold water. He went under and swam towards the girl he loved. He surfaced next to her and shook the water off his face. "Hey there." He said. She let go of the diving board and wrapped her arms around his neck. He hung on to the board with one arm, the other he used to pull her closer to him and kissed her gently on the lips. To his surprise she kissed him back, then giggled that earthy laugh of hers, lord he had missed that sound. He let his hand move downward and brushed it against the top of her thigh feeling the raised edges of the red scar. She pushed away and swam to the ladder but she didn't step up, instead she held onto the ladder, facing the concrete deck and didn't move.

Izzy had resolved to tell Keith everything when they were at the park. She knew that she loved him fervently. She had attempted several ways to tell him inside her head, but they all sounded stupid to her. She had instead decided to just show him, flash the scar at him, make him ask her questions but now that her plan was working, she was afraid to put it into words. Izzy had wanted to die. She had never said it outloud, not even in a quiet room by herself. Even her relationship with Ryan had come to fruition because she no longer cared what happened to her.

Keith let go of the diving board and with one stroke joined her at the side of the pool. She didn't look at him. Slowly he turned her head towards him with one finger and began gently lifting her chin. The anger was gone from his face, Izzy only saw his kind dark eyes. She knew that it wasn't out of pity, he had come to her without knowing of the accident but she was still afraid. Afraid of herself. She had refused to admit how much she needed him until now. She tried to look away but he held her chin firmly, he edged closer to her and nudged her forehead with his nose.

"I was in an accident." She confessed. "That's what they call it anyway. We were going so fast, it was like leaving everything behind. It made me feel like I had power." She laughed softly. "I've never had any power over anything in all reality."

"You have all the power." Keith answered. He held her gaze, not saying a word but his face said it all.

"She told you." She said bluntly. Keith nodded.

"The power is still all yours. Tell me what you want." He whispered softly.

Izzy looked deep into the eyes that had haunted her. She had seen that face in so many dreams. She had fought it, lied about it, avoided it, but his face had been with her throughout time. "I want you." She gasped. "I've always wanted you."

Keith took a deep breath, he wasn't sure what answer she was going to give him. He had pressured her in the corn field, and he had been so sure of himself so arrogant, the thought she could have found happiness with another man had never crossed his mind. He was so arrogant, and he knew it.

"She told me about Ryan. She said you were close, I was wondering how close?" He asked her.

Izzy narrowed her eyes. ""What are you asking me?" She asked. "It seems like you are being pretty possessive. I've been here since I got off the plane. Time doesn't stop, you know, it keeps going, it keeps moving forward, round and round and round."

"I suppose I am being possessive." He confessed. "I'm trying to figure out where I stand with you."

Izzy's face softened. She wrapped her legs around Keith's waist. He could feel the floor of the pool so he let go of the ladder. He wrapped his arms around her and kissed her soft buttery lips.

"Does it matter to you?" She asked. "Who I have loved if I love you now?"

"At least you said love as opposed to loved," Keith whispered. "I like present tense adjectives."

Izzy splashed him and released her hold of him with her legs. She climbed up the ladder. The air was warm but the water had been cold and her nipples showed erect through the paisley print of her bikini top. Keith could feel himself growing hard so he let go of the ladder and fell back into the cold water. He gave himself a few minutes while she toweled off. She sat down on the hot cement and stretched her legs out into the pool. He swam back over to her, folded his arms on the edge of the pool and smiled. "It seems you attract older arrogant men." He smirked.

Izzy flipped her wet hair over her shoulder. "What makes you think he is arrogant? You don't know him." She retorted, rising to the challenge Keith had given to her.

Keith pulled himself out of the pool. His biceps bulged as he pulled himself out and water dripped from his thinning hair. His tan skin glistened with droplets from the pool, accentuating his well defined muscles. He turned around and sat beside her, he nudged her with his side and she laughed."

"I don't know he is arrogant," Keith confessed, "but I can make a logical guess. A brilliant young surgeon, saving the life of a beautiful young girl. A girl who no doubt needed a man in her life, one who would devote himself to her and not cause her heart to ache"

"Ryan is a good man." She confirmed. "And he really did save my life, you know."

"I did too." He reminded her. "Or have you forgotten already?" He asked, smiling softly.

"Do you mean the beach? Keith, I wasn't drowning." She said matter of factly.

"I know." He confirmed, muffling a laugh, "but I was terrified that you might have, doesn't that count for something?" He winked at her.

"Of course, you get ten points." She laughed. "Seriously, I know you always tried to protect me, to keep me safe. Hell, that's why you married me. But Ryan, he really did save my life."

Keith knew what she said was true, he also knew he was responsible for almost ending it.

"I was trying to do the right thing, I thought it was best for you." He whispered. "I never dreamed that decision would almost kill you."

Izzy took in a sharp breath, Keith turned to look at her face. "Don't you dare blame yourself." She chastised. "I got in that car, I knew it was going to be bad, I can sense things like that! I got in anyway, I had felt something bad would come of it all day. I still got in, no one made me. I liked the way it made me feel, it was like getting high, it took me away from everything. I didn't care about any sense of dread, I welcomed it. All that I wanted was freedom. Fast cars helped me forget what I did to you, how sorry I was for what I did!"

"What? Me?" Keith asked, confused.

"Yes, you." Izzy said. "I could have ruined your career, the thing you wanted most."

"Iz." He said gently. She had missed that sound, Keith calling her a shortened version of her name, it sounded so good. "Iz, I wanted you most. When we made love, well, I've never felt like that before. I swear that I could almost see the colors you always talk about. You were everything, everything I needed, wanted, but you were fifteen. The only reason I agreed to let you go was because I believed we would be together again in a few short years. You were fifteen."

"sixteen." She corrected, then laughed her earthy raspy laugh.

"Barely." Keith laughed. "You had your whole life ahead of you. I couldn't take that from you. I wanted you to have all the things normal highschool girls have. I never had a normal childhood, but I could make damn sure that you had one. If you still felt the same

towards me after a few years, then I was going to come get you"
He paused, searching her face, then continued "You needed to have
dates, dances, corsages and prom." Then he laughed again. "Believe
me I never dreamed you would land yourself a surgeon, I was
thinking of a jock football player."

"Ha! Dances, corsages, prom? Seriously?" Izzy snickered.

"Iz, I'm asking again with no pressure. Don't say yes to help with
my career, I don't need you to, I simply realized that the movie would
provide the opportunity for us, you don't owe me anything. I was
stubborn, I was angry, I never intended to let so much time pass, then
I let my pride get in my way. I should have come to see you, let you
know how I felt. I'm telling you now, I'm asking you now. Say yes if
you love me and only if you love me. I'm eleven years older than you,
I'll be an old man in no time. It would be a foolish decision for you
to agree to it, just foolish, but God I want you to be foolish. Can you
see a life with me?"

He paused and looked down. "And before you answer, consider
what you know. You know very well what the life of an actor is
like. After every job I wonder if that's it, will there be another role.
Will the money run out, will I be able to pay bills. I worry about
health insurance and savings accounts. Everyone thinks the life of an
actor is glamorous, but you have lived with my brother off and on,
you know that it is anything but glamorous. You've seen my brother
struggle with relationships, being separated for long periods of time
from the person you love, sometimes it is hard to trust one another,
it has wreaked havoc with all of Jack's relationships. Izzy you would
be so much better off marrying a doctor. A doctor could take good
care of you, you wouldn't have to work, you could start a family, buy
nice things." She interrupted him by answering his question with a
long passionate kiss.

"You talk too much." She said to him, then kissed him again.

Jack and Ruth were watching from the patio door. He took her hand and kissed the back of it. "Looks to me like you are going to have a movie star in the family!." Jack laughed, then smiled his knowing smile.

"A movie star, hmmmm." Ruth said. "I suppose there are worse things, but just think of the free health care I could have had in my old age if she had just married Ryan instead."

Jack snorted, he loved Ruth's sense of humor. He pulled her away from the patio doors and left his brother alone with the love of his life.

19

"So how far are you planning on taking this?" Ruth asked. "I'm already getting calls from reporters. The rumors are insane and the movie isn't even out yet." Ruth said. "A few people had reported seeing you at the airport and the hotel, then the story of the two of you at Izzy's school so rumors of Keith and my eighteen year old daughter are starting to circulate. So far, your plan has worked brilliantly for you Keith, but what are your plans for my daughter?"

"What are you asking Ruth?" Jack chimed in. "Don't beat around the bush."

"Look," Ruth said. "We all watched Watergate, we know where lying can lead. I don't want my little girl ambushed. I think you should own up to all of it. I mean, eventually the whole Tijuana thing will be found out, I don't want Izzy humiliated. There has to be a way we can tell the truth, but lie about it too. The headlines are all about Keith and his movie but there is not an explanation out there for my daughter."

"Ruth Meeks!" Jack scolded. "You want us to lie?" Jack laughed so hard he had to sit down. "I never thought I would hear those words coming from your sweet mouth, what would your church say?"

"Jack, don't you mock me!" She reprimanded him. "You know I'm right."

Keith stood up and paced just a little. "She is right Jack, it's just a matter of time before they start asking why Izzy, they will dig deeper until they will find out and I'd rather get ahead of it. I'm actually surprised that you hadn't already planned for this!"

"The best defense is a great offense, that is what Jim used to say." Ruth said.

"That's a football reference isn't it?" Keith asked, teasing his future mother in law.

"I'm not going to bite." Ruth laughed, "But you better be joking."

"He's joking." Jack laughed, "Now let's be serious, what are you thinking Keith?"

"So we tell them." Keith said. "We can tell them what I've always told myself." He paused, looking at his future mother in law. "I told myself that Izzy and I were married in Mexico, as a promise. It was like a promise ring. It was a gesture but not binding, we were promising that in the future, if we still felt the same way, we would do it for real."

"Okay." Ruth said. "That is sweet and I think that is something we can work with. I think Izzy would like that, she is a horrible liar. If she told a partial truth, it would be easier for her."

"What would be easier for me?" Izzy asked as she entered the room.

"Seems you are a horrible liar." Jack said to her.

Izzy laughed. "Tis true." She said, "What did I get caught lying about?"

"What have you lied about?" Keith asked suspiciously.

"I plead the fifth." Izzy giggled. "Tell me what you are talking about or my lips are sealed."

Keith stood behind Izzy and wrapped his arms around her. "You haven't lied, at least not that I know of." He said, then spun her around and scrutinized her face. Izzy laughed and kissed him on the mouth. "Your mother, brilliant woman that she is." He continued. "She is afraid that if we don't spill the whole truth, someone will discover it and make our lives a living hell."

Izzy squinted her eyes at Keith, then looked at Jack and her mother. They both nodded to her. "So you want me to tell everyone that I married you when I was fifteen?" She asked.

"Sixteen." they all answered in unison. Everyone laughed.

Keith explained to Izzy about the half truth. "Then if it is uncovered, it's already out there." He said.

"Hmm, a little strange, but the whole thing is strange." Izzy said. "The gossip was bad enough when Ryan kept showing up at the school, now I have two movie stars taking me out of class. Honestly, it is more fun than I thought it would be." Keith wrapped his arms around her again and held on tight.

"Oh yeah, the doctor." Keith said. "We were going to have a conversation about him weren't we? And Braden too?"

"I don't think I agreed to either of those conversations." Izzy said. Keith tightened his hold on her.

"Have you broken up with the good doctor?" Keith asked.

Izzy snorted. "I broke up with him before you two showed your sorry faces here." She said, "He was boring."

"Izzy!" Ruth said. "That is a very unkind thing to say about a man who saved your life."

Keith couldn't help grinning and swaying back and forth with Izzy still in his grasp.

"I should have known though, this is the longest weve gone without so much as a call from him. Why didn't you tell me you broke up?" Ruth asked her daughter.

"Clearly mother," Izzy smiled wickedly at her. "Clearly, I'm better at secrets than you knew."

Keith swung Izzy backwards and kissed her like in the movies.

"Stop necking." Ruth said.

"Nope." Keith replied

Izzy couldn't sleep. She kept thinking to herself she was getting married, for real this time. She was nervous but happy. So many times she and Keith had been together throughout time, The love always carried over, it was the most intense feeling she had ever known. They had been happy and miserable, but the love never changed. What would this time hold? She looked at the clock, it was 2:43 am, she had dozed a few times but kept waking up. Wanting a drink she got out of bed and softly walked down the hall towards the kitchen. The floor was carpeted and her footsteps went unheard. Jack was snoring, she could hear him through the closed door of the guestroom. Her mother was down the hall, her room was silent and she knew she was sound asleep. Izzy turned the corner heading towards the kitchen and bumped into Keith who was entering the hallway. He quickly covered her mouth so she wouldn't scream. "Are you okay?" He asked. Izzy nodded. He let go of her mouth and she released a silent gasp.

"What are you doing?" She whispered.

"I couldn't sleep, I was um, going to sneak into your room." Keith told her, she giggled and covered her own mouth.

"I can't sleep either." She confessed. "It will be quieter downstairs."

Keith smiled a slow sexy smile and took her hand. He had been sleeping downstairs in the finished basement. It used to be Kent's domain. Ruth had made it into the main television room but Kent's bedroom was still intact. Ruth had commissioned a neighbor who was a builder of custom homes to finish that side of the basement. Most of it had been made into a family room. He had built a beautiful wall that served as a divider out of knotty pine. The family room side had a bookshelf with rows and rows of books, the Tarzan series, the Hardy boys series, poetry, romance and even national geographics that lined the shelves. The other side of the divider in the bedroom had smaller shelves that held knick knacks, mostly part of Ruth's massive angel collection. There was no door to the bed area, but it felt very private. There were two window wells and both had homemade curtains that hung over them for privacy.

Keith led Izzy to the bed, he had planned on going slow but she was already peeling her t-shirt off over her head. It was an army green t-shirt that was way too large for her. Then he recognized it, "Hey, that's mine!" He said.

Izzy smiled. "Oops." she laughed.

"You took it?" He asked, obviously surprised.

"It smelled like you." She answered simply.

"I looked everywhere for that shirt!" He said.

"I needed it." Izzy said, "It smelled like you."

Keith nodded, he understood. He had missed all of Izzy's scents. He might have taken something of hers if he had thought of it. Stepping forward he held her for a moment, the lamp by his bedside was on and he could see her body illuminated by the warm light and he was amazed. She wasn't shy, she never had been, she stood still and let him take it all in. He remembered her boldness from before and smiled in the memory. Keith was wearing just a pair of boxers but had covered up with a robe that he had lifted from the Cornhusker Hotel. It seemed that they were both thieves and he smiled to himself.

He let his robe fall to the floor and he pulled Izzy close to him. He ran his right hand through the back of her hair and his left hand he placed on her slim waist. He pulled her even tighter and she aped his embrace, running her hands greedily down his back and resting on the waistband of his briefs. Gently she tugged at them. He turned her back towards his bed and gently pushed her onto it, stepping out of his underwear. She let her eyes move downward, she gently took hold of his erection and bent down. Slowly she ran her tongue up his shaft, Keith wasn't expecting it. She had certainly matured since the last time they had been together. He became a little angry, wondering where she had learned this act, he crawled onto the bed and positioned himself between her legs. Something in him let loose, he didn't make love to her, he had sex with her. He didn't kiss, he didn't stroke, he shoved himself in. She was so wet, it was warm and welcoming. He moved quickly, back and forth and she arched her back and then began moving her thighs in and out in a tribal rhythm. He didn't last long but came harder than he could remember ever doing. He stayed inside her and felt her muscles twitching all around him. She was still breathing hard and her skin glowed with sweet sweat. He was still angry and didn't kiss her, he pulled himself out and rolled on his back beside her.

Keith turned his head towards her and to his surprise, Izzy was slowly falling asleep beside him. He remembered how other women that he had slept with, always wanted to talk and how he just wanted to sleep. He laughed at himself because now he wanted to talk. He hated that he was angry with Izzy, he had no right to be angry. He was surprised that she hadn't felt his anger and questioned him about it. Maybe she had? He needed to talk to her and she was falling asleep!

He rolled on his side and watched her. His anger was subsiding. He slowly ran his fingers down her silky arm. She turned onto her side and faced him, slowly opening her eyes. She leaned forward and kissed his lips, he felt her lips part but he didn't oblige. He needed to know.

"Tell me about Braden and tell me about Ryan. I know I shouldn't be jealous, I'll get over it if you slept with them. I'm more afraid that you loved them, I've never felt so insecure." He said. Izzy's eyes widened.

"I forgot that you knew Braden was here" She whispered to him. Keith nodded but didn't say anything. "He stopped by a few days ago." She said, "We went miniature golfing." Izzy smiled a devious smile. "He wanted to hook up." Keith tried to stay calm, the thought of the two of them was driving him nuts. He could just see the guy, making love to Izzy, all that thick dark hair in her hands as she pulled him down towards her body. Izzy was watching Keith's face. "You and I weren't together, I mean not a word from you in years so I said what the heck and did him in the parking lot." Keith went pale and his mouth opened then Izzy laughed louder than he had ever heard her laugh before. His heart had almost stopped before he realized she was kidding.

"You should have seen your face!" She was giggling. Keith felt his face flush and was grateful for both the poorly lit room and his tanned complexion. Sometimes he forgot she was in highschool. She was teasing him like a playful child. It made him smile but he continued to press her for answers.

"What did you do with him?" Keith asked in a serious voice. "Clearly you have been learning from someone."

"Oh god." Izzy teased. "I do read and I also watch movies."

"That isn't in a movie that you are old enough to see." Keith said. He watched her face, he could tell if she was lying.

"Actually I can, I just can't legally get married or drink." Izzy argued. "Ironic isn't it?" She asked. "Aside from that, I do have urges just like anyone else and I am pretty sure I was acting on them." She looked into Keith's eyes and placed her hand on the side of his face. "Still, I want you to know that you are the only man I've ever been with. You're the only one I've ever wanted. I told Braden I appreciated the attention but my heart belonged to someone else. He didn't ask me who."

"Tell me about Ryan." Keith asked, feeling somewhat more confident.

"Ryan is a good and kind man." She said, "He didn't know what I was," Izzy could see that Keith's jaw was tightening, she knew she was making him angry again. She knew he was angry when they made love but she didn't know why. Now she was understanding, he had been with a lot of women and she knew it, he even had a child, but he had never been engaged. Maybe, he had never really been in love, maybe she was his first? She hadn't considered that before.

"Ryan assumed I was pure." Izzy laughed but it wasn't a laugh like she was enjoying herself. "He wanted to get engaged, he said we could wait until we were married." Izzy sat up and looked down at her pillow. She picked it up and covered herself with it. Keith understood, she was ashamed and was hiding, not of her nakedness but of her actions.

"Ryan knew I was messed up, I mean, that's how we met in the first place." She said, "But he didn't know how badly I was messed up. No one knew. I don't think he would have cared, you know he was more into the whole, I'm saving this girl thing, but it dawned on me if I couldn't show him who I really was, I had no business dating him, much less entertaining thoughts of marriage with him."

"Is that what you think?" He asked. "That you're damaged, messed up? That you aren't good enough? He asked.

Izzy wouldn't look at him but she nodded.

"I'm weird." She whispered. "I'm weird not just because of the things that I have done with you, but no one understands the colors that I see, no one gets that I know what they are thinking. No one believes what I know is true. I can't tell anyone about it. I just wanted it all to end."

Keith sat up and lifted her chin up with his fingers. "Look at me." He whispered kindly. He couldn't believe what he was hearing, that she had considered death as an option. The girl he knew was determined and self reliant, she had always known her destiny. His actions had made her question it, this was his fault.

Izzy slowly raised her eyes to look him in the face. She loved his eyes, she loved his voice, she loved his touch. She felt what he felt, he blamed himself. He didn't pity her and he loved her, she knew it.

"Iz, it just occurred to me that I've explained all my reasons for wanting to marry you now, again, but I've left out the most important thing." She tried to look away but he held her chin firmly. "Iz, none of the other reasons matter, they are sensible, but they are unimportant." Keith kissed her, then nudged her with his face. "Look at me Iz," He coaxed. " The reason that I want to do this is because I love you." Izzy looked into his eyes. "And I believe you, Izzy. I believe the whole story, I have for quite some time now." He hesitated for a moment, then continued, " I know what you have told Jack for years is true, I know it is, because I feel as though I have loved you forever." He said.

"I know you didn't believe me, not completely, back in California when I told you this same thing. You were probably right. I thought, I believed you enough." Keith whispered. He leaned in and kissed her neck, she dropped the pillow and gave him full access.

"Izzy." He whispered against her neck. "You can feel my thoughts, you know that I believe you. It's the only thing that makes any sense."

He pulled her close to him and held her, then kissed her neck again and inhaled. He could detect honeysuckle, but also lilac. He kissed her more, letting his lips work their way downward. He kissed her sides and pushed her down on the bed, then kissed her stomach. The Lilac was slowly dissipating. He put his lips on her tummy and blew, making a farting noise against her flesh. She laughed out loud, the scent of lilac was gone.

Once he was sure that she was feeling better, he laid his head on the pillow beside her. "You don't always have to be strong." He told her. "I'm here for you, together we are stronger. You can take strength from me, just like you took my shirt." He laughed.

"I shouldn't have stolen your shirt." Izzy said. "You should probably know now, I think I'm a kleptomaniac. It's not the first thing I've stolen."

"Iz." He whispered, laughing softly. "We are supposed to be together. There is no shame in love. If my shirt gave you strength, I'm glad that you took it. You are a kindhearted little witch that predicts the future and casts spells on grown men." Izzy giggled.

"It's true." Keith said. "I am bewitched."

"Keith." Izzy said his name softly.

"Just to be clear though." Keith said as an afterthought. "You haven't stolen anything else of mine have you?"

Izzy smiled and rolled over. She turned off the lamp and closed her eyes.

"Izzy?" Keith asked again.

"Shh!" Izzy said. "Trying to sleep."

"No, no, no you don't." Keith said. "I want to hear you say that you love me too."

She rolled over and faced him, her eyes had adjusted and she could see him quite clearly. She put a strand of his hair behind his ear, then left her hand against his cheek.

"I should think that is quite obvious." She said, "Of course I love you. You have always been the only one."

"You mean throughout all time?" He asked.

She nodded the affirmative. "The only one." She said, "I don't know if I would even know how to love anyone else. I also just figured something out, I'm the only one that you have ever loved."

Keith considered her words, she was right. No wonder it mattered so much to him! Love was something that Keith had searched for his entire life, he had liked all the women that he slept with and imagined that he loved them, but now he knew better. He only felt like this with Izzy, he guessed he had known it deep down for years.

"You're correct." Keith assured her. "I don't know when I first realized that, but you are absolutely correct. Secretly, three years ago I actually hoped you would be pregnant because I couldn't stand being separated. I think I was even a little angry that you weren't, like you did it on purpose." Keith laughed. "I mean, I was angry anyway so I let myself get mad at that too. Speaking of children, are we at risk again?" He asked her.

"I suppose so." she said. "I don't take birth control, there hasn't been a need. I don't really like the idea of what it does to a woman's body anyway." She replied thoughtfully.

"I don't either if you want me to be honest." Keith said. "We should probably practice some sort. I hate condoms but I'll use them if you want me to, in the meantime I can pull out. It isn't foolproof but I don't think you want a baby right away." Keith said, it was almost more of a question. He was 29, a child wouldn't be out of the question for him, he wanted children, he thought about the age difference between the two of them and decided they might as well discuss it now. There was a lot he and Izzy needed to talk about.

"It wouldn't kill me." She said, "I would like to wait until I'm at least 20, but I'm open to whatever fate holds for us."

"Do we have kids?" Keith asked, "Can you remember?"

Izzy's face became very solemn. She closed her eyes and tried to remember.

"I don't know how to explain it, but I'll try." She said, "It's different every time. You are always the same person, a person's family is usually the same, but not always. Sometimes my dad is alive, sometimes he isn't. Sometimes I have brothers, sometimes I don't. I have no doubt that each person comes back, I just don't know how it works. What I do know, is each time, you bring with you the same love and the same scars.

The morning light was starting to seep through the curtains, turning them orange. Keith scooped Izzy into his arms, she laid her head on his shoulder. He was content, he was happy, it was an unusual feeling for him. Keith had always felt alone, not lonely, it was different than that. It was a feeling that he was isolated inside his own body, almost like he wasn't able to connect fully with anyone. He tried, he loved his family, he recognized that they were human, that they had weakness as did he, but it was like there was an invisible barrier keeping him from feeling completely satisfied with any of his relationships. Women, he tried to be devoted to them, but he never felt like he was one with them. Something was different with Izzy, with her family, there was a familiarity, a sense of being comfortable with them. He was actually happy.

20

Izzy sat at her desk, she was trying to pay attention but it was so hard. She felt the stares from around the room, in the hallway there were whispers. Even her teachers looked at her differently now. She had tried her whole life to blend in. She dressed blandly so she didn't stand out, she seldom raised her hand to ask or answer questions in class. She did her homework on time, never complained, she didn't try out for plays or musicals or cheerleading. She just tried to be unnoticed. She didn't go to school dances, she didn't even eat lunch in the cafeteria. Anywhere she might be noticed, she would avoid it. Occasionally she would be invited to a slumber party or a get together, she would accept and have a good time, but kept in the distance. The others would giggle and laugh and talk about boys and secrets, Izzy would just smile and listen. If anyone asked her a question, she would just say she hadn't had a date yet. It was true, she and Keith hadn't dated. Remembering one story was easier than remembering many.

Now, all eyes were on her. The years she had spent hiding her past meant nothing, the whole school was aware of her relationship with Keith, she couldn't deny what they all had witnessed. She saw other students that she had known her whole life who now seemed almost afraid to speak with her. Boys stared at her as she walked by and she could hear the laughing and the whispers. Of course they would make it seem dirty, perhaps it was, Izzy wasn't sure of anything anymore. It felt to her as though the whole school had witnessed Keith kissing her in the parking lot and now the story had been released about the marriage in Mexico. It was written well, even sentimentally, it was very sweet, but highschool boys were gross and she was sure they knew it was more than a promise.

There was only a week left of school, kids were planning senior skip day. Izzy thought about going with them, but the questions would be more than she could deal with right now. Some of her teachers had approached her, they were worried of course that she was being taken advantage of, it was an unusual situation. A time where other girls her age were worried about prom dresses or getting a car for graduation or even taking their SAT's, Izzy was coordinating a relationship with a 29 year old man. She understood her teacher's concerns and she understood the whispers and even the laughter, understanding just made it worse.

The buzzer rang and class was dismissed. Mr Holojak commanded that Izzy remain behind which only made more people look at her. Then a familiar voice said from the doorway, "I'm sorry she can't stay late today." She looked up to see Keith waiting for her by the door. "We have someplace to be this afternoon." Mr Holojak was sizing Keith up.

"Why don't we plan tomorrow afternoon then." Mr Holojak said. "I would like both of you to be here."

He tried to stare Keith down but it didn't phase Keith at all, he just smiled and said that they were booked pretty heavily right now and that Izzy needed to leave with him because they were scheduled to get a blood test. She couldn't believe he said it, but now it was out there. She saw Mr. Holojak take a breath, Keith just leaned against the door and smiled. The Jocks on the other side of the room looked at each other with wide eyes. she was really going to be harassed tomorrow. Mr. Holojak didn't say a word, he just nodded to Keith, Izzy picked up her notebook and removed her purse from the back of her chair. She exited the room, Keith taking her arm and as they left, she couldn't decide if she was amused or terrified.

When they left the building she half expected to see the Porsche parked on the sidewalk again since Jack had clearly been attempting to draw attention to the pair of them, but the car was parked neatly by the curb, probably because Jack hadn't come this time. It was a beautiful day, the sky was bright blue and the temperature wasn't too hot. Keith walked his prize to the Porsche and opened the door for her. Once she was settled in, he gently closed the door and walked around to the driver's side. Izzy could sense the eyes on her, she didn't need to look. When Keith got in the car he motioned towards the front door of the school, she looked to see a mixed crowd of students watching their every move. Some of the hippies had moved up from the lower wall where they congregated to smoke, band members had come out the side door of the band room and of course her dependable jocks were watching and pointing as well.

"We garnered a lot of attention Iz." Keith laughed. Izzy nodded, she knew it was only starting, Keith had warned her about the press that was sure to come. She would prefer the press, kids were mean. "Can you handle it?" He asked. He knew it would be hard for even the most seasoned actors, he was expecting a lot out of an 18 year old girl.

"I can handle it." She said, She looked over her shoulder, the crowd was still watching. She took a deep breath and leaned over to Keith, she put her hands on the side of his face and kissed him. It was a long, luscious kiss. Keith was surprised but welcomed it. Her lips were so soft, her skin was so fresh, he couldn't imagine having ever considered anyone else.

"Wow." was all he could say. Izzy smiled big for the first time since he had come to Nebraska. He put the car in gear and drove off, the whole world lay ahead.

Jack's agent had leaked the Mexico story. Most of Hollywood was already talking about it. Nebraska papers had taken a little longer but now that reporters were aware of the connection between Hollywood and one of their own, everyone was talking.

"Mr. Holojak will try to talk us out of it." She said, "He wasn't aware that I was going to marry you again, thank you for that by the way, I was afraid maybe the gossip would stop."

"They will know everything by tomorrow." Keith told her. "Jack had his agent leak the proposal."

Keith laughed under his breath, Izzy was acting more like herself. The tone, the tease, the sarcasm, he felt as though maybe he could begin to relax, in fact even Ruth was coming around. After her initial anger, she tried to get to know him. They had spent the evening talking and sharing stories. He had told her about his own mother and father. There had been a bitter custody battle, his mother was troubled and his father was absent. Keith had never really felt loved, not the way he wanted to be loved. Keith tried to be a good son, make them love him. Most of his life, Keith felt lost. He never spoke of his need for parental love to anyone, but Ruth was so easy to talk to that he suddenly found himself spilling his every thought and fear to her. Ruth listened and comforted him and really for the first time in his life, he felt like part of a family.

"Tell me what you want, Izzy," Keith asked. He was looking into her eyes. They had just left the doctor's office, both had a cotton ball and a bandaid on their arms from the blood draw. "You haven't really asked for anything, you must want something?"

"I do." She confirmed.

"Then tell me." Keith asked.

"Alright." She nodded. "I want flowers, real pretty drippy flowers. I want us to dress up and I don't want sombreros!"

Keith laughed. "You don't think that was romantic?" He teased her.

"Um, no." She answered curtly.

"Do you want a ceremony? He asked, searching her face.

"You mean like a church? God no." She replied. "But I would like it to be more real this time."

Keith contemplated. "You know, I look awfully good in a tux." She looked at her fiance. How strange it was to even think the word, but he was also her husband and that was strange too. His hair was a little longer, sort of scruffy. He had a close, neatly trimmed beard and mustache, he had told her it was his look in the film. His hair was a little thinner now but lord he was sexy.

"You look good in anything. You look good without clothes too." She giggled. "I've seen you in a tux before. Not as many ruffles this time please." She commanded.

"Dooley noted!" Keith said, then smiled at his future bride. "I'll be honest, we were already planning on a ceremony. Your mother suggested the sunken gardens? We need to get you a dress, Jack and I already rented tuxedos, we got them for the whole week. We were afraid prom might cause problems and we wanted some nice photographs taken too." He lied. He and Jack had rented the tuxedos for both the wedding and her prom. "So you graduate in a week, we get married the next week, we have time to plan a little. I told your mother the gardens would be fine, I mean as long as there is shade." Keith laughed and so did Izzy, he just didn't do well in the Nebraska heat and humidity.

"That sounds perfect." Izzy exclaimed. "It's beautiful, and there is lots of room for reporters to spy and take pictures!"

Keith grinned, she was reluctant at first, but now she was full in. She was feeding the gossip and not backing down from the talk. He was proud of her. Intrigued, he asked, "Tell me more about these gardens."

"Well, the sunken gardens are in the middle of town and nestled between two very busy streets." She giggled. "But it is beautiful, tons of flowers and ponds with giant goldfish."

"Koi?" Keith asked. Izzy shrugged. "I'll put Jack on it, it sounds perfect."

When Keith and Izzy returned to Ruth's house, Keith was grinning from ear to ear. "Guess what?" he said to Ruth when they walked in.

"What?" Ruth asked, delighted at the relationship that she was developing with her future son in law.

"Izzy wants a ceremony, the courthouse won't do. She loves your idea of the sunken gardens?"

Ruth's face lit up with delight. "Oh baby, really?" She asked her daughter.

"Yeah." Izzy said softly. "I guess I do."

Ruth took her daughter's hand and pulled her towards her bedroom, closing the door behind them. She sat on the bed and patted next to her, Izzy minded and sat down. "This is a wise choice." Ruth said to her daughter. "I know you don't like being in front of people, but this is Keith's wedding too, you both were cheated."

Izzy nodded, her mother was right, Keith was very old fashioned, she knew he wanted a ceremony. It wasn't just for publicity, he needed it.

"I need to find something to wear. Keith is going to wear a tux!" Izzy confided to her mother. Ruth stood up and opened her cedar trunk at the foot of the bed. She pulled out a large white box and opened it. Underneath the tissue paper was a beautiful pale silver satin gown. "This was your grandmother's wedding gown." She said, " I was too tall for it, but it should fit you perfectly. It's an antique, I know you like those kinds of things. I'm sure Arlene can take it in if she needs to."

Arlene was one of Ruth Meek's favorite neighbors and was an incredible seamstress. She had sewn many things for the girls over the years.

Izzy gently lifted the gown from the box. It was stunning. The gown was simple, silver satin. It had a drop waist and the hem line was patterned with white pearls, silver beads and tiny little rosettes. There was not a sequin on it, it was elegant in its simplicity. Under the dress was a light silver tulle veil that had a simple rhinestone band that would be attached to her hair, the veil looked to be about long enough to hit below the waist.

"Mom!" Izzy exclaimed. "It's beautiful!"

"I saved it for you girls, Terry didn't like it, it wasn't to her taste. But I had a feeling that it would appeal to you."

"Satin will show everything." Izzy stated.

"It is a telling fabric, but you don't have anything to hide my love. At least not yet." Ruth laughed. "Not a roll of flab anywhere and that is perfect for the reporters, they won't be able to insinuate anything nasty. You are going to be the most beautiful bride, you will look like a princess."

"I'm going to need some petticoats and some under things." Izzy warned.

"We can do that." Ruth assured, then put her arm around her little girl and gave her a big hug. "We could look for a prom dress too."

"Mom!" Izzy exclaimed. Ruth tightened her hug.

"I have something else for you." Ruth said. She stood and went to her jewelry box and opened it. She pulled out a little velvet bag and handed it to her daughter. Izzy gently tugged on the strings and loosened the opening, she shook the bag and a man's gold ring fell into her hand. "It was your father's," Ruth said. "I think he would like for you to give it to Keith."

"Mom," Izzy said. "I never even knew Dad wore a ring."

"I only eyeballed Keith's finger, but I'm pretty sure this will fit. Ruth said.

Izzy slid it on her thumb, it went over easily. She did have thin fingers but so did Keith, when he had returned Jack's ring on Oscar night, Izzy had slipped it over her thumb while she had gone to put it away. This ring fit the same way as Jack's ring had fit on her thumb, she was sure it would slide on Keith's finger. "I think it will fit too." She confirmed.

"You can always get it sized later if he needs to." Ruth said. "I just don't think we have enough time to get it done before the ceremony."

21

"I don't want to go to prom." Izzy stated flatly.

Jack just smiled and ignored her. He was holding up a dark blue tiffany dress that he had bought for her. He held it in front of her, admiring the color against her pale skin. It, like the wedding dress, was simple and elegant. It had sheer half sleeves, a sheer collar above a fitted bodice and flowing hemline. The neckline was a little low for Izzy but the sheer fabric that covered the shoulders allowed for a decorum of modesty. "I got you these shoes too." Jack said, dropping the dress and handing her a shoe box that he had set down on the reclining chair in the living room.

"Why isn't anyone listening to me?" She asked her mother.

"The dress is stunning, Izzy." Her mother said, "Try on the shoes."

Izzy just stood there holding the shoe box and shaking her head. Keith had been watching from the dining room and was having trouble containing his laughter. No one was paying any attention to Izzy's insistence that she didn't want to go. Izzy stomped her foot at Jack but he just laughed and held the dress up to her again. "I think you should wear your hair up." He said.

"Mom!" Izzy whined in desperation.

"Oh darling, can't you see this isn't just for you?" Her mother said.

Jack looked at Izzy with a pouty look, he quivered his lip at her. "Stop it!" Izzy said.

"Honey, think of everything Jack has done for you in the past. Are you really going to deny this man a prom?" Ruth laughed. "Jack told me that neither he or Keith had gone to their own proms. Make the boys happy!"

"Oh, my god." Izzy said. Keith smiled watching it unfold. Ruth and Jack had agreed, the best coercion would be for Jack to want to go. Deep down, Keith thought it was true anyway, any excuse for Jack to show off and dance, he would want to take. He was sure reporters would be there as well, the story was beginning to leak in the local papers now, it wouldn't be long before reporters were outside the house. Jack had stopped parking in the garage, making it easier for their whereabouts to be found.

"Fine." She said, "I'll go. I'll have two movie stars as a date, how weird could it be? The whole school whispers when they see me anyway."

Keith stood up and came into the living room. He took Izzy's hand and made her face him. "Are you sure you can handle it?" He teased.

"She's fine." Jack said. "This girl is tough."

"I'm sure." Izzy answered. "Hell, it might even be fun. I guess we should get it over with, the sooner they run with the story, the sooner it will be old news."

"Now you're catching on." Jack smiled. "As you know, I've made a few headlines myself."

22

It was Friday afternoon, Prom was the next day. Most of the whispers had died down, or at least Izzy didn't hear them anymore. The classes Izzy had were for the main part just letting the seniors goof around. She had a final in Geometry but wasn't worried about it at all. Izzy really liked Geometry. Her mother had always told her that people were usually either good at either Algebra or Geometry but seldom both. Izzy hated Algebra but the theorems and proofs in Geometry made perfect sense to her, plus it required a good memory and Izzy certainly had that.

Mr. Holojak wasn't as giving towards the seniors as the other teachers at East High. He had assigned a last minute paper, he was demanding the students write their own drama. Izzy had one already written, she had sent it to Jack earlier that year. Thankfully Jack had remembered to bring it with him when he and Keith came to Nebraska. She pulled it out from her notebook and laid it on Mr Holojak's desk. He seemed very surprised, he had just assigned it two days prior. "I should have guessed yours would be first." He said. "I am surprised you found the time with your upcoming nuptials." He laughed.

The story had been in the morning paper. The headline read, One of Lincoln's own to marry Hollywood Royalty. The meat and potatoes story wasn't in the local paper, it was in the Globe and could be found at every grocery store near the checkout counter. It read, Keith Enidarrac to marry an eighteen year old in Nebraska. Illegal

300

marriage performed years prior in Tijuana. Izzy just grinned at her teacher, she honestly wondered if she opened his desk drawer, which news source she would discover inside of it.

Mr. Holojak's class was her last class of the day. The classes had all been cut short so the students could get ready for prom. The dismissal bell rang and Izzy gathered her things. Jake Mueller and Isacc Larsen, two of the football jerks that were in Izzy's class, lingered in front of her desk. She looked up at the two football players and smiled. She had been practicing different scenarios she might have with those two inside of her head for a week now. She was ready for them.

"Can I help you two boys?" She asked cheerfully, accentuating the word boys just to piss them off.

"So Izzy," Jake asked unphased. "Are the stories true?" Issac laughed and nudged Jake in the back.

Izzy was a little disappointed they hadn't picked up on the barb, but they weren't the brightest bulbs on the string of lights.

"Ask her chicken." Issac nudged.

"Like, if you were married already, then you probably had sex right?" Jake blurted out loudly then laughed. "And if you are already married, why are you doing it again?"

Izzy leaned against her desk and smiled sweetly at the boys. She had this answer well practiced. It hadn't been hard to imagine what questions the boys would ask of her, a well thought out question would have been beyond either of their abilities. She smiled to herself, they weren't good enough to be professional football players and they never bothered to learn anything in class. They would make nice janitors a few years from now. Then she felt guilty, every janitor that she had ever known worked hard and was nice, these boys were incapable of both.

"Well," She said, "Yes, of course the wedding was consummated and," she paused, slowly looking the two boys up and down, then she leaned in a little closer. They could smell the sweet essence of her perfume, it was a delightful blend of roses and sage. "If the sex hadn't been incredible, I wouldn't get married to him again." She smiled demurely at them.

"Shit!" Jake blurted out, "I told you Issac, the quiet ones are the best ones."

Izzy leaned forward and slowly licked her lips. Then stood up and turned around.

"Jesus." Issac mumbled. The two boys stood dumbfounded. Izzy glided past them only to see Keith waiting for her in the doorway, a proud look on his face.

"You weren't supposed to hear that." She laughed as they sped off in the Porsche. Jack had insisted that Keith pick her up every day in that ridiculous thing.

"Did you mean it?" He asked, smiling as he drove down the road.

"Yeah." She said, "I meant it."

"Well I bet you give those two jerks wet dreams tonight." He laughed. Izzy turned her head so Keith wouldn't see her laughing and looked out the window. She hoped they did have wet dreams about her. It felt so good to finally speak about Keith out loud. She had kept so much inside and locked away for years. She hadn't told anyone what she did on her visits to California and had only mentioned that her Aunt Dorothy lived there, that had been by choice. Ruth had told her that keeping it quiet would protect the Enidarracs and that she would never need to worry if someone was friendly with her because of who she was or who she knew. Izzy had agreed, it made sense. So she had kept the friendship secret. She had kept her writing secret, her feelings secret and finally her pain secret. No one knew when her heart was breaking, no one knew when she was terrified that she might have been pregnant. No one knew she had gone to Mexico and married Keith, no one knew that she had wished she was dead and no one knew she often screamed in her pillow at night. Now she could finally talk about it and she had to admit, it felt good.

The night of prom the three of them had arrived in a limousine. Most of the kids had come much the same way, but when Jack and Keith stepped out of the Limo, camera's started flashing. Keith reached in and took Izzy's hand and helped her out of the Limo. She hadn't thought it possible but even more camera flashes began going off.

Her dress hit about mid shin and as she stepped from the limo, her legs looked long and lovely. The shoes that Jack had picked out were very glamorous. They had high heels which Izzy hated. They were the same dark navy blue as her dress but had a few rhinestones on the toes and ankle straps. They were a brilliant selection, that was the first view of the mysterious young woman who had captured Keith Enidarrac's heart. When the rest of her emerged from the car, there was an audible gasp from some of the other prom goers. A young, slender woman with an incredible figure stepped from the car. Her hair was up in a loose french roll with wispy long blonde bangs on the side of her face. Jack had added a rhinestone comb into her hair that caught the camera flashes. She wore just a little make-up at Keith's direction, but in truth she didn't need it. She blushed enough getting out of the car that her cheeks were rosy and the dark blue of the dress matched her eyes, making her look extremely beguiling.

So many of Izzy's friends had just grown used to her casual clothing and white tennis shoes. She usually had a ponytail of some type and seldom wore make-up. Most of the kids at her school thought that she was pretty, but she was so painfully shy that she was often ignored. Watching her step out of the Limo was like watching someone they had never met. The boys all ogled her and the girls were growing to hate her.

Keith took her hand and led her in. The prom was being held at the Cornhusker Hotel. Izzy whispered in Keith's ear to watch out for the bathrobe police and he laughed. There was a red carpet laid down for the kids to walk on. Keith was still laughing when he told Izzy she might want to get used to this kind of thing. Izzy rolled her eyes and snorted. She was trying hard to not look stupid in the high heels that Jack had picked out for her. She leaned over and whispered to Keith "I changed my mind."

Keith squeezed her hand and continued to move forward. "Like you could get away from me now." He said in response.

"Mr. Enidarrac!" A reporter yelled. "Is it true you are marrying her?"

"Keith." another one yelled. "Can you tell us when you met?"

"Jack!" yelled another. "Jack, will you come talk to us?"

Jack slowed down a bit and whispered into Keith's ear. "Never doubt me, choir boy."

When they entered the Cornhusker Hotel, a large desk was set up in front of the ballroom. Mrs. Pitchka and Mr. Holojak both manned the table at the entrance, behind them blue lights twinkled and a band was playing Brick house by the Commodores. Lots of laughter emanated from the double open doors. Izzy started to step backwards, looking at the exit sign glowing above one of the doors, Keith held her hand firmly. Jack approached the table first, flashing his most charming smile and leaned down to whisper in Geraldine Pitchka's ear. She responded by holding onto his arm and giggling loudly.

"Mr. Holojak!" Keith said in greeting, extending his hand forward. Izzy's teacher accepted the handshake but eyed Keith suspiciously. "I don't believe I've actually introduced myself to you. Keith Enidarrac." Keith continued. "Izzy's fiance. She speaks highly of you, I suspect you are responsible for much of her writing talent. Maybe we can find time to talk later in the evening." He smiled.

Izzy had seen Jack pour on the Enidarrac charm many times, Jack was brilliant at it. Izzy had never witnessed Keith do it, the man was incredible. She knew both men well, they both were somewhat shy and had insecurities, she studied the pair now, they oozed charm and displayed nothing but confidence. She was surprised how good Keith was at it.

A small crowd had gathered around the table. When Keith introduced himself there were some obvious whispers. "Fiance." Mr. Holojak repeated the word and then shook his head disapprovingly. Keith continued to talk to him, exuding confidence.

"Technically, her husband." Keith laughed, "But the real ceremony will be next weekend. I know it must seem strange to everyone but the truth is our families have been close for years. Our families kept it secret, you just never know when someone is using you. Iz is a sweet shy girl, it was my duty to protect her."

Izzy noticed that Mr. Holojak was no longer shaking his head, in fact he was nodding it now. She thought to herself, my God, Keith makes it look so easy.

"I hope that we can have that conversation you wanted to have sometime this evening." Keith continued. "I appreciate that you care so much about her and the special interest that you have taken in her talent. She will go far in the industry and she will owe a great deal of it to you."

Izzy took Keith's hand and pulled him from the desk, he obliged and followed her into the ballroom. Jack paid for three tickets, then winked at Geraldine before he left the table. "Don't forget." He said. "One slow dance."

"Oh Mr. Enidarrac." She said, "You are such a terrible flirt!" Then she giggled her obnoxious laugh and Jack followed the other two into the ballroom.

Kerrie Pitchka was the first to greet Izzy. She turned to Keith and introduced herself. "Hi." She gushed. "I'm Kerrie Pitchka, Izzy and I are just fabulous friends."

Izzy tried hard not to snort again. Kerrie was dressed in a low cut emerald green dress with lots of sequins. Keith thought it looked like something her mother would wear, but smiled graciously at the girl. "Of course," He replied. "Your mother is an amazing woman, she tells me that you have a wonderful singing voice."

"She does." Izzy confirmed honestly. "We are in singers together."

"Singers?" Keith asked.

"It's the name of the choir!" Kerrie gushed. "And Izzy, that is just the sweetest thing for you to say. I mean about my voice!"

Keith tried not to laugh, the girl was laying it on thick.

Izzy was telling the truth, Kerrie had one of the prettiest voices she had ever heard, aside from Izzy's sister. They were both altos, but Izzy's voice paled in comparison.

"I would love the opportunity to sing with you Mr. Enidarrac." She continued to gush.

"I'd love to hear you sing Kerrie," Keith said. "But I don't do duets now." He smiled at Izzy and led her deeper into the ballroom.

"Did you hear that?" Izzy could hear Kerrie saying to someone. "Keith Enidarrac wants to hear me sing."

The stares never seemed to stop whether Keith and Izzy were dancing or sitting quietly in a corner talking. The Picture man was constantly snapping photos of the three of them. Jack danced not once, but three times with Geraldine. He was an amazing dancer, he moved so eloquently, Izzy could have watched him the entire evening. At one point, one of the band members invited Keith onto the stage. He graciously accepted the guitar that was handed to him and began playing his Oscar winning song. He kept his eyes on Izzy the entire time and the jealous looks she received from many of the girls at the prom, didn't escape her. Izzy felt extremely uncomfortable but couldn't stop the blush on her cheeks. There was nothing that he could have done that would have been sexier, she had to cross her legs and squeeze her thighs together. She wanted him so badly.

Prom was well underway when Izzy whispered in Keith's ear that she had had enough. He kissed the back of her hand and tapped Jack on the shoulder as he was dancing yet another dance with Geraldine. Jack nodded and Izzy and Keith began exiting the ballroom. Mr. Holojak was standing by the doors, his arms folded across his chest, halfway blocking the exit. It was apparent that although he had been impressed with Keith, he still had not been swayed. Keith bent down and kissed Izzy's cheek then let go of her hand and motioned for Mr. Holojak to step out of the ballroom with him. As soon as Keith was no longer at her side, Izzy was mobbed by her classmates. They all had questions and asked them all at the same time. Izzy tried to be calm and polite, she had known that it would happen and had tried to practice for it as best as she could, she explained that they had been family friends since she was eight years old and that over time she had simply fallen in love. The music ended , Jack came up behind her and took Izzy's arm.

"Where's Keith?" He asked. The crowd of young girls began to disperse from around Izzy.

"He's talking to my teacher." She answered.

They left the ballroom and found Keith and Mr. Holojak, sitting at the table by the door deep in conversation. They were both smiling and seemed to be having a decent time. Izzy was relieved, Mr. Holojak could be quite intimidating, she also knew he didn't approve of the relationship. To her surprise, when Jack and she joined them at the table, Mr. Holojak smiled broadly at her. He stood up and gave her a brisk hug. "Congratulations!" He said and Izzy could tell that he meant it.

Izzy wasn't sure how Keith had managed it, but her teacher seemed satisfied. She glanced upwards at her fiance from under her dark brown lashes. He could be a force to reckon with, she knew that personally. The Enidarracs always got what they wanted one way or another, she loved this man, and she understood the power of his charm. The charm his entire family possessed.

As they got into the Limo, more photographers were waiting. The camera flashes were blinding as she stepped into the Limo. "Are you engaged?" A reporter yelled. "Where is the ring?" He yelled again. The driver shut the door and a few moments later they were headed back home.

Izzy laid her head against Jack's shoulder. He was wound up. He sat across from Keith and was leaning forward on his knees, rolling his thumbs along the inside of his fingers, making a motion almost as if his fingers were rolling like a wave on each hand. It was Jack's tell again. He did this when he was really excited, when his mind was going a thousand times faster than anyone else's. He laughed as he rolled his fingers. "It's almost done!" He said, then slapped Keith's leg. "Did you hear the last question? You two need to go ring shopping." He said.

Izzy looked at Keith and moved her long wisp of bangs out of her face, they weren't quite long enough to tuck behind her ears and sometimes they really annoyed her. "Actually Keith." Izzy said. "If you would like, my mother gave me my dad's wedding ring. If you want to, you can wear it." Izzy shyly lowered her eyes.

Keith moved over next to Izzy and brought her chin up so she would look into his eyes. "That is the sweetest gesture I've ever heard of." He said. "I would be honored to wear your father's ring." Then he kissed her, gently on the lips.

"What about your fiance?" Jack asked. "The press would love to get pictures of you shopping for a ring. I think we should do it." Jack commanded.

"Don't worry Jack." Keith said softly. "I've got this."

That night as they lay in bed, they didn't talk. Ruth knew they were cohorting downstairs, but she accepted it. Keith held Izzy's hand in his and gently ran his fingers over hers. She rested her head on his shoulder, she loved the way he smelled.

"You have the tiniest fingers." He said. "Do you want a big old diamond?"

Izzy rolled over and gazed at his beautiful face. "I don't need a ring at all." She said.

"Well you are going to wear a ring." Keith said. "For when Braden comes sniffing around."

Izzy laid her head back down on Keith's shoulder. "The joy is in the vow, not the jewelry." She said, "If you want, I can ask my mom if she has a ring that we can use."

Keith had actually never considered a woman wouldn't demand a diamond ring. He played with her fingers a bit more and contemplated his future wife. She had never been like any other woman he had known. With Izzy, it was always about feelings, not things. He smiled in the darkness thinking of his choice, knowing he had made the right one. He felt so completely at peace.

"Are you nervous?" He asked her.

"Nah," Izzy laughed. "We've done this hundreds of times before."

"Cute." He said. "Do you really remember each time?"

Izzy was silent for a few moments. "We've never really talked about it have we?" She asked. Keith shook his head. "It's not like that." She continued. "I mean, there are things that you remember like yesterday. Your lyrics were like that, because you had wanted them so bad," Izzy rolled over again and stroked the side of Keith's face. She liked this look, this neatly trimmed beard. She remembered the Oscar look, the disheveled hair and scruffy beard. It wasn't Keith, Keith was tidy, Keith liked things where they belonged. He liked the counters clean, the laundry folded and the toilet paper on the roller not sitting on the bathroom counter.

"Mostly," Izzy continued, still thinking about Keith's face. "It's like the card trick. It's a feeling."

"Like deja vu?" Keith asked.

"No. not like that." Izzy began to play with a strand of Keith's hair. "Really my whole life is like deja vu." Izzy said. "It constantly feels like I've done it before. But the feeling that I'm talking about, it starts out inside of you, like a nudge, that little voice telling you what you are supposed to do. If you ignore it, it's more like a push, then a scream if you still aren't listening." Izzy let go of Keith's hair and rolled over on her back, her head on her own pillow, she looked at an imaginary dot on the ceiling."

"Go on." Keith encouraged her.

"Sometimes, you know it is going to be unpleasant." Izzy said. "I've run away from some of that as fast as I can. Sometimes, even knowing it might not be nice, I run towards it." Keith gently stroked Izzy's scar on her leg and she nodded.

"They follow you, you know." she said.

"What follows you." He asked

"Scars." Izzy stated flatly. "You can't escape them."

"You said that the other night. I should have asked more questions. So you're telling me you had this scar before?" He asked.

"I've always had a bad scar." She said, "Scars are part of who you are, you can't escape them, or at least I have never been able to. It's not just physical scars, you carry emotional scars with you too. I think that might be the point."

"To learn from them so you don't have them again?" Keith prodded.

"No." She answered. "To not be afraid of them, to face them head on. Scars make you stronger."

"I'm not sure that I understand." He said softly.

"Like, I didn't do very well this time." She said, "I didn't embrace the emotional scar at all, if I had, we would have spoken and worked through everything. That's what led to the physical scar, I gave up, I thought about dying."

"I gave up too." Keith said.

"No, you did what you were supposed to do. You were strong." Izzy said.

"Explain." He demanded.

"Despite all evidence, you reached out to me." Izzy whispered softly. "I'm the one who is supposed to remember us, but I gave up. You didn't. You came here with no expectations, very little hope but believed in our love enough to try."

Keith pulled her as close to him as he could and held on tightly. She was right, it was the first time he could remember heading into a situation so completely unprepared. She was worth the risk, she had loved him completely and he knew it, reaching out to someone who is dedicated to you and to you alone, that was the key. That sort of person would never let you down.

"I promise that next time, I won't give up." Izzy said.

"Maybe you were supposed to." Keith answered. "Maybe that is what made me look inside of myself and find out who I was. You know something else, you did the same thing when you were eight years old."

"Interesting." She agreed. "That might explain why I kept searching for your colors! It even explains the answer I found."

"What do you mean?" He asked.

"Do you remember back at the beach, when you asked me why I always made you angry?" She asked.

Keith remembered. He remembered every moment of that day at the beach. He remembered falling in love with her then.

"I couldn't tell our colors apart. I tried to make you angry because I wanted to see if they changed."

"Go on." Keith urged her.

"I noticed first in the corn field." She said, the corner of her mouth slowly curling upward. "They were much bolder than they had been in the past. I think, going with your theory, that you being angry with me and holding it in these last few years, made your colors more passionate! "

"I'm not sure I'm following this time." Keith said. Izzy and his brother, their minds went a million miles a minute, thinking several thoughts at once and blending them together. Keith wished he could get into her head, feel what she felt so he could understand better and connect even more with her.

"It wasn't enough, that's all I mean." She said, Keith shrugged and Izzy rolled her eyes. "Are you concentrating?" She teased.

Keith furrowed his brows and put his fingers on either side of his head.

"I am now." He said.

"Just remembering the love, it wasn't enough." Izzy said. She remembered Jack telling her how lighting can make or break a movie. She tried another tactic. "Your colors became more intense when we were apart. You were angry, but you loved me. It wasn't enough to remember our love, you had to feel it."

He rolled over on top of her. He kissed her on the mouth, then moved to her neck. He heard her gasp as he worked his way downward. He positioned himself between her legs and ran his fingers down her inner thigh.

Izzy closed her eyes and let herself feel. She could feel his colors. They were bright, almost glowing. Yellows and purples and bright blue. She felt him kissing her inner thigh as he slowly moved her legs further apart. She felt him lick her between her legs, it was a sensation she had never felt before. At first he teased her with his tongue, lightly flicking it across her vulva, then there was a slight sucking sensation as he had moved to the most erogenous area, sucking her clitoris with expertise.

Izzy could barely stand it. She wanted him to stop but she wanted more. Colors were exploding in her head. She cried out, unable to stop herself. She felt Keith enter her body, she pumped her thighs in a rhythmic dance for a few moments then felt her muscles contracting. She wrapped her legs tightly around his waist, driving him deeper inside of her.

Keith had meant to tease her, he wanted to show her how passionate he had become. He wasn't expecting to experience what he did. While tasting her, she cried out, an earthy primal sound that drove him almost to a frenzy. He got inside of her and she pumped her legs driving him to the edge of insanity. He felt her coming and then taking him further inside while pulling him downward with her soft silky legs. His head was exploding with colors, he could feel what she felt. He could feel himself explode inside of her and her muscles tighten around his erection, but he could swear he felt her pleasure too.

When they were finished, neither wanted it to end. He stayed inside of her until he no longer could and when he moved off of her she tried to hold him there.

"I'm not sure what that was." He finally managed to say.

"Did I do something wrong?" Izzy asked. "I'm still new to this."

"Iz." Keith said, turning to face her. "I've had sex with a lot of women. I've never felt anything like that before. No, you didn't do anything wrong, that was the most incredible thing I've ever felt. I saw colors!"

Izzy giggled. "Then the universe is telling us we got it right!"

"We most certainly did." Keith agreed. "Is it always like that for you? I might end up having a heart attack but my God I hope it is like that for me from now on." He thought some more about their conversation earlier.

"Do I have scars?" He asked. Izzy nodded. "Tell me." he prodded.

"I sense mostly, abandonment from you." She said, "It feels like something that might not ever heal. Like, trust is hard for you, like you want something so badly but these feelings get in your way."

Keith didn't know how she sensed what she did, but she was correct. The only one he trusted entirely was her. He didn't even completely trust Jack. Being with Izzy just felt natural, like an extension of himself. She provided more than just meeting his physical needs, what she gave him was intangible, but she gave him a sense of belonging that he had never felt before.

"Now Jack." Izzy laughed, "That man." Then she shook her head. Keith rolled to his side and gazed at her. "He has soooo many scars,"

"So answer me truthfully." Keith nudged. "Are you afraid?"

"I'm so frightened my hair is perspiring." Izzy laughed.

"I love your hair." Keith said, playing with the long golden strands that fell across her pillow.

"Were you disappointed that I cut it?" She asked.

"Of course not." Keith said. "It's your hair, I would love you no matter what." Keith said. "But why did you cut it?."

"It was the first step." She said,

"The first step to what?" He asked.

"Of being angry with myself. Cutting it helped me end part of who I was." She said, She was no longer ashamed of her emotions, she had accepted her feelings. She might have wanted to die, but she also fought to live. She had wanted both. It was just like the colors she saw in her head. Red, green, live or die, everything was connected. She turned toward him and he pulled her atop of him. He kissed her forehead, then nose, then chin and then neck. She tilted her head backwards and closed her eyes. She loved for him to kiss her like that.

"Are you sure that you want to marry an old man?" He asked.

"You aren't old, I'm just young." She laughed. "It's all relative."

"When I'm forty, you will still be in your twenties. When I'm sixty, you will be in your forties." He said.

"And you watch." Izzy smirked. "I won't be young enough and you will leave me for someone in their thirties. Hollywood sucks."

"It will never happen." Keith laughed. "I will only love you. Believe me, after what you just did to me, I would never enjoy having sex with anyone else."

Izzy smiled and pulled Keith down to her mouth, "I'm not worried about it." She said, then she kissed him again with all that she had.

23

Jack had been worried about what was going to happen to Ruth when Izzy left home. Ruth confided to him that she was going to move to San Juan Texas. Her best friend Beth lived there. Ruth and the girls had spent many summers with Beth when the girls were young. Before Terry's horse shows and before Izzy met Jack. They rented a condo on Padre Island and enjoyed the beach. Izzy had one of the worst sunburns of her life on Padre Island. She was almost fluorescent red and peeled three times. She had to lay on a sheet in nothing but her underwear in front of a fan for days. Izzy had such fair skin, Ruth and Terry tanned easily but Izzy burned. The doctor had prescribed a spray with aloe vera in it and Ruth had to spray her several times each day.

Once recovered, they were far more careful with Izzy. They made her wear a hat and kept her inside during the sunniest part of the day. At night, the girls would go out with flashlights and catch little sand crabs. They always let them go free after catching them, but the hunt was a lot of fun. There had been one evening that the girls found a large sea turtle laying eggs in the dunes. It was beautiful.

Ruth had always loved Texas. Beth owned a truckstop and brought home dinner every night. The plan was Beth would sell the truck stop and Ruth would join her, they would buy a condo or a duplex and enjoy their retirement together. Ruth was left comfortable, when her husband had been killed, he had a large life insurance policy and she also received payments from the veterans administration and social security. The government took good care of her. She had continued to teach for a while, but shortly after Izzy came home and seemed troubled, she had retired so she could focus on her youngest daughter. Ruth had already contacted a realtor to list the house. Beth was looking for their dream retirement home in San Juan. They were going to travel a bit and take life easy.

Jack lay on his back in the dark room, taking long drags from a cigarette he had borrowed from Ruth. He remembered the first night he had spent in this house and he had done the same thing. He took another drag, the end lit up red and glowed in the darkness. He had grown to love this room. He remembered how he felt the first time he had come. Ruth had spent the day shopping, giving him everything he needed. He still had the cowboy hat and boots. He kept some of his clothes in the closet and even after so much time had passed, he was surprised to see that they still hung there. Ruth had made him feel as though her house was his home. He thought about her selling the place and he ached inside.

Ruth tapped on the door frame. He had left the door open, but she didn't come in. "Jack?" She asked. "Are you alright?" She reached for the light switch but Jack stopped her before she flicked it on.

"Leave the light off Ruth." He said. His voice quivered a bit.

"May I come in?" She asked him.

"It's your house." Jack responded.

"Yes, it is, but it is your room." She said.

Jack wondered how she managed to know exactly what to say. He sat up and Ruth sat beside him. "Change is always hard." She said to him, "Did I ever tell you about when my husband died?" She asked him.

"No, you never really spoke about it." He answered.

"For the longest time, as I was drifting off to sleep, I would feel the weight of his arm across me." She said, "It gave me so much comfort. Then one day I told a friend about it. She told me that our minds play tricks on us, that our brain would convince us it was true so we wouldn't grieve. Do you know I never felt his arm over me again and for years I secretly hated my friend for ruining it."

Jack didn't speak. He waited for Ruth to continue, he was going to put out the cigarette but Ruth took it from him and took a drag, then handed it back to Jack to put out in the ashtray on the bedside table.

"Let yourself grieve." She said, "It's alright."

He wasn't sure why, but all of sudden he lost control and sobbed. Ruth held him like she had often held her children and rocked back and forth very gently, holding his head with her hand against her shoulder. "Shssh" She said, "It's alright, let it out."

Jack hadn't cried like that in years. He wasn't embarrassed, in fact it felt good. Ruth didn't let go until Jack let her know that she could.

"It's alright honey." She told him. "I understand. I want you to know, home isn't a place, home is where you are loved. No matter where I am, when you come see me, you will feel at home." She assured him. For the first time, he understood once and for all what family felt like.

"I can't believe you kept this room for me." He managed to choke out.

"I knew you would come home." She said, "Family always comes home."

"You want to hear something?" Jack asked her. "The hardest part about Keith and your daughter was wondering if I would ever see you again."

"All Terry's boyfriends used to tell me the same thing when she broke up with them." Ruth said. "There are a couple that still stop by."

"Is that true Ruth Meeks?" He asked.

"I can't believe that you would question my sincerity." She said, feigning indignation.

"Alright." Jack said. "I believe you. What do you do when they stop by?"

"I get out the jar of pennies, we play Indian poker." She said,

"The world is a better place with you in it Ruth." Jack said.

"Go on." She laughed. After a few minutes she nudged his shoulder. "I'm serious." She said, "Go on."

24

The sunken gardens were in full bloom. Ruth had arranged for a trellis and had it covered with white and pale pink roses, pink and lavender lilies and long trails of drippy white flowers. There were cameramen everywhere and people lined up on the street trying to catch a glimpse of the movie stars. Jack and Keith wore the same tuxedos that they had worn to the prom. They were simple black tuxedos, no tails and simple gray bow ties. They both looked extremely handsome. Ruth and Terry both had on silver dresses. Ruth was striking with her silver hair and silver eyes. Terry looked beautiful no matter what she wore, but the silver against her olive skin was striking. Izzy wore the antique gown. The satin shone in the setting sun and the beadwork at the bottom hemline sparkled. She had wanted to go barefoot, but Ruth insisted she wear shoes. She found a pair of silver sandals with kitten heels that Izzy reluctantly agreed to wear, Keith still towered over her but Ruth was satisfied with the look. Izzy carried a bouquet of faded pink roses and baby's breath. The ceremony was short. It had been arranged that way, Keith was just not getting used to the Nebraska heat.

It was late in the afternoon so most of the garden was in the cool shade, tall trees lined the west side of the hill and the rustling of the leaves sounded very peaceful. The judge read from a script with little inflection. It was clear he was nervous. Ruth cried a bit, Izzy's sister Terry had come to stand up with her and Jack stood by Keith's side. When the judge asked if they would exchange rings, Keith

320

nodded. Izzy seemed surprised and watched with intense interest as Jack handed a small box to Keith. He opened it, repeated the vow the Judge gave to him, then slipped a ring on her finger. Izzy stood very still as she gazed upon the ring on her finger.

It seemed so long ago that she was in a car at a pawn shop in Los Angeles. Keith had left her there and gone back into the store, he had changed his mind about purchasing an album. He hadn't taken long and returned with his package that he had just carelessly laid on the back seat of his car. They had gone to the beach, they had talked, they had spent the day getting to know one another. What she never knew was he had gone back in to ask about the ring she had been looking at. It was a delicate gold ring, the center had tiny diamonds in the center that formed a star, then it was cut out from the rest of the ring in the design of a celtic cross and surrounded by a small circle of white gold with four tiny diamonds beside each cut out. It was so small, it wasn't expensive. The pawn shop had it priced at fifty dollars, but Izzy had thought it was the most beautiful thing she had ever seen.

She looked down at her hand that now donned that very ring. Keith had gone back in and purchased it so long ago, he had never said a word, even when they were married in Tijuana. This time she couldn't stop herself from letting a tear roll down her cheek. She looked up at Keith just as the tear fell from her face. He kissed her hand and looked so smug. She slipped her father's ring onto Keith's hand and he winked at her. The judge was saying they were pronounced man and wife, he kissed her softly on the lips then she was surrounded by everyone, congratulating the couple. The crowd above them cheered. Her sister hugged her and whispered in her ear, "Good going kid, finally I'm not the trouble maker." Then she hugged her again.

The rest was kind of a blur, Jack made a quick exit, she saw her mother hugging him tightly. He was off to the airport, he had already stayed longer than he had intended. As he left the gardens there was a burst of questions from the reporters who had been waiting above, there were cameras flashing and reporters yelling. Keith squeezed Izzy's hands and looked down at her, he had shaved, he looked much younger without hair on his face. His toothy grin was more obvious but she couldn't see anything other than his beautiful brown eyes. "It's about to hit the fan." He said. "I hope you're ready." She nodded to him, she wasn't ready but she would give it her best.

Keith removed the jacket to the tuxedo and rolled his sleeves up. His face was a little shiny but otherwise he appeared cool. They sat together on the edge of the stone pond, koi swam to the edge hoping for food or maybe they were just curious. The police had placed a barrier around the garden and were holding back the reporters and curious onlookers. He took her hand in his and looked deeply into her dark blue eyes. "I know that I hurt you," He said, "I'm sure I will again. All I can do is promise you that I will try my best not to. I love you Iz, the world isn't always black and white, I can't guarantee I will always make the right choice." He looked up at the setting sun. Fireflies were beginning to blink in the shrubbery around the pond. "I'll never get used to those." He laughed. Keith took Izzy's hand and kissed the back of it once more. " Are you afraid?" He asked. She shook her head and he smiled, then he threw the jacket over his shoulder and stood up. Still holding her hand they climbed up the stone stairway that led out of the gardens. She held onto his hand with her right hand, her thumb slowly spun the ring he had placed on her left. She looked up at the man, guiding her out of the garden towards the setting sun. The world might not be black and white, but Izzy smiled knowing she had a strong sense of colors, when it mattered, she could tell the difference between them, and as the evening air filled her lungs, she knew at last that she was happy and free.

Don't miss out!

Visit the website below and you can sign up to receive emails whenever Elizabeth Meeks publishes a new book. There's no charge and no obligation.

https://books2read.com/r/B-A-LDZJC-HOGYE

BOOKS2READ

Connecting independent readers to independent writers.

About the Author

Elizabeth Meeks is happily married and lives in a tiny house in the center of Lincoln Nebraska. She adamantly believes that the world would come to a sudden and devastating end without tacos and dark chocolate. She is the daughter of a national hero who saved the lives of his crew and those below the flight path of his jet before bailing out to his death. He was awarded the distinguished flying cross posthumously. Her mother was a beloved kindergarten teacher whose kindness is still remembered today by those who knew her. Her beloved Auntie Lo helped her mother raise her and encouraged her to pursue her dreams. Elizabeth works in the financial industry and is also a respected breeder of Crested Geckos.

Read more at https://elizabethmeeks.com.

www.ingramcontent.com/pod-product-compliance
Lightning Source LLC
Chambersburg PA
CBHW061334160726
47995CB00001B/18